WHITE LIES

WHITE LIES

LISA RENEE

NEW YORK TIMES BESTSELLING AUTHOR

JONES

Entangled Publishing, LLC
644 Shrewsbury Commons Ave., STE 181
Shrewsbury, PA 17361
rights@entangledpublishing.com

Amara is an imprint of Entangled Publishing, LLC.

Visit our website at www.entangledpublishing.com.

Cover design by Bree Archer
Cover art by LJ Anderson, Mayhem Cover Creations
Stock Credit: ArturVerkhovetskiy/Depositphotos
Interior design by Toni Kerr

ISBN 978-1-64937-276-5
Ebook ISBN 978-1-64937-292-5

Manufactured in the United States of America

First Edition September 2022

10 9 8 7 6 5 4 3 2 1

To Julie, my cat daughter, who purred by my shoulder, and stayed on this earth until I typed The End. It was our last story we told together.

PROVOCATIVE

BOOK ONE OF THE WHITE LIES DUET

PROVOCATIVE PLAYLIST

"Sugar" by Maroon 5
"Ain't My Fault" by Zara Larsson
"Whisper" by Chase Rice
"i hate u, i love u" by Gnash
"World Falls Away" by Seether
"Sugar" by Maren Morris
"Make You Miss Me" by Sam Hunt
"Sex and Candy" by Marcy Playground
"Take Me Away" by Seether
"Stay" by Rihanna
"Dreams" by Fleetwood Mac
"Human" by Rag 'n' Bone Man
"Love on the Brain" by Rihanna

pro·voc·a·tive

adjective

    1. causing annoyance, anger, or another strong reaction, especially deliberately.

    2. arousing sexual desire or interest, especially deliberately.

CHAPTER ONE

Tiger

There are those moments in life that are provocative in their very existences, that embed in our minds forever, and sometimes our very souls. They change us, mold us, maybe even save us. But some are darker, *dangerous*. If we allow them to, they control us. *Seduce us*. Quite possibly even destroy us.

The moment I stepped into the mansion that is the centerpiece of the Reid Winter Vineyards and Winery wasn't one of those moments. Nor were any of the moments I spent weaving through a crowd of suits and dresses cluttering the circle that is the grand foyer of the 1800s mansion, fancy tiles etched with vines beneath my feet. Nor the ones spent declining three different waiters offering me glasses of various wines from one of the most established vineyards in Sonoma, meant to entice me to buy their bottles and donate money to the charity hosting the gathering. Not even the instant that I spotted the stunning blonde in a snug black dress that hugged her many lush curves proved to be one of those moments, but I would call it a damn interesting one. The moment I decided the blonde silk of her long hair belonged in my hands and on my stomach was also a damn interesting one. And not because she's fuckable. There are plenty of fuckable women in my life, a number of whom understand that I enjoy demands for pleasure, which I will definitely provide, and nothing more. This woman is too prim and proper to ever agree to such an arrangement, and yet, knowing this, as she and her heart-shaped backside disappear into the congestion of bodies, I find myself pursuing her, looking for more than an interesting moment. I want that provocative one.

I follow her path formed by huddles of two, three, or more people, left and right, to clear a portion of the crowd, scanning to find my beauty standing several feet away, her back to me, with two men in blue suits in front of her. And while they might appear to blend with the rest of the suits in the room, they hold themselves like the parasites I meet too often in the courtroom, those who most often call themselves my opposing counsel. My blonde beauty folds her arms in front of her chest, her spine stiff, and if I read her right—and I read most people right—I am certain that she's found trouble. But lucky for her, trouble doesn't like me nearly as much as I like it.

Closing the space between them and me, I near their little triangle just in time to hear her say, "Are we really doing this here and now?"

"Yes, Ms. Winter," one of the men replies. "We are."

"Actually," I say, stepping to *Ms. Winter's* side, her floral scent almost as sweet as the challenge of conquering her opponents that are now mine, "we are *not* doing this here or now."

All attention shifts to me, Ms. Winter giving me a sharp stare that I feel rather than see, my focus remaining on the men I want to leave, not the woman I want to make come. "And you would be who?" the suit directly in front of me demands.

I size him up as barely out of his twenty-something diapers, without experience, the glint in his eye telling me he doesn't realize that flaw, which makes him about as smooth as a six-dollar glass of wine everyone in this place would spit the fuck out. A point driven home by the fact that he's wearing a three-hundred-dollar Italian silk tie and a hundred-dollar suit, no doubt hoping the tie makes the suit look expensive and him important. He's wrong.

"I said, who are you?" he repeats when I apparently haven't replied quickly enough, his impatience becoming my virtue as my role as cat in this game of cat and mouse is too easily established.

Unwilling to waste words on a predictable, expected question that I'd never ask, I simply reach into the pocket of my three-thousand-dollar light gray suit, which I earned by beating opponents with ten times his experience and negotiation skills, and offer the unimportant prick my card.

He snaps it from my hand and gives it a look that confirms my name and the firm I started a decade ago now, after daring to leave behind a certain partnership in a high-powered firm. "Nick Rogers?" he asks.

"Is there another name on the card?" I ask, because I'm also a fearless smart-ass every chance I get.

He stares at me for several beats, seeming to calculate his words, before asking, "How many Mr. Rogers sweater jokes do you get?"

I arch a brow at the misguided joke that only serves to poke the Tiger. Suit Number Two, who I age closer to my thirty-six years, pales visibly, then snatches the card from the other man's hand, giving it a quick inspection before his gaze then jerks to mine. "*The* Nick Rogers?"

"I don't remember my mother putting the word 'the' in front of my name," I reply drily, but then again, I think, she didn't ask my father to change my last name, either. She just hated him that much.

"Tiger," he says, and it's not a question, but rather a statement of "oh shit" fact.

"That's right," I say, enjoying the fruits of my labor that created the nickname, not one given to me by my friends.

"Who, or what, the fuck is *Tiger* all about?" Suit Number One asks.

"Shut up," Suit Number Two grunts, refocusing on me to ask, "You're representing Ms. Winter?"

"What I am," I say, "is standing right here by her side, telling you that it's in your best interests to leave."

"Since when do you handle small-time foreclosures?" he demands, exposing the crux of Ms. Winter's situation.

"I handle whatever the *fuck* I want to handle," I say, my tone even, my lips curving as I add, "including the process of having you both escorted off the property by security."

"That," Suit Number One dares to retort, "would garner Ms. Winter unwanted attention in the middle of a busy event. Not that Ms. Winter even has security to call."

"Fortunately, I have a phone that dials 911 and the ability to call it without asking her."

"*If* she's your client," Suit Number One says, clearly inferring that she's not, "you're obligated to operate with her best interests in mind."

"My decisions," I reply, without missing a beat and without claiming Ms. Winter as a client, "are always about winning. And I assure you that I can think of many ways to spin your story to the press that ensure I win, while also benefiting Ms. Winter."

"This isn't my story," Suit Number One indicates.

"It will be when I'm finished with the press," I assure him, amused at how easily I've led him down the path I want him to travel.

"This is a small community with little to talk about *but her,*" he says. "She doesn't want her foreclosure to become the front-page story."

My lips quirk. "If you don't know how easily I can get the wrong attention for you here, and the right attention for Ms. Winter, you'll find out."

"We'll leave," Suit Number Two interjects quickly, and just when I think that he's smart enough to see the way trouble has turned from Ms. Winter to them, he looks at her and says, "We'll be in touch," with a not-so-subtle threat in his tone, before he elbows Suit Number One. "Let's go."

Suit Number One doesn't move, visibly fuming, his face red, a white ring thickening around his lips. I arch a brow at Suit Number Two, who adds, "*Now,* Jordan." Jordan, formerly known as Suit Number One, clenches his teeth and turns away, while Suit Number Two follows.

Ms. Winter faces me, and holy fuck, when her pale green

eyes meet mine, any questions I have about this woman—and the many I suspect she now has of me—are muted by an unexpected, potentially problematic, palpable electric charge between us. "Thank you," she says, her voice soft, feminine, a rasp in its depths that hints at emotion not effortlessly contained. "Please enjoy anything you like tonight on the house," she adds, the rasp gone now, her control returned. *Until I take it*, I think, but no sooner than I've had the thought, she is turning and walking away, the absence of further interaction coloring me both stunned and intrigued, two things that, for me, are ranked with about as much frequency as snow in Sonoma, which would be next to never.

Ms. Winter maneuvers into the crowd, out of my line of sight, and while I am not certain I'd label her a mouse at this point—or ever, for that matter, considering what I know of her—I am most definitely on the prowl. I stride purposely forward, weaving through the crowd, seeking that next provocative moment, scanning for her left, right, in the clusters of mingling guests, until I clear the crowd.

Now standing in front of a wide, wooden stairwell, I direct my gaze upward to a second level, but I still find no sign of Ms. Winter. A cool breeze whips through the air, and I turn to find the source is a high arched doorway, the recently opened glass doors to what I know to be the "Winter Gardens," a focal point of the property and a tourist draw for decades, settling back into place. Certain this represents her escape, I walk that direction and press open the doors, stepping onto a patio that has a stone floor and concrete benches framed by rose bushes. No fewer than four winding paths greet me as destination choices, the hunt for this woman now a provocation of its own.

I've just decided to wait where I am for Ms. Winter's return when the wind lifts, the floral scent of many varieties of flowers for which the garden is famous touching my nostrils, with one extra scent decidedly of the female variety.

Lips curving with the certainty that my prey will soon be my prize, I follow the clue that guides my feet to the path on my right, a narrow, winding, lighted walkway, framed by neatly cut yellow flower bushes, which continues past a white wooden gazebo I have no intention of passing. Not when Ms. Winter stands inside it, her back to me, elbows resting on the wooden rail, her gaze casting across the silhouette of what would reveal itself to be a rolling mountainside at daybreak. The way I intend for her to reveal herself.

I close the distance between us, and the moment before I'm upon her, she faces me, hands on the railing behind her, her breasts thrust forward, every one of her lush curves tempting my eyes, my hands. *My mouth.* "Did those men know you?" she demands, clearly ready and waiting for this interaction. "Did you know them?"

"No and no."

"And yet they knew the nickname Tiger."

"My reputation precedes me."

"I'll take the bait," she says. "What reputation?"

"They say I'll rip my opponent's throat out if given the chance."

"Will you?" she asks without so much as a blanch or blink.

"Yes," I reply, a simple answer for a simple question.

"Without any concern for who you hurt," she states.

I arch a brow. "Is that a question?"

"Should it be?"

"Yes."

"It's not," she says. "You didn't get that nickname by being nice."

"Nice guys don't win."

"Then I'm warned," she says. "You aren't a nice guy."

"Is nice a quality you're looking for in a man? Because as your evening counsel, Ms. Winter, I'll advise you that nice is overrated."

She stares at me for several beats before turning away to face the mountains again, elbows on the railing, in what I could see as a silent invitation to leave. I choose to see it as an invitation to join her. I claim the spot next to her, close but not nearly as close as I will be soon. "You didn't answer the question," I point out.

"You wrongly assume I am looking for a man, which I'm not," she says, glancing over at me. "But if I was, then no. Nice would be on my list, but it would not top my list; however, nowhere on that list would be the ability and willingness to rip out someone's throat."

"I can assure you, Ms. Winter, that a man with a bite is as underrated as a nice guy is overrated. And I not only know how and when to use mine, but if I so choose to bite *you*—and I might— it'll be all about pleasure, not pain."

Her cheeks flush, and she turns away. "My name is Faith." She glances over at me again. "Should I call you Nick, Tiger, or just plain arrogant?"

"Anything but Mr. Rogers," I say, enjoying our banter far more than I would have expected when I came here tonight looking for her.

She laughs now, too, and it's a delicate, sweet sound, but it's awkward, as if it's not only unexpected but unwelcome, and an instant later she's withdrawing, pushing off the railing, arms folding protectively in front of her body, before we're rotating to face each other. "I need to go check on the visitors." She attempts to move away.

I gently catch her arm, her gaze rocketing to mine, and in the process her hair flutters in a sudden breeze, a strand of blond silk catching on the whiskers of my one-day stubble. She sucks in a breath, and when she would reach up to remedy the situation, I'm already there, catching the soft silk and stroking it behind her ear.

"Why are you touching me?" she asks, but she doesn't pull away. That charge between us minutes ago is now ten times more provocative with me touching her, thinking about all the places I might touch next.

"It's considerably better than not touching you," I say.

"My bad luck might bleed into you."

"Bleed," I repeat, that word reminding me once again of why I'm here, why I really want to fuck this woman. "That's an extreme and rather interesting choice of words."

"Most bad luck is extreme, though not interesting to anyone but the Tigers of the world, creating it. You're still touching me."

"Everyone needs a Tiger in their corner. Maybe my good luck will bleed into you."

"Does good luck bleed?" she asks.

"Many people will do anything for good luck, even bleed."

"Yes," she says, lowering her lashes, but not before I've seen the shadows in her eyes. "I suppose they would."

"What would you do for good luck?"

Her lashes lift, her stare meeting mine again. "What have you done for good luck?"

"I came here tonight," I say.

She narrows her eyes on me, as if some part of her senses the far-reaching implications of my reply that she can't possibly understand, and yet still, the inescapable heat between us radiates and burns. "You're still touching me," she points out, and this time there's a hint of reprimand.

"I'm holding on to that good luck," I say.

"It feels like you're holding on to mine."

With that observation that hits too close to the truth, which I have no interest in revealing just yet, I drag my hand slowly down hers, allowing my fingers to find hers before they fall away. Her lips—lush, tempting, impossibly perfect for someone I know to be imperfect—part with the loss of my touch, and yet there is a hint of relief in her eyes that tells me she both wants me and fears me.

A most provocative moment, indeed.

"Have a drink with me," I say.

"No," she replies, her tone absolute, and while I don't like this decision, I appreciate a person who's decisive.

"Why?"

"Good luck and bad luck don't mix."

"They might just create good luck."

"Or bad," she says. "I'm not in a place where I can take the risk for more bad luck." She inclines her chin. "Enjoy the rest of your visit." She pauses and adds, "*Tiger*."

I don't react, but for just a moment, I consider the way she used my nickname as an indicator that she knows who I am, and why I'm here. I quickly dismiss that idea. I'd have seen it in those pale green eyes, and I did not. But as she turns and walks away and I watch her depart, tracking her steps as she disappears down the path, I wonder at her quick departure and the fear I'd seen in her eyes. Was the root of that fear her guilt?

That idea should be enough to ice the fire in me that this woman has stirred, but it stokes it instead. Everything male in me wants to pursue her again, and not because I'm here for a reason that existed before I ever met her, when it should be that and nothing more. It *is* more. I'm aroused and I'm intrigued by this woman. She got to me when no one gets to me. Not a good place to be, considering I came here to prove she killed my father, and maybe even her own mother.

CHAPTER TWO

Faith

I stand at the library window on the second level of the mansion that I've called my family home, but not *my* home, my entire life. Nick Rogers exits the front door, pure sex and arrogance. He stops to talk to the doorman, both men laughing, before Nick palms the other man a tip and then rounds his shiny black BMW that I'm fairly certain is custom designed. He begins to get in but hesitates, scanning the grounds immediately around him, and then, to my complete and utter shock, his gaze lifts and lands on my window. Stunned, my heart begins to race all over again, the way it had when he'd touched me in that garden, but it's impossible for him to see me. I know it is, but somehow, there is no question that he knows I am here. He holds his stare in my direction for several beats, in which I cannot breathe, and then lifts two fingers, giving me a wave before he disappears into his car. Moments later, he drives away, and I let out the breath I'm holding. Hugging myself, I am both hot and cold, aroused and unsettled, exactly as I had been when I was with him in the garden. Every look and word I exchanged with that man was both sexual and adversarial.

Rotating, I sit on the window seat of the grand library that was once my father's, bookshelves filled with decades of books lining the walls left and right, all with answers to questions that we might not even ever ask. Which is why I read incessantly and why I wish I knew which one to open for the right answers to why Nick Rogers felt so right and wrong at the same time, and why so many other things are wrong in ways I'm not sure I can make right. But that would be too simple, and I am suddenly reminded of a poem

I wrote long ago in school that started out with: *The apples fall from the trees. The wind blows in the trees.* I'd proudly handed it into the teacher and quickly found myself scolded for my display of simplistic writing. I didn't understand. What was wrong with being simplistic? The words and the concepts fit together. That is what mattered. That was what was important to me. The way the pieces fit. The way it made sense. It seemed so simple to me, when in truth, little in life is simple at all. And that's exactly why I keep that poem pinned on my bedroom wall. To remind me that nothing is simple.

Except death, I think, my throat thickening. One minute you're alive, and the next you're dead. Death is as simple as it gets. At least for the person it claims. For those of us left behind, it's complicated, haunting. Mysterious and maybe even dangerous. And death, I have learned, is never done with you until you are gone, too. My mind returns to Nick Rogers and the way he'd known that I was in the window. The way he'd stared up at me and then given me that wave, and every instinct I own tells me that Nick Rogers is a lot like death. He's not done with me, either.

CHAPTER THREE

Faith

Gasping for air, I sit up in bed, my hand on my throat, my breath heaving from my chest, seconds passing eternally as I will my heart to calm. Breathe in. Breathe out. Breathe. Just breathe. Finally, I begin to calm, and I scan the room, the heavy drapes that run throughout the family mansion that I grew up in casting it in shadows, while my mind casts the horror that woke me in its own form of darkness. Every image I think I can identify dodges and weaves, then fades just out of reach, like too many other things in my life right now.

Suddenly aware of the perpetual chill of the centuries-old property, a chill impossible to escape seeming to seep deep into my bones, I yank the blanket to my chin, the floral scent of the gardens that my mother loved clinging inescapably to it and to me. I glance toward the heavy antique white nightstand to my right to find the clock: eight a.m., a new dawn long ago rising over the rolling mountaintops hugging this region to illuminate the miles and miles of vineyards surrounding us. It's also the dawn of my thirtieth birthday, and really, why wouldn't it start with a nightmare? I'm sleeping in my dead mother's bed.

It's an uncomfortable thought, but not an emotional one, a reality that makes me even *more* uncomfortable. When my father died just two years ago now, I'd cried until I could cry no more, and then did it again. And again. And again. But I'm not crying now. What is wrong with me? I didn't even cry at the funeral, but I'd been certain that when alone, I would. Now, eight weeks later, there are still no tears. I had my problems with my mother, but it's not like I don't grieve for her. I do, but I grieved for her in life as well, and maybe I grieved too much then to grieve now. I just don't know.

Rolling over, I flip on the light, then hit a remote that turns on the fireplace directly in front of my bed. Sitting up, I stare at the flames as it spurts and sputters to life, but I don't find the answers I seek there, or anywhere in this room, as I'd hoped when I'd moved from the identical room down the hall to this one. I'd been certain that being here, in the middle of my mother's personal space, the scent of the gardens she loved clinging to virtually everything, including me, would finally make the tears fall. But no. Days later, and I'm still not crying; I'm having nightmares. And whatever those nightmares are, they always make me wake up angry. So there it is. I *do* have a feeling I can name. Anger is one of them. I'm not quite sure what that anger is all about, but right now, all I can hear is my mother shouting at me: *You're just like your father.* An insult in her book, but there was no truth in it. I was never like my father. I always saw who and what she was, where he only saw the woman he'd loved for thirty years—the same amount of time I've been alive.

Throwing off the covers, I rotate, my feet settling on the stepstool that is a necessity to climb down from the bedframe. My gaze lands on Nick Rogers's business card where I'd left it on the nightstand last night, after spending the minutes before sleep replaying every word, look, and touch with that man. This morning I'm admitting to myself what I had not last night. He woke me up, and because of him, there is at least one other emotion I can feel: *lust.* If lust is really even considered an emotion, but whatever the case, there is no other word for what charged the air between myself and that man, for what I felt and saw in his eyes when he touched me, but *lust.* And the more I think about that meeting, the more I know that there wasn't anything romantic or sweet about our connection. It was dark and jagged. The kind of attraction that's unforgiving in its demands. The kind of attraction that's all consuming, proven by the fact that, even now, hours after our encounter, I can still feel his hand on my arm and the sizzle that had burned a path through my body. I can still feel the hum of my body that he, and he alone, created.

And while I cannot say if that man is my friend or my enemy, I know where this kind of collision course of dark, edgy lust leads. I've lived it, and it is not a place you want to go with anyone that you don't trust. I'm not sure it's a place you can even find with someone you really do trust. I think it's dark because it's born out of something dark in one or both people, maybe that they bring out in each other. Which means it's not a place anyone should travel, and yet, when you feel it, I know that you resist it. But you cannot deny it, or the person who creates it in you. It's exactly why I am certain that, despite my rejection of Nick Rogers last night, I'll be seeing him again, which brings my mind back to one particular exchange we'd shared that keeps playing and replaying in my head.

"You're still touching me," I'd said, and he'd replied with, *"I'm holding on to that good luck."*

Logically, he was inferring that meeting me was good luck. He'd already stated that coming here to the winery was good luck. It was simple flirtatious banter. So why did it bother me then, and why does it bother me now? Chance meeting or not? The timing... the men...the dark lust. It never comes from a good place. Maybe I'm wrong about him. I have plenty of darkness of my own right now. Maybe my energy fed our energy together. But it doesn't matter. He's dangerous. He's taboo.

He's not going to touch me again.

My cellphone rings, and praying it's not some crisis in the winery, I grab it and glance at the caller ID. At the sight of my attorney's number, and with the knowledge that his office just opened, my heart races, and I answer the line. "Frank? Do you have news?"

"It's Betty," I hear. Betty being Frank's secretary. "Frank wants to know if you can be here at eleven."

"Is there a problem?"

"He's in court. He wants to see you, and he said it had to be today. That's all I know. Can you be here at eleven?"

"Can he see me sooner?" I ask, my nerves racketing up a notch at the "had to be today" comment.

"He's in court."

"Right. Eleven it is, then."

My phone rings again, and I glance at the unknown number, hitting decline. At least the bill collectors waited until sunrise today. Three seconds later, the ringing begins all over again, and this time it's a San Francisco number. Repeating my prior action, I hit decline, and this time I have the luxury of blocking the number. I don't need to talk to the caller to know they want a piece of me that they can't have, and yet another of my exchanges with Tiger comes back to me. I'd asked, *"Does good luck bleed?"* And his reply had been, *"Many people will do anything for good luck, even bleed."*

Bleed.

Isn't that what my father did? Bleed? And bleed some more?

And why do I feel like I'm bleeding right now?

And why does that thought remind me of Tiger?

I glance down at my balled fist and open it to discover I've crumpled his card into a ball in my hand.

My phone registers five more unknown callers by the time I complete the fifteen-minute drive to my attorney's office, which is in one of my favorite places in the city: the quaint downtown area, where there are stone walkways leading to stores, restaurants, and a few random businesses; some areas are even framed with ivy overhangs. I park by a curb, in front of a row of side-by-side mom-and-pop shops, right in front of the path leading to Frank's office, but I don't get out, nervous and with reason. The winery was everything to my father, and to save it, I did things I didn't want to do—things I regret. And the guilt I feel is overwhelming. Maybe I can't cry because it's eating away at me, like acid that just won't stop burning away my emotions.

I straighten my funeral-black pencil skirt, which I've paired with a funeral-black sweater and black, knee-high boots, the thick tights beneath it all meant to fight the chill of an October mountain day. But nothing can take the chill off death, which is my reason for choosing funeral-black attire yet again today. I don't remember the day, week, moment, that I stopped dressing this way after my father died. I guess it just happens when it feels right, and it doesn't yet. My cellphone rings again, and I grab it from my well-worn (also black) briefcase that doubles as my version of a purse. Eyeing the caller ID, I see that the new San Francisco number has apparently called me twice now. I block it and one other, certain from the past two weeks of hell that yet another caller will start showing up on my ID any second.

I turn my ringer off and slip my cell back in its pocket, my gaze landing on the gold Chanel logo pressed to the outside of the bag, my fingers stroking the letters. It was a gift from my father when I'd graduated from UCLA with eyes set on selling my art and buying lots of Chanel. My father declared this bag a "taste of luxury" to inspire me. And it had been, but then things had happened and—

"Damn it," I murmur, my eyes pinching shut. "Now I'm teary-eyed? What the heck is wrong with me?"

I grab my bag and settle it on my shoulder, opening the door of the black BMW that I'd inherited from my father, while my mother's white Mercedes still sits in the garage back at the mansion. Even their cars were opposite, I think. They were opposite in all things. I stand, and the card I'd balled in my hand earlier falls to the pavement. I bend down and pick it up, standing to straighten it and read: *Nick Rogers, Attorney at Law.* Mr. Rogers. Right. Well, he's no sweet, sweater-vested kid's television personality, for sure.

Deciding to ask my attorney about the notorious "Tiger," I stick the card inside the pocket of my briefcase and get moving. I hurry under one of those overhangs to travel past a candy store, a candle store, and then finally reach the law office I seek. As I'm entering the office, the receptionist greets me.

"Hiya, sugar," Betty greets me, her red hair glowing maroon where last week it had been more of an orange hue, her bold style in contrast to her boss—a true case of opposites attract. But my mind goes back to Tiger and me. I don't think we're opposites. Thus the dark energy. "Frank's on a conference call," she says, bringing me back to the here and now rather than last night. "He should be done any moment."

"Thank you," I say, claiming one of the half dozen leather seats in the small, familiar lobby I'd often frequented with my father in my youth, hanging out here until he finished meetings, which was when we'd then grab ice cream. Usually when my mother was nowhere to be found.

My throat thickens with that memory, and I'm about to set my bag down when Frank appears in the doorway, looking fit and younger than his sixty years in a well-fitted black suit, his gray hair neatly trimmed, his face lightly lined. "Come in, Faith." He backs into his office to offer me room to enter.

I'm on my feet before he finishes that statement, crossing the lobby and entering his humble office with a desk, two chairs, and a window. It's simple, but it's personalized with a collection of University of Texas memorabilia as well as his diploma. But he doesn't need to be fancy. He grew up in Sonoma and took over his father's trusted practice, becoming a local favorite about the time I was born.

Frank lingers behind me and shuts the door, that thud a trigger for my nerves to bounce around in my belly. So, okay. I do feel things. I'm not numb about anything but my mother's death. I claim a seat, and he rounds the desk to sit down, elbows on the wooden surface, his gray eyes steady on my face. "How are you?"

"Better when I know what this meeting is about," I say. "Did the state finally approve you as executor of my mother's estate?"

"I'm afraid not," he replies. "The bank filed a formal objection based on my role as your attorney, which, they claim, works against their best interests."

I scoot to the edge of my chair. "But I'm the rightful owner of the property with or without my mother's will. She inherited it from my father with the written directive that I inherit it next."

"The bank claims otherwise," he says.

"It states it in his will."

"They claim the debt allows them to supersede that directive."

"That note my father took is large, but it's not anywhere near the value of the winery. Can they even make this claim at all?"

"They can claim they own the White House," he says. "That doesn't mean they do. Your mother failing to register a will complicates this, but your father's will specifically stated that she inherited the winery on the condition that you were next in line. But you do need to pay the bank debt your mother left behind. We're at six months tardy at this point."

"Five," I say, my role as acting CEO not much different than my role the past two years. And I still don't have access to the empty bank accounts. "I made a payment."

"Is the winery making money?"

"Yes. I've run that place and kept the books since my father died."

"Then why was she four months behind on the bank note when she died?"

"I don't know. And not just the bank note. Everything. Every vendor we use wants money. I can't catch everyone up at once. I need time. Or I need access to her personal accounts. That has to be where the money is."

"I've filed a petition with the court to appoint a neutral executor appointed with no allegiance to the bank," he says. "But they could easily come back with names we have to reject."

"Which is what the bank wants," I assume, and suddenly there is a light in the dark tunnel. Not necessarily an end quite yet, but a light. "They think time will place me so far in debt I have to surrender the property. That would be insanity, and I'm not insane. It would be easier to get my hands on the money my mother pulled from the accounts, but I told you. The winery is making money. If we drag this out long enough, I'll pay off that note. Drag it out."

"You're sure?"

"Positive," I say firmly.

"Have you had any luck at all finding the money she pulled from the company?"

"None," I say. "Have you had any luck finding anything that might point me in the right direction?"

He reaches into his drawer and sets a card in front of me. "You need a private investigator. He's good and affordable."

"I can't afford to hire a private detective."

"You can't afford not to," he counters.

"We're making money. I just need you to buy that time."

"What if you have another surprise you don't expect?" He slides the card closer. "Call him. Talk about a payment plan."

I reach for the card and stick it in my purse. "I'll call." My mind goes to my newest surprise. "Do you know Nick Rogers?"

He arches a brow. "The attorney?"

"Yes. Him."

"Why?"

"A couple of bank goons showed up last night, and he was at the winery. He stepped in and scared them off."

"He's a good friend and a bad enemy."

"There's no chance that was a setup and he's already an enemy?"

"Nick Rogers doesn't need to play the kind of games that comment suggests. He has the prowess of—"

"—a tiger."

"Yes," Frank says. "A tiger. He'll—"

"—rip your throat out if you cross him or his clients," I supply.

"I know his reputation, but what I don't understand is how he, above others in his field, is so well-known."

"He's one of the top five corporate attorneys in the country, and he's local to our region." He narrows his eyes on me. "But back to you. Do you have any other questions about what I shared today?"

"Not now."

"Then let's get to what's important. Happy birthday, Faith."

"Thank you," I say, my voice cracking, forcing me to clear my throat and repeat, "Thank you."

"It's a rough time to have a birthday, I know," he says. "You lost your father at about the same time of year."

"I did," I agree. "But at least every year it's all concentrated in one window of time."

"Your birthday."

"Birthdays are for kids."

"Birthdays are for celebrating life," he says. "Something you need to do. I'm glad you didn't cancel your appearance at the art show tonight in light of your mother's passing. It's time you get back to your art, to let the world see what *you* do. And a local display with a three-month-long feature is a great way to get noticed again."

Again.

I don't let myself go to the place and history that word could take me to. Not today.

"Your agent did right by you on this," he adds.

"Josh overstepped his boundaries by accepting this placement, and had he not committed in writing before I knew, I'd have declined. He was supposed to simply manage my existing placements and related sales."

"Declined?" he asks incredulously. "This is an amazing opportunity, little girl."

"Le Sun Gallery is owned by one of our competitors, a winery that infuriated my mother."

"Your mother was selfish and wrong," he says. "I know she's

gone, but I'm not saying anything we don't both know. And Le Sun is owned by a rock star in the art world and the godparents of said rock-star artist. Every art lover who visits Sonoma wants to see Chris Merit's work at that gallery, and when they see his, they will see yours. And you've put your life on hold for too long. If you decide to keep the winery—"

"I am," I say. "It's my family legacy."

"You're sure your uncle wants no part of it?"

"Yes," I confirm. "Very." And even if he did, I add silently, my father would turn over in his grave if that man even stepped foot on the property again. "Bottom line," I add firmly. "I'm keeping the winery."

"Make the decision to keep it after you achieve some breathing room. After your show and the chance to remember your dreams, not his." He reaches inside the drawer again and retrieves an envelope, holding it up. "And after you read this and give yourself some time to process it." He sets it in front of me.

My gaze lands on my name and a birthday greeting written in my father's familiar script. I swallow hard, my stomach flip-flopping, before my gaze jerks to his. "What is that?"

"He asked me to give it to you upon his death, if it was after you turned thirty or on your thirtieth birthday, should he pass before that date."

My hands go to the back of my neck, under my hair; my throat is thick, and I have to turn my head away, my eyes shutting, a wave of emotions overwhelming me. "And yet my mother didn't even have a will," I murmur.

"People don't want to believe they're going to die," he says. "It's quite common."

I jerk back to him, anger burning inside me at my mother, and at him for protecting her. Again. "You do what's responsible when you hold a property of this value. You just do." I grab the envelope my father left for me. "Please just buy me time."

I stand and walk to the door, and just as I'm about to leave, he says, "Faith."

I pause but do not turn. "Yes?"

"I know you're angry at her, and so am I, but it, like all things, will pass."

I want to believe him. I do. But he wouldn't be so confident if he knew all there was to know, which I will never allow to happen. And so, I simply nod as a reply, then leave, thankful that Betty is on the phone and has a delivery driver in front of her, which allows me to pass by her without any obligatory niceties. Exiting the office, the cool air is a shock I welcome, something to focus on other than the ball of emotion the envelope in my hand seems to be stirring. Maybe I didn't want to feel again after all, and eager to be alone, I quicken my pace, entering a tunneled path beneath an ivy-covered overhang, and don't stop until I'm on the other side. Clearing it, I turn left to bring my car into view where it's parked on the opposite side of the street, my lips parting, my feet planting, at the sight of *Mr. Rogers* himself leaning against it. And he isn't just leaning on it. He's leaning on the driver's-side door, as if to tell me that I'm not leaving without going through him first.

CHAPTER FOUR

Faith

I now know the source of the dark lust and energy I'd felt with Nick Rogers wasn't just about sex. It was about betrayal. Because the fact that Mr. Rogers—no, *Tiger*—is here at *my attorney's office*, leaning arrogantly on my car, watching me with arms folded in front of his chest, ankles crossed, can mean only one thing. He's working for the bank. And he's doing it in a custom-fitted dark blue suit that I don't have to see up close to know is expensive. Because apparently ripping out someone's throat requires style. And he wears that suit well, too; it doesn't wear him. He has a way of owning everything around him that I'd actually thought attractive last night. I'd allowed myself to be drawn into a flirtation with him. And I might have embarrassment in me if I wasn't so damn furious with myself for being foolish and him for being an asshole.

I charge toward him, and he tracks my every move with those striking navy blue eyes. I actually got lost in them last night. I also know them to be intelligent and brimming with arrogance, which I plan to use to knock him down a notch or ten. Crossing the road, I don't stop until I'm standing in front of him. "Get off my car," I say before adding, "*Mr. Rogers.*"

His lips, which are really too damn pretty and full for a man, but still somehow brutal, quirk with amusement. "You don't take requests well, I see, *Ms. Winter*," he says. "I told you to call me anything but Mr. Rogers."

"I can think of *many* names to call you right about now," I retort. "But Mr. Rogers was the kindest. I don't like being played with."

He arches a brow. "And…you think I'm playing with you?"

"I know you are."

"You're wrong," he says immediately.

"If I'm wrong, how did you know I'd be here?"

"Your staff," he replies simply.

My anger kicks up about ten notches, and I can almost feel my cheeks heat. "Do you win all your cases by lying? Because my staff didn't know I was here." I turn away from him, click my locks with my keychain, and open the door despite him leaning against it. He moves without argument, but my win is short-lived as the earthy male scent of him rushes over me, and I whirl around to find myself caged between a hot, hard male body and the hard steel of the car.

"Talk to my lawyer," I order before he can speak. "Not me."

"I have no interest in talking to your lawyer," he states. "I *am not* working for, nor am I associated with, your bank." He steps closer, so close we are a lean from touching. So close that I can feel the warmth of his body and, if I wanted to, I could trace the barely-there outline of a goatee. "And I don't lie," he adds, a hardness to his voice, a glint in his eyes that tells a story beyond this moment. "In fact, I hate liars, and I don't use the word 'hate' liberally."

"Wrong," I say, *hating* the way my body wants to lean toward his. "My staff—"

"—told me you had a meeting," he supplies, "and it was fairly obvious after last night that it would be with your attorney, and I'm resourceful enough to have that bring me here."

"Why would you even do that?"

"You interest me, *Faith*," he says, his voice lower now, my name intimate on his tongue, a soft rasp that still manages a rough, seductive tone, etched with a hint of something in his voice, in his eyes, I don't quite read or understand. "And unless I've developed a colorful imagination, I interest you, too."

"You don't work for the bank?" I ask, my anger easing but not gone.

"No," he confirms. "I *do not* work for the bank, and to be clear, I do not work for anyone who has your business interests in mind. I work for me, and I have *you* in mind."

"If this is all true, then explain to me how you thought showing up here, knowing what you learned about my situation last night, was the way to get from no to yes?"

His hand settles on the window beside me, somehow shrinking my small space, somehow creating more intimacy between us. "We were red-hot last night, and you know it."

"That's not an answer."

"That's not a denial, but I'll answer your question. If I'd shown up at the winery today, you would have disappeared into some corner again until I left, like you did last night. I wasn't prepared to let you run again."

"I didn't run," I say. "I simply decided you could be playing me. And I don't need more enemies than friends."

"And now?" he challenges softly. "Am I a friend or an enemy?"

"I haven't decided."

Something flickers in his eyes, gone before I can name it, before he asks, "All right, then. I'll settle for either as long as you keep that old saying about enemies in mind."

"They aren't the nice guys."

"If you have an enemy who's a nice guy, it's no different than having an attorney who's a nice guy. You might as well call him a friend."

"But you're not a nice guy. You said so."

"What I am is the man who made you drop that ten-foot wall of yours when I touched you last night." His gaze lowers to my mouth, lingering there before lifting. "And I've been thinking about touching you again ever since. About tearing down that wall and keeping it down."

"That wall is to keep men like you out."

He narrows his gaze on me. "Who burned you, Faith? And what scars did he leave?"

That wall of mine slams back into place, and damn it, he did tear it down, and he did so without touching me. He's dangerous. He sees too much. Things I don't want to show anyone ever again. "I'm leaving," I say, turning back to the car, but as I do, my purse strap falls from my shoulder. I try to catch it, and only then do I realize I'm still holding the card from my father, and it tumbles to the ground. I suck in air, hating the idea of it on the ground for reasons I'll analyze later. Turning and squatting down, I intend to grab it, but Tiger is already there, and it's in his hand. I wobble on the toes of my boots just enough to instinctively flatten my hand on his powerful thigh to catch myself. The impact of that connection is electric, instant, that wall he'd mentioned falling. I can't breathe, and my heart is instantly racing. I try to pull back my hand, but his covers mine.

That breath I'd sucked in moments before is lodged in my throat, and my gaze lifts to his, the impact punching me in the chest, heat waving between us, that dark lust charging the air. I tell myself to stand up, but I don't. I tell myself to jerk my hand back from where it rests against him. But he smells so good, a cocoon of earthy masculinity that seduces me to stay right where I am, lost in those deep blue eyes of his.

"Touching you again," he says, his voice as earthy and warm as his scent, "or, rather, you touching me this time, is better than the first time." He offers me the card. "Happy Birthday, Faith."

I don't ask how he knows it's my birthday. It's on the card. It's also on documents that he, no doubt, studied before he came here today. I reach for the envelope, but he doesn't let it go. He holds on to it and me, and it hits me that the two things in life that I've learned you can neither explain nor control have now collided: *death and lust*. And I have never needed control more in my life than now.

Tiger reaches up and strokes the hair from my eyes, his hands settling on my cheek, a stranger who somehow feels better than anything has in a very long time. And just as I feared, I'm reminded of how good an escape that dark lust can be, how addictive. He's right. I *am* afraid. I'm afraid of losing what little control I have right now.

I stand up and go on the attack. "You researched me like a client or someone you're prosecuting," I charge, knowing it's a ridiculous reason to be mad. I would have researched him, too, had I gotten in earlier last night, but I don't like it right now. I don't like how he's taken my life by storm. "You knew it was my birthday before you came here."

"I researched you like a woman I want to know. And I *do* want to know you, Faith."

His tongue strokes my name again, soft yet rough-edged, which somehow screams sex to me. *He* screams sex to me. "Stop saying my name like that."

"Like what?" he asks, and in that moment, with his long hair tied at his nape, his deep voice roughened up, he is lethal for no logical reason.

"Like we're intimate," I say. "Like you know me, because the internet doesn't determine who or what I am."

"Then you show me who you are."

"Why?" I challenge. "You already read me like a book. I need to get to work." I turn and climb into my car, as I should have before now.

He kneels beside me, and I brace myself for the touch that I am both relieved and disappointed doesn't follow, but I can feel him compelling me to look at him. "This is what I do," he says, undeterred when I do not. "I push and I push some more to get what I want."

I look at him before I can stop myself. "You officially pushed too hard."

"If you're still running, I haven't pushed hard enough."

"This doesn't work for me."

"Good. It doesn't for me, either."

I blink, confused by a reply that conflicts with his pursuit. "What does that even mean?"

"Our shared state of mind simplifies the attraction between us and even explains it. Bottom line: we both just need to fuck a whole lot of everything out of our systems, including each other."

"Who even says something like that to someone they don't know?"

"Me, Faith. I might not always show my hand, but as I said, I don't like lies. When I say something, it's honest. It's real."

"You don't think not showing your hand is a lie?"

"Do you?" he counters.

"Good dodge and weave there, counselor," I say. "There's more to you than meets the eye, Nick Rogers."

"I could say the same of you, now couldn't I, Faith Winter?"

"Yes," I dare, because most likely he already knows this as fact, and anything else would challenge him to prove otherwise. "You could."

He arches a brow. "I expected denial."

"Seems you didn't learn everything about me on the internet that you thought you learned."

His eyes glint with something I can't name. "The internet was never going to give me what I want from you anyway."

I tell myself not to take the bait, but there is more to him than meets the eye. More that I don't just want to understand. More than I almost feel I need to understand. And so, I do it. I dare to ask exactly what he wants me to ask.

"Which is what?"

"You. Not the you that you show the world. The one behind the wall that intrigued me last night and now. The real you, Faith, stripped bare and not just exposed. *Willingly* exposed." He stands up, backs away, and shuts the car door.

CHAPTER FIVE

Faith

I leave downtown with Nick, or Tiger, or whatever I decide to call the man, on my mind, and he stays on my mind. Five minutes after my encounter with him, much to my dismay, I can still feel that man's touch and the warmth of his body next to mine. Ten minutes later, the same. Fifteen. The same. This, of course, was his intent when he suggested we fuck and then left without so much as another word. He wanted me to crave his touch. He wanted me to be ready for next time, which we both know will come. And it worked.

I hit the twenty-minute mark with Tiger haunting my thoughts, but I finally have the blessed distraction from him as I pull onto the long, winding path leading to the place I call home. The white country-style house I'd bought with my inheritance six months after my father's death. I'd finally accepted that my mother would run the winery into the ground if I didn't leave my life in L.A. behind. I'd had this crazy idea back then that I could merge my world with that of the winery. I'd been wrong, but today is my birthday, and I'm giving myself the gift of a weekend with my art, including a brush in my hand.

I park in the driveway rather than the garage, then quickly grab my bag, hurrying up the wooden steps to the porch that hugs the entire front of the house. Once I'm inside, I clear the foyer and hurry across the dark wood of the floors of the open living area to my bedroom. I enter the room I haven't slept in for a month, everything about the space artsy and clean, done in cream and caramel tones. A cream leather-framed bed and fluffy cream area rug. Caramel-colored nightstands. A cream chair with a caramel ottoman. My painting, a Sonoma landscape, is the centerpiece above the headboard, because hey, I can't afford a Chris Merit, though Josh loves to tell me I could be the *next* Chris Merit. I'd be happy to just be the next me and actually know what that meant, which reminds me of the card from my father. I set my bag on the bed and pull out the card, staring at my father's script. I run my fingers over it, missing him so badly it hurts, but I remember that he saw my art as a hobby and the winery as my future. I've accepted that destiny. I'm protecting our family history and his blood and sweat. But I can't open a card tonight and risk gutting myself before a night I've already committed to surviving. I set the card down and whisper, "I love you, and I'm going to make you proud."

My eyes burn, and the guilt I have over the tears I haven't shed for my mother has me rushing to the closet off the bathroom to change. I need to paint. I need to get lost with a brush in my hand. I turn away from the bed and enter the bathroom—done in the same shades as the bedroom, including the checked tiles, with an egg-shaped sunken tub—and continue to my walk-in closet. Once there, I change into jeans and a T-shirt, as well as sneakers.

A few minutes later, I'm on the second level of the house, which I had converted to my studio, with a smock over my clothes, a blank canvas in front of me, a brush in my hand for the first time in months, and my phone on the table beside me. And impossibly, somehow, Nick Rogers is still on my mind. I don't like arrogance. I don't like men with long hair. I don't like men like Nick Rogers. And yet, that man is haunting me. I go to work, determined to paint him off my mind, long strokes, heavy strokes. Soon my creation begins to come to life, a work that is like no other I have ever created, and I am driven—obsessed, even—to finish it.

Time passes—an hour I think, maybe more—before my phone rings. I set down the brush and wipe my hands on the smock before picking it up. "Hi, Josh," I say after noting my agent's number on caller ID.

"I'm finally here," he breathes out, sounding decidedly grumpy.

"Finally? What time is it?"

"Five," he says. "And why the hell do you not know that, Faith? This is a big night for you. Chris Merit won't be there, but he donated a never-before-seen painting for the charity auction. The event's been sold out for months. And this is your event, too."

"It's his event. I'm showing my work."

"It's your event, too, and I will spank your pretty little ass if you say otherwise again."

"You do not need to say things like that to me."

"Because I scandalize you? We both know that's no more true than Cinderella. Besides, A) you'd bust my balls if I ever tried anything with you, which I would not, because B) I like submissive types. You are so far from that it's laughable. If you were, I'd already have you past this nonsense that you can't paint and run your family business."

I grimace. "Where are you going with this, exactly?"

"You should be at a spa getting a facial or whatever you women do before fancy black-tie affairs that would never cross our male minds."

"Actually," I say, blowing out a breath, "I was"—I stop myself, not wanting to give him the wrong idea about where this is going—"about to take a shower."

"Please tell me that sentence was supposed to finish with the word 'painting,' because that's the only answer acceptable in my mind."

I inspect the project I've been working on for hours, my inspiration coming from an unexpected place.

"Faith?" he presses.

"Yes. I've been painting."

"Thank you, Lord," he says, his voice exaggerated relief. "I have to see whatever it is before I leave Sunday."

"No," I say quickly. "This is nothing like the black-and-white landscapes I'm known for. This is just for me."

"Now I'm really intrigued. And after tonight, you'll be a hot mama in the art circuit. Maybe this new project is the one where we make big money together."

"You know that doesn't matter to me," I say. "I just needed to pay my outrageous L.A. rent, and selling my work helped."

"You mean you downplayed your dream of quitting the art museum and painting full-time every chance you got. I've told you before many times. There is *nothing* wrong with dreaming big and getting paid big for your work. I need new work to keep that dream alive. You've given me nothing in a year."

"I don't have anything to give you," I say despite the dozen covered easels around the room that say otherwise.

"Liar," he accuses. "We both know you can't live without that brush in your hand. I want to see what you did before I leave."

"No," I say. "No, this one is for me."

He's silent a beat. "Do you know how long I've waited to hear you say you were painting for you again?"

I inhale and release a shaky breath. "Josh—"

"Don't tell me the reasons why you can't paint, because I know it's in your blood. It's like breathing to you, and I also know that you've been secretly painting. But tonight isn't about me pressuring you to paint. It's about celebrating the success of the work that you've already given me and the art lovers of the world. This night is my birthday gift to you. So. Happy birthday, Faith."

"Thank you," I say, always amazed at how he remembers this day when others who should remember have often forgotten. "How are you so bad with women and so good with your clients?"

"Being single is not about failure. It's about choice. I want what I want, and I won't settle—something we both know you understand."

The man knows far more about me than most of the people who I called friends back in L.A., but then, he lives in the art world, as I once did. "I walked right into that one," I say.

"Yes, you did. Meet me at my hotel at six thirty. I'll see you soon, sweetheart." He hangs up, and my lashes lower, a hotspot in my chest and belly where emotions I don't want to feel have formed. Emotions I swore I *wanted* to feel when I moved into my mother's bedroom. I was wrong. Emotions weaken me. They make me feel instead of think. They change my judgment calls. Yes. I was definitely wrong about welcoming them back into my world. Just like I was wrong two years ago when I bought this place, thinking I could paint and help at the winery and give up nothing. I can't do both, and when I dip a toe back into the art world, that's what I want to do full-time. I wish tonight wasn't happening. I wish I had said no. And yet, I need to go change and dress.

Still holding my phone to my ear, I shake myself out of my reverie and stick my cell inside my jeans pocket. I have to shower and get dressed. Tearing away the smock, I toss it on the wooden stool beside the table. I exit the studio and rush down the stairs and back to my bedroom, then finally reach my closet. Flipping on the light, I walk into the giant box-shaped space and stop at the far wall, where my party dresses hang. I remove two choices, both still with tags, both splurges meant for shows I was to attend just before my father's death. One is a deep royal blue, made of lace with a V-neck and gorgeous sheer long sleeves. I love those sleeves, but my favorite part of the dress is that it's ankle length with a classic front slit. I like classic. I like the way it makes me feel like the woman I forgot I was until I met Nick Rogers. I'm not sure why he woke me up. I'm pretty sure I will wish he didn't later, but tonight, I need to feel like me, like Faith Winter, not an employee of the winery.

I refocus on the second dress, which is… Well, it's a black dress. That's the problem. No matter what it asserts otherwise, its color is my deterrent; it says death to me, a reminder of all loss. Of the people I love. Of hope. Of dreams. Of so many things. I don't know if I can survive this night while being reminded of all those reasons I can't allow my past to be my present. But tonight is about that past and about my art, though I really don't know what that means to me anymore. It's a hobby and nothing more. It can't be. It's… Wait. My spine straightens. Josh said tonight could set me up for a good payday, and I already know a second mortgage on a new mortgage won't do for me. But do I dare believe my art, my past, could help me get out of this hole that I'm in with the winery? Or at least buy me some time to find the money my mother has to have somewhere? I hope.

I set the blue dress on the bench in the middle of the room and turn around, then sprint from the closet, through the bathroom and bedroom. Running back to the stairs to my studio, I start pulling sheets off easels, staring at each of the dozen pieces I've completed, one by one. Looking for the ones that Josh might think are worthy of his representation. And the truth is, I never think any of my work is worthy of representation, so why am I even trying to figure this out? But I've sold work for up to seven thousand dollars. Okay, only a couple of pieces, and they took time to sell, but if I could sell just some of these, I could buy that time I need. And if I wasn't so damn confused about how my two worlds fit together, I might have already thought about this. I'll just show them all to Josh. I rush to the office in the corner, ignoring the glass desk in the center, and walk to a closet, where I remove a camera.

Returning to the studio, I snap photos of my work. I'm about to head back downstairs, but somehow I end up standing in front of the freshly painted easel. A portrait. I never paint portraits, and not because I don't enjoy them or have no skills in that area, but rather because of the way the brush exposes secrets a person might not want exposed, and I value privacy. I value my secrets staying my secrets, and I assume others feel the same. But I want to know Nick Rogers's secrets, and I know he has secrets. Which is why I haven't gone to the internet for answers, where I will discover only sterile data. Instead, I found myself painting him, and the hard, handsome lines of his face are defined, but it's his navy blue eyes that I've fretted over. Eyes that, along with what I've sensed and spoken of with him, tell a story I don't quite understand, but I will. I have the weekend off from the winery as my gift to myself, and I plan to finish the painting. I plan to know that man more and figure him out before I see him again. Doing so feels important, for reasons I can't quite say right now. Maybe he's my enemy or maybe he just enjoys the dynamics of playing that game. Perhaps I'm just trying to feed myself a facade of control by trying to figure out the unknown that I simply won't and don't have with that man. I wonder if he knows he doesn't have it, either.

Whatever the case, it won't matter tonight. As Josh said. The event has been sold out for months. No one, not even Tiger and his arrogance, can snag a ticket. And since I'm not going back to the winery until Sunday night, I suspect he'll have gone back to wherever he practices by then. In fact, maybe I'm wrong about seeing him again. If he gets back to work and gets busy, he might even forget whatever challenge I represent. My painting might actually be the last I see of the man. This should be a relief. It's not.

By the time I email the photos to Josh, I have only an hour to shower and dress. By the time I fret over underwear and thigh highs as if Tiger might show up and rip them off of me, then move on to change from the blue dress to the black dress twice, I'm running late. Finally, though, I return to the blue dress, then rush through fussing with my makeup and curling my hair, which I usually leave straight. Even choosing shoes becomes an ordeal, but I settle on strappy black heels, along with a small black purse with a little sparkle that is also Chanel, purchased by someone I'd rather not think about.

I'm in the car, starting the engine, ten minutes before I'm supposed to meet Josh, and it's a thirty-minute drive. He calls me at fifteen: "Where are you?"

"The traffic was bad."

"There is no traffic. Faith—"

"I sent you photos of the work I have done." All except one particular portrait.

"Did you now?" he asks. "I'll take a look now and you're forgiven."

"You don't have time now. I know that."

"I'll make time. Meet me at the gallery instead of the hotel. Go to the back door. Expect security." He hangs up.

I let out a breath I didn't know I was holding. He's looking at them now. I suck another breath in. What if he hates them? What if dabbling at my craft has made me forget what my craft is all about? "What was I thinking?" I pull up to a stoplight, and I know exactly how to make myself feel good about this decision again. I grab my phone, tab to my voicemail, and hit the button to play all messages. One after another, harsh messages play from the bank or a vendor that is past due. Each a brutal reminder of why I chose to send those photos to my agent. I have to get everyone caught up, and one by one, I've been working to do just that.

It's right at seven when I turn into the Chateau Cellar Winery that is home to the gallery. It's literally a stone castle, covered in ivy with a dungeon-style front door. Just the sight of it has my nerves jolting into action, fluttering in my chest and belly, and not just because I'm late. I've never been featured in a show this high profile. And while I tell myself this night is one last hurrah, as I turn into the parking lot, I see every space is filled, and all I can think is that this is my dream. This is still my dream. I pull on around to the back of the building and find the lot equally full, those nerves expanding, but I dare to allow myself some excitement as well. How amazing would it be if my dream saved my father's?

I park, and I've just killed the engine when there is a knock on my window. I roll it down to find Josh in view, his dark hair trimmed neatly as always, his handsome face clean-shaven. "They're waiting on you to make announcements."

"Oh no. Oh God. I shouldn't have taken the photos tonight." I click the locks, and he immediately opens the door, offering me his hand. I snag my purse and flatten my palm in his, struck by how good-looking he is in his tuxedo and how unaffected I am by his touch, even before I'm standing and under the full impact of his dark brown eyes giving me a once-over.

"You are stunning, Faith Winter." He releases me and waves a hand in the air. "I see it now. You in a bathtub on the cover of a magazine with a headline: sexy, successful, and talented." He doesn't give me time to reply. He shuts my car door and snags my arm. "Let's go."

I double step to keep up. "I'm never going to be naked on a magazine."

"Not if you keep smashing grapes instead of painting."

My heart sinks. "You hated the photos. You think I lost my touch."

He stops walking and settles his hands on my arms. "They're magnificent, like you are. Go in there and be a painter, because I don't represent winemakers."

The door opens, and a woman steps outside. "Josh. Now."

"Let's do this," Josh says, taking my hand and leading me into chaos. There are greetings and handshakes, and before I know it, I'm sitting in a chair on a spotlighted stage with two other artists I don't know but admire on either side of me, the gallery around us in darkness, the crowd standing around us.

"Welcome all," the announcer says from the podium in front of us. "As you know, we have three new artists to introduce you to tonight, but because I know you are all anxious to see the Chris Merit release, I want to explain how this works. We'll unveil the painting in exactly one hour. Highest bidder wins, and all proceeds—one hundred percent—are donated to the Children's Hospital. In the meantime, we have our three featured artists here tonight. They will be donating twenty percent of all sales tonight to the Children's Hospital as well. Please visit them in the crowd tonight. Please visit their displays and our many others." He has each of us stand, and after a few more words the lights come up. I stand and look left to find Josh waiting for me at the steps, but something intense, something familiar, compels me to look right, and I suck in air. Nick Rogers is standing there, looking like dirty, sexy, delicious lust in a tuxedo.

CHAPTER SIX

Tiger

I don't lie. I meant that when I said it to Faith earlier today. She *does* intrigue me, and the reasons are many. For starters, I like a challenge, and she is that, both in character and physical perfection. She doesn't look like a killer, but rather a beautiful woman, who is somehow delicate and strong at the same time. She doesn't smell like a killer, but rather like the garden where I'd first touched her. She doesn't even read like a killer on paper, but then I knew that when I sought her out. And right now, with her standing on the stage, staring at me, stunningly beautiful in a blue dress, I vow to know her body as well as her mind, vowing to feel every curve that dress hugs—of which she has many—next to me before this night is over. Right after I find out if she tastes like the killer and enemy I still, regretfully, suspect her to be.

I watch now as she recovers from the surprise of my appearance, the shell-shocked look on her heart-shaped face fading, her composure sliding back into place remarkably fast. She walks toward me, grace in her steps, those long legs of hers peeking out from the slit in her dress, teasing the fuck out of my cock in the process. Legs I want wrapped around my hips, but not before I've licked every last inch of them and her. She stops at the edge of the stage, at the top of the stairs while I'm at the bottom, those full, lush lips of hers painted a pale pink, subtle and yet beautiful, the way she uses a brush on a canvas. She's talented, gifted as few are, and capable of making a living on her own, without involvement in blackmailing or killing my father.

"You look beautiful," I say, and I allow my desire for this

woman to radiate in the deep rasp of my voice. "You *are* beautiful."

To my surprise, her cheeks flush red, shyness in the lowering of her lashes, as she says, "Thank you," and once again proves she's a contradiction, a beautiful, complicated fucking contradiction that I have to understand. But I'm adding another level of complication of my own that I *want* to understand.

I take the bottom step, leaving only two between us, and offer her my hand. She looks at it and then me, and when those green eyes lock on mine, the connection delivers a punch to my chest. I'd revel in how alive this woman makes me feel, in how much I want to fuck her, if I didn't think there was a 90 percent chance that she's a blackmailer and a killer, but the facts are clear. Her chin lifts defiantly, but she offers me submission, settling her palm on mine, her eyes flickering with the contact. My cock twitching with the contact. Her hand slides against mine, delicate and small, and I close mine around hers.

"Free will," I say. "Exactly what I wanted from you."

"I didn't want to make a scene," she counters, allowing me to walk her down the stairs to stand at the side of the stage.

"That's a coy response," I say, daring to settle my hand on her slender waist, pleased when *her* hand settles on my arm rather than pushing me away. "It's beneath you," I accuse.

"You're right," she surprises me by saying. "It was coy, and I don't do coy. You're touching me because I let you."

"That's true," I say. "You are letting me. Why?"

"Because you touching me is better than you not touching me."

Heat courses through my veins, perhaps because I'm playing a dangerous game with a beautiful woman who might just kill me, too. Or perhaps simply because I want Faith Winter in a way I don't remember wanting anyone in a very long time.

"How are you even here?" she asks. "The tickets were sold out."

"I know Chris Merit."

"Of course you do."

I arch a brow. "What does that mean?"

"You seem to know everyone, or they know you."

"Why is that a problem?"

"It's not."

And yet, I can almost hear that wall of hers slam down between us. I step closer to her, my free hand settling on her waist as well. "What just happened?"

"Nothing that matters."

"And if I think it does?"

"Then I'll rephrase. Nothing that I plan on explaining."

"I don't like secrets."

"It's not a secret just because someone doesn't choose to share it with you," she says. "It's simply that person's right to privacy. Besides. You want me naked. That doesn't require deep conversation."

"I didn't say I wanted you naked," I counter. "I said I want you stripped bare and not just exposed. *Willingly* exposed. The two are vastly different."

"And what exactly do you expect to expose?" she replies.

I lower my head, my cheek near hers but not touching. "All of you," I say, lingering there, letting my breath trickle warmly on her cheek and ear.

"We'll see," she says, her hands settling on my chest as if she means to push me away or pull me close, but before she can do either, we hear a male voice say, "Faith."

At the sound of her name from behind and to the right, my jaw clenches and Faith jolts, her hands falling away from me. In unison, Faith and I rotate to face our intruder, my hand settling possessively at her lower back, reminding her—and anyone else that might hope otherwise—that I'm here to stay tonight.

"Josh," Faith says, greeting the tall, dark-haired man I recognize from my research as her agent, Josh Miller. Age thirty-eight, bank account status—not as rich as me, but rich enough to declare his success.

"You did wonderfully during your introduction," he says,

glancing at me and back at her before he adds, "but you need to mingle with the masses."

"This is Nick Rogers," she says, as if he's nudged for an introduction I suspect he'd rather not have at all. "He owns a law firm in San Francisco."

"I know that name well," he says, looking at me. "You represented our top football player when he sued us to get out of his contract with our sports division."

"Who was that?" Faith asks.

"Connor Givens," I say. "Damn good quarterback."

"And what happened?" Faith asks.

"He left the agency," I say. "We won."

"And we lost," Josh says, flicking a look between Faith and myself. "I'm not sure how I feel about that."

"It's business," I say. "Like Faith is to you." There's a message in those words. I know he wants to fuck her, or he wouldn't have had his hands all over her when they entered the gallery tonight.

Josh narrows his eyes on me. "Business I take seriously," he says, an obvious warning in those words that he'd have been better off not delivering. He'll discover that soon, but now, now he dares to give me a two-second stare before cutting his gaze to Faith. "Let's mingle."

"Yes, of course," she says, looking at me, her body angled in my direction, a silent question in that action. I take her hand and draw it to my mouth. "I'll be close," I promise, kissing her knuckles, and I don't miss the tiny tremble of her hand in mine.

She nods, and I release her, and the way she hesitates in her departure tells me that I've taken her "no" to a "yes" and done so faster and easier than expected. But then, there is a reality here neither of us can deny: we really are red-hot together. She departs, and Josh latches onto her arm, touching her yet again, but she never touches him. She doesn't seem to know that he not only wants to fuck her but perhaps is even in love with her, which, considering how intelligent she is, amazes me. But then, women who don't return a man's feelings often don't see what is there to be seen. I, however, have made my intentions clear. Her naked. Me naked. Lots of sweaty, hot, dirty fucking.

I watch her chatting with one guest and then another, remembering my conversation with the star artist of the night, who I'd met while representing a mutual friend.

"Chris Merit, artist and superstar," I'd said. *"I need tickets to the event at Le Sun Gallery tonight."*

"I didn't know you were into art."

"I have a Chris Merit on my wall."

"Really? You never said a word. But, hey, man. I'm always honored to hear someone chose my work over someone else's."

"You're humble as fuck, man."

"You sure as fuck are not."

I laugh, and so does he, but he's not laughing when I add, *"How about a ticket in exchange for a fifty-thousand-dollar donation to your charity?"*

He whistles. "I'll give you the tickets, man."

"Happy to donate. It's not a problem or I wouldn't have offered."

"All right, then. That's generous as hell. I'll call my godmother and arrange a ticket. Or do you need two?"

"Just one."

"Got it. It's business, then."

"I wouldn't call her business. What do you know about Faith Winter?"

"Not much personally, but my wife and I are the reason she's in that display. I saw her work in L.A. and had a flashback to her visiting me at Le Sun a good several times a decade ago and with big dreams in her eyes. She's talented, and it's clear from looking at her work that she took some inspiration from mine, which I find flattering. She executed her work not only well but with her own style."

"Most people wouldn't like that inspiration."

"Most people are insecure." He'd laughed then. *"Funny side*

note about Faith. She'd felt like she was betraying her family by visiting me at Katie and Mike's vineyard. I told her that Katie and Mike not only knew her father well, they knew that I don't give a damn about wine. She told me she didn't, either."

"She didn't what?" I'd asked.

"She didn't give a damn about wine, and yet I hear she's now running her family vineyard, and that, my friend, could be where her dream dies, if she lets it. My wife reminded me how easily that could have happened to me when I inherited my mother's cosmetic business."

"Thus you made sure Faith was on the ticket tonight."

"Exactly."

"Does she know that?"

"No, and keep it that way. I offered her an opportunity. It's up to her to decide what to do with it."

I return to the present, watching Josh's damn hand settle on Faith's back as they stand talking with two older, distinguished men. Possessiveness rises in me, and I clamp down on the urge to go break his damn arm, reminding myself that I want to fuck Faith and then fuck her over, not marry her. Irritated at myself, I turn away from her, walking to the Chris Merit displays, admiring his skill, these particular pieces all San Francisco skylines in black and white that of course even a damn near blind eye to art would call brilliant. Interested in Chris's reference to Faith's inspiration, I cross the white tiled floor of the gallery to a corridor that has Faith's name on it, two high, glass-blocked walls creating her walkway.

Entering her display, I find ten or so guests viewing random paintings, and I decide to continue past them to the farthest corner to view from the end of the display forward. At the far corner, I find myself standing alone and studying a painting of the Reid Winter Mansion, rolling hills behind it that most would craft with the brilliant colors of Sonoma's many grapes, flowers, and trees, while Faith does not. Instead, this work is black and white, a technique

Chris also favors, but there are differences between the two. Chris sticks to various shades of gray and whites, but as with this painting, Faith always adds a splash of red. In this case, a bloodred moon.

"I'm afraid to ask what you think."

At the sound of Faith's voice, I turn to find her a few feet away, her blonde hair brushed behind her shoulders, her neck as creamy white and delicate as the rest of her. "You know you're talented," I say.

"No, actually," she says, a flicker of something in her eyes. "I don't. I never..." She lifts a hand and gives a wave. "I just don't."

I close the space between us, stopping toe to toe without touching her. "Well, you are."

Her face flushes a pretty pink like her lips. "Thank you."

There are footsteps to our left before we hear, "Ms. Winter."

At the sound of her name, Faith turns to the several guests now beside us, who in turn rave about her work. She signs autographs for them, and they declare their intent to buy one of her paintings. They depart on that note, but another couple steps forward. This continues in a rotation of guests for a good half hour or more.

"You don't take compliments well," I say when an announcement about the Chris Merit auction approaching clears the hallway, leaving Faith and me alone again.

"Everyone can't be as arrogant as you," she says, an obvious teasing note to her voice.

"Confidence isn't arrogance," I say.

"Is that what you are?"

"No. You're right. I'm arrogant, but it works for me and against my opposition."

"You'd make a bad enemy," she says. "My attorney says so."

I close the space that distractions have placed between us, my hand settling at her hip, and I do not miss the slight tremble of her body in response. "And what do you think, Faith?" I ask.

"That there are a million reasons in my head right now that say you're a bad idea."

"Then why am I touching you right now?"

"Because you touching me still feels better than you not touching me," she says, surprising me with her quick, direct answer. "And because tonight, I'm allowing myself the freedom to be someone and something I cannot be tomorrow. That's my hard limit. No tomorrow."

"Hard limit," I say, the term implying knowledge of a world I know well but did not expect her to know at all.

"I know that this is mine," she says, neither confirming nor denying her understanding of a broader, kinkier meaning.

"Negative," I say. "I do not accept that limit."

"It's my *hard limit.*"

"I *don't accept* that limit," I repeat.

"Then we end before we begin," she says, backing away and leaving me two choices: let my hand fall away from her hip or pull her close.

"It began the minute we met," I say, letting my hand fall away from her rather than pulling her close. Seeking that free will I've told her I both want and will have. "And if we're really done," I say, "why are you still standing a step from my reach, instead of walking away? And why are we both thinking about how fucking good fucking each other will be?"

"One night," she breathes out.

I close the step she's put between us, but I don't touch her, my voice low, for her ears only. "I could spend one night with just my tongue on your body and never get inside you. In fact, if I had my way, your dress would be up, and I'd be finding out how sweet you are right now."

"That was—" she begins.

"Dirty?" I supply. "Yes. It was. And I am. And so are you, or you wouldn't know what a hard limit is." I lower my head, my lips near her ear, breath intentionally warm on her neck. "You have no idea how dirty I can be," I say, "but you will. And soon."

"You think—" she begins, only to be cut off as we both hear,

"Faith," spoken from behind us.

My jaw clenches at the sound of Josh's voice, which denies me the end of that sentence, my head lifting, as Faith faces Josh and I step to her side. "They're unveiling the Merit piece in less than twenty minutes," he says, focused on Faith. "It would look good for you to be there." He glances over at me. "Are you going to bid?"

"Depends on what it looks like," I say.

His expression sours. "It's a Chris Merit one of a kind."

"And if it fits well with the one already on my wall," I say, "I'll buy it."

"You already own one?"

"He knows Chris," Faith supplies. "I'm pretty sure he can get a painting when he wants one."

Josh arches a brow. "Is that right?" he asks, looking at her, but I watch his eyes narrow, noting the sly intent they register before he looks at me and adds, "You know. Since you're obviously trying to win over Faith, supporting her work would go a long way. If you can afford that Chris Merit painting, why not buy her entire collection?"

Faith gasps. "No," she says firmly. "No, he will not." She looks at me. "I don't want you to do this. Please don't."

Her reaction, which is far from that of a blatant, money-grubbing killer in a financial bind, pleases me, but I need to know it's not a coy show. "I think me buying your work is an excellent idea."

"No," she snaps, looking between myself and Josh. "No. This is not an excellent idea." She rotates to face me, giving Josh her back. "I *do not* want you to do this."

"A portion of the sale does go to charity," I point out.

"You donated to the charity to get your ticket," she argues. "And I'm going to tell the gallery not to sell to you."

"That's like telling them to deny a donation."

"No," she repeats. "You *will not* do this." Her jaw sets, and her eyes narrow on me. "I don't understand where you're going with this, but I *am not* for sale." She turns and starts marching away. And since that conclusion really is shoving a square peg in a round hole, considering she's already agreed to fuck me, I've obviously hit a nerve.

And judging from the smirk Josh casts my way, he knows it and planned it. "I guess you had better bid on the Merit auction," he suggests before pursuing Faith, and no doubt doing so with the certainty that he's now gotten rid of me, but I am not dissuaded from what I want, ever. And I want Faith Winter. And in truth, Josh has given me a gift—a couple, actually. He's allowed me a glimpse into what makes Faith tick, and at her core, there seems to be pride, not greed. That doesn't make her innocent of the crimes I suspect her of committing, and in fact, it might simply make her a perfect criminal, able to hide behind a perfect facade of innocence. But that second gift Josh gave me was the realization that at some point, maybe even from that very first provocative moment when I first made eye contact with Faith, my original agenda has changed. I stopped looking for ways to prove her guilt and started looking for ways to prove her innocence. That might seem as if it works for her, but the truth is, it doesn't. Because when I want to believe in someone and they let me down, they betray me, my wrath is vicious.

I start walking, pursuing Faith myself, not about to let her get away. When I reach the end of the hallway, I find the immediate area a ghost town, the main gallery area cleared. An announcement sounds over an intercom: *The Chris Merit auction begins in twenty minutes in Room 4C. The painting is available for viewing in ten minutes.* In other words, the guests are now piling into room 4C, and so, likely, is Faith. I'm about to hunt it—and her—down when I spy Faith crossing the corridor toward the "staff only" door, clearly trying to use the twenty-minute gap before the auction to escape and compose herself. I decide to lend her a hand.

With long strides, I pursue her and manage to arrive at the door she's exited only sixty seconds after she disappears on the other side. Following her, I open it and enter the next room, shutting it behind me to find myself at a crossroads. Forward is the exit, and I'm about to step in that direction when a sound catches my attention, and I look right to find Faith hurrying down a narrow hallway. Again, I follow, and as I pick up my pace, she gives a quick glance over her shoulder at me but doesn't stop walking. Just before I catch up with her, she turns and enters a doorway.

I give the "Women" sign an inconsequential look, and as I know she knows I will, I push open the door and enter.

CHAPTER SEVEN

Tiger

I step inside the two-stall bathroom only to have Faith whirl on me and attack, obviously waiting for this moment. "I meant it," she declares, her eyes flashing with anger. "I can't be bought. And why would you even try? I can't figure it out. I said I'd fuck you, and yet you still do that? Is it a power play? A way to stroke your ego?"

I lock the door and step toward her, expecting her to back away, but she fearlessly stands her ground, and I swear this woman gets more interesting by the moment. She's also made it easier for me to shackle her wrist and pull her flush against me, her hands settling on my chest. "How people handle other people's money tells a story of who they are."

Her fingers close around my lapels. "I gave you *no reason* to believe I was that kind of person."

"I don't know you, sweetheart," I say, "and you don't know me. But I do know that I've seen many a thief in virgin clothing."

"You mean you got burned. Well, I'm not her, whoever she was, and why does this even matter? You just want to fuck me out of your system."

"Because I do the fucking. I don't get fucked," I say. "A motto I live by, and I don't intend to change that for you or anyone else."

"Sounds to me like you have trust issues that aren't my problem," she accuses.

"A bit like you thinking I was trying to buy you when you already agreed to fuck me," I say, tangling my fingers into her hair and not-so-gently tugging her gaze to mine. "I'm not him," I add, "whoever he was, but as you said. Why does it matter? You just want to fuck me out of your system."

"*Why* do I want you?" she breathes out. "You're such an arrogant bastard."

"The arrogant bastard who's going to fuck you better than you've ever been fucked, sweetheart," I promise, my mouth closing down over hers, and I can feel her breathe out in reaction, as if my kiss is what she's been waiting for, and it turns me on. Fuck. She turns me on. Too fucking much, considering I sought her out to destroy her.

Angry with myself for losing focus, and at her for being that damn distracting, I tear my mouth from hers, my hands settling at her hips. Staring down at her swollen lips, I see that her lipstick is untouched, but she will not be, in every possible sense, when I am done with her. "You want one night?" I ask. "That's your hard limit?"

"Yes," she confirms, grabbing my lapels again and tilting her chin up to add, "that's my hard limit. Take it or leave it."

"Then here's my hard limit," I say. "We agree that I'm going to change your mind about *your* hard limit."

"No," she says in instant rejection. "That essentially makes my limit obsolete."

"Your limit stands," I say. "But I'm telling you up front. I'm going to change your mind. Starting now."

"Are you asking for my agreement or demanding it?"

"Stating a fact and sparing us time, considering we have about ten more minutes before that auction starts and you're missed."

"Fine," she says. "I'll save you lost energy while you spare us lost time. You can't change my mind."

I react to the absoluteness in her tone, lifting her from the wall and turning her to face the sink, her hands settling on the counter, my big body caging hers from behind. Her reaction is a lift of her chin, her gaze meeting mine in the mirror with defiance in the depths of her stare. "One night," she repeats, adding a smooth "Tiger" to the end of the sentence, as if she wants to poke the very tiger she's just called me.

"Do you know how much I enjoy a challenge?" I demand, tugging her lace dress up to her hips, her nearly naked ass now under my palms.

"Too much," she replies, not even sounding breathless. "In fact, some might say that indicates you're insecure at your core."

Amused, *challenged*, I give her backside a teasing smack that earns me a yelp before I turn her to face me. "Tell me if it's too much, and I'll stop."

I pick her up and set her on the counter, spreading her legs, my hips settling between her knees, hands on the lace bands of her thigh highs. "Then again," I say, my fingers sliding up her naked thigh to rest just at the edge of her silk panties, "since I'm such a bastard, if you tell me it's *not* enough, I might not care. But I'll try to be polite about it all."

"Polite?" she asks, giving a choked laugh, her hands covering mine on her thigh. "You?"

"I'm so fucking polite," I say, "I deserve an award for proper manners." I stroke the silk between her legs, her spine arching as I do. "I'll carry your bag for you," I continue. "I'll hold the door for you." I lean in and press my cheek to hers, mouth at her ear. "I'll make you wet," I say, shoving aside her panties and stroking the slick heat of her body, my reward in the soft moan that slides from her lips. "I'll let you come when I'm ready for you to come. I'll even warn you right before I rip your panties off." I grip the silk in my hand and yank it away, shoving them in my pocket before settling on one knee in front of her. "And now I'm going to lick you in the very spot you want me to lick you, but I'm not going to let you come." I lean in and run my tongue along the exposed skin just above the lace of her hose, then caress a path to her sex, where I pull back just enough to allow my breath to trickle over her, my cock so fucking hard it hurts.

She makes a sexy, desperate little sound, her hips arching ever so slightly, urging my mouth closer, and I give her nub a tiny lick. She moans, and I swear I feel that sound like a stroke of her tongue on my cock. Restraint is my friend and her satisfaction, and for that reason, I suckle her gently, then tease her with a long swirl of my tongue. And damn I do want more, I want everything right here and now, but waiting for the sweet taste of her orgasm, and that perfect moment that I bury myself deep inside her, is all about anticipation, about submission. *Her* submission.

I pull back, my fingers flexing into her legs. Her eyes go wide, a pained moment in her eyes when she realizes I'm really not going to let her come. "You're evil," she says as I stand and set her on the ground.

"But polite," I remind her. "I warned you in advance." I pull down her dress. "I even put your clothes back on."

Her eyes flash, and she reaches into my pocket and grabs her panties. "You don't get to keep these," she declares, scooting past me to walk to the trash can, where she tosses them.

I shackle her arm and pull her to me, her hands on my chest, my hand at the back of her head. "I didn't want the panties," I say. "I wanted this." I slant my mouth over hers, my tongue licking long and deep into her mouth, and I don't give her time to object or submit. "Now we both will taste like you for the rest of this event," I say. "Until we both taste like you at the end of the night."

"Like I said," she whispers. "You're evil."

"Your torture is mine," I promise. "I'm hard as fuck and want to be inside you, but without limits. And this bathroom is one big limit."

As if proving my point, knocking erupts at the door. "Faith! Are you in there?"

At the sound of Josh's voice, Faith's eyes go wide, her fingers curling on my lapels again. My hands come down on her shoulders, and I lean in close to her ear. "Easy, sweetheart. Answer him." I lean back, and she takes a deep breath, giving me a nod.

"I'm here," she calls out.

"Did you fall in or what?" he demands. "The auction's about to start."

"I'm coming," she says, her voice a bit louder now, and when I smile, she glowers at me and adds, "I'll be right there."

I barely contain a laugh, and she must think I won't, because she pushes to her toes and presses two fingers to my lips. The flare of heat between us is instant, and I take her hand, leaning in to brush my lips over hers before my lips find her ear. "This is our secret. Go. I'll follow." I lean back, and she nods, but when I would move away, she grabs my sleeve and gives me a confused look that turns to gratitude before whispering, "Thank you."

And once again, she is nothing I expect and, it seems, everything I want. I give her an incline of my chin and step around the corner and into one of the stalls. I can hear her moving around, fixing herself before the click of the lock sounds and she opens the door. "What the hell, Faith?" Josh demands. "You need—"

The door shuts, but I still hear her reply—"You embarrassed me"—and the way her voice trembles with accusation with those words. "Why would you ask him to buy my work?"

I don't hear his reply, their voices moving farther down the hallway, but I heard what was important. She's embarrassed. But is she really, or is it an act? "Fuck," I murmur. I want it to be real. I want to prove she's innocent, but the facts are inescapable. There were checks equaling damn near a million dollars written to her mother by my father, and notes that lead me to suspect blackmail. And my father and her mother died of unexpected heart attacks, and my father died after her mother. That points to Faith double-crossing her mother, but if she did it for the money, where's the damn money?

I push off the wall and press my fingers to my temples. Maybe her mother had another partner who took the money. Or maybe Faith is in bed with that partner, who's hiding the money. I unbutton my jacket, my hands settling on my hips. I don't do stupid, and I'm not going to start now. My father ran through women, including my mother. He didn't write them checks, and he damn sure wouldn't write nearly a million dollars to one woman. And no one proves guilt while trying to prove innocence. I cannot lose my focus. I have to kiss Faith to taste the murderess beneath the woman, and I have to tear down that wall of hers to ensure she can't hide behind it. I'm not here to save her. I'm here to expose her, even destroy her. And I have to make sure that every moan I get from her is one step closer to one, or both, of those goals.

I walk to the door and yank it open, stepping into the hallway, my stride measured, with purpose. Find Faith. Get her out of here and alone. Fuck her. Expose her. *Own her.* With this intention driving my every step, I find my way to room 4C, where the mostly seated crowd encircles another stage, the easel on display there still covered. Scanning the chairs middle, left, and right, as well as the rows of people standing behind each, I locate Faith standing behind the chairs in the center row, Josh by her side, and I watch as he pats her shoulder, then leaves his hand there. And she lets him.

I inhale on yet another rush of possessiveness over this woman that could easily lead me to Faith's side, pulling her to me. But I am not a man to act rashly or without calculation. My mentor back in L.A., the smart, hard-ass bastard that he was, used to say that if you have a bird and it flies away, if it doesn't come back you never had it in the first place. He was talking about clients and reliable witnesses, but I've found that premise to have broad reach. I've pursued Faith. It's time for her to come to me. It's in that moment of decision that an elegant woman I estimate to be in her late fifties to early sixties takes the stage, her dress floral, her hair long and gray.

"Hello everyone," she says. "I'm Katie Wickerman, Chris Merit's godmother, and I am so very proud to share his newest release. This one is special to him, and while I believe you will find it rather different for him, as well, I believe it's his most brilliant work to date. But I won't talk your ear off. Without further ado…" She reaches for the sheet. "I give you Rebecca."

My spine straightens at the name of the painting, and when the sheet slides away, gasps and murmurs fill the room, while the familiar scene the work depicts punches me in the chest. It's a beachfront, on a pitch-dark night, and yet you can make out the hundreds of people gathered there with lights in their hands. Honoring a woman named Rebecca, who, after months of being missing, was declared dead.

"And now I'll hand the stage over to Kenneth Davis, our auctioneer," Katie says while a short man with a Santa Claus beard joins her.

"We'll open the bidding at fifty thousand dollars," he announces, but right now, I'm not in this room. I'm back on that beach, reliving that night that was less than one year ago now. The cold wind. The heavy emotions. The profound way one woman brought together a city and touched so many hearts and lives. She certainly did mine.

"One hundred thousand," the auctioneer calls out, snapping me back to the present, my gaze pulling left to find Faith still standing with Josh, and, delivering way more satisfaction than it should, his hand is no longer on her shoulder. I inhale and glance at the painting again, and I am suddenly far more connected to the many dark secrets of Rebecca's life, death, and murder than ever before. I want this painting.

Decision made, I walk to the table positioned by the door and register to bid. Faith appears by my side, my beautiful bird returning to me at the same time "three hundred thousand dollars" is shouted out from the stage. "You're going to bid?" she asks.

"I'm going to win," I tell her, accepting my paddle as I hear "four hundred thousand dollars" shouted out. Not about to allow the auction to close before I win, I give Faith a nod and start walking, looking for a spot near the stage. A moment later, Faith catches up to me, pursuing me now, and then and only then do I snag her fingers with mine, guiding us to the right side of the stage, close enough for the auctioneer to see and hear me. "Five hundred thousand dollars," he calls out. "No," he amends quickly with another raised paddle. "Make that six hundred thousand."

I release Faith's hand, and she murmurs, "My God," at the

dollar figure and links her arm with mine. Touching me by choice, that free will she is showing motivating me to win my auction sooner rather than later and get her out of here. I hold up my paddle and call out, "One million dollars."

The room seems to let out a collective gasp, but the auctioneer is not fazed. "We have one million dollars," he says. "Do we have a million one?"

"A million fifty thousand," a woman calls out.

I scan the crowd. A forty-something woman in a red dress is directly across from me giving me a wave, a smug look on her gaunt, overly made-up face that says she thinks she's won.

"A million one," I say loudly, lifting my paddle.

The woman scowls, and the room fills with murmurs before the auctioneer says, "Do I have a million two?"

My competition purses her pre-puckered lips and lowers her paddle, then sits. The auctioneer delivers final warnings, and it's done. I've won my painting. Faith steps in front of me, gripping my lapels as she had in the bathroom. "You just bid a million dollars on one painting."

A million one, I think, but I don't point that out. "It's a charitable donation," I say instead.

Josh appears beside us and goes on the attack. "How the hell does an attorney have the money to pay that kind of bid?"

"Josh," Faith snaps. "Stop."

"I've invested well and inherited well," I tell him. "Not that it's any of your business."

"I want to invest where you invest," he snaps.

"I'll give you my guy's name," I say drily, "but I have to warn you. I make most of my own picks."

"Of course you do," he says, repeating the exact words Faith had used about me knowing Chris Merit earlier. I arch a brow, and he smirks. "Bottom line. You have money to throw around, and you thought you'd use it to impress Faith."

He's trying to take us back to our bathroom argument, and

I'd shut him down, but Faith steps in first. "Josh," Faith chides and looks at me. "I'm sorry."

"Don't apologize, sweetheart," I say. "I do want to impress you, but not with my money." I glance at Josh. "Because what your agent here fails to understand is that smart people do not surround themselves with those chasing their money, or with any misplaced agendas."

His eyes sharpen with hate before he spouts back with, "My agenda is to protect and support Faith."

"I wasn't aware we were talking about your agenda at all," I say, making his misstep obvious.

It's in that moment that Katie chooses to join us, smiling at us all, her greeting first directed at Josh and Faith before she focuses fully on me. "Nick Rogers," she says, offering me her hand. "Thank you for being so very generous."

"It's a special painting," I say, shaking her hand. "It caught me off guard, but in a good way. I had to have it."

"Chris told me when he called about your ticket that you'd understand the painting in ways others would not."

"Rebecca not only means something to me," I say in confirmation. "But I was on the beach the night that painting depicts."

"You knew the woman who inspired the painting?" Faith asks.

"I knew her," I say, thinking of the many times I saw Rebecca with my client in what is now my sex club. She was his. He just didn't know how much he wanted her to be his. But that isn't information for Faith or anyone else. "I was involved in the investigation into her disappearance and represented someone close to her."

Josh jumps on that. "Someone suspected of murdering her?"

"Rebecca was killed by a woman who was jealous of my client's love for her," I say.

"Thrown in the sea," Katie supplies. "Chris's wife found her journals, and ultimately she was a key to solving the crime."

"Really?" Faith says. "That's…incredible. How must she feel being a part of such a tragedy?"

"She feels like she knows her," Katie says. "Chris did know Rebecca, and it guts them both that she's gone. Though, I admit, I keep hoping she'll show up one day, and we'll find out she's been on some island somewhere, living life well."

"We all do," I agree, "including everyone on that beach that night who didn't know her but knew her story."

"Indeed," Katie agrees. "Indeed." She inhales. "Onto brighter topics." She turns to Faith while Josh slips away, hopefully shamed into staying away. "Faith," Katie says, taking her hand and patting it. "You are so very talented. We're honored to have your work here."

"Thank you," Faith says. "I'm honored to have it here."

"Your father would be proud," she says. "Reid *was* proud of you."

I watch Faith's delicate little brow furrow. "You knew my father?"

"I did," she says. "And your mother. Our neighbors are like family. We loved hearing your father tell stories about the many Reid Winters before him. We actually used to get together with them when you were a young girl."

I watch confusion slide over Faith's face. "But I thought you were competitors. My mother said—"

"We were competitors? I mean, technically yes, but variety is the spice of life. It's not us or you."

"I'm very confused right now. My father—"

"Loved your mother very much, and we had a falling-out with your mother before you even hit your teen years. But Reid and Mike spoke quite frequently. And just so you know, my husband wanted to be here tonight, but we had a private party at the winery that got a little rowdy. Perhaps you can come by for dinner one night." She glances at me. "With you, of course."

A woman in a suit dress, clearly not here for the party, appears beside us, her attention on Katie. "Sorry, Katie, but I have a situation."

"What is it, Laura?"

"The bidder who lost the auction insists that Mr. Rogers cash out before she leaves."

Katie flushes with obvious embarrassment. "That's inappropriate."

"It's perfectly fine," I say. "I'll cash out now."

"It's not necessary," Katie assures me.

"It's really not a problem," I say, looking at Laura. "Where's the cashier?"

"I can help you," she says.

I glance at Katie. "I'll calm the beast in red for you." I refocus on Faith. "I'll be right back."

She nods, and I motion to Laura, who leads me out of the room and through the gallery to an office, where a college-aged male clerk attends to my paperwork. I fill out a promissory note with my banking information and connect him with my personal banker. "One last form," the man says, shoving his heavy-rimmed glasses up his nose. "This indicates delivery location and instructions."

My mind goes to Faith, and I fill out my information but put a huge note at the bottom: *Hold for guest viewing until Faith Winter's display is discontinued.* I hand the man the form, and he glances at me. "Are you sure about this?"

"Completely. Let your customers enjoy it." Impatient to get back to Faith, I enter the gallery, the crowd thinned to almost nothing, and end up walking toward Katie.

"Paperwork signed," I say. "Let me know if you need anything else."

"Of course," she says. "I'm sorry again."

"It's really fine."

Her lips curve. "But you just want to get back to Faith. I know that energy you're putting off. She's in the Chris Merit display area." She pats my arm and steps around me, but my feet stay planted.

A muscle in my jaw starts ticking. What the hell kind of energy am I putting off? Damn it, this woman is *way* too far under my skin if I'm reading like a man who has a woman under his skin. I really do need to fuck her out of my system, and there is no better time than tonight.

I start walking, crossing the gallery, and find an entire room dedicated to Chris, but the only person left inside is Faith. She's standing in front of a painting I recognize as the Paris skyline, but if she senses I'm here, she doesn't turn. I close the space between us and step to her side, my hand settling at her back, and touching this woman fires me up in ways something so simple should not fire me up.

She glances over at me. "The lady in red didn't attack you, did she?"

I laugh. "No. The lady in red did not attack me."

"It's an incredible painting," she says. "Obviously special. Rebecca's story touched me, and I barely know it."

"It's not an easy story to know," I admit.

She studies me a moment. "Not a nice guy, but he has a heart."

My lips curve. "I'm human despite my best efforts not to be."

"Don't worry," she says. "Your secret's safe with me." Her lashes shut as if her words have hit a nerve, and she quickly turns away, changing the subject. "He's incredible. I really can't blame the lady in red for wanting the painting. And he has such supportive godparents."

"Spoken wistfully," I observe, certain she's still thinking of that conversation with Katie, and, looking for revelations, I add, "People have secrets, Faith. It's part of being human."

"My mother sure did."

I turn her to face me. "What kind of secrets, Faith?"

"Her kind of secrets. Like you have secrets. *Tiger.*"

"My enemies call me Tiger. You call me Nick."

"Why do I keep feeling like you're the enemy?"

"Why are you looking for an enemy?"

"Why are we standing here talking when we agreed this was

about sex and then goodbye? Because this, whatever it is, still doesn't work for me."

"All right, then," I say. "Let's go fuck." I take her hand in mine and start walking, aware that she's using sex as a distraction, another version of her emotional wall. Certain that her "hard limit" understanding means that she's played the kind of sex games that make sex an escape, not a commitment. One might say I'm perfect for this woman. Except that I'm not, because the naked truth awaits. I just have to reveal it.

CHAPTER EIGHT

Faith

Nick.
Not Tiger.
Friend.
Not an enemy.

I still don't know if "not an enemy" is true, and actually, he didn't clarify our status outside of a name. Tiger is for his enemies. Nick is for me. Technically, that makes me a friend. But as we walk toward the main hall of the gallery, having already determined we're both parked out back, him holding me close with his arm at my waist, my bet is on me being neither friend nor enemy. I am simply a challenge to Nick Rogers. And he has proclaimed how much he enjoys a challenge. Once I move from challenge to conquest, he'll be back in San Francisco, where he lives and works, and I suspect I'll be forgotten. And that works for me. It's the reason I stopped pushing him away. I get my one night with him, lost in the fierce masculinity of a man who is so big, bold, and demanding, and he's already proven that he will leave no room for anything else. No guilt, anger, or thought of the new revelations about my parents that just keep adding up every single day.

Just Nick.
Just passion.
Just escape.

Nick and I cross through the center of the gallery, thankfully without delay, the crowd no longer a crowd, using the back employee exit I've been granted access to, and other than a few people milling around with no interest in us, we are undeterred.

We exit to the dimly lit parking lot, a cool breeze lifting my hair and then traveling straight up my dress. I shiver and squeeze my thighs together, reminded not just that my wrap is in the car, but that Nick ripped away a crucial piece of my clothing.

"Apparently, panties serve a purpose outside of looking pretty," I murmur, hugging myself.

He laughs, a deep, sexy sound, and suddenly that cold spot between my legs is hot. "It's not funny," I chide, shivering again, deeper this time.

He halts our progress and surprises me as he shrugs out of his tuxedo jacket. "This should help," he says, wrapping it around me, but he doesn't move away, his hands gripping the lapels as I had earlier, his big, broad, wonderful body crowding mine. The chilly air around us is suddenly as warm as that spot between my thighs. "Better?" he asks, his voice gravelly, sexy, the overhead light catching the warm heat in his blue eyes.

"Yes," I say, the intimacy of me wearing his jacket doing funny things to my stomach. I swallow hard. "Thank you. But I thought you weren't a nice guy?"

"I'm not a nice guy," he says, his voice that hard steel I've already come to know from him. "But," he adds, his eyes lighting with what I would almost dare call mischief, "I *am* a very polite guy. Remember?"

"Your *bad* manners are why my panties are in the trash and not in your pocket," I say, finding his teasing rather charming, despite the way he tormented me in that bathroom.

His full mouth, which I now know feels really good on my mouth and other parts of my body, curves. "As long as the panties are off, I'm a happy man." He slides his arm around my shoulder and turns us toward the cluster of ten or so random cars.

"I'm on the right far row," I say, and we quickly walk in that direction while I dig my keys from my purse and unlock my car. Proving he's polite all over again, he opens my door, which has me biting back curiosity about his mother, but if I ask questions, he'll ask questions that I don't want to answer.

I step into the alcove created by the car and door, and when I turn to face Nick to determine our plan for travel, once again I'm trapped between hard steel and this hot, hard man. But unlike last time, I don't want to escape. I want to get lost in the way he smells and the way he feels and... "Where are we going, Faith?" he asks.

I wet my lips, jolted out of a fantasy that was headed toward him naked, and me enjoying the fact that he was naked. I'm now back to a hard reality: the decision between inviting him to my private space and personal sanctuary or daring to go to his hotel, which isn't much of a decision at all. "Small towns have wagging tongues," I say. "And I really don't need that right now, with all I have—I don't need that."

"I'm in a private rental house," he says, seeming to read my thoughts. "We can go there if you're worried about your staff."

A private rental house should be a safe zone, but in that moment, I know I need the known of my home, to balance the unknowns and the powerful force that is this man. "I own a house also close to the winery, and I'm staying there this weekend. We can go there."

He considers me for several beats, a keen look in his eyes telling me he's read my need for control, and I wait for him to insist he retain it all. Maybe he'll push me too hard. Maybe this is a bad idea—but that isn't what he does. Instead, he does the exact opposite. He arches a brow. "Interesting. I thought you'd pick my rental."

"Why is that?"

"It fit your hard limit of one night."

"My space. My control."

His hand slides to my hip, and he pulls me to him, his hips aligned with mine, my hand settling over his heart, and I am surprised to find it thundering beneath my palm. "Sweetheart," he says. "I'm going to demand control, because that's who I am and what I need. I can read you on this, just like you do me."

He's right. I do. Because I'm drawn to men with his type of appetites. Because apparently, that's who I am. "I do know that about you. But ultimately, I have control. I say yes or no."

"As it should be," he says. "But I'm going to make sure you don't want to say no and that you never forget me for all the right reasons. That's a promise." He covers my hand where it rests on his chest and lifts my wrist to his lips, caressing the delicate skin before pressing my hand to his face, as if he's getting me used to touching him. But he leans into the touch as if he craves it, and then he kisses my palm, and I swear, it affects me. It's tender, and sensual, and probably the sexiest thing anyone has ever done to me, and I am not without experience, but he affects me. Intensely, deeply.

With obvious reluctance, he releases me and takes a step backward, his hand on my door. "I'm two rows over. I'll pull around to follow you. I'm in a—"

"—black custom BMW," I supply, letting him know that yes, I *was* watching him at the window before I slip back inside the car, fully intending to, for once, leave him with a revelation as he did me today. But I should have known Nick Rogers would not leave his curiosity piqued without resolution.

He squats down next to me. "You *were* at the window."

"Yes," I confirm, turning to look at him. "How did you know I was there?"

"I felt you watching me." He lowers his voice to a deep rasp. "Like I can feel you now, Faith, and I'm not even touching you." And once again, like this morning, with a bombshell statement, he is gone, doing to me what I failed to do to him moments before. He's already standing, the door shutting, and without question, as he's intended, I am left in a sea of simple words that are not simple at all. And this time I do not have hours and a paintbrush to try to make sense of the way this man so easily affects me, the way my heart is thundering in my chest at this very moment.

He can feel me without touching me. I can feel him without

touching him. I think back to my past, to the relationship that gave me the hard limits—a turbulent, addictive, completely-wrong-for-me relationship. Was it like this and I just can't remember? I don't think so, and yet it *was* passionate. It *was* intense. But it wasn't this. And yet this isn't romance. It's sex. I mean, my God, we almost had sex in the bathroom. So, what makes Nick Rogers different? And I still can't get past that sense of something darker than just our passion between us, that battle of friend versus enemy that should have scared me away. Earlier today, it would have.

Headlights now burn behind me, telling me that I am out of time, with no answers, and I accept this is how it must be, unless I plan to go panty-less and unsatisfied, which I don't. I quickly turn on my car. Or I try. The engine clicks but doesn't come to life. I try again. "No," I whisper. "No. No. No." The lights flickered when I unlocked the door. The battery isn't dead. I try again with the same result. The headlights behind me shift, and Nick pulls in beside me. I try the ignition again, but the car doesn't start. There's a knock on my window, and I sigh, caving to my inevitable circumstances.

I open my door, and Nick rounds it, once again, squatting beside me. "Has this ever happened before?"

"No," I say, "but I hate to admit this, because it's completely irresponsible, which is not who *I am*, but I can't remember the last time I took it in for maintenance. And it's a BMW. They're high maintenance."

"Yes, they are," he says, and to my surprise he doesn't make me feel more stupid than I already feel. "But they handle the San Francisco hills and the Sonoma cuts and curves like no other car. We'll get it towed and fixed in the morning. Let's take my car."

In the morning.

The inference being that he's not planning on leaving tonight, but that rattles me far less than him feeling me without touching me. But right now, I need to deal with my car. "Yes," I say. "That works." I rotate to get out of the car, and he snags my fingers, and then my waist, to help me stand, and suddenly I'm flush against him, his hands at my waist.

And while moments before he'd held me captive with words, with the idea of touching him, now it's the way he feels when he touches me. The way I can't breathe unless he's breathing with me when we're this close. "I'm going to go inside and tell them we're leaving your car," he says, warmth in his voice.

"There you go being polite again," I accuse.

"I guess my mother raised me right after all," he says, stroking a wayward strand of hair from my forehead, and not only do I barely contain a shiver, I barely contain my desire to ask a question about his mother, which he doesn't give me time to ask anyway. "Come," he says—or, rather, orders, which I've decided is as natural to him as that need for control we just talked about, and I don't mind. It's actually sexy when done at the right time and place by a man who knows that time and place, which is preferably while naked. And we're both already mentally undressed.

In a few steps and moments, I'm sliding inside his BMW, its soft cream-colored leather encasing me while that earthy scent of the man himself surrounds me. "I'll be right back," Nick says, shutting the door, and I inhale that alluring scent of him again and pull my seat belt into place, the sound of soft music stirring curiosity in me. Turning up the volume, I find it's classical music that I know well. Somehow, it fits Nick.

The driver's door opens, and he joins me, and I swear the man has this energy that consumes the very air around him. And me. He consumes me. Suddenly, the car is smaller, more intimate, and I am warmer, my heart beating faster. "That was fast," I say.

"A guard just showed up and made that easy on me," he explains. "He's letting Katie know the situation." He reaches for the gear shift but pauses, seeming to listen or think before casting me a sideways look. "You found my music, I hear."

"I did," I say. "'Symphony No. 5'. I know it well. It suits you."

"Don't let that fool you," he says, starting the engine and backing out of the parking spot before placing us in gear. "I'd just as easily have Kid Rock or Keith Urban on the radio. It depends on my mood and where my head is at the time."

"And tonight it was classical. Why?" I ask, casting him a curious look.

"It's a work state of mind," he says. "When I'm prepping for court, opening and closing statements in particular, words distract me, but music helps me set the tone in my mind."

"Are you working on opening or closing statements now?"

"Actually, in this case," he says, driving us through the narrow path connecting the gallery to the winery, "it's deposition prep for next week. If you do them right—and I do—you convince the enemy that you're going to win in court, and they make a deal out of court."

"There is that word again," I say, my gaze scanning the Wickermans' castle as we turn toward the exit.

"What word?" Nick asks, pulling us onto the highway.

"Enemy," I say. "I don't like it, but I guess for you, that's not a word but a rule of life. You always have a new enemy, right?"

"In most cases," he says, "I have opponents."

"You said enemy."

"In this case, enemy applies. I used to work with the opposing counsel back in L.A. We cochaired an insider trader case for one of the biggest clients in the firm."

"And what happened to make him an enemy?"

"I like to win," he says, "but I do it the right way. With my brains. He likes to win as well. By playing dirty."

"And you never play dirty? They do say you'll rip someone's throat out if they cross you."

"If someone hires me to do a job, my job is to win. Not to feel sorry for the person coming after my client, or even the person aligned with the person coming after my client. My client needs to know that if he or she is with me, he or she is protected."

"And what if the witness is pulled into the case without wanting to be pulled into the case?" I ask. "Are you still that coldhearted to that witness?"

"Yes," he says with zero hesitation, even doubling down. "Absolutely. Because I didn't pull that person into the case. The person attacking my client did, and my client has the right to protect themselves. And believe me, if you were the one needing that protection, you'd be glad I was the one on your side."

"That sounds vicious."

"It is vicious, and I'm unapologetic about it. But there's a difference between being a coldhearted asshole and breaking the law. And the man I call an enemy broke laws to obtain evidence, which could have gotten us both disbarred."

"What did you do?"

"I was forced to throw out what would have been good evidence if obtained legally and find another way to win."

"And the enemy of yours, he agreed to throw it out?"

"No. I threatened to go to the board at the firm, and he read my willingness to do it accurately."

"And you won the case?"

"Yes. I won."

I rotate to my side to face him. "Can you tell me about it?"

He glances over at me. "You want to hear about the actual case?"

"I want to hear about how you won it under those circumstances, yes."

"Why?"

Because I need to hear about someone else overcoming another person's crimes and winning, I think. But I say, "Because you intrigue me," and it's true. He does.

He laughs at my play on his earlier words, the passing lights illuminating his handsome face. "Aren't you the witty one, Ms. Winter?"

"Actually, not many people call me witty."

"You sure about that? Because that comeback in the bathroom where you called me insecure was pretty witty."

"That was snarky."

"So, you're known for your snark?"

"No," I say, "but I am known for excellent pancakes and an incredible knack for sprucing up a box of Kraft macaroni and cheese like nobody's business."

"You're known for your paint brush," he amends.

"I'm *almost* known," I correct before I can stop myself, but I've said it, so I just wade on into it. "Which is like almost winning a case to you, I suspect."

"You downplay your achievement," he says. "Chris Merit wanted you in his show. That's pretty damn powerful in the art world."

"Our families share a connection," I say. "Apparently more so than I realized." I change the subject that I wish I hadn't broached. "Tell me about winning that case."

"I'd rather hear about you. Tell me about your art."

"You teased me with part of a story," I press. "I really want to hear about how you won the case."

His phone rings, and he hands it to me. "Tell me who's calling so I don't drive us into a cliff."

Stunned by something that feels rather private, I nevertheless take the phone and glance at the caller ID. "It says North. Why don't you use Bluetooth?"

He grabs an earpiece from the visor and attaches it to his ear. "Hackers love Bluetooth, and I deal with confidential information for powerful people. And I need to take that call, sweetheart. It's my associate working on the depositions with me."

"Of course," I say, the endearment doing funny things to my belly all over again.

"Punch the button for me, will you, before he hangs up?" he says, battling his headset.

"Yes," I say, turning down the radio for him, "but take the next right and it's going to be about five miles before we turn again."

"Got it," he says, and I hit the button to answer the call, then face forward, sinking into my seat. I feel as if I'm intruding on his world now, when really, I haven't even searched him on the internet or otherwise, as he has me. It's a thought that does not sit well. I really don't want him in my world—just in my bed. I don't want anyone in this hell with me right now. I inhale and shut my eyes, listening to him speak, and I don't remember ever being so attracted to a man's voice. But there is something about his deep, masculine voice that is almost musical, and judging from the warm heaviness in my body, it's a song that plays all the right notes for me.

"No," Nick says to the person he's labeled as "North" in his phone. "Don't ask him that. He'll walk right around the topic, and you'll alert him to what comes next." He pauses to listen. "No. Explain your reasoning, and you're going to need a miracle to get me to agree to this."

As his conversation continues, I'm struck by how certain Nick is about everything he says and does, wondering how long it's been since that was me. And it was. There was a time when I was young and thought I could rule the world with a paintbrush, back when I was as confident as he is today. When I'd thought big dreams and hard work would get me to the level of success Nick is at now. But I wasn't Nick. I wasn't hard enough. Life chipped away at me, and right now, that makes me feel more of that anger I've been feeling. Only I realize it's not really my mother's fault at all. She did what she did, but she didn't make my choices for me. I did. I chose how I let me handle me.

"And I'm off," Nick announces.

"And all is well?" I ask.

"All is well when I finish a deposition with a settlement." His brow lifts, and he surprises me by turning the radio back up and testing my musical knowledge. "Do you know this one?"

"'Dawn' from *Also sprach Zarathustra*, Richard Strauss. Did you know that this is the opening to the movie *2001: A Space Odyssey*?"

"Did *you* know that Elvis used it for his entrance to concerts?"

"I did," I say. "Mostly because I had an art teacher who not only thought painting to classical music gave the work depth, but she was also insanely in love with Elvis. Painting to Elvis gave the work sexiness."

He laughs, a deep rumble that feels real to me when not much else has lately. Maybe that's why I need this man so much. That lust we share can't be faked. It's real. "Is that art teacher the reason you know classical music?" he asks, pulling me back to the present.

"Oh yes," I say. "That's how I know classical music and every word to every Elvis song ever recorded. Doesn't everyone know the words to every Elvis song ever recorded?" I laugh, his lighter mood lightening mine as well.

That is until he asks, "Do you still paint to classical music and Elvis?"

I am instantly thrust back in time, to the excitement I once woke up to every day to just hold a brush. "Sometimes I'd just turn on the music and let it run through songs until one inspired me." Except today, I think. He was my inspiration.

"Why was that statement past tense?"

"It's complicated."

"I think I've made it pretty obvious that I'm good at complicated," he counters.

"I'm not. And take the next right. You'll go down about a half a mile and then turn at the white gate. That leads to my property. You can park in the driveway. I left the garage door opener in my car, and the door sticks half the time anyway."

"Back to complicated," he pushes.

My phone buzzes with a text, and I lift his jacket, searching for my purse under the sea of cloth. By the time I have it in my hand, my phone buzzes again, and I unzip my purse, digging it out to glance at a text from Josh: *Where are you? Your car's still here, but I can't find you.*

"Oh no," I murmur, "I didn't say goodbye to Josh." I turn to Nick. "What was I thinking? He's my agent, and I said nothing to him."

"Text him, sweetheart, or we'll never get to those morning-after pancakes."

"Who says you'll be around for pancakes?"

"Me."

"You know, I don't like arrogant men."

"Since we both know I make a living being arrogant, what's my appeal? My money. My good looks." His lips curve. "I'm just so damn polite that you can't help but lose your panties?"

"You're bad."

"Dirty. And bad. So, is that the appeal?"

"It's definitely not your money," I say while he pulls us onto the driveway by my house, dim lights casting us in a glow.

"Most women like the money," he says, killing the engine.

"Which means you can't ever know if a woman wants you for you or for your money. There's a reason you're what, thirty-five or thirty-six, judging by your career, and either divorced or never married."

"Thirty-six," he says, turning to me. "Never married and never plan to be married. I don't believe in marriage."

"Then I guess we are perfect for each other," I say.

"Are we now?"

"For tonight," I confirm, and when his lips quirk, eyes lighting, I quickly add, "That's not a challenge."

"Of course not," he says, and there is the distinct vibe radiating off him that he knows something I don't know.

"What does that mean?"

"Whatever I make it mean," he says, giving a low chuckle before he adds, "I'll come around and get you," and he's already exiting the car, clicking the locks before he departs. I turn to my door and try to open it, but it won't budge. Frowning, I try again, and still it won't move. Nick grabs the door and opens it, and I twist around to get out, and to go right along with the rest of my day, my skirt catches on my heel. Much to my distress, as I rotate to face him, the slit down the middle of my dress tears straight to my bare-naked crotch.

I gasp, and as much as I want to cover myself, my heel and my skirt are still not where they should be. But when embarrassment would kick in, Nick is suddenly squatting in front of me, his hands on my knees, his gaze sliding to my sex, lingering and then lifting to mine, the connection stealing my breath.

"If you're trying to seduce me," he says, his expression all hard lines and passion, before he adds, "it's working."

It's cold outside, and I am warm all over. "I… That wasn't the idea."

He leans in and kisses my leg just above my thigh high, and then, to my shock, he leans in and licks my clit, and then he's doing this slow teasing swirly thing with his tongue, and now I really can't breathe. I brace myself on the dash, and just when I think I might melt right here in this car, Nick pulls back and stands, taking me with him.

I pant with the impact. "You can't keep doing that to me," I whisper. "Seriously. That is—"

He leans in and kisses me, hand at the back of my head, his tongue now doing that same slow, sexy tease he'd just done in much more intimate places, before he speaks: "I won't stop next time. That's a promise."

CHAPTER NINE

Faith

Nick laces his fingers with mine and guides me away from the car, shutting the door. Somehow, though, instead of walking forward, we're standing toe to toe again, and when our eyes meet, there is this flutter that turns into heat radiating across my chest and down my arm to where our fingers touch. To where he holds my hand, and with all I have dared sexually, with good and bad outcomes, with all I know he will dare of me, this is still what affects me.

"You hold on to me like you think I'm going to run," I murmur. "You wouldn't be here if that were my plan."

"I hold on to you like a man who doesn't want to stop touching you." He reaches up and caresses my cheek, the touch tender, my body reacting, my breasts heavy, my nipples puckered under the lace of my bra. That flutter in my chest repeats. "Let's go inside where I don't have to," he adds.

"Yes," I say. "Please."

His lips curve. "Please."

"I'm polite, too," I say, but I don't add anything about my mother teaching me right, because she did not. My father did.

"I wonder if you'll be so polite when I finally get you naked."

"Don't count on it," I say, and it's meant to be playful, but there is this pulse of adrenaline in me that makes it more raspy and needy.

He knows it, too. I see it in the darkening of his eyes. "Come," he says, draping his arm around my shoulders and turning us toward the door, leaving my hands free to tug his jacket around all my gaping, naked places, while I'm thinking about being truly naked with this man. And with each step we take, I am aware of how our legs move together, hips aligned. How he holds me close, touching me just as he said: like he doesn't want to stop touching me.

We've just reached the eight steps leading to the dimly lit porch when my cellphone rings in his jacket pocket, I'm still wearing and I stop dead in my tracks. "Oh no," I say, digging in the pocket. "I didn't send Josh that text. It's going to be him, and where is my phone? I can't find it, but I hear it."

Nick moves to the step in front of me, and he reaches in the opposite pocket from the one I'm struggling with, retrieving my phone, which has stopped ringing. "Thank you," I say, reaching for it, and I have no idea how this man handing me my cell has turned into something sexual, but he's holding it and my hand.

"I still don't have you inside the house," he murmurs softly, walking backward to lead me to the porch, only steps away from the door. "I still don't have you naked."

And that's when my phone starts to ring again.

Nick sighs. "I'm starting to feel like this is a threesome." He releases me. "Talk to the man so I can have you to myself."

"Sorry."

"Don't be sorry. Just be done."

I nod and answer the call. "Josh." And then I say that word again: "Sorry. I just saw your text."

Nick walks to the door and leans on it, and while I intend to walk to the security panel to key in my code, I instead find myself standing just above the steps, embracing my first opportunity to fully appreciate Nick without a suit or tuxedo jacket on. His white shirt stretches across an impressive broad chest, his arms—also impressive, from what I can tell—folded in front of said impressive chest.

He notices my attention, of course, because how can he not when I'm boldly watching him? He arches a brow, the look on his face a wicked invitation. Josh says something about the parking lot followed by, "And I texted and tried to call you," while I have no idea what else he's said.

Cutting my gaze from the distraction that is Nick, I reply with, "It didn't ring," and cross to the keypad on the wall, right next to the spot Nick leans on.

"And you didn't think about finding me before leaving?" Josh demands.

"I had car problems I was dealing with." I key in my code to have it beep in rejection.

"Which means you were leaving without finding me," he accuses.

Giving up on the code to the door, wishing now that I didn't let the security company convince me to use this keypad system, I rotate and rest against the wall next to Nick. Focusing now on surviving this conversation with Josh, I say, "You disappeared along with the crowd."

"Where are you now?" he asks. "Do you need help with your car?"

"I got a ride home."

"A ride with Nick Rogers," Josh says, disapproval in his voice.

"Josh—"

"That's a yes," he says. "He's an arrogant bastard who will fuck you and leave you. You know that, right?"

A fizzle of unease slides through me at the harsh words that do not fit Josh, but then again, he's still close to a past that I've left behind. A man I've left behind, and I'm not going to go there with him with Nick standing here—or ever, if I have my way. "Thank you for the advice," I say, trying to recreate the professional barrier between us that seems to have fallen. "And for everything tonight. I'm excited that you liked my new work. I can't wait to see what happens with it." I can feel Nick's eyes on me, heavy, interested.

"In other words," Josh says, "he's with you, and you don't want to talk."

"Now's not a good time," I confirm.

"Right." He's silent several beats. "Just be careful."

"I always am."

"We'll talk before I head back to L.A." He hangs up, and I stuff my phone back in the jacket pocket.

"Well, that went well," I say, glancing over at Nick. "And I have to call the security company. I don't have a key. I use the keypad."

Nick pushes off the wall and steps in front of me, big and overwhelmingly male, but he really makes overwhelming delicious. "What's the code?" he asks.

"8891, but I tried it twice. It won't work."

He keys in the code, and the front door clicks. "Of course it opens for you," I murmur.

"You were focused on Josh," he says, and instead of making a move for the door, he presses one hand on the wall above my head, those blue eyes of his too intelligent, too probing as he repeats Josh's words. *"An arrogant bastard who will fuck you and leave you,"* he says.

"You heard. Obviously."

"I heard. And *obviously*, he doesn't know that the description 'arrogant bastard who will fuck you and leave you' makes me perfect for you. Why is that, I wonder?"

"I could ask you the same."

"You could," he agrees, "but right now, we're talking about you. Should I guess the reasons you like your men here and gone?"

"Should I guess the reasons you like your women here and gone?"

"Go for it, sweetheart," he says, and the challenge is clear. If I make my guess, he can make his without my rightful objection. But I do object, deny, and reject the idea of this man, who sees too much as it is, seeing anything more than my body. The rest is off-limits.

"No," I say. "I don't want to know. Who you have in your bed or in your life, aside from a wife you've said you don't have, is none of my business. And we've already filled this night with too many words. Tonight isn't about conversation."

I dart away from him to the door, opening it, but I also know that I do not have to rush. He won't rush after me. He's a man of control. A dominant that will follow at his pace, pursue in his way. And he'll catch me, but it won't be for conversation, which is exactly why I'm making him pursue me. Entering the house, I notice that the light is on, when I don't remember it being on, but then, it was daylight, and I was in a rush. Dismissing the concern as nothing, I walk down the hallway, and I'm almost to the living room when I hear Nick's steps in the foyer, the door shutting behind him, locks turning. Adrenaline rushes through me, no longer a slight bump in energy but a fierce surge, but really, how can it not? Nick Rogers is nothing if not an injection of adrenaline. And while I call him a dominant, that isn't just a personality trait. He is a sexual dominant, and, as I expected when I threw out the term "hard limit," he has experience in a world where that word has heightened meaning. That knowledge should have been enough for me to decline this encounter, and yet, it wasn't. I don't know what that says about who I am, or what I want or need, and I haven't for two years now. Maybe before, but maybe that's the gift Nick will give me. I'll figure it out through him.

Entering the living room, I turn the dial on the wall that brings the lights to a soft glow, a chill clinging to the air. Nick's footsteps grow closer, and I move deeper into the room, walking past the kitchen to my right and around the overstuffed chocolate brown couch and chairs, my destination the fireplace directly in front of them. Once I'm there, I flip the switch on to heat the room, and I can feel the moment Nick joins me, feel his energy, his dominance. It crackles and snaps, the way the gas fire does not, charging my skin, and suddenly, I am hyperaware of the tear in my dress that goes nearly to my belly button.

Inhaling, I turn to face him, and I don't use his jacket to cover myself. I let it gape open, my lower body exposed. He's leaning one broad shoulder on the wall just inside the archway that encases the hall, directly in front of me. "I thought you weren't running from me, Faith?"

"I told you. I'm not running from you, or you wouldn't be here."

"Then why am I over here and you're over there?"

"That's your choice, not mine."

"Is it?"

"Yes," I say, shrugging out of his jacket and tossing it on a brown stool in front of the fireplace, a fluffy cream-colored rug beneath it. Exposed now for Nick's viewing, I straighten, a silent command from me to him that he look at me, but he does exactly what I expect—what any true dominant would do—and that's not what I've bid. His gaze is fixed unwaveringly on my face. His way of telling me that he is in control, that he looks and touches at his own inclination, as will I. It's simply his way, a part of who he is, and even a huge portion of what turns me on about him. But my mind flashes back to a time when another dominant was in my life. When I was naked and exposed, tied up. Submitted, and it was pleasure, and then it wasn't anymore. And that has nothing to do with Nick and everything to do with my choices and my own self-discovery. I am not a submissive, but I want this man who will want that of me, and I do not understand it, or myself, right now.

Certain Nick is going to read my trepidation, if that is even what I'd call it, I need something to fill the room other than him and my hyped-up, crazy energy. Ruling out the television behind me above the fireplace, I decide on music and quickly walk to the artsy, built-in entertainment center in the corner. Once I'm there, facing a portion of the dozen shelves that gradually get shorter and smaller as they climb the wall, I can feel Nick move again. God. I can feel him just like he said he could me, even when he's not touching me, which is exactly why he is nothing like my past. Nothing made me feel this then. No one made me feel this.

I reach for the CD player and hit power and then play, knowing that it contains a CD of random downloaded music that is about as eccentric as the taste he described in the car. Music fills the air, an Ed Sheeran song, and with another deep breath, I rotate, finding Nick sitting on the ottoman to one of the chairs, angled toward me. And while sitting might seem a submissive position, it's not. It's him watching me. It's him on the throne of power, while I stand in front of him. Which is exactly why I sit down on another stool I keep by the shelf, meant to reach the books on the bottom row now behind me. And I do so with my knees primly pressed together, aware that while my lower belly, legs, and thigh highs are exposed, I've denied him a view of what's in between.

Our eyes lock and hold across the small space of several feet, separating us, a challenge in the air, which I've created by choice this time. Can he make me submit? But it's not a real question. We both know he can. And I don't have to fear that is all there will be between us, that he will think he can bend my will every moment he's with me. There is only this moment, this night.

The song skips, and just when I fear I'll have to break this spell with Nick and change it, it changes on its own to an old nineties hit: Marcy Playground, "Sex and Candy," and that's exactly the lyrics that fill the air: *I smell sex and candy here. Who's that lounging in my chair?*

Nick arches a brow at the rather appropriate words and says, "Sex and candy?"

My hands press to the cushion on either side of me. "Sometimes, you just need sex and candy."

"Indeed, you do," he agrees, leaning forward, his forearms on his knees, his sleeves rolled up to expose several tattoos I cannot make out, and I don't try. Not when his piercing gaze lingers on my face, and the song continues with: *Yeah, mama, this surely is a dream.*

"And there she was," he says, his blue eyes burning with that dark lust we share. "Like double cherry pie," he adds, followed by the command of, "Open your legs, Faith."

My breath hitches, and I don't know what happens. I want

to do it. I plan to do it, but nerves erupt in me like I'm some inexperienced schoolgirl. I'm not a schoolgirl, nor am I suppressed or reserved sexually. I didn't get raped. I don't fear or dislike sex. And yet I haven't had it in a very long time. And my heart is racing again, or maybe it never stopped; my mouth is dry. So very dry. Somehow, I'm standing without consciously making that decision and I'm darting toward the connecting kitchen. I enter the archway, open the stainless-steel fridge, and grab a bottle of water. I open it and start guzzling.

Nick is suddenly in front of me, reaching for the bottle and taking a drink, his hand on my hip, leg aligned with mine. "Water?" he asks, looking at the bottle. "I thought you were going for liquid courage, but I didn't think it would be water."

"I don't like to dull my mind with booze," I say. "My mouth gets dry when I get nervous, but this was really not smart because nothing like a girl needing to pee to ruin the mood and I—"

He kisses me, and the lick of his tongue is cold from the water, and fresh, and I have no idea why, but it calms me. Him touching me, not watching me, calms me, but the kiss is too short and his question too fast. When he pulls back to look at me, he takes the water, setting it in the refrigerator. "Why are you nervous?" he asks.

"I don't know."

"Hard limit," he says. "That phrase comes with experience." He rotates us slightly and kicks the door shut. "You've been a part of a world that doesn't match your nerves."

He's right. It does. "It's been a long time."

"How long?"

"Two years."

"Since you were in that world or since—?"

"Nothing for two years."

"It's just like riding a bike"—his voice lowers—"only you'll be riding me." He rotates me and presses me against the island, his body lifting from mine, hands pressed on the dark wood of the counter behind me. "Were you someone's submissive?"

"No. I'm not a submissive."

"But you were with someone who wanted you to be."

"Yes."

"I don't want you to be."

"But you're dominant."

"I don't take submissives, and you have to sense that, or you wouldn't be with me."

"You think I could *sense* that?"

"I think we're remarkably in tune with each other for virtual strangers. Which is why we're both here right now. I like control. You like making me earn it. But as we've established, I like a challenge. And you, Faith, are that and so much more. Which means I'm okay with earning control, and you get the control you want, because you decide when I get mine."

And there it is. The many reasons I want this man. His power. His control. The challenge I enjoy delivering and he enjoys conquering. But there is more there, too. There is the reason, a few moments ago, that nerves controlled me instead of our game and him. And it had nothing to do with who tried to control me in the past—at least, not sexually. He sees too much. He knows too much when he should know nothing. It's illogical, but he's right. I did know him without knowing him, and he knows me without knowing me. And that makes him, and this, dangerous. But now that I know what is happening and why I should run, I have less desire to do so than ever.

I want him. And, as if his mind is in the same place, he says, "I want you, Faith," and then reaches down and rips my dress all the way open. I gasp, shocked, aroused, more aroused. His hands end up at my knees, where the final tear allows my dress to fall open, but they do not stay there. They glide from my knees, my thighs, and over my hips to the front clasp of my bra, which he manages to unhook. It falls away like my dress, replaced by his hands. "I want you, Faith," he repeats. His thumbs stroke my nipples, his cheek pressing to mine. "Like I don't remember ever wanting in my life."

I might reject these words, but there is this raw, almost tormented quality to his voice that tells me he doesn't want to feel this…whatever it is that is happening any more than I do. It tells me that he has a past, as do I. It echoes with every spiraling emotion inside me, right now, and deep inside every night that I cannot sleep. He pulls back, his eyes meeting mine, and while his expression is impassive, there are shadows in his eyes that he doesn't hide, that he lets me see, and I think… I think this is to let me know that I am not alone. But I am alone, and the fact that I've had this thought is confusing—and yet, somehow, I'm *not* alone with this man, not this one night, when we dare be whoever it is we are together.

He lifts me, sitting me on the counter, his hands on my knees, which are now pressed together.

"Now open for me," he orders softly, but he doesn't press them open himself. He waits for me to open them, giving me the control and taking it at the same time. The look on his face, the warmth in his touch on my legs, promises me salacious, wonderful rewards, and a deep throb radiates in my sex. I open my legs, and my dress hangs from my body. His hands settle on my shoulders, branding my skin under the silk and lace of both the dress and my bra. His gaze lowers, sliding over my breast, a heavy caress that is not a caress at all, but my nipples pucker, my sex clenches.

Slowly, he inches the material down, over my back, and when it falls to the counter behind me, I slip my hands away from it. "I loved this dress," I say.

"I'll buy you a new one," he says.

"No," I say immediately, my hands going to his hands where they rest on my thighs. "No. I do not want you to buy me a dress. I don't want your money, and don't make this about that."

"Make this what?"

"I don't need anything from you but an orgasm. Or two or three, *if* you're up to it."

The blue of his eyes burn, hot coals and simmering heat. "A

challenge we can both accept."

"But I still think you need to pay for my dress."

His eyes narrow. "You said—"

"That I don't want money but I want an even playing field." I reach in the drawer beside me and grab a knife, removing it.

I don't even get it beyond the counter before Nick grabs my hand, pulling it and the blade between us, his jaw steel, his voice tight. "What are you doing, Faith?"

CHAPTER TEN

Tiger

My fingers wrap around Faith's slender wrist, that knife between us, but as I look at her, I think that if she intends malice, she's far better an actor than any opponent I've ever faced. I see no intention in her face, nor do I sense any in her energy, see any in her eyes. But this moment damn sure reminds me that I'm not here because this woman rocks my world like no other, despite the fact that she does. I'm here because my father and her mother are dead. Because she is the only logical place murder leads, even if it now feels illogical to me.

"Trust issues much, Nick?" she challenges. "Who was she? Because clearly she fucked with your head."

"You're the one who plays with knives, sweetheart."

"I don't play with knives," she says. "You inspired me."

"Forgive me if I'm not flattered."

"Do you have any particular fondness for that shirt?"

"Actually, I do. It's one of my favorites."

"Good. I felt the same about my dress. You owe me my revenge."

"Revenge is not a word a man wants to hear from a woman with a knife in her hand."

"Trust me and let go of me. I know that's hard for a dominant like yourself, but fear isn't a good shade for you, Tiger. And if it makes you feel any better, if I was going to kill you, I'd get that orgasm you've denied me not once, but twice, first."

"The name is Nick," I say, my gaze sweeping over the knife that just happens to be right in front of her beautiful breasts, before I refocus on her face and add, "unless you attempt to stab me. Then you meet Tiger." And I think I'm losing my fucking mind, because I've decided that letting her have the knife is a good character test. I release her and press my hands on the island on either side of her.

"Now what?" I challenge, the current in the air electric, the push and pull of control between us damn near explosive.

Her eyes narrow, mischief in their depths, but again, I find no malice. More seduction and playful sexiness, which I rarely partake in. I like sex. I like fucking. I don't like games that I don't dictate, and my games are not playful. But this woman is not like the others; she does not affect me like anyone before her, and the jury is out on whether that is good or bad.

She grabs my shirt and pulls it from my pants, then takes the knife to the last button. It pops and flies into the air, hitting the ground with a magnified sound. Her gaze lifts to mine, and she says, "Still scared?"

"Don't poke the tiger, sweetheart. You won't like the results."

"I'm not scared," she promises, popping another button, then another, her free hand on my stomach, and if she wasn't holding a knife, I'd move that hand to the damn throbbing in my cock. Instead, she just makes that throb worse, that hand following the path of the knife higher, farther away from where I want it and her. I endure the torture of not touching her, and patiently at that, until she is finally at my tie, a little too close to my neck for comfort. I grab her wrist again, taking the knife this time, and tangle my fingers in her hair. "Are you going to buy me a new shirt?"

"You can buy your own," she says, her fingers tangling in the hair on my chest, and not gently—that bite of pain, adrenaline in my veins, her determination to challenge me proving relentless. "And we both know you wouldn't have it any other way," she adds.

I toss the knife into the sink to my left, and before it's even landed, I'm kissing her, drinking her in, and this time, unlike the kiss by the refrigerator, I don't hold back, and neither does she. Our tongues connect, stroke, battle...but it is one I *will* win. I will demand everything she has to give me. I want her free will. I want her as exposed as I vowed to make her, and it's not to prove she's a killer. It's for me. For the man in me who not only wants to own this woman but will. And when she tries to resist, when I sense her trying to withhold even a piece of herself, my hand covers one of her breasts. My fingers stroke her nipple with delicate, sensual touches that become rougher and rougher.

She pants into my mouth, and satisfied that wall she just tried to put up has fallen, I nip her lips, lapping at the offended area before I pull back, fingers still tangled in her hair. I yank at my tie and unbutton the last two buttons still intact, but I don't move away. Not yet. I kiss her again, hard and fast, and while the resistance is gone, the taste of challenge remains on her lips, but it will soon be submission. She just doesn't know it yet.

My hands go to her hips, and I lift her off the counter and pull her to me, molding every soft perfect female part of her to my harder body, one hand cupping her sweet little ass. My lips linger just above hers, and damn it, there is this deep ache in me for this woman that is unfamiliar, unwelcomed. The lies I've told her are a fist in my chest that I reject. I have to know the truth, and it's not a truth someone just tells.

I squeeze her ass and then draw back and smack it, testing her, feeling out the depth of those nerves she showed me, her comfort level with where I might take her. Making a judgment on where I think she wants me to lead her. She doesn't jolt with the impact. She doesn't act shocked or angry. She leans into me, her body already submitting to me even if her mind has not, her hand covering my hand where it covers her breast. Her message is clear: She wants the kind of escape I've just offered. She wants me to push her to go to places that consume, to leave room for nothing else but the here and now. No fears. No nerves. No emotion, which I hope like hell does not include guilt.

Whatever particular sins she wishes to escape—and to me, emotions that control us are sins—she doesn't just want someone to fuck. She wants that invisible something that she believes I can give her. After two years of trusting no one, she's chosen to gamble on a man who's here to expose more than her passion. If she is guilty of murder or blackmail, or both, I'm a master in every sense of the word. If she's innocent, I'm a bastard in every sense of the word. I kiss her again, and this time there is anger on my tongue, accusation, my own lies, and maybe hers.

And when I pull back, my anger, my own torment over my actions, her trust, her possible sins and mine, have shifted the mood between us. Intensity that wasn't there moments before pulses between us, a living thing, a band wrapping us, pulling us closer, but in a dark, volatile way. Her hands grip my arms, fingers flexing into my skin. Our breathing is ragged, heavy. I scoop her up, aware of how naked she is but for her thigh highs and her high heels, aware she is mine to own now, and mine to destroy if I so please. And she doesn't know it. There is something powerful and arousing about this idea that I'm pretty sure makes me a sick fuck, and I'm accusing her of being no better—she just doesn't know it. But I reject the guilt that pierces a tiny part of my black, steel heart for her and her alone. I'll make being owned feel so good for her.

I carry her to the living room, but I don't take her to the couch. I take her to the rug in front of the fireplace and lower her to her feet in front of me. She reaches for me, and damn, as much as I crave those hands on my skin, I resist and catch her wrists.

"You touch me when l say you can touch me from this point forward."

Her eyes flash with defiance. "And if I don't agree?"

"Then I don't touch you." I walk her to me, her elbows bending, arms resting between us. "We both know what you want from me."

"Which is what?" she demands, a hint of vulnerability in her voice that I find sexy as hell.

"An adrenaline rush. The kind that pushes your limits but comes with a burn for more tomorrow, not with the regret your nerves fear I'll give you. But your hard limit pushes for just that. It says, all or nothing tonight. It says, go there now or there is no chance to go there later. I won't go there now just to live up to your hard limit."

"I didn't set sexual limits. I set a time limit."

"If you didn't have a sexual limit, you wouldn't have gotten spooked earlier, and you wouldn't have gone untouched for two years."

"That two years has nothing to do with us tonight."

"It does to me. You have limits. Someone broke them."

"I don't have limits tonight."

"Except one night. And that creates a limit for me. I won't take you too far and find out it's too far too late to turn back time. Consider that my new hard limit, added to my promise to make you want more than tonight. Because I do."

"If you plan to treat me like a delicate flower, this ends now."

"I don't do delicate flowers, sweetheart. Cowering females don't get me off. But you aren't that, and you do. You get me off, Faith. But submission isn't weak. It's fearless. It's pleasure. But it's also trust. You have to trust me like I did you with the knife. Trust for trust."

"That's why you let me use that knife."

"I gave you what I give no one. My submission."

She laughs. "That wasn't submission."

"As close as you'll ever get from me. But that's not what you want from me anyway, now is it?"

"No," she whispers. "It isn't."

"And I want your trust, but I'm not demanding it. I'm asking you to let me earn it."

"You're asking?"

"Yes. I'm asking. Do what I say, but tell me to stop at any time. Just say stop. Or no. Or whatever language you want to use. I'm not the man who'll tell you no means yes. Understand?"

"I understand that you are not what I expected."

"Is that good or bad?"

"I haven't decided."

"That's a good answer. Because you shouldn't, and if you did, you wouldn't be the woman that has me this fucking hard." I lean in and brush my lips over hers, licking into her mouth, before I add, "You taste like temptation, and I am never tempted." I inhale. "And you smell like amber and vanilla, not flowers tonight. This suits you better than the flowers."

She breathes out with those words, her face lowering as if I've punched her in the chest. I release her wrist and cup her face. "What was that?"

"You talk too much and ask questions I don't invite. Fuck me or leave."

Her tone is defensive, but I've observed and pushed enough people in depositions and in the courtroom to know torment when I see it. And I don't like where torment leads us. I don't want to be there with her right now. "You're right. Too many words." I rotate her and press my hands to her shoulders, stepping into her, lowering my head. "Trust for trust. On your knees, Faith."

She inhales deeply, but she does as I order, kneeling in front of me, and her spine is straight, her hands on her knees. A submissive position, and more and more, I am curious about her past, her sexual coming of age that she then denied until tonight. I squat behind her, stroking her hair away from her neck, my hand on her naked shoulder, my lips at her ear. "I own your pleasure for the rest of the night." I brush my lips over her earlobe. "And we're going to start by getting you out of your own head." My lips trail down her neck to her shoulder, where my teeth scrape before my tongue soothes that bite. "A nice guy doesn't bite."

"And you're not a nice guy," she whispers.

"Nice guys are boring," I say, caressing down her arm and back up again, my fingers stroking the edge of her breast in both directions, "but you already know that, now don't you?"

"But safe. They're safe."

"Like I said"—I gently tease her nipple—"you didn't want a nice guy." I cup her breast and meld it to my palm, two fingers tugging at her nipple. She reaches up to cup my hand, something I've noticed she does often, and I lean into her. "You don't touch me unless I tell you to touch me."

"I want to touch you, Nick."

"And I want you to touch me, sweetheart. But not yet. Now, you let me take you where you want to go. Put your hands on the stool."

She pants out a breath and does as I command, her palms flattening in front of her, and I notice her nails, a simple gloss, not manicured and fake. I don't think she's fake. Just guarded. I cup her face and lean around her. "Don't move," I murmur against her lips, kissing her, a slow lick of tongue against tongue before I release her, standing and removing a condom from my wallet. I tear it open, making sure she hears it, that she knows she doesn't have to think. I'm protecting her. I shove the package back into my pocket and unzip my pants, rolling the condom over my painfully thick erection, but I leave my pants on, removing the ease of slipping inside her, which is tempting, but now is not that time.

I go down on a knee beside her, my hands on her lower back and slender belly. "Elbows on the stool," I order, and the moment she complies, I lift her hips, placing her on all fours, my hand on her lower back, my lips pressing between her shoulder blades. She arches forward, and I reach under her, teasing one of her nipples, my hand sliding to her backside. "Do you know what I'm going to do to you?"

"Spank me," she whispers.

"Yes," I say, squeezing her backside. "I'm going to spank you, but I won't hurt you."

"What fun is that?"

There is that challenge again, and I caress her shoulder blades with one hand while the other pinches her nipple, tugging it roughly. She arches forward while her backside lifts into the air, just as I expect. I immediately give her nipple another tug, moving my other hand down to her backside and over it, stopping right above her sex. I give her a slight smack there, not meant to cause any pain, just pleasure. I earn a gasp and can hear her breathing now.

"What's your tolerance level, Faith?"

"I don't know."

But she does know. No one plays in this world—and leaves it—without knowing her limits. She just doesn't want to give them to me. That answer, the knife, the lack of sexual limits. They fit a pattern that says hard limit. One night. I get nothing else, not even all of her tonight, but there is another layer to this. The layer that screams abuse. I lift her and move her to the stool, placing her hands on my knees.

"Tolerance level, Faith. I'm not—"

"I don't know," she hisses. "Don't you get it? I don't know, Nick. That's an honest answer. I don't know what worked for me. I don't know what felt like too much because of who I was with and what was too much because it hit the wrong buttons for me. All I know is that I wanted this tonight. And I want you to put me back on my knees and finish what you started for once."

There she goes. Pushing me. Challenging me, but I don't let anyone push me. I study her, search her face, and she says, "That is as honest as I have been with anyone in a very long time, Nick. I need—"

I pull her to my lap, straddling me, my hand at her face. "I know what you need," I say, kissing her, tasting that need, tasting what I've wanted to taste on her lips every time I've kissed her. Honesty. Hunger. Need. But it's real now. She's real; at least one part of her wall has crumbled. "And I'm going to give it to you."

I stand up with her, carrying her to the couch, where I sit down next to the arm with her still on top of me, those gorgeous legs of hers spread across me. Her hands press to my shoulders, and I fill my hands with her breasts, my thumbs stroking her nipples, my head lowering, tongue lapping at one stiff peak and then the other. "Please tell me why you still have clothes on," she whispers, sounding desperate, breathless, and I like her breathless.

"I'd be inside you already otherwise," I say.

"What's wrong with you being inside me?"

My hands settle at her waist. "It's not time," I say, my gaze raking over her body, her long blonde hair draping her shoulders, touching the tops of her high, full breasts. Her plump, tight nipples are rosy red. "On your knees beside me, and then lay across my lap, Faith."

CHAPTER ELEVEN

Faith

I want him to spank me. I want to feel his hand on my backside. I want that sting and shock that leaves no room for anything else. No worry. No loss. No death. No guilt. And no room for the way Nick makes me feel too much. The way Nick sees too much. The way he seems to peel back layers I don't want peeled back. The way he exposes me emotionally. I just want him to fuck me. I just want this to be what it was supposed to be. Nameless, empty sex.

I move to bend over his lap, but he catches my hips, his gaze probing mine, penetrating, and I want to look away, but I have learned that will only make him look harder, dig deeper. So I meet his stare, and I mask my emotions that I can't even name. His eyes narrow on me, a flicker of something I also cannot name in their depths. His hands fall away from me, a silent offer of freedom and that free will he vowed to pull from me. And he has it. I want this and him. Of that, I cannot even begin to deny, nor did I intend to when I invited him here.

And so, I take that free will and settle my knees on the couch facing his legs. But nothing with Nick is just fucking, which is what I know, what I understand. He wraps his arm around my waist, tangling fingers in my hair, leading my mouth to his, and then kissing me until I think I might shatter. "I'll warn you before I spank you," he says. "Understand?"

"Yes," I whisper, and just hearing him say "spank you" has my sex aching and my nipples tingling. As if he realizes this, as if he can read my mind, or perhaps just my body, he leans over and licks one of the stiff peaks, swirling it with his tongue and then sucking it deep, teeth scraping ever so slightly, the pull on my nipple like a pull on my sex.

His hands move to my hips, mouth trailing lower and lower, and suddenly, I don't want that spanking as much as I want his mouth on the most intimate part of me. But he stops short, pressing his mouth to my belly and lingering there, his tongue flicking, licking, before he looks at me and says, "Not yet, Faith. I want you across my lap, on your elbows, backside up." There is a command to his voice that I have always resisted from others—resented, even—but for reasons I cannot explain with this man, I'm aroused, vulnerable in just how much he affects me. But most striking is the moment I dare to submit, to spread my body across his, his hands on my belly and lower back. There are nerves tingling and fluttering through me, but no dread, no fear. Things I know as preludes to pain that lead to oblivion—things that perhaps I wanted tonight, because I feel like I deserve them, but just aren't here now, and I do not know why. I don't know this man. I can't trust this man, but my body appears to disagree.

"Ah, Faith," he murmurs, running a hand up my spine. "How did you manage to go untouched for two years? You are too beautiful to be left untouched." His voice is low, gravelly.

I was too damaged to be touched, I think. I needed a break. I needed something that I couldn't have. I needed something that felt as right as this man's hands on my body. His teeth scrape my hip, his tongue following, and I'm really starting to like that combination. That tongue that I know is wicked magic, but that always denies me the reward of that magic. He caresses a path to my backside, and at the same time, his other hand finds my sex, cupping it. And then he is stroking my bottom at the same time as he is stroking my clit, teasing me, touching me until I am so wet and aroused that the ache in my sex is as fierce as the ache I know will come from his palm.

"Faith," he breathes out, and I don't know why, but it feels like a question. Am I ready? Am I okay? Am I sure?

"Yes," I say. "Yes. And yes."

His reply is not in words. He begins to pat my backside, just above my sex, while deft fingers slide through the wet heat of my body, an attack on my senses from all directions. And we are never going to get to the spanking because I'm going to come. Or maybe that's the idea. He wants me to come. He wants the sting to be lost in the pleasure. But I don't want that. I want the sting. I want— "Nick," I pant out again, so close I am about to tumble over.

His hands still, and he replies with, "That's what I wanted, sweetheart," seeming to understand exactly what I was telling him. "You on the edge but not there yet. I'm going to spank you now, Faith. Seven times. The first two will be the hardest, but they will get softer from there. Count them out. Repeat that."

"Count," I say, adrenaline setting my heart into a gallop. "Harder, then softer."

"And then I'm going to fuck you, Faith. I'm going to turn you around, and you're going to ride me. Understand?"

"Yes. Please stop talking or my heart is going to explode from my chest."

"Deep breath, sweetheart. This isn't new to you, but I am. And I'm not going to hurt you."

I have no flippant remark this time. His hand is caressing my cheeks, warming them, as it should be, but too often, I have known a hard palm with no preparation. But he doesn't rush. One second. Two. Three. Four. "Nick," I plead.

"Now, sweetheart," he says, and I barely have time to realize the impact of that endearment before his palm is on my backside, a hard sting that arches my back, and oh God. It's back. "Count," he orders.

"Two," I breathe out.

And another. "Three." I can't breathe, and fingers are stroking my sex. I forget to count, but he does it for me. "Four," he says, and then another palm, softer now, just as he promised.

"Five," I breathe out.

"Six," he says. That gravelly tone to his voice is back now, the force of his palm on my skin following.

"Seven," I breathe out again, and it's done. He smacks my backside, and then, to my shock, his mouth is on it, kissing it, a strange tenderness to that act that I swear has me as breathless as the spanking. And then he is turning me to face him, cradling my body against his, his mouth coming down on mine, and it, too, is tender, a slide of tongue, but I can feel his passion, his need that he controls, as he has me.

"Tell me you're okay," he demands.

"I am," I say, shocked that he's asked, that I believe he cares.

"You're sure?"

"Yes," I promise, my hand on his face. "I liked it. I like it so much that it's…"

He kisses me again then, and this kiss is different. This kiss is hungry—greedy, even—and fierce. Addictive. Seductive. And it unlocks those things in me. I am kissing him back, and kissing him and kissing him. And he is touching me, and I am touching him, hard, sinewy muscle beneath my palms. And I can't get enough, and that is what I feel from him. It's not enough, but we try to find that place where it is, where it will be. And some part of me knows that he's given me what I want. There is nothing but this man, and yet, this experience is nothing like I expected. It's good now.

I am so lost in Nick that I barely remember him pulling me around to straddle him or how his pants got down. But they are, and his thick shaft is between us. I reach down and stroke it, and I revel in the low groan that slides from his lips. "I feel like I've needed this since before I ever fucking met you." His hands go to my waist, and he lifts me while I guide his cock to my sex and press him inside me. He's so hard, so big, stretching me, filling me, and it's been so long, and I can barely catch my breath. I breathe out as I take all of him, and finally, we've reached the place where we are here, wherever here really is.

But we don't move. We're staring at each other, and there is this magnetic pull between us that has nothing to do with sex. Or maybe it does. I just don't know. But I feel this man inside and out. I feel him and see him as he does me, and it's not what I wanted, and yet, I am hypnotized by this moment, by him. A charge seems to spark suddenly between us, and we snap. He moves first, or maybe we move together, but he's cupping my head and my breast, and as our lips collide, I reach around him to the band at his hair and pull it free, sinking fingers in the long strands that surely must touch his shoulders. I tug on them, using them as an outlet for all the crazy sensations pulsing through my body.

Nick deepens the kiss, and then we are moving, swaying, *fucking*. Slow. Fast. Slow again. Our mouths lingering a breath apart before we erupt into wildness again. And I don't want this to end. I don't want to go back to reality. I want to stay lost in this man. And I fight to make that happen, to stay right here with him, but the build of pleasure is fierce; the passion on his tongue, in his touch, consumes me, and I have been so on edge for so long. And when he pulls me hard against him, thrusting into me as he does, I am there, in that sweet place that tenses my body.

The next moment, I'm tumbling over, my body spasming around him, my head buried in his shoulder. He wraps his arm around my waist and thrusts again, a guttural sound sliding from his lips as he shudders beneath me. Time spirals and sways until we collapse into each other, and for long moments, neither of us move. We just lay there, breathing together, heavy, then slower and softer. And still we linger. It's Nick who breaks this silence. "Faith, sweetheart," he says softly, cupping my face. "As much as I want to hold you like this the rest of the night, and I will again, I had better take care of this condom before we make baby Tigers."

We won't, I think. We can't, but I don't say that to him. "Yes. Of course."

I start to move away, but he shifts us and rolls me to my back, pulling out before he says, "Always trying to run."

My brow furrows. "How was that running?"

"It was in your eyes."

"It wasn't in my eyes."

"No?"

"No."

I wrap his hair in my hand. "Why does an attorney of your stature get away with long hair?"

"I am nothing anyone expects. And that works for me. Does it work for *you*, Faith?"

I release his hair, and my fingers curl on what I now know to be perpetual stubble on his jaw. "It pisses me off," I say honestly, because I still don't want to want this man, and I am so far from fucking him out of my system, as he'd suggested, that it's almost laughable.

His eyes darken. "I'll take that for now." He covers my hand with his and brings it to his mouth, kissing it. "Where's the bathroom, sweetheart?"

"My bedroom is the closest one," I say. "The door right behind you." He kisses me and grabs a blanket from the back of the couch to cover me.

"I'll keep you warm when I get back." He stands and adjusts his pants.

I sit up. "You didn't even get undressed."

"The night is young," he says, giving me a wink that sets that flutter in my belly to life again before he heads to the bedroom.

I watch him cross the room, the muscles of his back flexing, confidence in his every step. He's gorgeous and unexpected in every way. *I'm* unexpected with him. I've been tied up, flogged, paddled, displayed, clamped, and more, and, as time went on, taken to extremes that didn't arouse me or make me cower. They made me angry. They made me withdraw, but not out of fear. Out of self-respect, something the past few months made me lose, I realize now. And so I went with Nick, telling myself he would take me back to that punishing place, but he was right. On some level, I knew that wasn't true.

He is the unexpected.

Different than what I've known. And I'm different with him. He didn't spank me hard, he didn't push me to uncomfortable places, and yet he pushed me. I felt exposed and vulnerable with him in ways that I have never felt before. I don't want to be exposed, and I glance at the bedroom, and in light of these thoughts, I wonder why I've sent him to my most private space alone. I stand up, and the straps at my ankles cut into my skin, reminding me I still have my heels on. I sit back down and quickly unclip them and kick them off, then wrap the barely there throw around my shoulders and hurry across the living area. Entering the bedroom, I hear Nick talking on the phone. "It's nearly midnight, kid. I give you an A for dedication but an F for strategy. You still aren't going at this the right way."

Relief washes over me as I realize his delay isn't about nosing around my room—as if a man like Nick would care about my personal items. He's talking to his associate again.

"Okay," Nick says. "Let's try this another way. How do you think he perceives himself? That's what you need to find out in questioning him, then use that to finish the questioning." He's silent a moment before he says, "Because how he perceives himself reveals strength and weakness, and we need to know what both of those things are."

My brow furrows with Nick's comment. How do I perceive myself? I think about this. And I think some more, and I don't have an answer. I don't know me anymore. Maybe that's why I don't know the woman who Nick just brought to her knees in so many ways. Who Nick seemed to know when I did not. My gaze catches on the card on the bed, and I walk to it. I stare down at my father's script, a knot in my belly. I pick it up and sit down, the low pedestal allowing my feet to easily touch the ground, and when the blanket begins to fall from my shoulders, I don't even try to catch it. I just stare at the card, trying to convince myself to open it, but what's the point? It won't surprise me the way Nick has. I know what it says. I know what he thinks of me and what he expects. Those thoughts and expectations have driven every moment of my life for two years. I just don't want the reinforcement of him saying it again from his grave on this particular day.

"Faith."

I look up to find Nick standing in front of me, and I never even heard him approach. He goes down on one knee, draping my pink silk robe around my shoulders. "I thought you might want this."

There is a protective quality to his actions—again, unexpected and unfamiliar in every way. No one protects me, and I don't know what to do, how to react. It scares me how good it feels to have someone actually care about what I feel or need, and I know that I cannot allow myself to want or need. But it's a moment in time, one night, and I cannot wish it, or him, away, any more than I could the chance to experience that art display tonight.

I stuff an arm into the robe and shift the card to my opposite hand, then do the same on the other side. Nick reaches down and grips the silk, his gaze raking over my breasts, a touch that is not a touch, my nipples and sex aching all over again. But he doesn't touch me. He doesn't turn this into sex. He pulls the robe closed and ties it for me, our eyes locking and holding as he does. And it is then that I see the shadows in the depths of his stare, and for the first time since meeting him, I see beyond the arrogance and sexuality of the man. I see his own torment. I see a man as damaged as me, and I think, maybe, just maybe, that's why our connection is so very intense. That *something* I felt when we were naked and lost in each other moves between us again, a living, breathing thing that bands around us. "Is it from him?"

I don't play naive. He means the card, and he knows there was someone in my life. "No," I say, and I shouldn't say more, yet I do. "I don't talk to him."

"Ever?"

"Ever."

"For how long?"

"Most of those two years I mentioned."

"But the card—"

"It's from my father. He died two years ago but apparently left it with Frank for my thirtieth birthday."

Nick glances at his Rolex, but I am looking at the craftsmanship of the black-and-orange tiger tattoo covering his entire right forearm. "You still have fifteen minutes to read it on your birthday."

I give a humorless laugh and set the card on the bed. "If I read that, I might need you to spank me again, but harder and longer this time."

"Then you should read it before I have to go back to San Francisco Sunday night."

I don't miss the implication he's going to stay with me until then, but any right or wrong I might feel from that is muted by the fact that he'll be gone. This will be over.

He sits down next to me, and his hand settles on my knee, allowing me to catch another glimpse of his tattoo, the black and orange ink evident now. Curious, I reach for his arm and turn it over to study the detail of the beautifully designed blue-eyed tiger etched into his skin. "It has your eyes," I say, glancing up at him. "*Tiger.*"

"That was the artist's idea."

"Who did it?"

"I had it done six months ago by someone Chris knows in Paris, actually. A guy named Tristan."

"He's incredible. I'd be terrified to ink someone's skin."

"Your ink would be as incredible as your art, Faith."

I look up at him. "You don't have to keep complimenting me."

"I'm no sweet-talker, Faith. Surely you know that by now. You're talented, and like my tattoo, your art is a part of you, Faith."

Rejecting the many places those words could take me right now, I quickly grab his other arm and study the ink there. Just words that read: *An eye for an eye.*

"That one, I got in college," he says, but I barely hear him speak, the phrase replaying in my mind: *An eye for an eye* clawing at me to the point that I feel like I'm bleeding inside. I can feel the rise of emotions, when only yesterday I was afraid because I could feel nothing. I jump to my feet and try to escape Nick, but he grabs my arm and turns me to face him.

"What just happened, Faith?"

"I don't know if I should admire you or fear you, Nick Rogers. *Tiger.*"

His eyes narrow, his energy sharpening, and he pulls me between his legs, hands on my hips. "Why would you fear me, Faith?"

CHAPTER TWELVE

Tiger

I stare at Faith, waiting for her reply, and while I do not share my father's name, I cannot dismiss the possibility that her reaction to my tattoo is about her knowing who I am. That she always knew and she's a damn good actor. That she knows that the words "*an eye for an eye*" etched in my arm motivated me to come for her and she's trying to manipulate me as I suspect her mother did my father. And the idea that he and I, men who do not get manipulated, could be manipulated by a mother and daughter grinds along my nerve endings. Or maybe my tattoo and the words it spells out simply stir guilt in Faith over the sins I suspect her of, which isn't much better. Or it could be something else entirely, and considering the way she's rocked my world, I hope like hell it is.

My fingers flex at her hips where I've pulled her between my legs. I repeat my question. "*Why* would you *fear me*, Faith?"

"I said admire or fear." Her hands close down on mine. "Why are you honing in on the fear?"

"It's a strange thing to say, sweetheart."

"Don't call me sweetheart with that condescending tone. And you're shocked about the word fear? Really? This from a man who admitted to me in the gallery bathroom that people fear you?"

"But not you. You said not you."

"I don't fear the Nick Rogers with me now. But the words 'an eye for an eye' imply that you might love hard, but you hate harder. That's who you are, right? You'll tear my throat out if I ever cross you? Which I guess makes it a good thing that I have that hard limit. We fuck. You leave. *Now*, if you want."

Relief washes over me, and the intensity of it—my desire for her innocence—shakes me to the core. I do not get personally involved, but then, I don't fuck my friends or enemies, either. I fuck for release. For pleasure. And she's personal. In more ways than I expected. "I don't want to leave, and until you saw my tattoo, you didn't want me to leave."

"I don't want your kind of viciousness in my life."

"You knew I was Tiger before you ever invited me here. But let's clear up who Tiger is. Who *Nick Rogers* is. I don't hate. It's a dangerous emotion that feeds irrational actions. And as for 'an eye for an eye'...I began my career in criminal law and, in fact, did a two-year stint in the DA's office that started when I was a law student. I got my tattoo after putting a man on death row for brutally raping and killing a fifteen-year-old girl. So, fuck yeah. An eye for an eye. Only, he's not dead yet, but you can bet I'll be in the front row when he does."

She breathes out. "Oh."

"Yes. Oh." I fist my hand and show her my forearm again. "Those words," I say. "They do matter to me. I read them often when I'm protecting someone who's been done wrong. I deliver justice."

She stares at my arm for long seconds before she reaches down and covers the tattoo with her hand, her eyes meeting mine. "I'm sorry. I'm afraid I reacted prematurely and convicted you for someone else's sins."

"Him," I say, referring to the man in her past who I have a good idea is the artist she lived with in L.A.

"You keep going back to *him*."

"Because he's in the room now, and he was with us when we were fucking, Faith."

"This is one night," she argues.

"This is whatever it turns out to be," I amend. "And for the record, I don't stay the night with women or have them stay with me, but I'm not leaving without a fight and at least three more orgasms. Yours. Not mine. And as for *him*, I keep going back to him because he's the reason you might try to insist that I leave. He's the reason you just tried to push me away over my tattoo. And if I'm right, he's the reason you keep everyone at arm's length."

"You don't know me well enough to make a statement like that."

I've studied her for three weeks, obsessed over the details of her life like I do every case I take on, because I win. I always win. I know her better than she thinks. But I settle for, "I know enough."

She studies me for several long beats, her expression tight, her voice tighter as she says, "Macom Maloy. That's his name, and 'an eye for an eye' was his justification for doing something I consider unforgivable."

"Unforgivable," I repeat. "That sounds personal." And, I silently add, perhaps like murder and blackmail.

"I'm not going to talk about this or him," she says firmly, her gaze meeting mine, no coyness. No cowering, no lowered lashes and turned head. Just straight up. No more conversation. She's not having it.

"I'll let it go," I concede, clear on the fact that if I push, she'll push back and I'll end up at the door. "But I'm not him." I show her the tattoo again. "I do believe in these words. I do live by 'an eye for an eye,' but I apply that in a controlled fashion, and I fight for those I protect."

She covers the tattoo with her hand again, but she searches my face, studying me, looking for the truth in my words before she says, "I believe you, but sometimes the need to punish—*an eye for an eye*—gets out of control, Nick. Maybe it hasn't for you. Maybe it has. But be careful. It could."

I cover her hand with mine where it rests on my arm, my eyes never leaving hers. "That's a sign of weakness, and I am not weak."

"Until you are."

"Not gonna happen, sweetheart. I have a spine of steel."

"There's that arrogance again."

"Yes. There it is. Like I said. It works for me." My jaw clenches with my need to ask her more questions that I just promised not to ask. "How about those pancakes, sweetheart? I haven't eaten since about three today."

"That's it?" she asks, sounding dumbfounded. "You aren't going to press me for more? I'm used to you pushing too much and too hard."

"I told you I wouldn't." I stand up and cup her face. "I pushed to get you to say yes to me, Faith. I pushed to get here. I'm not going to push to get kicked out the door. And free will, sweetheart, does not just apply to sex. So." I pause and ask again, "How about those pancakes?"

She blinks at me, seemingly stunned by me actually doing what I said I'd do, which tells me more about Macom. I might be a bastard, but I'm not his kind of bastard. "I can't make you pancakes, Nick," she says firmly.

"I pissed you off that bad, did I? You're going to starve me?"

She smiles, and damn she's pretty when she smiles. "I actually don't have eggs or milk in the house. I'm not here often."

"I see. What do you have?"

"Cereal."

"But no milk."

"Right. And boxes of macaroni and cheese but—"

"No milk."

"Right." Her eyes light. "But I do have lots of ice cream. This is my cheat place. I eat junk here."

"Ice cream it is, then."

She points to the bathroom. "But I'm going in there first. I'll be right back."

"I'm going to the car to get a T-shirt."

"You have a T-shirt in your car?"

"I always keep an extra suit, jeans, and a T-shirt in the car." I give her a wink. "You never know when someone might slice off all your buttons." I pull her to me, kiss her, and head for the door as her laughter follows. I pause under the archway, and she does the same at the bathroom entrance.

She laughs again. "You should have seen your face when I pulled that knife, Nick. I mean, I get it. I should have known it would freak you out. I'm a stranger and all, but you looked like you'd just realized you'd gone home with Chucky's Bride." She turns earnest. "But don't worry. I'm not as easily provoked as she is." She laughs again and disappears into the bathroom, leaving me to scrub my jaw and run a hand through my hair. *Holy fuck.* She's joking about being a killer, and the ways that could fuck with my mind right now, if I let it, are too many.

Exiting into the living room, I head down the hallway, and when I reach the foyer I stop dead in my tracks as darkness greets me. The light was on when we came into the house. Suspecting a bad bulb, and feeling rather protective of this woman I ironically came here to prove is a killer and who ironically just joked about being one, I walk to the switch and flip it on. Frowning, I decide it must be on a timer the security company has installed. I unlock the door, exit to the porch, and make my way to my car, where I open my trunk, and when I would grab my overnight bag, I am instead drawn to the identical one next to it. I unzip it and pull out the two death certificates on top, both with the same cause of death: heart attack. A month apart. Also in the bag is every detail of Faith's life, and her family's, heavily focused on her mother, none of it leading me to a clear answer. But I've looked in the eyes of more than one killer, and I'd bet my practice that Faith isn't a killer, but not my life. Not quite yet. Not when I'm smart enough to know that I want this woman beyond reason. But if I'm right and she's innocent, where that conclusion leads me, I don't know. But the woman. She leads me right back in the door, to her.

I grab my overnight, open it, and pull on a white T-shirt, slipping it over my head, and then pull the zipper and settle the bag on my shoulder. Shutting the trunk, I waste no time crossing the lawn and reentering the house. I lock up and flip off the light, having no intention of going anywhere tonight but Faith's bed.

Traveling the hallway, I find Faith in the kitchen, standing at a pantry with her back to me, my lips curving at the sight of her bra hanging on the door handle. Her dress is laying on top of the trash can, and I make a mental note to find that dress and buy her another one, pretty damn certain good ol' Macom is behind her dislike of other people's money. Which sure doesn't lend to the premise of Faith being involved in blackmail.

Walking to Faith's bedroom, I'm presumptive enough to drop my bag inside the door, and then I return to the kitchen. She obviously hears me this time, glancing over her shoulder from the pantry she's still studying. "I have cherry Pop-Tarts," she says, facing me. "Cool Ranch Doritos, protein bars, and microwave popcorn."

"The protein bars and popcorn don't fit the cheating-while-you're-here theme."

"Sometimes I feel guilty after all the Doritos and ice cream and force myself to eat protein bars and popcorn."

"Ah," I say. "Makes sense." And it makes her all the more adorable, and she doesn't seem to know it. "Not to dismiss the delicacy of cherry Pop-Tarts, Doritos, protein bars, and popcorn," I continue, "but what happened to the ice cream?"

"My favorite choice is well stocked," she says, opening the bottom-drawer freezer and waving a hand across it. "I have Häagen-Dazs only because it's my favorite. My top choice: pralines and cream, which is so very, *very* incredible."

"Two verys. That sounds serious."

"It is. It's addictive."

Like her, I think, when normally it's simply fucking a beautiful woman I find addictive, until it's over.

"I also have rum raisin," Faith continues, "and I promise you, you can't go wrong with rum raisin."

"I've heard that," I say, my tone serious. "You can never go wrong with rum raisin."

She smiles. "Don't joke. I take rum raisin very seriously."

"Only one 'very,'" I point out. "I predict you choose the praline."

"I'm still deciding," she says. "And so are you, because I also have two pints of coconut pineapple, which sounds simple, but it's creamy and sweet and addictive." Her hands go to her hips. "And each of these pints contain my entire day's calorie intake, but I haven't eaten all day, so I don't care."

"Nerves over the show?"

"Yes. Nerves and the birthday thing. You know. You self-analyze and do all those things the big birthdays make you do. But it's over. No more of that." She points at the freezer, but not before I see the flicker of emotion in her eyes I can't quite name. "What's your sin?" she asks, glancing back at me, her expression checked now.

You, I think, but I say, "I'll take the coconut pineapple," and reach down, grabbing a pint before adding, "because sweet and addictive is exactly what I want right now." I watch her cheeks flush over that comment, when, in contrast, her bold order for me to spank her had not inspired the same flush. Beautiful, sinful in bed, and sweet when she's not. I might be fucking in love. "What about you?" I ask. "What's your sin, Faith?"

"I'm pretty sure it's you," she dares to say. "But as for the ice cream. Praline." She grabs her pick, shuts the freezer, and then walks to a drawer to grab two spoons, which she holds up. "No knives. I promise." She clunks her pint on the counter. "Though I think I might need to cut this, it's so solid."

I motion to the living room. "The fireplace will soften it up."

"And warm me up," she says, shivering. "The freezer gave me chills." She darts past me, my gaze following her to note her bare legs and pink fluffy slippers. Adorable, all right, and I'm so fucking hard all over again, she might as well be wearing leather and a G-string, which is exactly why I need to keep my pink-fuzzy-slipper-wearing woman away from the knife drawer until I'm 100 percent sure she isn't a killer.

CHAPTER THIRTEEN

Tiger

Pursuing Faith, something I've been doing since I first learned she existed—she just doesn't know it—I follow her into the living room. I find her snuggled under a cream-colored blanket I saw on one of the chairs, her ice cream already by the fire. I join her and sit down with my back against the stool I'd had her sprawled over earlier, then set my pint next to hers by the fire.

She gives me a thoughtful look. "You *know*," she says. "I'll believe you're staying when you take your shoes off."

I chuckle. "Is that the way you know a man's staying the night?"

"It seems like a good marker," she says. "Not that I've had to make that determination any time in recent history."

I'm not sorry at all, nor am I chuckling anymore. "Do you want me to stay, Faith?"

"Hard limit," she says, her voice a bit raspy. "I get tonight." And when I arch my brow at the less-than-conclusive answer, she adds, "Yes. I do." Definitive. No shyness to her.

I don't even try to hide the satisfaction in my stare. I reach down and unlace one of my shoes. She unlaces the other for me, tugging it off. I toss the other one. "How's that?"

"Better," she says, giving me a once-over. "It somehow makes you less assuming and more down-to-earth."

"Assuming," I say drily. "That's right up there with arrogant."

"But arrogant works for you," she says. "You said so." Her brow furrows. "And how are you here when you have a big case next week?"

"I do my best prep work locked away from the rest of the world,"

I say. "And I've got another situation here. I actually rented a house for three months."

"Three months," she repeats, and this time she looks away, reaching for her ice cream, but I lay down beside her on my side, resting on my elbow.

"Faith."

She inhales and looks at me, her expression guarded. "Yes?"

"The ice cream hasn't had time to thaw, and what you're really thinking about right now is the fact that I'm here for three months."

She sets the ice cream back down. "You didn't tell me that."

"I'm telling you now."

"I don't know what to say to that."

"There's a first. You usually snap right back."

"I still don't know what to say to that."

"Well, then, just remember this. You can hate me in the morning just as easily if I have a rental house here or if I don't."

"Am I *going* to hate you, Nick?"

"*No*, Faith. You are not."

She studies me for several beats, then says, "You owe me a story."

"A story? I thought I owed you an orgasm."

"I'm pretty sure you owe me three orgasms, but just one story."

"What story are we talking about?" I ask, and it hits me then that she doesn't blush when we're talking sex, and yet, her art, her beauty... These things make her blush. She's sterilized to sex, not so unlike myself. It's physical. It's not emotional.

"Your trial story," she replies. "The one that made your opposing council on your new case your enemy. You said you had to throw out good evidence because he obtained it illegally, but you still won the case."

"What interests you about that story?"

"Aside from the fact that I like stories where people beat the odds, how you handled that case seems to me to be a crossroads for you. You chose to go the hard road rather than the easy road, and still you're a success."

I narrow my eyes on her, certain this is a masked reference to herself, maybe even to her walking away from blackmail and murder.

"What kind of case was it?" she asks.

"Insider trading," I say. "We were representing the CEO of a large tech company. I'll spare you the dirty accusations against him, but he was set up by a competitor. I managed to find someone who not only testified to the setup but had documents and recordings to prove it. But I found her in the eleventh hour, let me tell you."

"And you and your co-chair became eternal enemies."

"Considering I went to the board afterward and reported him, yes."

"After telling him you wouldn't?"

"The devil is in the details, sweetheart. I didn't lie to him. I never told him I wouldn't go to the board. But he lied to me. He told me he'd destroy the illegally obtained evidence, but he kept it until the day of closing. And I already told you. I can't stand a damn liar, and I damn sure wasn't giving him another chance to burn me or the firm."

"And you got him fired," she assumes.

"That's the insanity of this story. The board chose to reprimand him instead of fire him."

She blanches. "After he broke the law?"

"Yes. After he broke the law. They also offered me partner, and at twenty-six, that would have made me the youngest in their history."

"And you declined."

"In two flat seconds. If they felt his behavior was appropriate, I damn sure wasn't signing up for a bigger piece of that liability."

"And he's still with them?"

"They gave him my partnership spot, which tells you they're born of the same cloth."

"So this case is personal to you," she adds.

"No case is personal to me," I say, my own words an unfriendly reminder of the fact that I've made her personal. "When you get personal," I add, a warning to myself as I speak it, "you end up on the bottom with everyone else on top."

"Yes," she agrees, and when she says nothing more, again reaching for her ice cream, that one word becomes loaded.

"Yes?" I prod as she removes the lid to her ice cream and jabs her spoon inside.

"Yes," she says, offering nothing more but my pint of ice cream, which she shoves into my hand. "It's ready." And then, before I can press further, she moves on, "Did you leave and open your firm, or did that come later?"

I pull the lid off my pint. "I left and opened my firm. Ten years ago next month."

She hands me a spoon. "Why San Francisco and not L.A.?"

"I can do everything I can do there in San Francisco, with fewer assholes and less traffic."

"Yes," she says. "There are."

"You're very agreeable," I say. "That's different for you."

"You haven't said anything outrageous for me to call you on in at least fifteen minutes. But I'm sure you can remedy that if you try really hard."

"That's more like it," I say, watching as she scoops up ice cream and takes a bite.

"Hmmm," she sighs. "I love this stuff." She motions to me with her spoon. "Try yours. I'm dying to know if you like it."

I reach over and take a bite of hers. "Yes. It's delicious."

She smiles and sticks her spoon in my ice cream before taking a bite and then says, "A spoon for a spoon."

"Like trust for trust?" I ask.

Her mood is instantly somber. "Trust does matter to me, Nick."

I feel a punch in my chest with those words and my betrayal, but I have to know she's innocent, and this is about murder. Evidence is everything. "No lies," I say, hoping like hell mine are the only ones between us. "Tell me something about you."

She settles back underneath her blanket, the withdrawal in the action easy to read, even before she says, "You already know about me. You researched me."

"Tell me what documents and the internet can't. The important parts. Who are you, Faith?"

She takes a bite of ice cream, and I do the same times three, its sweetness easier to swallow than the idea that she might not be what she seems—what I want her to be. "Faith?" I press when she doesn't immediately reply.

"I'm just trying to figure out what there is to tell outside what you know. I mean, the checklist is pretty obvious. My father died two years ago. My mother died two months ago."

"That's how you define yourself?"

"Death does a lot to define us."

"I disagree," I say. "Life defines us. And yes, before you ask. I've known death. My mother died in a car accident when I was thirteen. My father died a month ago."

She stares at me, her expression remarkably impassive. "I'm not going to offer you awkward condolences."

"I appreciate that, but most people *don't* offer me condolences."

"I guess that's the difference between women and men, which is really pretty messed up."

"The difference is, I not only wasn't close to my father, but no one around me even knew him. And I'm an obvious hard-ass."

"My mother was well-known in Sonoma," she says. "You said you weren't close to your father. Didn't he raise you after your mother died?"

"The many versions of a nanny my father wanted to fuck raised me after I ended up back with him."

"I see," she says, and I sense she wants to ask or say something more, but she's too busy rebuilding that wall to let it happen.

"Why'd you leave L.A.?" I ask before she finishes shutting me out.

"My father died, and my mother was struggling to handle the winery. I came back to help."

"For two years?"

"It was supposed to be a few months. At six months, I figured out she just couldn't handle it."

"And you bought this house."

"Yes. I spent my inheritance on it, which, in hindsight, was a poor use of my cash. But at the time I needed something that was mine. I had it remodeled, actually. The entire top floor is my studio."

"Because your art is everything to you."

She sets her ice cream and her spoon down, and when she refocuses on me, she says, "You didn't ask about why I might admire you."

"I promised to stop pushing you before I got the chance."

"All right, then. I'll tell you now. When I saw the tiger tattoo, and despite now knowing the meaning, even the 'an eye for an eye' tattoo, those tattoos told me a story about you. They told me that you know who you are. You own it. You claim it. You have the tattoos to prove it."

"You're an artist, Faith."

She picks up her ice cream again. "I think I'll eat the rest of this pint before I respond to that."

"That statement was a fact. It doesn't require an answer. Why black, white, and red?"

"Black and white is the purest form of any image to me. It lets the viewer create the story."

"And the red?"

"The beginning of the story as I see it. A guide for the viewer's imagination to flow. I know it sounds silly, but it's how I think when I'm creating."

The red isn't blood. It isn't death. It's life. "You mentioned your new work to Josh."

"It's really six months to a year old," she says. "He just thinks it's new. I haven't painted recently."

"You paint about life."

"Yes."

"And yet you just defined yourself by death. No wonder you can't paint."

Her eyes go wide. "I…I hadn't thought of it that way." She glances away from me and back again. "I painted today. It was amazing."

"And what music did you paint to today? Elvis?"

"No Elvis today. No music today. I was inspired before I picked up the brush."

There is something in her eyes, in her voice, that I can't read, but I want to understand. "By what, Faith?"

"Life," she says, indicating my ice cream, her brow crinkling in worry, with the cutest dimple in the center. "You've hardly eaten that. Do you want the Doritos?"

"No." I laugh. "I do not want the Doritos. I'll stick with ice cream." I set my pint down, spoon as well, and move closer to her, taking *her* spoon from her again. "I'll share yours."

"Okay," she says, awareness spiking between us. "I'll share."

I take a bite of the ice cream, sweet cream and praline exploding in my mouth, and I cup Faith's cheeks and pull her mouth to mine. My tongue licks into her mouth, and she sighs into the kiss the way I've come to know she will, as if it's everything she's been waiting on. And it is fucking hot as hell. I deepen the kiss, drinking her in like the drug she is, then slowly pull back. "You taste good," she whispers, stroking the edge of my lip.

"So do you, sweetheart." I pull the blanket away, her robe parting, one rosy nipple peeking out of the silk, and I'm inspired. I take a bite of ice cream, set it aside, and, with the cold sweetness in my mouth, pull Faith down to the ground with me, aligning our bodies, my mouth finding her exposed nipple.

I suckle it while she sucks in air, her hands going to my head. "It's cold," she pants, arching her back.

"I'll warm you up," I promise, taking another bite of the ice cream and kissing her again, and damn, every moan and sigh she makes affects me. She affects me. For once, I'm with a woman and not thinking about tits and ass and fucking her to take the edge off before I get back to what's important: work. I'm thinking about Faith's next moan and sigh. And my mouth and hands are on a journey for more of everything Faith will give me. A journey that leads me to that sweet spot between her legs and a promise I made: next time, I won't stop. And I don't. I lick her clit. I lick into her sex. I fuck her with my mouth and pull back. Then I tenderly lick again, teasing both of us in the process. And do it all over again. I take pleasure in driving her to the edge, but this time, I take even more pleasure in that last desperate lift of her hips, the way she trembles with my fingers inside her, right before she shatters under my tongue. And what I'm left with is a journey that hasn't changed. It's still the quest for more. I want more from this woman, who might just literally be the death of me if I'm not careful. And yet, that doesn't matter.

I still want more.

CHAPTER FOURTEEN

Tiger

I blink awake to the scent of vanilla and amber, the silky strands of Faith's blonde hair tickling my nose, and the sweet press of her naked next to me. The fireplace is burning to my right, the rug is beneath me, and the sun is burning through a window in a blinding bright light. Someone is also holding their damn finger on the doorbell.

Faith jolts awake and sits up, the blanket falling to just the right spot to expose her creamy white back and to cover my morning wood. I'd have claimed her if not for the incessant doorbell ringing. "Any idea who that asshole is?" I ask irritably, preferring to wake up with this woman in a much different way.

"I'll handle it," Faith says, avoiding my query, her fingers diving into her hair before she pops to her feet and takes the blanket with her. The result: my wood is officially on display, while someone is now pounding on the door.

Faith lets out a low, frustrated sound. "I need to throw on clothes," she says, rushing toward her bedroom, sadly never even noticing said morning wood, which only makes me more irritated at the incessant ringing now consuming the entire damn space.

I push to my feet and grab my pants, and in the thirty seconds it takes me to pull them on, the doorbell has stopped ringing and started again. Running hands through my tangled hair, compliments of Faith's fingers, I walk to her bedroom, my gaze landing on that card on the bed before the empty space leads me through to the bathroom. I find Faith standing in her closet, pulling a T-shirt into place and already wearing black sweatpants. "Who the hell is that?" I ask again.

"I don't know," she says, shoving her feet into Keds, "but as embarrassing as this is about to get, I'm guessing it has to be one of the bill collectors from the winery."

"As in plural?" I ask. "There's more than the bank chasing you for money?"

Her expression tightens, right along with her reply. "Yes. It's every vendor we use, and no one would stay this long, and this rudely, who wasn't here to collect money."

Protectiveness, as unfamiliar as the possessiveness she stirs in me, rises in me, and I go with it. "I'll handle it," I say, heading back to the bedroom and onward toward the front of the house, my mind processing the implications of Faith's embarrassment and circumstances. And I come to the obvious conclusion, which has nothing to do with my rapidly growing interest in this woman: no one with access to the funds my father wrote to her mother would put themselves through this with such genuine emotional response. If Faith was involved in whatever scam occurred, which I highly doubt, she doesn't have the money now. And if she wanted to take the money and run, why put herself through this? Why not give the winery to the bank?

"Nick," Faith calls after me, her voice echoing from the distance. "Nick. Stop."

"Not on your life, sweetheart," I murmur, doubtful she can even hear me, but my actions speak for themselves.

The pounding grows louder right about the time I reach the foyer, as if the asshole just took his boot to the door—or his fists. I disarm the alarm, unlock the door, and right when I'm about to open it, Faith calls out from behind me, "You have on no shoes, no shirt, and no underwear, and your pants are unzipped."

I open the fucking door, and there stand the two stooges I'd called suits at the winery two nights before. This time they wear matching khakis and white-collared shirts, because apparently khakis are supposed to be intimidating. "Mr. Rogers," Stooge

Number One says, and while I can remember his name, I just don't care to give him that credit. "I... We..."

Stooge Number Two tries to fill in the blanks. "We didn't know you were personally involved in this."

"Card," I demand.

They both blink at me like I've just spoken another language they don't understand any more than their own.

"Business-fucking-card," I say. "Now."

They both fumble with their pockets, and I have two cards shoved at me. I grab one and look at it. Then the other. Both employees of a collection agency that I happen to know the bank that holds Faith's note hires often.

"We both know the ways you've broken the law," I say. "Don't do this again." And with that order, I slam the door on them and lock it. I don't immediately turn to Faith, who is hovering nearby. I step to the slit of a window beside the door and watch the stooges all but run to their car.

Rotating, I find Faith standing under the archway dividing the hall from the foyer. "They won't be back. I'll buy you some time at the bank, but we need to sit down and talk. I need to be fully armed with information when I talk to the bank."

"No," she says. "No. I can't pay you."

I give her a once-over, her nipples puckered under her pink tee, her hair a wild, sexy mess. Her lips are natural and swollen from my kisses, of which I plan for many more. "I'm doing this for you, Faith. Not money." I take a step toward her.

She backs up and holds up a hand. "Stop. You don't get to fuck me and then take over my life, Nick. I didn't even invite you into my life. I invited you for one night. Hard rule, Nick."

"I've had my share of one-night women, Faith," I say, voicing what I've only just concluded myself. "You aren't one of them." I firm my voice. "I'm not leaving. You need my help, and you're going to take my help."

"You don't get to just decide that. I'm not some girl who's gaga over you, Nick. I'm a grown woman who lives her life and makes her own decisions."

"Who now has help. There is nothing wrong with needing help besides not having it."

"You can't bulldoze me, Nick. I won't let you."

"If I could, you wouldn't be interesting to me, Faith. And you are. More now than the moment I met you, and that's new for me. Usually, a fuck does the job and I'm not interested anymore."

"There it is. The exact reason I'm reacting like I am. You basically just confirmed my thoughts. You'll help me until the interest fades. I pay not in money but by entertaining you and fucking you, until I have the misfortune of sating your appetite. I don't need what you just made me feel in my life right now or ever again. Leave, Nick." She turns on her heel and starts marching away.

I stand there, mentally dissecting all the reasons she's just kicked me to the door, which I don't plan on exiting. Something to hide. Embarrassment. The something to hide might not even be about a crime, but that embarrassment. Macom. He was obviously part of her life, and a bad one, and I've stormed into hers without giving her time to breathe or to reject me. But I don't have a choice. I can't let that happen. Not under these circumstances, and as it turns out, I don't want it to happen for my own personal reasons, which I'll examine when the heady scent of her isn't driving me fucking insane.

I pursue her yet again, finding her in the kitchen, her back to me while she stares at a Keurig dripping coffee into a cup. She knows I'm here. I can sense it, but she walks to the refrigerator and pulls out some kind of flavored creamer. I want to storm around that counter, pull her to me, and kiss her until she melts for me. I want to strip her naked and fuck her right here on the solid wood island I didn't fuck her on last night. But doing those things would only drive home her accusation that I just want sex from her.

Clamping down on all those male urges and a hell of an

overload of testosterone, I walk to the barstool opposite her at the island and sit down. She walks to the Keurig, fills her cup with creamer, and then turns to face me, that cup cradled in her hands. "I am not your plaything."

"No," I say. "You are not. And I'm not yours, either, Faith. That isn't what this is."

"It feels like it is."

"We are, as I said before, red-hot together. That doesn't make it all we are."

"You can't just come into my life and try to take over," she repeats.

"I'm not."

"You *are*. It's your way."

She's right. It is. "Usually people are relieved when I want to help them."

"Aside from the ridiculous arrogance of that statement that isn't working for you right now, Nick Rogers, have you just fucked and spanked *those* people?" She holds up a hand. "Don't answer that. I don't want you to tell me what I want to hear."

"What do you want to hear, Faith?" I ask, her statement speaking volumes about where her head is, and it isn't focused on kicking me out.

"Nothing," she says. "I told you—"

"Let's talk about *my* hard limits with women," I say. "They're really quite simple. No tomorrows. No conversation. No confession about my many nannies, who I tell no one about. For me, I just want to fuck."

"Why did you tell me about the nannies?"

"Because my gut said that you needed to hear it. Fuck. Maybe I needed to say it to someone who needed to hear it. I don't know what this is between us, Faith, but it's not what you're trying to turn it into."

"You said that we just needed to fuck each other out of our systems."

"I know what I said."

"And now—"

"And now I want more. That is exactly what I keep thinking with you. I want more. What the hell does that mean? I don't know, but I need to find out, and I think you do, too."

"Arrogance again?"

"Not this time. Just facts. Just possibilities. And I can't promise where that leads, but I can tell you that for me, it's not just sex. If it was, you'd be naked and on the counter right now, because that's exactly where I wanted you when I walked into this kitchen."

She doesn't blush. She looks me in the eye. "You said you didn't want more."

"I didn't, but I have learned in life not to run from the unexpected. And I'm not running from this, and I'm not letting you run from it because of a past that I'm not a part of."

"The past is a part of me."

"But I am not," I say, "and in the foyer, you responded to me like I was."

She turns her head, obviously struggling with where this is leading, seconds ticking by before she sips her coffee and then sets it on the island, her eyes meeting mine. "You are very assuming, Nick."

"Agreed," I say, reaching for her coffee cup. "But only about things that matter to me, and it appears you do." I turn the cup so that my lips are aligned with the exact spot where hers were moments before, the act telling her we're connected now, that possessiveness I've felt on numerous occasions with Faith back again.

I drink, taking a sip of the chocolatey concoction that would taste better on her lips, against my lips. "I'm beginning to get the idea you have a sweet tooth."

"I do," she says. "And yet there is nothing sweet about you, Nick."

"You might be surprised. If you give me a chance."

"You aren't going to bulldoze me."

"So you told me," I say, sipping her coffee again, then setting it back in front of her. "And since you seem to need to hear it again, if I could, you wouldn't be interesting to me." I soften my voice. "Don't let pride, or fear of us, get in the way of a solution to a problem you need to solve."

She picks up the coffee, takes a drink, and then another, and when she sets it back down, I arch a brow at her interest in drinking, which she's used to calm her nerves. I like that she can be nervous and overcome those nerves. That makes her strong, as proven by her next smart question. "Isn't sleeping with me and representing me some kind of ethical issue for you?"

"Not so long as the relationship existed prior to me becoming your counsel."

"Frank is my attorney already. I have him on retainer."

"Frank's an estate attorney on the verge of retirement. He is not going to make the bank his bitch. I will." I soften my voice. "Talk to me, Faith. Let me help, and I promise that help comes with no conditions. Whatever happens with us personally, I'm with you on this until the end."

"I *hate* airing my dirty laundry to you. And it's not even that I barely know you. It's that I don't want this to be how I know you."

It's an honest answer. I hear it in the rasp of her voice. I see it in the torment in her eyes. And every honest answer she gives me makes me trust her more. "We all have our dirty laundry, Faith. I told you my father fucked all of my many nannies. I don't talk about my father. Or the many nannies."

"You don't?"

"No, Faith, I don't."

"You thought I needed to hear that," she says, but it's not a question, and she reaches for the cup again, withdrawing.

"Why did you just try to shut down on me?" I ask.

She sets the cup down, a few beats passing before her eyes lift and meet mine. "I appreciate that you shared that with me."

"But you withdrew."

"No. I just... I was taking in the impact of your statement. Taking stock of myself, too, and my reaction to...you, Nick. And I don't mean to seem unappreciative of your offer to help. I'm sorry. I am embarrassed about this. And you *are* very unexpected."

"I met you while those two assholes were trying to collect from you at the winery. I knew what you were going through when I pursued you."

"You knew you wanted to get me naked," she says, giving a humorless laugh. "There's a difference."

"I repeat. I'm here. I'm not leaving. I'm helping you. If that makes me a bull, let's fight about it and get past it."

"I don't want to fight with you, too."

It's not hard to surmise the "too" means the collectors, but my gut says it's more; avoiding an emotional trigger right now, I focus us on business. "If you don't want to replace Frank, I'll manage Frank. But I need details from you first."

"Details," she repeats.

"Yes. Details. If it's easier, I can tell you what I learned when I was researching you."

"Please don't. I'd rather not know. Bottom line, without the family drama. My father left the winery to my mother on the condition I inherit on her death. She had no will, and she was apparently six months behind on a note my father took from the bank five years ago. Actually, she was behind on most things. Taxes, vendors, the bank."

"Has the winery been losing money?"

"No. That's just it. She didn't run it. I did. All of it for most of the two years since my father died, and I had a tight rein on our profit and loss. We were—are—making a net of forty grand a month before her income."

"But she wasn't paying the bank note and obviously select vendors."

"Several months before she died, I started getting collection calls. I confronted her, and she said she had it handled."

"Define handled."

"That's exactly what I said, but she shut me out."

"And you have no idea where the money is?"

"I'm locked out of her accounts because the bank keeps rejecting every executor we try to name with a conflict-of-interest claim."

I tap the table, my mind working. If her mother needed money, blackmailing my father makes sense. But she clearly didn't use it to pay the bills. Was Faith's mother being blackmailed along with my father? Was her mother planning to leave the winery behind and run off with someone?

"It's bad, right?" Faith asks when I don't immediately respond.

"We'll back the bank off," I say. "And we'll get you your executor and buy you some time. I can't promise how long, but some time. Have you paid the taxes?"

"Yes. I used what I had left of my inheritance from my father. And I'm paying the vendors for current services and then some, which worked for some. Not all. I would have taken a loan on this house, but the note is too small, and I can't sell it with a profit."

"How much are you behind with the bank?"

"Sixty thousand dollars, and there's another hundred thousand owed to vendors."

And yet, my father wrote her mother a million dollars in checks. It just doesn't add up. I glance at the loan papers she's given me. "This note isn't even close to what your property would be worth. Have you had the winery valued? Once I clear this probate issue, have you considered—"

"No," she says, reading my mind. "I can't sell it. I promised my father it would stay in the family, and I'd never sell it before the bank foreclosed anyway."

"So your mother knew that if you didn't take care of the place, you'd inherit a disaster."

"Yes. She knew. But it wasn't about the inheritance to me. This was never my life or my dream, but she knew that my father's wishes were—and are—sacred to me."

And so Faith gave up her art and her life—which to some would be a motive to kill her mother—grabbed the reins, and tried to end the hellish cycle of the past two years, but that just doesn't ring true to me. The ways I could fit my father into the equation are many. However, that he found out about the murder doesn't support a reason for the checks he wrote to her mother.

"My mother has to have money that I can get to and handle this," she continues. "And even if she doesn't, which is completely illogical, I have a great manager at the winery. We're a great team. We're making money. As long as I stay involved, I have the tools to keep succeeding. I just need time to catch things up."

"You're sure you're making forty thousand a month?"

"Yes. Very. Forty thousand after expenses, which means with my mother's love of men, Botox, and clothes, she had to have savings on top of the money she hadn't spent on bills."

"Men," I repeat. "Was there some young thing she was spending the money on?"

"There was always some young thing, Nick, even when my father was alive. At least your father's affairs were not when he was married to your mother."

"The only difference between you and me, sweetheart, is that my mother left my father, and I wasn't blind or young enough to not understand why."

"At least she has self-respect. My father knew about my mother's affairs, but he wouldn't leave. He made excuses for her. That's why I went to L.A. for school and stayed there. I loved my father, but it hurt me to watch him get hurt over and over again. And the behavior didn't fit what I knew of him."

In other words, her mother could have partnered with any number of men to blackmail my father, with an end game that might or might not have included a bigger plan. For instance, running off after draining the winery's funds and leaving Faith to suffer, which ironically is what she did anyway.

"Nick," Faith pleads. "You keep going silent, and it's making me a little crazy. What are you thinking?"

"Has there been a recent man you know of?" I ask, looking for a suspect that isn't Faith.

"Her attention span was short, but she also knew I didn't approve. She didn't bring them around me. She'd taken a number of trips to San Francisco this past year, though."

To see my father, I surmise, and in that moment, I wish like hell I was in a place where I could say that to Faith, but I'm not. Even if I was certain she was innocent, if she knew the truth of why I sought her out, she'd shut me out before I could help her. "You have no idea where she went or who she saw?"

"No. I don't. I asked, but she'd simply say 'a friend' lived there. *Nick.* What are you thinking?"

"Something doesn't compute, Faith. You have to see that."

She inhales, her lashes lowering. "I do," she says, looking at me again. "I'm going to find out she gave the money to some hot, young thing, just like you've inferred, and I'm angry. I'm really damn angry." She straightens, determination in her face. "But whatever she's done or not done, I return to my certainty that I can still save the winery. I just need time."

I study her for a long few moments, and there are some cold, hard facts about how the bank may have handled this that I decide to save for later. "I need to talk to Frank. I need us both to talk to Frank so he knows you're on board with this." I glance at my Rolex. "It's only eight, and it's Saturday. Unlike the two stooges who just came by here, let's give him a few more hours to sleep. Not to mention, I have a call with North that I need to prep for." I glance at my watch. "I'm going to set it up for noon."

"Oh God," she says. "Your deposition. Please, just put this aside until it's over. I've made it this long. I can make it another week."

I don't tell her the bank might try to pull a dirty trick I'm not going to give them a chance to pull. "I have my work in the car. I'll sit down at your kitchen table, and we'll call Frank after I finish up with North," I say, walking around the island and pulling all her soft, tempting, fuckable curves to me. And when her hand settles on my chest, that morning wood is back. I'm hard. I'm hot. And I want her. "But I'm going to need something to eat other than ice cream," I add, "and a cold shower, since I don't have time to fuck you properly right now, and I really want to fuck you right now."

"You know," she says, her hand flattening on my naked stomach, her eyes lighting with mischief, the worry and anger of the past few minutes at least momentarily lost, if not gone. "I considered telling you we should cool things down. But your pants are open, and your cock is right"—her fingers touch the head of my shaft—"here. And you really need the edge off if you're going to do a good job for you and me. I feel obligated to help."

"Do you now?"

"Yes," she says, and holy fuck, she is going down on to her knees, and she already has my cock out of my pants and wrapped in her hand. "And I feel that this is the way to it." She strokes the head of my cock with her tongue and smiles up at me. "Salty. You really did need this, didn't you? And just in case you're wondering, don't hold back. I intend to swallow." And with that evil, seductive comment, she draws me into her mouth. And damn, Faith is good. She suckles. She licks. And when my hand goes to her hair, my body pumping into her, she makes these hot little sounds, like she needs this as much as I do, which has my balls tight, my body burning in all the right ways.

She wraps her hand around my thigh for leverage, and I'm close. So damn close. "That's right, sweetheart," I murmur, my voice low, gravelly. "That's good." My hand twines into her hair, urgency surging through me. I pump harder, pushing my cock deeper into her throat, and she takes me, sucks me harder, even, and that does it for me. She does it for me. I'm there, a hoarse moan sliding from my lips with the release that follows. My shaft spasms in her mouth, and she does exactly what she said she would. She swallows, but she is in no rush to end this. She drags her tongue and lips up and down me, slowly easing me to the completion of the best damn blow job of my life.

Only when my chin lowers, my eyes finding hers, does she slide her mouth from my body. She pushes to her feet, and I drag her to me. "You know that wasn't—"

"Payment for services? Damn straight it wasn't. Free will, Nick. And now, I'm going to shower and go pick up food so you can get your work done." She pushes away from me and takes off walking. Damn, that woman rocks my world. I hope like hell she's innocent, because I'm in deep now. And about to be deeper, because she's about to be naked in that shower, and so am I.

CHAPTER FIFTEEN

Tiger

It's nearly eleven by the time Faith is ready to leave to pick up food, and I walk her to my BMW outside her house, while her car waits for the tow truck we called a few minutes ago. Both of us are in faded jeans and boots, me in a black T-shirt with the classic royal blue BMW logo on it and her in some sort of pink, long-sleeve lace shirt that hugs her breasts just right. Which I notice because, unlike my hair, which is knotted at the back of my head, her long blond hair is not only free and smelling like vanilla and amber again, it's resting over her nipples, which I just had in my mouth fifteen minutes ago.

She dangles my keys between us. "I'm nervous about driving your car."

"Don't wreck it and everything will be fine."

"Thanks for that comforting thought and vote of confidence."

"That's what people like about me," I say. "I'm warm and fuzzy *all the damn* time."

Her sexy mouth curves, and damn, I'm thinking about it on my cock again. "Like I said, Nick Rogers," she says as if she's just heard my thoughts, "there's nothing sweet about you."

I pull her to me and give her a long, drugging kiss, and I swear I can taste that amber-and-vanilla scent from her hair on her lips. "How's that for sweet?" I demand.

"Your kisses aren't sweet, any more than you're a nice guy," she says. "But you're right. Nice is overrated, and so is sweet."

I give her pink-painted lips a glance. "Why the *fuck* does your lipstick never come off?"

She laughs. "Such fierceness over lipstick. It's not supposed to. They make it that way."

"Hmmm. Good. I think I like a challenge."

"Your challenge is your deposition next week. Let me get to the grocery store and pick up that Italian food I promised, so you can get your job done."

"I don't think I've ever had a woman scold me about my work," I say. "It's surprisingly arousing. But I'm pushing my call back to one." I release her and open the car door. "Go now before I need to push this call back to two."

She starts to climb inside but pauses. "Make yourself at home. Just don't burn down the place and everything will be fine."

Laughing at her play on my warning, aware that she manages to keep the playing field even at all times, I watch as she disappears into the BMW. I shut her inside, backing up to watch her depart, and as she puts the car into gear, I decide there's something very wrong, and yet right at the same time, about a woman I'm fucking in my pride and joy, my custom BMW Hurricane. But then, there is something about Faith that's both wrong and right, all the way around. She disappears around a curve, and I sigh. All I can do is hope like hell she's as good at driving it as she is at riding me.

I cross the drive and march up the stairs. Entering the house, I shut the door and prepare to start a search. But damn it, it's impossible not to feel the betrayal of Faith's trust in that act. It feeds my need to prove her innocence and not her guilt, which I've already established is a problem. At this point, I'll take innocence any way I can frame it, and she's logical and smart. It will be a blow to realize why I sought her out, but she'll understand. Forgiving me might be another story, but right now, I just need to find a murderer that isn't her. I glance at my watch: eleven fifteen. I need time to review the material North has certainly already emailed me, but by the time I do this search and eat with Faith, that's not going to happen. Not willing to compromise the prep for the deposition or my management of North, I snag my cellphone from my pocket and text him: *Move to two o'clock.*

He responds so damn fast I don't know how he has time to type: *Copy that, boss.*

I smirk and shove my phone back in my pocket. "The kid's eager," I murmur. "I'll give him that."

In the interest of time, I head for Faith's bedroom, where most people keep their secrets. Once I'm there, I place my hand on a dresser drawer and hesitate. Damn it, I hate doing this, but I have no other option. I pull open one organized drawer after another, finding nothing out of the ordinary. The nightstands are next, and I find more of the same. The bed's a platform, which means there are no hiding spots beneath it, but my gaze lands on the painting above Faith's bed—one of her own works, this one of a vineyard, with a streak of red on one vine. She's talented, stunningly so, which brings my attention to that card from Faith's father she didn't want to open. Why do I know that card is all about his confidence and pride in her for taking over the winery, with a negative spin on her art, her passion? And yet, even in death, she wants to please him, craving his love. Not a problem I had with my father. I never craved anything from the man. Hell, he probably only gave Meredith Winter a million dollars so it was a million less that I'd inherit.

Rejecting the grind in my gut with that thought, I turn away from the bed and head into the bathroom, searching the drawers there, and then I move into Faith's closet. My digging there includes checking pockets and shoes, but the results are the same. Nothing. From there, I make my way to the opposite side of the house, where I find a small library with a couple of overstuffed chairs and art books filling the shelves. I don't have time to check those books. I need to find an office. There has to be one, or at least a place where she keeps her documents, and this isn't it.

Glancing at my watch, I estimate I have thirty minutes before Faith returns, and I track a path to the kitchen, do a quick search. Realizing that I have no place but Faith's studio left to search, I hesitate. That feels like a place she should take me, but there could be an office up there somewhere, and I have to look for that. For now, though, I walk into the dining room, where I've left my briefcase, which I retrieved from the car before Faith left. I sit down at the rectangular dark wood table and glance at the credenza, which has no drawers, before I unpack my MacBook and files to make it look like I've been working.

Next, I have to make a phone call before Faith returns, even above searching the studio for an office. Moving to one of the floor-to-ceiling windows framing the credenza, I pull back the curtain to keep an eye on the driveway before removing my phone from my pocket, dialing Beck Luche, a tatted-up former CIA agent who now does private hire work, and not for a small price. He also did five years undercover as a rogue US hacker deep inside a Russian hacking operation. It's a detail about his past I learned when he was under consideration for a hundred-thousand-dollar paycheck from one of my high-tech clients. He got the job, and I hired him personally three days ago after waiting two weeks for him to be free from another job. But I didn't want this screwed up.

"Nicolas," he answers, using that name despite me explicitly telling him not to. "How's the meeting with the would-be black widow if she ever got married?" he asks.

I grind my teeth at the dagger he's just thrown. "She's either innocent or a damn good actor."

"The best criminals are always the best actors."

He just keeps on throwing daggers. "Macom Maloy. Have you checked him out?"

He snorts. "If you thought I was an amateur, why'd you hire me and pay me so damn much money?" He doesn't wait for a reply he has no intention of getting in the first place, moving on. "Of course I checked out the ex-boyfriend. And that dude is a tool, but he's not smart enough to pull off the blackmail and murder, especially living in another city."

"But he's got money to pay someone else to do it."

"That man isn't thinking about Faith Winter, and he has no connections to Meredith Winter at all. That man is thinking about money, art, and some private fuck club like the one you own. He used to take Faith to it, but now he just takes himself—as in several times a week."

I had no idea Beck knew about the "cigar club" that fronts for the sex club I bought from a friend and client last year when he went off and got married. But then if he didn't, he wouldn't be worth hiring. And the fuck club Macom took Faith to—and replaced her with—explains many of Faith's references to her sexual past. It also indicates another uncomfortable disclosure with this woman I'm not looking forward to anytime soon.

"Let me run down what I know," Beck says. "Thanks to the security feed from your father's house, I've determined that Meredith Winter visited your father once a week for six months before she died. The checks he wrote her began at two months."

I inhale a jagged breath. "So she did visit him."

"She went to his home during those visits, and she stayed there for hours when she did. I have a few instances of them kissing by his door. He was banging her, but it went further than that. They had regular phone conversations in between their visits. No emails, unfortunately. But the bottom line here. A relationship between the two pokes holes in the blackmail theory. He sounds like he was giving her the money by choice. Paid sex, perhaps."

"My father liked his women thirty years his junior," I say. "He wasn't paying a fifty-something-year-old woman for sex."

"She was still a gorgeous woman."

"That's not it. Moving on. Meredith wasn't paying the bills at the winery. She was taking his money and the money made at the winery and doing something with it."

"I was coming to that. Her bank accounts were dry for that four-month window she was taking checks from your father. She'd deposit those checks, let them clear, and then clean every penny out of her accounts. I don't know yet where it went, but I'm working on it."

"She was giving it to someone," I surmise.

"Or stashing it," he says. "Meredith had a revolving bedroom door. She'd have a great many candidates for cohorts or enemies, but one option stands out. Jesse Coates was seeing Meredith for the few months before your father. Twenty years her junior and a successful stockbroker who moved from New York to San Francisco. He might be behind a scam."

I scrub my jaw. "My father was too smart to be scammed. Blackmailed, yes, but not scammed."

"Blackmail is a scam."

"Blackmail is blackmail. Being seduced by a woman and stolen from is another."

"You wouldn't believe the people I've seen scammed, my man," Beck says. "It would blow your mind. And if that's what went down, it was done smartly. I see no contact between Meredith and Jesse in the six-month window that she was seeing your father, but that really doesn't matter. That could be part of an end game."

"What are we thinking was the big end game?"

"I don't make assumptions I can't back up. And what doesn't add up to me is that Meredith wasn't paying the bills at the winery. She could have sold the place for a small fortune."

"Faith inherited on her death as a stipulation of her mother's inheritance, which would mean her mother could not sell without Faith's willingness. And I can tell you that woman appears to be holding on to a sinking ship because it's her father's wishes."

"Yes, Faith. I'm still working on figuring out that hot little number."

That possessiveness flares in me again. "And?" I ask tightly.

"And right now she looks clean, but so does Jesse. Not to mention the fact that you just gave her motive. She wanted to keep the winery; her mother did not. Maybe her mother was trying to force her hand into selling by not paying the bills and destroying the vines. The mother wanted the payday that property would be worth. Faith didn't. Maybe your father was in on the payday."

"Sell for the massive profit margin the property and operation are worth, or have them taken away."

"That's the theory I'm going to work on."

"Working that theory, Faith would have to have connections to my father, who she'd need to have killed, right along with her mother."

"Which I have yet to find."

"What about her sharing a link to anyone connected to my father?"

"Nothing, and I dug through layers as deep as a phone book."

I consider everything he's said to me. "Meredith forcing Faith to sell and taking off with a hot young thing for the money makes sense to me. What doesn't is how my father fits into this. Why the fuck was he writing her checks? Wait. *Fuck*. He wanted in on the sale of the winery."

"Then why pay Meredith the money?"

"A down payment on him buying it is my guess."

"But they're both gone, and so is the money."

"Which means you need to—"

"Find the money. I plan on it."

"Call me," I say, but when I'm about to end the connection, he says, "Nicolas."

"I'd tell you to stop calling me that, but it clearly won't matter."

"Be careful with Faith Winter. She could have the money. She could want to sell herself."

"Then why go through this hell?"

"Because not going through it makes her look guilty. Like I said, man. Be careful."

With that blow, he ends the call, and I stand there, aware that I am guilty of not wanting her to be guilty, but no matter how many times I warn myself of this danger, it doesn't change. I'm going there again. It is what it is. I want her to be innocent. I'm boring myself with the repeat of this conclusion. Accepting what is allows me to manage what is.

Moving on to what I just learned. Yes. Faith has motive to act against her mother, with financial gain, but I don't believe she wants to sell the winery. More like save it from her mother selling it, but she could have done that through the court system. But to believe that she would have, or could have, plotted out and killed my father and her mother is a stretch I can't make. I scrub my jaw. But I don't want to make it, either. I just admitted that.

I glance at my watch and then scan the horizon with no sign of Faith. I estimate I have fifteen minutes until Faith will be here. Just enough time to nose around upstairs if I hurry. Scanning the horizon one last time, I settle the curtain back into place, then waste no time making my way to the stairs. I don't hesitate when I start the straight climb up. I'm helping her. She just doesn't know it, and I'd be fine with her never knowing it, but that's not possible.

At the last step, I turn right under an archway, and I find myself in a room with a steepled ceiling that literally stretches the entire top level of the house. The wood floor has been glossed with some sort of finish I assume is easily wiped clean. There are two arched windows consuming the wall in front of me, both endcaps to the space. And there are random easels sitting around the room, all uncovered, all demanding attention I can't give them. My gaze lifts to a door to my left, which I hope is an office. Moving in that direction, I enter and flip on the light, and sure enough, I find a heavy dark wood desk, a deep leather chair in the corner, and random works of art on the wall that are absolutely Faith's signature strokes and colors. And damn, there really is something sexy about a talent I'll never have.

Another arched floor-to-ceiling window sits behind the chair and illuminates the room, allowing me to round the desk and sit down without a light, and then to quickly locate random financial documents. I pull out my phone, set my alarm for five minutes, and start snapping photos. It goes off right as I find her father's will, and I risk the extra minute to click shots of it. Out of time and nowhere near done, I stand up and exit the office. I fully intend to hurry to the archway, but I notice the table and color palette sitting next to one easel, which means it has to be what she was painting yesterday. I take two steps in that direction and stop myself, some instinct in me telling me that looking at that painting is far less forgivable than searching her house, at least now that I have every intention of saving her from the hell she's in.

I turn back to the door, and that's when I hear the front door open and Faith's footsteps downstairs. *Fuck.* I run a hand through my hair and make an instant decision. I have to own up to being up here, and if I let her walk around looking for me, that's only going to make this worse. Inhaling a jagged breath, I walk to the archway and step to the landing above the stairs. As if she sensed I was up here, she's at the bottom, looking up at me, her blond hair tousled from the wind, her hand on the railing.

She doesn't speak. For long seconds, she doesn't move. And then suddenly she is walking up the steps toward me, her pace steady, controlled, anger crackling off of her. She stops in front of me, her eyes meet mine, and it's not anger that gets me. It's the wounded look of betrayal. "This is not my house. This is my private workplace. This is my sanctuary." She doesn't give me time to reply. "You saw it, didn't you?"

"Faith—"

"I knew it." She cuts away from me and walks into the studio.

Fuck. What does she think I found? What the hell am I about to find out about this woman that I don't want to know? I follow her inside the room, but she isn't headed to the office. She's standing at the painting she started last night. She stares at it. "Do you know why I painted this?"

I walk toward her. "Faith," I begin again. "I didn't—"

"Look at this?" She waves her hand in front of it and turns to face me. "You came up here, and you didn't look at my work?"

"I am intrigued by your work, Faith. I was drawn up here, but I got here and realized it was a mistake. I knew this was your private domain, and I—"

"A liar is not a better shade for you than fear, Nick Rogers. No. Tiger. Because that's who you are." She grabs the easel, struggling with it, and I move toward her, but before I can get to her, she's flung it around until it lands in the space left between us. My gaze lands on the painting of myself, and I suck in air, a reaction I'm not sure I've had more than a few times in my life.

"Do you know why I painted that, *Tiger*? Because I was trying to figure out why I want to trust you but can't."

CHAPTER SIXTEEN

Tiger

The painting of me lays between Faith and me, our eyes meeting, hers still alight with anger and betrayal. And I want to call her reaction over the top, but she clearly senses I came to her without pure motives. "Faith," I begin, and for once in my life I'm not even sure how I'm going to finish the sentence. But I never get the chance.

"Leave," she orders, her voice as strong as her evident will. "I want you to leave."

I reject her demand not in words she won't hear, but actions. I'm around that painting before she can blink twice, pulling her against me, all her damn soft, fuckable, perfect curves pressed to my body. "You want to know me? Look into my eyes, Faith. See what's there, not what you choose to paint."

Her hand settles on my chest, elbow stiff. "You are such an asshole, *Tiger*. You are—"

"I know what you think of me," I say, cupping the back of her head. "But I don't accept it anymore." I lower my head and kiss her, licking into her mouth, the taste of anger and the betrayal I'd seen in her eyes on her lips, and it guts me. I *am* betraying her, and I have no way out of where I've gone or why I can't tell her the truth. "And my name is not Tiger," I say, tearing my mouth from hers. "I'm Nick to you, Faith."

"You had no right to come up here, *Tiger*. You had no right—"

"You're right," I say. "I was wrong, Faith, but I swear to you, I didn't look at any of your paintings."

"Liar."

She's right. I am. Just not about this. "I *didn't* look."

"The best liars are the best actors."

That play on Beck's words hits a nerve that I reject like her command for me to leave, cupping her face. "I didn't look at your work, Faith," I say again, and because I won't lie where I don't have to lie, I add, "but I wanted to. And I wanted to because I, too, want to know who you are. I want to know your secrets. I want to know what the hell you are doing to me that no other woman has done."

"You barely know me."

"But I want to. That's the point."

"You are—"

"*Obsessed* with you," I say, and this time when my mouth closes down on hers, I let her taste those words on my tongue. I let her taste my hunger for her. I let her taste how much I want her and how much I don't want to want her, and yet how high I am on this addiction. Maybe it's the forbidden. Maybe it's her. I don't know. And in this moment, I don't care. And this time, she doesn't, either. She answers every unspoken word I deliver on my tongue with conflicted need.

I pull her shirt over her head, and I have her bra off in seconds, touching her breasts, teasing her nipples, my mouth devouring her mouth. And her hands—talented, gifted hands—are pressed under my shirt, burning me where they caress my skin. I unbutton her pants, fully intending to strip her naked. "Your meeting," she breathes out, grabbing my hand.

I pull back to look at her. "Are you actually thinking of my meeting right now?"

"Yes," she murmurs. "But with regret."

"I moved it to two," I say, scooping her up and carrying her toward the office, my steps tracking a path that doesn't stop until we're at that oversize chair, where I set her down.

I'm on a knee in front of her in an instant, and we're both removing her boots with hurried hands. The minute I'm over that obstacle, I pull her to her feet, unzipping her pants, my lips on her belly, and the male in me, the man who is obsessed with every inch of this woman, revels in the trembling that quakes her body.

I pull down her pants, panties as well, wrapping my arm around her waist before tugging them away. One hand at her hip, the other cupping her sex, two fingers sliding into her wet heat, where I press them inside her, a tease I quickly remove. She moans in protest, and I stand up, cupping her face again and swallowing that tormented, delicious sound.

"Hurry," she pleads, reaching for my pants. "I need—"

I kiss her again. "I need," I murmur, reaching into my pocket for the last condom I have there, but I come up dry. I search the other. I've got nothing, and her hand has just made its way into my jeans and into my underwear, her fingers wrapping my cock with delicious pressure.

I reach down and cover her hand with mine. "The last condom I had fell out somewhere."

She pulls back to look at me. "Oh," she says, regrettably easing from my body.

My hands go to her waist, eyes raking over her naked breasts, before I promise, "We'll improvise."

"I have one," she says. "I have a condom. A birthday prank at work. They said I— It doesn't matter. It's here." She slips around me and hurries to the desk, naked, beautiful, and suddenly pulling the papers I'd taken photos of from a drawer, flinging them on top of the desk. And as hot and hard as I am, I can think of one thing in this moment. She has zero concern about something in those files exposing a secret or a lie. And I feel her actions as both a relief and a punch of guilt. "I can't find it," she announces, pressing her hands to the desk, her head lowered, long blonde hair draping her shoulders. Her back arches, backside in the air. Her beautiful body is exposed, but there is so much more of herself she's showing to me right now without knowing. "This is wrong on so many levels."

I move toward her and turn her to me, hands shackling her

waist. "Back to improvising."

"I'm on the pill," she announces. "I stayed on despite Macom— Okay. Why did I just say his damnable name?" She presses her head to my shoulder and raises it again. "I know you probably don't want to without one, and I shouldn't, but I just—"

I kiss her, and no, I do not have sex without a condom. Not ever. But there is trust in what she just offered me that I have not given her. And the sweet taste of her tongue on my tongue is now a part of my new obsession, as is her body pressed to mine, and her—just her—I forget the condom. I forget everything but touching her, kissing her, and then there is that moment when I end up on the chair but she slips away, kneeling at my feet.

"My turn," she says, yanking at my boot, and if the woman wants my boots off, they're coming off.

I reach down and take care of the other one before she slides her hands into my pants again. "We're going naked," she says. "I want *naked*."

"Naked it is," I say, kissing her hard and fast before I undress and pull her to my lap, her long, sexy legs straddling me, and she is sliding down my *naked* cock, the wet heat of her naked body gripping me, and it is pure fucking bliss.

But more so is the moment that I'm kissing her, and then I'm not because we're just breathing together. I feel this woman in ways I didn't know it was possible to feel a woman, and I just met her. I feel her everywhere, burning me alive. And maybe I'm making the biggest mistake of my life with her, but if I die, I'll die happy. And when we do kiss again, it's slow, sexy kisses. And slow, nerve-stroking slides of our body that meld our breathing, our tongues, our bodies, until we both shatter into release. Until I release inside her as I have with no other woman since I was a young fool, and I bury my face in her vanilla-and-amber-smelling hair.

And I hold her.

When I never hold women.

It sends the wrong message.

And yet, I hold Faith now. I inhale the scent of her hair.

"Tell me you don't regret that," she murmurs against my neck.

I lean back to look at her. "What the hell am I supposed to be regretting?"

"Not using a condom."

"No man or woman has a regret over a missing condom unless the result is later regrettable, but since I don't fuck without a condom, you're safe."

"I don't, either, Nick. Never with Macom. I… He liked… I didn't."

I want her to fill in those blanks, but I sense that this is another one of those moments where pushing is the wrong choice. "We're naked in every way and safe," I say softly. "*Except* that now we have to get you off me and save your chair from our mess."

"Kleenex on the table," she says, and without warning, she leans over and starts to tumble. I catch her, but not without a lean that puts us both on the floor, her on her back, me over the top of her, and us both in an eruption of laughter.

And when that laughter fades, we don't move. We stare at each other, and I have this sense that we both are trying to read the other; I damn sure am her. That we both are trying to understand what this is between us. Sex? Really damn good sex? Or…what? I don't know what the hell it is, but it's a powerful force between us, a magnet with a pull that won't be escaped. Seconds tick by, and I pull her to her feet, our gazes colliding before we both dress. And as we do, the reason for the explosion that led to taking our clothes off in the first place comes full circle, expanding in the air between us. The minute we're dressed, I pull her to me. "Faith."

"I probably overreacted," she says, reading where I'm going.

"You didn't," I say. "I had no right to come up here. And I repeat, I didn't look at the painting. I am, however, as intrigued by your art as I am you. It is you. It's a gift you alone possess."

Her lashes lower, her expression etched with torment before she looks at me again. "Thank you for saying that." She covers my hand with hers. "Let's go heat up the food."

She's slammed the wall down again, evidence that I've hit a nerve. And as much as I want to push and know this woman, for right and wrong reasons, I let it go. But I've made my decision. I'm not letting her go. Guilty or innocent, she's mine now, even if she doesn't know it. And guilty or innocent, wherever that leads.

CHAPTER SEVENTEEN

Tiger

Once we're downstairs, Faith sticks our food in the microwave while I unpack the groceries she's bought, which include milk, eggs, and... "Pancake mix?" I ask, holding up the instant mix. "I don't get your famous pancakes?"

"I guess I didn't mention that they're famous because that's all I ever make."

I laugh. "No, you didn't." I walk to the pantry and find the proper spot to stick them before turning back to her. "I might have to make you pancakes."

"You cook?" she asks, setting bottles of water on the island where we plan to eat.

"I picked up a few tricks from one of my many nannies who had a thing for cooking contests."

She opens the microwave. "The food should be ready," she says, inspecting it and then removing the container. "We're good to eat." She sets our sealed containers on the counter, and I move to the spot directly across from her, both of us claiming our seats before returning to our prior conversation. "As for cooking," she says. "I don't. Neither of my parents cooked, and I didn't have to learn. I grew up at the winery, and there are two chefs on staff. One for the restaurant and another for the staff." She lifts the lid to her food to display spaghetti and meatballs, and I do the same.

"Looks and smells amazing," I approve, the scent of sweet-and-spicy tomato sauce almost as good as her amber-and-vanilla scent right about now.

"It is," she assures me. "An Italian family owns the place. And

I'd offer you wine, but I don't keep it here."

I arch a brow. "Aren't you supposed to be a wine lover?"

"I like wine," she says, "but when I'm here, I just want to escape everything to do with the winery." She picks up her fork and clearly makes a move to change the subject by adding, "I'm starving, and real women eat everything on their plate."

"Sweetheart," I say, wrapping pasta around my fork, "you keep up with me on everything else. I'd be disappointed if this was different." I take a bite.

Faith watches me with intense green eyes. "Well?" she prods.

"Damn good," I say. "And I've eaten my share of pasta in Rome."

She sighs. "Oh, how I'd love to go to Italy. My parents went a good half-dozen times for 'wine research,' as they called it. My father loved those trips. My mother was all his then. I can't imagine wanting someone so badly that you'd allow yourself to be treated that way. I never understood."

Which, judging from what I know of her, is why Macom got kicked to the curb after only a year. "There's a fine line between love and hate," I assure her. "Lovers become enemies. I see it all the time with my work."

"But you do corporate law, right?"

"Personal relationships are common disruptors to business. The worst kind because they get emotional and dirty." I stay focused on her past. "Who stayed with you when your parents were traveling?"

"A friend of my parents who passed away a few years ago. And Kasey, the manager at the winery, has been there for twenty years."

I study her a moment. "Why, if he's good at his job, can't you paint, Faith?"

Her answer comes without hesitation. "Kasey and my father were a team. A few years back, we were just getting by, but they'd built our retail sales to a huge dollar figure the year before my father died. That's why I was able to buy this house with my inheritance."

"And your mother inherited well, I assume?"

"He had life insurance and money from the winery, which is why I need into her bank accounts."

Which Beck tells me are empty, I think.

"When my father passed," she continues, "my mother insisted she was taking over that role my father held, but it was, as expected, a disaster. My mother angered customers and made rash decisions."

"You lost business," I surmise.

"A ton of business." She stabs a meatball. "That's when I took over and tried to earn the deals back. But it got worse before it got better. We lost one section of our vineyard to a bad freeze because she declined normal procedures as too costly. Kasey was at his wit's end, and I convinced him to stay. That freeze," she says, stabbing another meatball, "makes the forty thousand a month a real accomplishment."

"Don't artistic types hate the business end of things?"

"I know this place," she says. "I bring knowledge and the name to the brand." She waves that off. "Enough about that. Did you always want to be an attorney?"

"Yes. My father was an attorney, and I wanted to be better than him. And I wanted him to know I was better than him."

"Are you?"

"Yes," I say, offering nothing more, and nothing more is how I always liked that man.

"How did he die?"

"Heart attack."

"My mother, too, and I'd say that's an interesting coincidence, but it's a common way to die."

"It *is* common," I say, and I silently add, *And the perfect cover up for a murder. Or two.*

She sets her fork down. "Right. Common. And this is a bad subject. I think I'm done eating."

"You've hardly touched your food, Faith."

"I just...like I said. It's a bad subject." She starts to get up, and

I catch her hand.

"Sit with me." She hesitates but nods, settling back into her seat. I glance at her plate, then at her, letting her see the heat in the depths of my eyes. "I'm going to make you wish you ate that."

She studies me right back for several beats and then picks up her fork. "I'll eat, and I'll do so because my growling stomach will distract me when I paint, and then I'm going to paint while you get ready for your call."

"Not about to let it be about me, now are you?" I challenge, but I don't give her time to fire back. "Are you going to finish painting me?"

"Maybe," she says, her eyes filling with mischief. "We'll see if you inspire me again."

I remember the way she'd thrown that painting on the ground, the way she'd shouted at me. "If inspiring you means making you think you can't trust me, I'd rather not."

"There are other ways to inspire me," she says, taking a bite of her food.

"How should I inspire you, Faith?"

"I'll consider letting you know when it happens."

"All right, then. When did you first get inspired to paint?"

"I always wanted to paint. From Crayola to paintbrush at age five. And Sonoma is filled with art to feed my love."

Now she says love, but she's used the word "like" when talking about wine. "And you went off to college with a plan to turn it into a career."

"I did."

"And your parents had to be proud."

"They were supportive enough, but as an aspiring artist, I'm just like half of L.A., trying to make it to the big or small screen. No one takes them seriously until they do it."

"And Macom? Did he take your art seriously?"

"He's an artist."

"So he understood the struggles."

"Yes," she says, reaching for the bottle of water. "I suppose you could say that." But something about the way she says those words says there's more to that story than meets the eye.

I open my mouth to find a way to that story when her cell phone rings. I finish my food while she pushes to her feet and walks to the counter where her purse, which looks like it's seen better days, sits. She retrieves her phone and glances at the screen. "The mechanic." She answers the call.

I stand and dump my takeout plate into the trash, and Faith seals hers and walks to the fridge as she listens. "Okay. Yes. No. Just please tow it to the winery. Thank you." She ends the call and stuffs her phone into her jeans.

"That didn't sound good."

"All I heard was the price, and I'm not spending that without another opinion and some time. I have another car at the winery. I'll just have to ask you to please take me to pick it up when you leave."

"And when am I going to leave, Faith?"

"According to my hard limit, before we sleep tonight."

"No sleep, then," I say. "So be it." I don't give her time to argue. "Let's call Frank."

"My paperwork related to the winery is all upstairs. We should call with the documents in front of you. And if you want, you can just work up there while I paint. Or not. You're welcome to stay down here."

"Upstairs," I say, the significance of her going from not wanting me up there to wanting me up there not something that I miss. Neither is the fact that she just invited me to sit at that desk, where I can nose around in anything I want. And she has to know this. I gather my work, and we head up to the studio. Faith straightens the desktop but sets a stack of files on the desk. "Taxes. My father's will. Collection letters. Random other items. If you need anything specific that isn't there, just ask."

I reach for a file that catches my eye and flip it open, looking at the forty-five-million-dollar valuation of the vineyard with the note for thirty-five. "Faith, you could sell for ten million?"

"That evaluation was done before that freeze and the substantial loss of business that followed. I still believe it would sell for a profit, but nowhere near that. But I'm not selling, Nick. This is my family business."

"Did your mother know the value had gone down?"

"I tried to tell her that, but she didn't care enough to listen."

Or she did listen, and the freeze lowered the price and made the vineyard a steal for someone like my father, who would rebuild it. It makes sense, except for the fact that my father wouldn't put money down on something Meredith Winter had no right to sell. He was not that stupid. Not to mention the fact that both of them are dead now. "Let's call Frank."

She pulls her cellphone from her pocket and dials on speaker. "Faith," Frank answers. "What's happened? Is it the bank harassing you again?"

"I'm here with Nick Rogers."

"Ah, yes. Nick. I knew this call was coming when you brought up his name. I might be old, but I still have instincts. Am I being fired?"

"No," Faith says quickly, her eyes meeting mine, a silent plea for me to say the right thing right now.

"I'm going to play second counsel," I say. "But I need to be brought up to date."

Frank doesn't hesitate. "Well, for starters, we have no will, and the bank sees this as a chance to make a profit, thus they have a substantial interest in claiming the property."

Speaking to Frank, I say, "Which is an asinine claim that will never hold up in court. I can name five ways to Sunday how they're pushing the limits of the law."

"I couldn't agree more."

"Have we made it clear to the bank that you'll counterattack?"

He gives a long, rambling answer that amounts to "no" and

does not please me. "We need to order another evaluation of the property," I say.

"It's not her property until we clear this probate issue," he argues.

"The bank has an end game here," I say. "The way I see this, they're either representing a buyer who has some interest we don't yet know in this property, thus wants to force Faith to sell—or frankly, *Frank*, they're hoping you're weak enough to let them take it from her before she can sell for a big payday."

Faith's eyes go wide, and I hold up a hand while Frank says, "I don't want to let Faith down."

Faith shuts her eyes and then says, "You won't, Frank. You won't."

"We need to get you out of probate," Frank says. "Then you can take out a loan on your winery and pay off the debt your mother left you."

"But the bank won't let that happen," Faith says.

"They will," I assure her. "I'm taking care of this." Her eyes meet mine, shadows and worry in their depths, and I repeat, "I'm taking care of this."

She gives a tiny nod. "And I'm going to leave you two to your attorney talk." She tugs on her shirt to whisper, "I'm going to go change."

I nod this time, watching her depart before I take Frank off speaker phone. "Tell me the players in this game."

He begins a detailed rundown of who is involved with what and what's happened, which on his part is a pathetic example of legal work. He has no fire left in him, and Faith needs fire on her side right now. Fifteen minutes later, Frank and I end the call just before Faith appears in the doorway, now wearing paint-spattered jeans and a T-shirt. "Well?"

"He's not done enough. I will. We'll talk through a plan before I leave."

She studies me several long beats. "Thank you, Nick."

"Tiger on this, sweetheart. That's a promise."

"Tiger," she says. "There's a coffee pot in the corner. And a mini fridge with random creamers, which shouldn't be expired because they last a scary long time when you think about it."

"Thanks, sweetheart," I say. "You're going to paint?"

"I am."

"Will I get to see the results?"

She gives me a coy smile. "Maybe." She slips away, and I glance down at the paperwork in front of me, craving time I don't have to review it in more detail.

I grab my briefcase from the ground beside me and pull out my MacBook and review what North has sent me. That's when Mozart fills the air, a sign that Faith remembers I work to classical music. And what's crazy is that no other woman has ever known that about me. I've only just met Faith, and I've let her see parts of me no one else has. I stand and walk to the door to find her standing at the easel, my painting no longer on the ground. It's in front of her, pleading for her brush, and I wonder if she's still looking for the lies that I've sworn I despise but can't stop telling her.

CHAPTER EIGHTEEN

Faith

Nick and I spend the rest of Saturday afternoon and into the evening inside my studio, him in my office, me sitting in front of a once-blank canvas with a brush in hand. And I do what I love—what I have denied myself for far too long.

I paint, and I do so without hesitation.

I paint without what I now believe to be the fear of the past few months. Fear of failure. Fear of disappointment. Fear of seeing myself through my brush when I do not like who and what the past few months have made me.

I paint Nick.

His strong face.

His piercing eyes.

His tattoos. The tiger. The words: *An eye for an eye.*

And I do all of this while trying to understand a man who seems to understand me perhaps too well. I also do so quite entertained by the way he paces my office, throws paper balls at a trash can, talks to himself, and then repeats. *His* creative process. And what I like about seeing this is that the hard work shows me what's beneath the arrogance.

Amazingly, too, at random times, I look up from my canvas to find him standing at the office door, his broad shoulder resting against the doorway, a force that consumes the room while he intently watches me work, and I do not withdraw. I'm okay with him being here. I'm okay with him observing my creative process when I have *never* allowed anyone to watch me work, including Macom. But then, Macom was always critical of every creative choice I made, and Nick…is not.

But then, Nick and I are new to each other, and time changes people. I've often wondered when my father became my mother's man-child rather than her husband. Was it instant? Was it at one month? One year? Ten years? Every question leads me back to the paint on my brush and the man in my office. That's the great thing about a one-night hard limit: it never has time to go sour. The person can never see too much or know too much. And yet, any minute now, Nick and I will be at two.

Unless I send him away.

As if he senses where my thoughts are, I feel him, rather than see him, step back into the doorway of my office. And after hours of this push and pull of wordless energy between us, I don't have to look at him to know that one of his broad shoulders rests on the doorway. Or that those piercing blue eyes of his are on me, not the sun fading and washing the green from the mountainsides, soon to disappear and leave them black. But this time, I do not allow him to watch me work.

Instead, I clean my brush and remove my smock. Then and only then do I lift my gaze to meet his. He doesn't speak, but his eyes are softer now but still warm. So very warm. Not the kind of warm that says he's about to strip me naked and remind me why I can't resist him, but warm with affection. And that kind of warm, mixed with the fact that he sees too much and knows too much, should be exactly why I send him on his way.

Hard limit: *One night.*

Inhaling, I tell myself that limits are not made to be broken. My limit was meant to protect me.

I start walking toward him, and I know immediately why I need that protection. Because he affects me on every possible level, inside and out. Because as those warm eyes of his track my every step, I feel his attention like a touch when it's not a touch at all. I feel this man in so many ways that I have never felt with another. And I have only just met him. What impact might he have on me, what things might he see in me that I do not want seen, if he were with me beyond my hard limit?

There is little time for me to answer this question, as my path to him is short, and when I stop in front of him, he doesn't touch me. *Free will.* The decision about tonight is in the air.

"All done painting?" he asks.

"For now," I say.

"That's a good answer. It means you plan to pick up that brush again tomorrow. Do I get to see today's work?"

"No," I say without hesitation. "You already saw it before it was finished."

"And what, Faith, makes a painting of me 'finished'?"

"I'll know when it happens."

"But we've established it won't be tonight."

"No," I say. "It won't be tonight."

There's an implication there that he will be around to see it another day—or night—but, unique for Nick, he doesn't push. Instead, his gaze lifts beyond my shoulder, and he scans what I know to be the now shadowy horizon. "It's peaceful here," he says. "I see why you were drawn to this place."

"It's easy to feel alone here."

"Is that a good thing?"

"Yes," I say, my stare unwaveringly on his, my answer the truth, for so many reasons I will never explain to anyone.

His eyes hold mine as well, and that warmth I'd seen in his stare minutes before expands between us. "Tonight, Faith?"

"No," I say softly, because while alone is good, he feels better. "Not tonight."

His big hands come down on my waist, and he pulls me to him, our bodies flush, and when his gaze lowers to my mouth and lingers, I know he is thinking about kissing me. I desperately want him to kiss me. But he does not. Instead he says, "How about those gourmet pancakes?"

"Mine or yours?" I ask, finding a smile isn't as hard to come by with this man as I'd once thought.

"I'm thinking we better go with mine," he says. "But we're going to have to make a run to the store."

To the store.

With Nick.

Hard limit number two: *Just sex. Don't get personal.*

I have to put the brakes on everything but sex.

I should tell him this, but he's laced his fingers with mine, and he's leading me toward the stairs.

I repeat my new hard limit often for the next hour. In my head, and not to him, and I do this for what I consider a logical reason. He likes a challenge. I'm not going to issue him one on something I can't afford for him to win. So over and over, I mentally recite: Hard limit number two: *Just sex. Don't get personal.*

The first roadblock to maintaining that limit is that I go to the store with Nick in the first place. I should have said no to this trip, but the fact that he's absolutely consuming, assuming, and arrogant while there should have made limit number two easy to follow. The opposite proves true. I learn little things about him, and he learns little things about me, like that I hate mushrooms and he hates olives. He loves orange juice, and so do I. Cereal is a necessity, the more marshmallows the better.

In other words: Hard limit number two is a *failure.* And when it comes to Nick Rogers, resistance is futile.

The man finds ways to touch me the entire time we're in the store, drawing attention to us that he seems to enjoy, while I dread the wagging tongues to follow. And I know every moment that I should tell myself to back him off, but I don't. Instead, I help him load up bags with nuts, strawberries, cream, and various other items, and before long we are back in my kitchen, both of us working on his specialty pancakes. And we're talking too much.

We have on too many clothes. This is not what I signed up for, but I don't stop it from happening. Somehow, we end up on my bed with our clothes on but no shoes, eating pancakes. Talking again.

There is so much—too much—talking going on. And yet I'm doing a lot of the talking. What is wrong with me? "Tell me about your most memorable courtroom experiences," I prod, my excuse for prodding my need to finish my painting, to finish the story in his eyes.

Nick laughs. "Where to start?" He considers several moments. "Okay. How's this for memorable? I'm giving the biggest closing argument of my very young career at the time, and I have enough adrenaline pumping through me to fuel an eighteen-wheeler. I'm halfway through it, and it's going well. Really damn well."

"And you nailed it."

He laughs again, that deep, sexy laugh that seems to slide up and down my spine before landing in my belly. "No. I would have, or so I tell myself to this day, but the judge let out a burp so loud that the entire courtroom went silent and then burst into laughter that went on eternally."

"Oh my God. Did you— What did you do?"

"I had to finish, but no one was listening. Thankfully, no one listened to the opposing counsel, either."

"Did you win?"

"I won," he says, setting our empty plates on the nightstand behind him before adding, "and I was proud of that win then, but looking back, the case was a slam dunk anyone could have won."

I study him, charmed by this man who gave me humor over the grandeur I've expected. "Humble pie from Nick Rogers? Really?"

That warmth is back in his eyes. "There's much about me that might surprise you, Faith."

"So it seems," I say, but I do not tempt fate, or his questions, by once again telling him the same is true of me—nor do I have a chance to be lured into that misstep. He reaches for me and pulls me to the mattress, his big body framing mine, his powerful thigh pressed between mine. "There is much about you that has surprised me, Faith Winter, and I should tell you that I am so far from fucking you out of my system that I haven't even begun."

He doesn't give me time to react, let alone speak, before his lips are on mine, and he's kissing me, a drugging, slow kiss. And it seems now that I feel every new kiss he claims deeper in every possible way. He is the escape I'd hoped for, but he is so much more. And eventually we are once again naked, but it's not kinky spankings and naughty talk. It's not *just sex* at all. It's passionate and intense, yes, but it's softer and gentler than before, in ways I don't understand but feel.

Until we are here and now, in this exact moment when the lights are out, the TV playing a movie with barely audible sound. His heart thunders beneath my ear, telling me that he is still awake as well. I inhale, breathing in that woodsy scent of him, wondering how one person can feel so right and so wrong at the same time. Macom had felt right and then wrong, though the wrong took me longer than it should have to admit, but he was never both at once. Ironically, too, when I look into Nick's eyes, I believe he feels the same of me.

I'd told Nick that it's easy to feel alone here in this house, but I didn't tell him just how good that usually is to me. I didn't tell him that alone is safe. I didn't tell him that alone allows me to be me without fearing what someone will see or judge. Alone is a place where I take shelter and can breathe again. But as necessary as being alone feels right now, Nick has awakened something in me, and not just the woman. I am painting again, and suddenly I realize that painting is how I learn, grow, and cope.

My mind starts to travel back to the past, to how solitude became my sanctuary, and I meld myself closer to Nick and somehow find myself asking, "Did you speak to your father often?"

"No," he says simply.

"Do you feel guilty about that?"

"No," he says, no hesitation. Just straight up. This is how it is.

This is what it is.

"Have you cried for him?"

"No," he says again. "I have not."

"Me either," I say, and I don't mean to say more, but in the safety of darkness, my eyes hidden, my expression with them, I do. "And it feels bad," I add. "Like I'm supposed to be crying for her."

"If the person didn't deserve your love in life," he replies, "they don't deserve your tears in death."

I know he's right. My mother doesn't deserve my tears, but death is her friend and my enemy. Death is the gaping hole in your soul that just keeps spiraling into blackness. "Do you have siblings, Nick?"

"No."

"Other family?"

"No."

"Then you're alone now, too."

"Sweetheart, I was alone when that man was in the room."

As was I with my mother, I think, memories trying to invade my mind that I do not want to revisit. I shut my eyes, inhaling Nick's woodsy sent, losing myself in him. In sleep, I hope. And the shadows start to form. The darkness, too, but then suddenly, I don't smell Nick any longer. That woodsy scent is replaced by flowers. So many flowers. Daisies. Roses. Lilacs. The scent of the Reid Winter Gardens. The scent of my mother that clings to my hair and clothes almost daily. I will my mind away from the place I sense it's taking me. I fight a mental war I lose. I am back in time, living my tenth birthday.

My father has just picked me up from school, and we've returned to the mansion, and I cannot wait to find my mother, a drawing in my hand, a present for her, while my father has promised mine will come soon. I push through the doors leading to the garden. I drop my drawing and gasp when it starts to blow. I run and catch it, picking it up and staring down at the colors. So many colors. So many flowers. I've drawn my mother's garden, and I know she will be proud.

With my prize back in hand, I rush to the gazebo where I always find her but stop short when I spy a tall, dark-haired man with her. "I told you not to come here," my mother says.

"Return my phone calls, Meredith, and I won't."

"You do understand I'm married?"

He grabs my mother's arm and pulls her to him. "I also understand you want me," he says, and then he is kissing her, and I open my mouth to scream, but nothing comes out. I turn away and start running, and just when I reach the door to the mansion, it opens and my father steps outside. And he's big and tall and like a teddy bear that loves and loves, and I want to protect him like he protects me.

"Daddy!" I shout and fling myself at him, hugging him.

"Hey, honey. Did you find your mother?"

"She's inside," I say. "We have to find her. I need cake."

He laughs and takes my hand, leading me to the mansion. "Let's find her and have cake."

My lashes lift, my eyes pierced by sunlight, and I blink away slumber with the sudden realization that Nick is gone. I jolt to a sitting position, pulling the blanket over my nudity, a ball of emotion I refuse to name in my chest. Of course he's gone. Why wouldn't he be gone? That ball in my chest expands, and I reject it, refusing to name it. Glancing at the clock, I'm appalled to discover it's after nine. I have the rest of today here before I go back to the mansion, and I'm wasting it in bed, which admittedly was more appealing when Nick was in it, but I'm damn sure not letting today suck because of him leaving without saying a word.

Throwing off the covers, I walk into the bathroom and pull on my pink robe and shove my feet in my pink fluffy slippers. By habit, I brush my teeth and hair, and I note the smudges of mascara under my eyes. "No wonder he left," I murmur. I look like the scary chick from that horror movie—*The Grudge*, or something like that. Only she had dark hair, meant to be goth and scary. At this moment, I'm a close second to her, though, for sure. I decide I don't care, either. There is no one to care but me, and I just want coffee. And I think I might make me some gourmet pancakes my way. I need to stick to doing things my way. And bill collectors or not, I need to stop staying at the mansion. I need my space. I guess that is the gift Nick Rogers left me with.

Me again.

Or maybe that will turn out to be a curse, and I will in turn *curse him* for months to follow.

I walk back into the bedroom and note that he is, indeed, polite. He took our plates to the kitchen when he left. For some reason, that really irritates me. I walk into the living room, and my mind goes back to the dream, to my tenth birthday, and without a conscious decision to do so, I cross the living room and enter the library. Once I'm there, I walk to the bookshelf and pull out a worn brown journal and sit down on the chair beside it, opening it to pull out a piece of old, worn paper that was once balled up like one of the pieces of paper Nick used for paper basketball in my office yesterday.

"Faith."

I jolt at Nick's voice, looking up to find him standing in the doorway.

"You scared the heck out of me, Nick," I say, my hand at my chest, while his chest is hugged by a snug black T-shirt he's paired with black jeans and biker-style boots, the many sides of this man dauntingly sexy.

He starts laughing in reaction, his jaw sporting a heavy stubble, while his hair is loose and damp, because apparently he took a shower and I didn't know.

"It's not funny," I scold.

"No," he says, crossing the room to sit on the footstool in front of me. "It's not funny, but I hate to tell you, Faith, as beautiful as you are, right now you look like the girl from—"

"*The Grudge*," I supply, remembering my makeup. "I noticed

that, but I thought... I noticed."

He narrows those too blue, too intelligent eyes on me. "You thought I was gone?"

I could deny the truth, but he already knows, and games are better when naked or trying to get naked. "Yes," I say. "I did."

His eyes fill with mischief. "And miss a chance to see how you look this morning?"

I scowl, and he leans in to kiss me before saying, "Minty fresh. I find it interesting that you brushed your teeth and left your mascara like that."

"Maybe I wanted to scare you away," I say. "And fair warning. I'm cranky without coffee."

"We can fix that in about two minutes." His gaze goes to the drawing. "What's this?"

It's a testament to how this man distracts and consumes me that I've forgotten what I'm holding in my hand. "The past," I say, and when I would fold it, Nick catches my hand.

"Was this your work as a child?"

"Yes," I say. "It was."

"You saw things in color then. When did that change?"

That day, I think, but instead I focus on the next time I created anything. "Sixteen."

"What made you change?"

"Life," I say, and because I have no intent of explaining, I add, "I really need that coffee. Actually, I really need a shower."

He studies me several beats, then releases my hand. "I'll be armed with coffee in the kitchen." I shut the journal, and Nick glances at it. "You're a journal writer?"

"No," I say. "I paint. I don't write. It's actually my father's."

He tilts his head. "Did you read it?"

The question cuts right along with the answer. "Every page many times over, and I understand him less now than I ever thought possible." I stand and shove it back on the shelf, thinking of the words inside with biting clarity. "He loved her so damn unconditionally." I look at Nick, who remains on the stool. "And affection to me is, as you said, with tears. It has to be earned."

"As it should be," he says, and this leaves me curious about him, but I tell myself it's time to just stay curious about Nick. To stop talking.

I walk toward the door, but that curiosity wins. I pause before exiting. "Has anyone earned that from you, Nick?" I ask, turning to find him standing by the stool now, facing me.

"There were a few swipes I tried to turn into something right, but they were always wrong."

"Why?"

"The only answer I have is that I don't believe in happily ever after," he says. "That doesn't sit well with most women."

And just like that, he validates an acceptable reason for me to continue to bypass my hard limit of one night. "Since I don't, either," I say, "we really are the perfect distraction for each other, now aren't we? It's really kind of liberating. I don't have to worry about you falling in love with me, and you don't have to worry about me falling in love with you."

I don't wait for a reply. I exit the library.

CHAPTER NINETEEN

Faith

No love.
No happily ever after.

In these things, Nick and I are kindred souls, but that begs the question: can one soul know another before the two people realize that to be true?

This is what is on my mind as I shower, then dress in faded jeans and a T-shirt, concluding that with Nick and me this must be the case. It's the only explanation for the right and the wrong of us together. We aren't so much about dark lust as I'd started out thinking, as we're damage attracting damage. He's damaged. I'm damaged. We see each other. We know each other. The understanding between us exists beyond the short time we've known each other. But do damaged people cut each other deeper? Or do they heal each other when no one else can? I don't know this answer, but I do know that in a short time, Nick has changed me. Or maybe just opened my eyes.

As if it's not enough to feel this, I am staring at the logo on my T-shirt that reads: Los Angeles Art Museum. My ex-employer, where by day I embraced art, and then by night I went home and embraced it again with a brush in my hand. I've let the past invade the present. No. I've let me be me. I'd say that is a good thing, but it exposes things I can't afford to expose. I think it's bad, like Nick—but, also like Nick, it feels good. But bad is bad. Why can't I remember that with this man?

This thought lingers in my mind as I finish flat-ironing my hair and apply light makeup, a brush of pink here and there, and no more. Satisfied that I no longer resemble a chick from a horror flick, I walk to the closet, stick my feet into black UGG sneakers, and then head toward the bedroom, only to stop dead in my tracks. On the white tiled ledge that frames my equally white tub is Nick's bag. I just didn't look for it. Maybe I didn't want to see it. Maybe I just wanted him to be the asshole I've called him because that would be simple. But he's not simple, and I don't feel like *we're* simple together at all. I like simple. It's easy to explain and control, and yet, I find myself walking toward the living room, seeking Nick out, with simple feeling overrated for the first time in my life.

I know he will make demands. I know he will want too much. I know everything for me should be too much right now. And I don't care. I just want to find him again and inhale that scent of his, which is positively drugging in all the ways Nick is right and wrong. God, I love it.

As I exit the bedroom, I'm drawn toward the kitchen by the low rumble of Nick's confident voice. Rounding the corner, I find him sitting at the island in profile to me, his hair now tied at his nape, his orange-and-black tiger tattoo displayed as he holds the phone to his ear. The art is detailed—exquisite, really, but somehow simplistic and fierce. While the man, too, is fierce, there is nothing simple about Nick Rogers or what he makes me feel.

"Damn it, North," he growls into the phone, glancing in my direction, his eyes warming as they find me, and when I might expect him to somehow make this moment sexual, he does not. He lifts his cup to offer me his coffee, an intimate gesture that does funny things to my belly. I start in his direction, and he scowls at something North has said. "Think like the enemy," he scolds the other man. "I would have prepped my client for every question you gave me for this witness."

I reach the island and pick up Nick's cup, my eyes meeting his as I place my lips where his lips may well have been moments before, but the instant the hot beverage touches my lips, the harsh taste of plain black coffee has me scowling. Nick laughs, and apparently North is confused, because Nick says, "No. That wasn't funny, and you will get your ass handed to you by opposing counsel and then by me."

Yikes. North is in hot water, and I decide to let Nick focus. I set his cup back down, and I walk to the coffee pot and get another cup brewing for me, listening as he goes back and forth with North for the next couple of minutes. My coffee has brewed and I'm just pouring white chocolate creamer in my steaming cup when Nick says, "Just meet me at my place at five. We're going to be ready in the morning if we're up all night." He ends the call.

And I feel the end of the weekend like a punch in the chest.

I stand at the counter, my back to him, not about to turn until I figure out what the heck this reaction is that I'm having. What I'm *feeling*, which I guess is another curse and gift Nick has given me. I am feeling things again because of him, but he's about to leave. And of course he is. It's Sunday. And, rental property or not, he lives and works in another city, and I'd planned on telling him to leave anyway. Hadn't I? No. I hadn't. I'm just trying to make myself feel simple and in control. And I am those things. This is a fling. This is a *weekend* fling. It was supposed to be one night. It's just a—

Nick steps behind me, his hands at my waist, his touch radiating through me with more impact than any man should ever have over me, especially since this is the last time I might ever touch him. And it *feels* much worse in practice than I'd imagined.

He leans in and nuzzles my hair, inhaling like he is breathing me in. And God, I really love when he does that. "Come to the city with me," he says.

Shock rolls through me, and I face him, my hands landing hard on his chest. "What?"

"Come with me, Faith. I have to go back to San Francisco. If you're with me, then we can deal with the bank together. And you need a break from all of this. We'll come back here for the weekend."

"I have to run the winery, Nick."

His eyes darken, and not with disappointment but rather awareness I have not yet realized. "At least you didn't decide your new hard limit includes me leaving and never seeing you again."

He's right. I didn't. This man is unraveling every carefully crafted plan I had, and I can't seem to care. And I should care. This is trouble. He's trouble. *I'm* trouble. "What are we doing here, Nick? What is this?"

His hands settle on the counter on either side of me, his big body crowding mine without touching me. "I don't know, Faith," he says, "but let's find out."

"You don't— We don't—"

"I could supply a number of phrases to end that statement, but it would be words. Just words. I'm not done with you, and I hope like hell you're not done with me, Faith."

"I wish I was," I say, angry at him for complicating my life. Happy that he has at the same time, because yes, I'm still fucked-up.

"Ditto, sweetheart. We're here now, though. Agreed?"

"Yes," I say. "Agreed."

"Then let's make a new hard limit. The only hard limit that exists, until we decide together otherwise, is we take this one day at a time."

Until we decide together. I realize with those words part of Nick's appeal. He's this uber alpha male. He's sexy. He's demanding. But he has this way of knowing when to back off, when to ask. This is new to me. This is right, not wrong. "One day at a time," I agree.

"Come to San Francisco with me."

I want to, I realize. I want to know who he is in his own domain, but want doesn't equal need. And I need to be here. "I can't just leave the winery."

"You have a manager. A good one, you said."

"Kasey is amazing," I say, "but I do my best to protect him and the staff from the bill collectors who stalk us during the week. I can't leave, Nick. I won't. Not now."

The doorbell rings. "Holy fuck," he says. "This isn't helping my case." He starts to move away, but I catch his arm.

"Damn it, Nick," I warn. "Our agreement to take this day by day is not an invitation for you to take over my life. I run my life."

"I know you run your life, sweetheart. I can't tell you enough times—I get it. Let me be clear. It makes me hot. It makes me want to bend you over the counter. But let me also be clear. I'm now your attorney, Faith. Unless we've deviated from that plan, I'm getting that door."

I purse my lips and release him, only to have him lean over and kiss me, and then he's on the move in about two flat seconds. "At least he has his pants zipped this time," I murmur, taking off after him, overwhelmed by Nick's desire to protect me, and I tell myself to be smart enough to accept it but strong enough not to count on it, now or ever.

Clearing the hallway, I enter the foyer at the same moment that Josh, dressed in khakis and a button-down, walks in the front door, but he doesn't seem to notice me. He shuts the door and faces Nick, the two men crackling with opposing male energy. "Nick Rogers was the name, right?" Josh asks, and I'm not sure if he's being a smart-ass or playing coy, considering he knew Nick's name immediately at the art gallery.

Nick doesn't respond. As in, at all. Seconds tick by, and then more, and I can't take it. I have to break the tension before Josh does and it ends badly for him. "Josh," I say, hurrying forward, remembering now. "I forgot you were stopping by."

"Obviously," he says, his tone acidic. "And clearly this isn't the time to have a serious business discussion. Call me Monday, and we'll talk through decisions that need to be made, or perhaps forgotten." He turns and walks out the door.

Certain this is about Macom—that this is personal, not professional—I'm instantly angry and indignant, and I charge after him, not bothering to shut the door behind me. "Stop," I call after him, a cold gust of morning wind blasting me, but I'm too hot-tempered to care.

Thankfully, he does as I've ordered, halfway down the stairs, turning to face me. "Now is clearly not the time, Faith."

"Because I dare to have a life again?" I demand, walking to the edge of the porch.

"That man in there is none of my business," he says. "But you are."

"My work is your business," I snap back.

"Exactly," he agrees. "And when I find out you've finally started painting again, that's a good thing. A distraction is not." He motions to my shirt. "You're wearing an art shirt. This gives me hope that we're back on track. You need to stay focused."

"I painted *Nick*," I snap back before I can stop myself. "He inspired me to paint. Having a life again inspired me to paint."

He goes very still. "You painted a portrait?"

"Yes. I did. And I might do more. I might do a lot of things, but not now. Now, I have to save the winery, and you know what, Josh? I know you need people who make money for you. I understand if you can't wait this out with me."

"I do need to make money, Faith. But more than anything, I need clients who are actively involved in the career I'm representing them for. You need to be painting. I need to be placing your work. I got a call after the show from a representative of the L.A. Art Forum. They're interested in your work for next month's show."

My eyes go wide at the mention of one of the most prestigious events in the art world. "They are? They never—"

"They are now because you actually got out there and did something for your art. But I'm not saying yes when you're telling me now is not the time. So think about that, Faith. How much can you fit in your life right now? Cut what won't work, and if that's your art and me, I need to know and know quickly." He turns and walks away.

And I stand there, watching him cross to his white Porsche,

because why wouldn't my agent drive a Porsche like my ex, who he's best friends with. Still pissed, really baffled about what just happened, I don't wait for him to leave. I walk into the house. The minute I'm inside, Nick shuts the door and pulls me to him.

"That wasn't about your art, sweetheart," he says, his hands at my waist. "You know that, right?"

"I don't know what the hell that was."

"He wants to fuck you. He's probably in love with you."

I blanch. "What? No. No. No. He's best friends with my ex."

"Come on, Faith. Some part of you knows that man wants you. And you need a new agent."

"Because you think he wants to fuck me?" I demand, angry all over again at these men trying to run my life. I push away from him, darting down the hallway, where I can have some coffee and get more wired and angry at the rest of the world.

Nick's on my heels; I can feel him, a heavy force of alpha pain-in-my-ass man right now, which, while sexy as hell at moments, is not now. I enter the kitchen and round the island, fully intending to keep it between us, but he has other ideas. I turn, and he's already with me, pressing me against the counter, his big, delicious, pain-in-my-ass body crowding mine.

"He wants to fuck you, Faith. He's thinking with his dick, not his head. That isn't good for you."

"And what are you doing, Nick?"

"Sweetheart, I have no hesitation in telling you that I want to fuck you and then do it all over again. But this isn't about me and you fucking. This is about your career."

"You don't know me enough to care about this."

"When do I get to care, Faith? One week? One month? Two? Tell me. Because this is new fucking territory for me."

"You can't—"

"I do, and the one thing that your dickhead agent and I agree on is the fact that you need to paint. And I'm going to make you paint. And when you do, you need an agent who isn't thinking about fucking you instead of selling you."

"He's my ex's best friend," I say, returning to the explanation I've given myself every time I felt awkward with Josh.

"You said that already, and it still changes nothing."

"You want me to change agents because he wants to fuck me and so do you."

"Sweetheart, I'm going to make sure you're well enough fucked that he never has a shot. And that's only going to piss him off more. Be ready. His wrath is coming, but before it comes, tell him to set up that show he mentioned."

"It's not that simple," I argue. "You don't understand."

"I understand that I want to fuck an artist. So you're going to be an artist."

I blink at the ridiculousness of that statement. "So I have to be an artist because you want to fuck an artist?"

"You *are* an artist, Faith. End of story, and everything else you do is simply a distraction."

"Including you?"

He strokes a lock of hair behind my ear. "I'm okay with being second to your art."

Once again, Nick surprises me, delivering an answer that is nothing that I expect and everything I didn't even know I want.

"Second to your art," he adds. "But not another man. New hard limit." He cups my face. "Whatever this is, it's exclusive. You fuck no one else until we decide it's over."

"And you, Nick?" I ask. "Will you fuck someone else?"

"Sweetheart. You have my full attention, and not only do I want no one else, I want all of you and I'm not going to settle for any less."

I'm not sure what he means by this. *All of me.* And I don't ask, because he can't have all of me. Which is why this should be the end. But when he kisses me, I'm alive. When he touches me, I'm on fire. When he's with me, I'm not alone, even though I would be with anyone else. So when he says, "Hard limit, Faith. Only us," I don't push him away, and I don't push back. I live dangerously. I say, "Hard limit. Only us."

And just like that, Nick has proven I was right about him from the beginning. He is dark lust. He is all-consuming. He is an escape I crave. Maybe he's even an obsession, as he'd called me. But more so, he *is* dangerous. I sense it. I feel it like I feel this man in every part of me, inside and out.

But then, so am I.

CHAPTER TWENTY

Faith

Nick packs up his work and most of my documents, and we head to the winery with the intent of having lunch there and reviewing his legal plan with the bank. And now, sitting in the passenger seat of his car, I am aware of this man next to me in ways I have never been aware of another man. It's not about looking at him and being aroused. Or looking at him and thinking about how sexy he is. It's about how I feel him inside and out. The way I know him beyond logic and reason. And maybe that means things are going too fast, but to where? We agreed. No love. No forever. This is just "us," and "us" makes me *feel* something that isn't guilt and pain. And I need that. I guess that means I need him, and that's a terrifying thought, to need someone else. My father needed my mother, and that made him a fool.

"What are you going to do about Josh?" Nick asks.

I breathe out. "Have a heart-to-heart with him."

"You can't reason with a man who's thinking with his dick, sweetheart."

"I really hope you're wrong about his feelings for me, but even if you're not, he kept me on despite Macom telling him to drop me, *and* he placed my work when I was doing nothing to support it myself. No agent would have done that."

He glances over at me. "Macom told him to drop you?"

"Yes," I say. "I learned that he's all about an eye for an eye. I left him. It wounded his ego. He lashed out. And as much money as he makes Josh, Josh had the courage to tell him that professional and personal are two different things. I'd like to think that's about my work, not some personal agenda."

"Your work is exceptional, Faith," Nick says. "And any inference you took from my evaluation of Josh's interest in you otherwise was not intended. I also know his reputation. He's a good agent, but he's a good agent acting badly. He indirectly threatened you today when he said he'd cancel your appearance in the forum, and he did so because I was at your house."

"You're right. He did, but he deserves to have me talk to him, not drop him right when I might find some success that he helped create. Like I said, and this is big: that man kept me on and helped place my work when I was doing nothing to support that work."

He turns us into the winery property and glances over at me again. "Loyalty is a good quality, but once a man is in the place he's in with a woman, there's no room for delicate conversation. My advice that you didn't ask for: be frank."

"You say this like it's from experience."

"I've never been shameless over a woman. Ever. But as I said. Love and hate wear a fine line, and I've fought many a battle in court over that line."

"Noted, counselor," I say. "Be direct. I really don't have a problem with direct."

He gives me a sexy half smile. "And yet you're damn good at talking in circles. You would have been a hell of an opponent in court."

"Oh no," I say. "I hate the spotlight. I would have hated the way people would stare at me and be hanging on my words."

"And yet your art puts you in the spotlight."

"My art is the spotlight," I say. "And that's how I like it." He turns us into the drive of the mansion. "And speaking of the spotlight. Because I've never brought a man here, everyone is going to be talking about the two of us."

"Not even Macom?"

"No," I say simply, saved from more when we pull to a halt at the front of the mansion.

But Nick still tries. "Just no?"

"Just no," I say as the valets open both of our doors, but my mind is already on the way my father hated the idea of me with an artist, and how much I was certain my mother would like me with Macom a little too much. Not for the first time, I wonder how my father would have justified forgiving that one.

I make small talk with the valets, and Nick rounds the car to join me, his hand settling at my lower back, and the heavy weight of their stares stiffens my spine. "They'll get used to me," Nick promises, and the fact that he knows what I feel, and that he's made it clear he's sharing that burden with me, is more impactful to me than anything else he's done to this point. It's not about sex. It's not about legal matters. It's about a small moment of time that he recognized as mattering to me.

We walk the steps, and as we reach the top level, the doors are opened for us, and just inside the foyer, Kasey greets us. Tall and silver-gray at fifty, he is a good-looking man who is friendly, well-liked, and still manages to be reserved in his personal life. "Fair warning," he says. "We have a bridezilla in the house. I'd recommend taking cover."

I laugh. "You are a bridezilla expert," I say, and as he glances at Nick, surprise in the depth of his stare, Nick offers him his hand.

"Nick Rogers."

"Kasey Gilligan," Kasey greets, and the two men shake hands and exchange small talk that doesn't last. Kasey's walkie-talkie goes off on his belt.

"Trouble in the garden," a voice says.

"That's about the bridezilla," he says. "I need to go focus her on her vows."

Guilt over his dilemma and my weekend away washes over me. "Do you need—"

"No," he says. "I do not need your help. I'm quite capable of running this place."

"I know that."

"This weekend gave me hope that you might mean that statement."

He leaves me no room to argue. In a blink, he's gone, and Nick glances down at me, arching a brow. "It's not about how he handles the management of the winery. It's about the challenge that was my mother, and now the bank."

"Then let's go talk about overcoming those things," he says. "Because my hard limit was made with an artist." He urges me forward, and I guide him to the stairwell and a path behind it with a second stairwell leading down. The way he pushes me to paint affects me in ways I'll analyze later, alone.

Once we're in the basement level, where there is a gift shop and a restaurant, we find our way to a rare vacant table among the fifteen that are mostly occupied, the floral tablecloths and designs in the center my mother's choice.

"What do you recommend?" Nick asks, grabbing the menu on the table, and I wonder if he knows the way he fills the room, or the way men look at him with envy and the women with desire.

"Any of the five quiche choices," I reply. "The chef trained in France, and apparently, that's a thing there. She knows her quiche."

"Quiche it is," he says right as Samantha, our waitress, appears.

Nick turns his attention to her, and I watch, waiting for her gorgeous brunette bombshell looks to affect him, but if he notices, he shows no reaction at all. In fact, his hand finds my knee under the table, his eyes looking in my direction more than not.

And it's only moments after we've ordered that, compliments of another waiter, we have coffee in front of us, and I find myself in the center of Nick's keen blue eyes. "I can't believe you've never been to Paris, considering the wine culture."

"My parents went. I stayed home."

Awareness that shouldn't be possible flickers in his eyes. "They invited you. You didn't want to go."

"I wanted to go," I say. "Just not with them."

"How bad was your relationship with your mother?"

"I'd say it ranked about where you describe that of yours with your father."

"And everyone here knew?"

"No," I say. "We put on a good show."

"But Kasey knew."

"Kasey didn't know until after my father died and I was forced to become the wall between the two of them. Honestly, it's made Kasey and me closer. He loved my father and was confused by his relationship with my mother as well. I mean, my father was tough, charismatic, and dynamic in business. His willingness to take my mother's abuse was illogical."

"Love is blind," he says wryly. "Or so it seems." He changes the subject. "I like Kasey, by the way."

"He's a good man," I say. "And a friend."

"How have you explained the bill collectors?"

"He knows there are probate issues, which, knowing my mother as he did, does not surprise him."

"So you aren't going to lose him?"

"No. Not now. But I'm nervous about this dragging on too long and giving him cold feet."

"I'd like to talk to him next week, if you're okay with that?"

"Why?"

"I'm looking for any insight into your mother's activities he might give me that, as an outsider, might stand out to me, and not you."

"Of course," I say. "That seems logical. I'll tell him you'll call, but you have your deposition, Nick. You need to focus on that."

"I can walk and chew bubblegum at the same time, sweetheart. I do it all the time."

Our food is set in front of us, and in a few moments, we are both holding forks, and Nick takes a bite. "Well?" I ask.

"Excellent," he approves. "No wonder you never learned to cook when you could eat here."

We chat a moment, and I'm struck by the easy comfort I have

with this man in any setting. It's not something I have with people, and I've often thought that I stayed with Macom so long because I needed a connection to another human being. Not because I needed him.

"Tell me about the show Josh mentioned," Nick urges a few bites into our meal.

The show again. He's mentioned it twice, and I haven't even let the possibility of being in that show sink in yet, nor do I want to talk about it. "You listened in on the entire conversation between myself and Josh, didn't you?"

"Unapologetically," he says, his eyes challenging me to disapprove.

But I don't. I feel envy instead at his ability to be frank and unapologetic about pretty much everything. Who he is. What he is. How he feels about his father. God. To be that free. What would it be like?

"You told him you painted me," Nick says.

"I shouldn't have," I reply without hesitation.

"Why?"

"Because I used it to justify me being with you."

Surprise flickers in his eyes. "I realized that," he says. "I wasn't sure you did."

"Otherwise, I'm not sorry I told him. You did inspire me to paint, Nick."

"By being an arrogant asshole you aren't sure you can trust?"

He's right. That is what happened, but somehow that feeling I'd had about him no longer weighs on me as it had. "I don't trust easily."

"Those who do get burned," he says, and there's something in his eyes, in his voice, that I cannot name but wish I could, and I never get the chance. He circles back to where this started. "The show, Faith."

"The show," I repeat, my mind tracking back to those years in L.A. "Being picked for it has always been a dream for me. For years, my work was presented to them. For years, I was declined."

"And this time they came to you," he observes.

That hope and dream inside me rises up with panful insistence, and I shove it back down. "An inquiry means nothing."

"Have they inquired before?"

"No, but they may rule me out."

"But if they want you, you're not going to decline."

It's not a question. It's a command, and while I don't take commands well, this one is well-intended—but also ineffective for reasons out of his control. "They aren't going to accept me. It's a month away."

"Don't do that, Faith." His tone is absolute.

"Don't do what?"

"Downplay how big this is for you. Don't find a way to make it not matter."

I stare at him, trying to understand how this man I barely know can be this supportive. Is it real? Is it just a part of his temporary obsession with me? He arches a brow at my silent scrutiny, but I am saved a real answer when more food appears. But it's not a true escape. The moment we're alone, Nick returns to the topic. "What does the show do for you?"

"If you're spotlighted, you've made it. Those are the artists people want to have in their stores and on their walls." Unbidden, my mind goes back to the day I'd told my father I had a full scholarship to UCLA. There had been hugs. Excitement. Smiles. Then he'd said, "I can see it now. Our wine will be in every gallery in the country because you know the wine that pairs with the art." And I'd been devastated. My art was never going to be more than a hobby to him.

Nick's knees capture mine under the table, and my eyes jerk to his. "What just happened, sweetheart?" he asks, that tender warmth back in his eyes, and a knot forms in my throat.

"If I can get into the show, I can sell my work and save the winery."

Nick's eyes narrow on mine, and I swear, in that moment, it feels like he's diving deep into my soul and seeing too much again. "When you get into the show, it's about you, not the winery."

"But the money—"

"Let's talk about the winery and money with my attorney hat on."

I shove my plate aside, and Nick does the same. "Okay. I don't like how that sounds."

"Money isn't your issue," he says. "If that were the case, I'd take advantage of a good investment, write you a check, get a return, and we'd be done with this."

"I'm not foolish enough to miss the way you framed that in a way you think I'd find acceptable, but you giving me money—which I wouldn't take, no matter how you presented it—isn't your point."

"No. It's not. Obviously, Frank has you focused on money being your salvation when it's not."

"You yourself wanted to know the financial status of the winery," I point out.

"Because if it's a sinking ship, there's no reason to save it. That isn't the case, so we move on to your primary problem. The absence of a will is the issue."

"I have my father's will, which said my mother inherits on the stipulation that I inherit next."

"But we have no idea what documents came after that will that might say otherwise. There may be none. The bank may just hope they can pressure you into walking away. They may even have an investor who wants the property and wants you to sell cheap."

"Can they be a part of that? Can they do that?"

"There are a lot of things that shouldn't be done that get done. And I'm having someone on my research team look into the money trail and the mystery of your mother's barren bank accounts."

Guilt assails me again, and it is not a feeling I enjoy. It's heavy and sharp and mean. "Please don't spend money on my behalf."

"I have people I'm already paying," he says. "I promise you, the bank will know what we don't. And we won't have, nor will I allow us to have, that disadvantage." He slides my plate in front of me. "I got this. Stop worrying."

"Faith."

At the sound of my name, I look up to find the restaurant manager, Sheila, standing beside us, and the distressed look on her face has my spine straightening. "What is it, Sheila?"

"There's a man at the door asking to see you who looks like... He looks like..."

My blood runs cold. "My father," I supply without ever looking toward the door. "I'll be there in a moment."

She nods and leaves, and Nick glances at the man by the door who I know to be tall, fit, and with white hair that was once red. "Bill Winter," he says. "Your uncle, your father's twin, and the CEO of Pier 111, a social media platform that's giving Facebook a run for its money. He was also estranged from your father for eight years before his death."

"Reminding me that you studied me like you were picking a refrigerator out isn't a good thing right now, Nick."

"As I've said, I studied you like a woman who intrigued me," he reminds me. "And I'm not going to feign naïveté I don't have, and I know you well enough to know that's not what you want."

"No," I concede. "I wouldn't. I need to go deal with him. And it won't take long."

He considers me for several moments before releasing my knees, he's still holding. "I'm here if you need me."

Has anyone I wanted to say those words ever said them to me? "Thank you."

I stand and turn toward the door, and sure enough, there stands Bill Winter, and I swear seeing him, with his likeness to my father, turns my knees to rubber. But it also angers me, and my spine straightens. I start walking, crossing the small space to meet him at the archway that is the entrance to the restaurant. "What are you doing here, Bill?" I ask, my voice sharp despite my low tone.

Towering over me by a good foot, he stares down at me, his blue eyes so like my father's it hurts to look at him. "How are you, Faith?"

"What are you doing here, Bill?" I repeat.

"I'm your only living family. I'm checking on my niece."

"You're my blood but not my family. My father would not want you here."

"Your father and I made peace before he died."

"No, you didn't," I say, rejecting what would add another irrational personal decision to my father's track record.

"We did, but regardless," he says. "I owe him. And that means protecting you. The bank called me. I understand there are financial issues. Let me help."

I am appalled and shocked that the bank went to Bill. "I don't want or need your help, and if I did, my father would roll over in his grave if I took it."

"I told you. We came to terms before he died."

"I don't believe you, but it doesn't matter. I don't care."

Nick steps to my side, his hand settling possessively at my back, his presence drawing Bill's immediate attention. "Bill Winter." My uncle introduces himself. "And you are?"

"Faith's loyal servant," Nick assures him. "And everyone else's nightmare. The name is Nick Rogers." He doesn't extend his hand, nor does Bill extend his own.

Bill's eyes narrow at the name. "I've heard you're a real bastard."

"And here I thought I got rid of my nice-guy reputation. I understand you're leaving. We'll walk you out."

Bill gives a smirk that almost borders on amused, then looks at me. "I'm staying at the cottage. I'll be close if you need me." He turns and walks away.

Nick flags Sheila. "Make sure he leaves, and if he doesn't, call Faith." I nod my approval to Sheila, and Nick turns to me. "Where can we talk?"

"This way," I say, motioning us into the hallway that leads nowhere but an exit door, and the minute we're there, Nick's hands are on my hips.

"What cottage?"

"He owns a property up the road, but he's rarely here, and when he is, I don't see him. He says the bank called him about the default. Can they do that?"

"Context is everything, and he holds the family name. Does he want the winery?"

"He's a billionaire, Nick. He doesn't want or need this place."

"Then why was he here?"

"To help, he said. Basically, to repent for his sins."

Nick's energy sharpens. "What sins, Faith?"

"He's the reason I stayed in L.A. after my graduation. He's also one of the reasons I don't believe in happily ever after and therefore make such a good fuck buddy. He slept with my mother. She got mad at him and, to get back at him, told my father, who predictably forgave her but not his brother. And that was it for me. I was out of here."

I blink, and Nick's hands are on my face, his big body pinning me against the wall. "Don't do that," he says for the second time since we arrived. "Don't decide what we are or are not based on that man or anyone else. We decide otherwise, or they win and we're weak. We are not weak."

Emotions I swore I wanted to feel, but don't, well in my chest. "Nick, you—"

"I am not my father, and you are not your mother. We decide who we are, Faith. Not them. Say it."

"We decide," I whisper.

"We decide," he repeats, stroking my cheek a moment before his lips brush mine. "I fucking hate that I have to leave you right now. Come with me."

"You know I can't. You have to see that."

He looks skyward, seeming to struggle not to push me, before he says, "Let's make sure uncle dearest has left before I leave."

A full hour later, I finally convince Nick he has to leave. My uncle is gone. His number is in my phone. He has a deposition he has to prep for. I walk him to his car, and despite the many people most likely watching, he pulls me to him and kisses me soundly on the lips. "I'm going to miss the hell out of you, and I don't even know what to do with that." A moment later, he's in his car, as if he fears he won't leave. Another few moments, and I'm standing on the steps of the mansion, watching him drive away, a storm brewing inside me while I replay his words: *I am not my father, and you are not your mother.*

The problem is, I have a whole lot more of my mother in me than Nick Rogers knows.

CHAPTER TWENTY-ONE

Tiger

What the hell is this woman doing to me?

That's one of many thoughts I have as I leave behind Reid Winter Winery, and Faith with it. Leaving her kills me, and I have never in all the many fucks I've shared with a woman given two fucks about the morning after—or the second morning after, as it may be—and what do I do? I choose Faith, a woman I went looking for to destroy. She's not the killer I thought she was, but she might be when she finds out who my father is and why I sought her out. And she'll have to know there's no way around it. Really, this is poetic justice. I told Faith I'm not like my father, but running through women and not giving two fucks is something he did well and I do better. How profound that the one I give a shit about is going to hate me like she's never hated before.

I pull onto the main highway, and taillights greet me. "Fuck," I growl, forced to halt behind a line of cars, debating the pros and cons of turning around, throwing Faith over my shoulder, and taking her home with me. Something feels off with her uncle. Something feels wrong in general, and it's not her.

Looking for answers and action, I fish my phone from my pocket and use Siri to find the shop that has Faith's car, making arrangements to pay for it and have it delivered to her over the weekend when I plan to be with her. By the time I end the call, the traffic still hasn't moved, and I dial Beck. "Nicholas," he greets.

"The uncle," I say.

"Filthy rich snake of a bastard," he says, clearly aware of who I'm talking about.

"He fucked Faith's mom."

"Who didn't?" He laughs. "That woman saw more action than ten Taco Bells on Friday night at two a.m."

"The uncle," I repeat.

"He had random contact with Meredith Winter over the years, but nothing notable after the obvious falling-out between him and her husband. And I'm sure you know that he's married to one of the billionaire Warren Hotel heiresses now."

"I knew," I say, having done plenty of my own research. "That's how he got the money for his startup. Any contact between him and Faith?"

"Aside from him attending both her mother's and father's funerals, none."

"Find out if he, or anyone for that matter, has an interest in the property the winery is sitting on," I say before moving on. "Josh—"

"The agent," he says. "What about him?"

"Could Macom have used him to connect to Faith's mother or my father?"

"Interesting premise when I thought of it as well," Beck says, "but I cross-referenced phone numbers and emails. There's nothing."

Grimacing, and with plenty of taillights and time in my future, I lead the conversation to the bank and draw Beck into a debate over their motives, before my mind takes me to a place I don't want to go. Not with Faith in Sonoma and me in San Francisco. "What if Faith isn't a killer, but now she's the one in the way of whoever is?"

"Any time a million dollars plus is missing and two people are dead of the exact same cause two months apart, the possibility of someone else ending up dead exists. But unlike you, apparently, I won't conclude a murder or murders were committed until you get me your father's and Meredith Winter's autopsy reports. And for the record, I'm far from thinking Faith Winter is innocent. She and her mother could easily have been a scam team. Always remember that in the absence of evidence, there is someone making sure there's an absence of evidence. I'll warn you again. Watch your back. You have my excessively large bill to pay."

He hangs up on the warning I'd feel obligated to give me, too, but I'm not a fool. I read people with a lot less of a look into their lives than I have into Faith's. I dial Abel Baldwin, my closest friend, one of the best damn criminal attorneys on the planet. "I was starting to think you might be dead, too," he says when he picks up. "What happened with Faith Winter?"

I glance at the clock on my dash. "Can you meet me at my place at four?"

"Now I'm really curious. I'll be there."

I asked him to help me destroy her. Now I need to pull back the reins and have him help me save her. And I return to: *What the hell is this woman doing to me?*

Just after four, Abel and I sit in the living room of my house, him on the sectional that occupies most of the room, me on a chair across from him. One of his many Irish whiskey picks he brings by my place weekly is in our glasses, and while the sectional he occupies is a pale gray, my mood is decidedly darker. "Good stuff, right?" Abel asks, refilling his glass.

"One of your better picks," I say, but when he lifts the bottle in my direction, I wave him off. "I need to stay sharp. I have work to do."

"I'll hang out and get boozed and ask stupid questions to piss you off, because what are friends for?"

"You're a hell of a friend, Abel. One hell of a friend."

He downs his whiskey. "I love watching North geek out and start reciting facts."

"The kid's an encyclopedia," I say, motioning to his severely buzzed blond hair. "You thinking about going back to the army or what?"

"Starting a trial next week," he says. "The judge is a former SEAL."

"And you plan on reminding him that you are, too."

His lips quirk. "Gotta work what you got." He narrows his

eyes at me. "And you got me, Nick. Put me to work here. What's the elephant in the room you want to talk about but haven't?"

"What's it going to cost me to get those autopsy results sooner than three weeks from now?"

"We just filed the order," he says. "You can't buy your way past a medical procedure. This isn't a crime TV show, and you know it. Toxicology, which is what we're looking at, will take weeks and even months."

"Understood," I say, "but we both know we can move certain aspects of this to sooner rather than later. Whatever it costs, make it happen."

He narrows his eyes on me, and after a decade of friendship, I'm not surprised at what comes next. "You fucked her."

"I've fucked a lot of women."

"This one got to you. Nick, damn it. You got me involved in this because of one word: murder. Let's recap. You find a million dollars in checks written by your father to this woman's mother, who is now dead by the same means as your father, thus making Faith Winter the biggest suspect, and you choose to fuck her."

"I'm crystal clear on the details. And murder is still on the table. I just don't think she did it."

The doorbell rings, and I curse. "Leave it to North to be early."

I scrub my jaw, and I'm about to get up when Abel says, "Nick. Man. Many a good man fell over a woman, and I'm pretty fucking sure the same can be said in reverse. Watch where you stick your cock."

"Says the guy who can't stop banging his ex," I remind him, standing and heading for the door, my booted feet heavy on the pale wood of the living room floor, only to have him shout out, "She has magnificent breasts."

I laugh, and she must, because that's not the first time I've heard that. But his warning about fucking Faith has hit a nerve, and my own warning replays in my mind, when I swore I wouldn't let it again. You never find guilt when you're looking for innocence.

I open the door to find North standing in front of me, looking like Clark Kent if Clark Kent was skinny and geeky. But that's the thing about North. There's more to him than meets the eye. He will slay you with facts. Superman-slay you. And damn it, there is more to Faith than meets the eye, too. I know it. I feel it. And I need to find out what and now, before a surprise slays me.

It's eleven when I finally have my house to myself again, and I walk into my office and bypass the pine carpenter-style desk that is the centerpiece. Instead, I walk to the oversize brown leather chair in the corner, a floor-to-ceiling window beside it, and sit down. Beside it is a stack of paperwork from my father's office and another from his home, which led me to Meredith Winter in the first place. I've been through it all ten times, and there is nothing that gives me the answers I need. Who killed him? I've told myself that it is simply my need for closure, but the truth is, the idea that that man was thwarted by anyone but me in his death claws at me. Bastard that it makes me, I wanted the man around just to show him his son would always be better. Someone took that from me. And my gift to myself is to find that person. That's my form of grief. There is no guilt to it.

Guilt.

That's what I keep sensing in Faith, but my mind goes back to lying in bed with her last night. When she'd asked if I had cried for my father. When she felt she should have for her mother.

Guilt.

Acceptable guilt that I can live with and help her live with. It's nothing more than that. I let that thought simmer for several minutes, with space between myself and Faith, and I still feel the same. She didn't kill my father or her mother.

I remove my phone from my pocket and dial her. She picks up on the second ring. "Nick," she says, and damn it, how is it that my name on this woman's lips can make my cock hard and my heart soft?

"Hey, sweetheart."

"Did you finish your prep?" she asks, once again showing concern about my work that I've never given another woman a chance to express. Maybe they would have. Maybe they wouldn't have. I just didn't care to have them try.

"We're ready," I say. "We'll kill it at every turn."

"I'm glad," she says. "I was worried I'd distracted you."

"You do distract me, Faith, but in all the right ways. Where are you?"

"My house," she says.

"I thought you were staying at the winery?"

"I was inspired to paint."

I lean back in the chair, shutting my eyes, imagining her standing at her canvas, beautiful, gifted, focused. "Are you painting me, Faith?"

"Yes," she says. "Actually I am. I'm still trying to understand you. Now that you're gone…"

"Now that I'm gone, what?"

"I don't know. Something."

"Something," I repeat, opening my eyes and standing up, facing the window, the glow of the lights on the Golden Gate Bridge before me. "There is something, Faith," I add, wanting her to tell me what I sense. "What is it?"

She's silent for several beats. "Are we talking about you or me, now?"

"You," I say. "I'm your attorney and the man in your bed and life. What haven't you told me?"

"We're new, Nick. There's a lot I haven't told you."

I feel those words like another claw in my heart, and every warning that's been thrown at me the past few hours digs it deeper. I have never been a fool who thinks with his dick. I'm not starting now. "I want you to tell me, but you know I'll find out."

"Of course you will. You enjoy a challenge. Good night, Nick."

She hangs up.

CHAPTER TWENTY-TWO

Tiger

That conversation with Faith haunts me most of the night, and by seven in the morning, I'm at work behind my desk on the fifth floor of the second tallest building in San Francisco. By eight, I've woken up three clients and drafted a contract. All while wearing a black suit with a royal-fucking-blue tie that reminds me of Faith's dress. Her ripped dress, and that moment in the car when I'd leaned in and tasted her. The pencil in my hand snaps.

It's at that moment that North pops his head in the door. "Can we—"

"No," I say. "If you aren't ready now, you won't be. You have three hours before they arrive, and you need a set of balls. Go find them."

He shoves his glasses up his nose. "I actually know the location of my balls. The use of said—"

"I'm not going to teach you how to hold your balls," I bite out. "Go play with them alone."

He has the good sense to leave. Unfortunately, my assistant, Rita, appears in the spot he's just left. "I have coffee," she says.

"You never bring me coffee," I say, but nevertheless, in a rush of bouncing red curls and sweet-smelling perfume, a cup is in front of me. I glance at it and her. "When I ask for coffee, you say 'fuck you.' What the hell is going on?"

"It's my twentieth wedding anniversary," she says, waving fingers at me. "I woke up to a sapphire this morning. I guess at fifty I've still got the goods."

And at fifty, she's beautiful and devoted to one man, where

Meredith Winter was devoted to many. "Happy fucking anniversary. Use my card and go to a ridiculously expensive dinner, and I need two things from you."

"Item one," she prods.

"I need a dress."

She arches a brow. "Is there something you need to tell me, boss?"

"Royal blue. A slit in the front. Expensive."

"I need more than that, starting with size."

"Petite."

She grimaces. "I'm good or I wouldn't be working for you, but that isn't good enough."

"Look up artist Faith Winter. It's for her. Make your best guess."

"Am I shipping it to her?"

"Reid Winter Winery in Sonoma," I say and hand her a sealed note. "Include this and have it delivered by tomorrow. And I need a gift to celebrate an artist's success that says art. A necklace. A paintbrush. Both. I need options. Lots of options. I'll know when I see it."

Her eyes go wide. "Do I dare believe a woman finally has your attention?"

"I hope like hell the one standing in front of me." I push to my feet. "I need to know where Montgomery Williams of SA National Bank is by the time I get to my car."

"You have a deposition here in two hours."

"Good thing this won't take two hours." I round the desk and head for the door, on a mission to see a man I despise and try not to think about the woman I can't stop thinking about.

Considering I work in the financial district a few blocks from SA National, Montgomery Williams isn't hard to find. He's at a coffee shop a block from my office, and given that he's short, fat, bald, and has a twenty-something girl sitting next to him with her hand on his plump thigh, I have no issue interrupting.

I walk to their booth and sit down across from them. "How's the wife?" I ask. Montgomery turns red-faced. The girl straightens and looks awkward. I simply arch a brow.

She purses her ridiculously red lips. "I'll see you tonight, honey." She slides out of the booth.

"Was she talking to me or you?" I ask.

"What do you want, Rogers?"

"Faith Winter," I say, and while I mean it in the literal sense, he simply registers the name.

"Why do you care about Faith Winter?"

Aside from the best blow job of my life, she's as talented and intelligent as she is good in bed, but I leave out the details. "I'm representing her."

"You work for some of the biggest companies on planet Earth. You don't do probate."

"I'll supply a cashier's check for a hundred and twenty thousand dollars, which covers her back payments and six additional months. In exchange, I want you to stop holding up the execution of the probate and drop all claims aside from the promissory note to the winery."

"We want a reevaluation of the property before we agree to anything."

"With what end game?"

"We'll decide when we have the reevaluation."

"And you ask why I'm involved," I say. "I'm involved because we both know this isn't just probate." I lean closer. "And we both know you're shitting your pants that I not only know you're fucking around on your wife but that I'm now involved."

I stand up and head for the door, my gut telling me that the winery is connected to murder. And the murder is connected to Faith. I step outside and dial Beck, who answers on the first ring. "The bank wants the winery, which means someone powerful wants that winery. You need to find out who and now. And get someone watching Faith around the clock," I say, doing what I should have done before. "Today."

"I assume we don't want Faith to know she's being watched?"

"No," I say. "We do not."

"Then you don't trust her."

I inhale deeply, cool air blasting me right along with his words, which he's using to bait me. He wants me to argue my reasoning, outside of her guilt. But I don't give people ammunition to analyze me, and his paycheck is all the justification he deserves. "Just do it," I say. "I'm headed into depositions. Text me when it's done." I end the call.

CHAPTER TWENTY-THREE

Faith

I woke on the hard floor of my studio, a smock over my clothes, and I have no idea how I let that happen. Or maybe I do. Nick was on my canvas and in my mind, but he wasn't in my bed downstairs, where I'd be alone again. And those words: *I'll find out.* They'd haunted me then and do now as I sit at my desk inside my tiny office at the winery. Those words made me ask again: are we friends or enemies? I'm confused and irritated that I somehow ended up in a black skirt and royal blue blouse today, the color reminding me of that damn dress he'd ripped. Of that moment he'd leaned in and licked me and then promised—*I won't stop next time.*

"Why are you flushed?"

I look up to find Kascy in my doorway, his gray suit and tie as perfect as the work he does here at the winery. "Too much caffeine. Can you shut the door when you come in?"

"Of course," he says, doing as I've asked and glancing around my box of an office. "Why do you stay in this hole? There are three bigger choices, including mine."

"You get the corner office," I say as he sits down. "You're the boss. I'm just your assistant."

"You never wanted to be here. It hurts me that you feel you have to be. I can handle this place, Faith."

For the first time in a long time, I take those words to heart, despite knowing they're true. "You can run this place. You *do* run this place. But there was my mother. No one but me could manage her."

"Yes, well," he says. "That's a conversation we should have,

Faith. She's gone. I hate to say it, but that changes things. You are an artist. You have a budding career. You had a show again, which I still hate I couldn't get a ticket to, by the way. How was it?"

"Wonderful," I breathe out, because I just can't stop myself. "It was really wonderful."

"Good," he says, his eyes warm with a pride I never saw in my father's. Not in regard to my art. "There is no reason you can't get back on that path."

"Right now, we need to talk about the legal issues."

"And the bill collectors," he says. "We've been avoiding the elephant in the room for too long. Why wasn't your mother paying the bills? What don't I know?"

Nick's words echo once again in my mind: *What haven't you told me, Faith?* And I shove them aside. "I don't have the answer to that question. We're making money. Not what we were before we lost part of the vines, but we're making money. And we never stopped making money. Right now, without a will, I'm locked out of her accounts, and there are legal steps I have to take to protect us. Nick Rogers, who you met yesterday, is coming on board to help."

"I looked him up, and I was hoping like hell you were going to say that."

I breathe out, thankful to Nick for the relief I see in Kasey's eyes right now. "He wants to call you. He's weeding through this mess and needs input."

"I'm not sure how I can help, but of course," he says. "Anything to get this mess behind us and get you out of this office." He narrows his gaze on me. "There are at least three people here on staff that could step up and take on more, so you can get back to being you."

"You know my father—"

"Was obsessed with you running this place. We all know that, but Faith, life is short. This place is my life. It's why I get up in the morning and do so with excitement. Have you said that for even one day of your life that you've spent here?"

Yes, I think. This past Friday, when I knew I had a show and I was going to stay at my house.

"I didn't think so," he says when I haven't answered quickly enough. "You pay me well, little one. I get incentives that made a difference before we lost the vines. This is not your dream. Go chase your dream."

"The bill collectors—"

"You must think I'm a delicate flower," he says. "I am not. You have Nick Rogers now. You'll get your mother's bank accounts unlocked and get everything up to date."

I pray he's right. And as confused by Nick as I am right now, I'm glad he's involved.

"Your mother threatened to fire me," he adds, "and I believed she'd do it. That's why you had to run interference. The bill collectors can't fire me. Only you can, and frankly, getting you the hell out of here is job security."

His walkie-talkie buzzes. "I need you, Kasey," comes a female voice.

"I'll be right there, Shannon," he answers, speaking to our garden manager before refocusing on me. "Stay at your house, like you did this weekend. It's a start. And I'll talk to Nick and whoever else needs to help you get past this probate issue." His walkie-talkie goes off again. "Ah. I need to go." He's on his feet and at the door, gone before I can issue the words, "Thank you."

I let out a breath and turn my attention to my computer, doing what I haven't done up until now. I google Nick Rogers. The minute his picture fills my screen, my stomach flutters, and I know that I am in trouble with this man. He affects me. He peels back the layers that are safer left in place. And he doesn't trust me, which means he's going to keep peeling. And why do I want to be with a man that doesn't trust me?

My phone buzzes. "Faith, you have a call," the receptionist tells me. "Bill—"

"Winter," I supply, anger spiking through me. "I'm not available."

"Understood."

I inhale and let it out. My father did not forgive him. I don't believe that for a minute. I key up my email, and my heart skips a beat at Nick's name, when I haven't even given him my email address. I hit the button to open it and read:

Faith:
What the fuck are you doing to me?
Nick
P.S. Don't stop.

I sit back in my chair and pant out a breath, feeling so much right now. Feeling too much. I am one big emotion, and I can't even name it. Maybe because I stopped recognizing anything but guilt. Guilt over not wanting this place. Guilt over my answer to my father. Guilt over so many things with my mother, when she doesn't deserve to make me feel that. I know that. But I still feel it.

But these feelings Nick stirs in me... They aren't guilt. But I think there's some fear. Yes. Fear. I hate fear. It's a weakness. But I am afraid of Nick, and yet that fear is almost a high. Everything about that man is a high that I crave. Maybe I'm obsessed, because he's on my computer screen right now and I want to feel him next to me again. I want to call him and hear his voice.

And yet I don't.

I can't.

Why am I being this stupid?

He will find out who I really am. He will.

I stare at the email, and I wonder how his deposition is going. I imagine him sitting in some big conference room, his suit as perfect as his body, those keen eyes of his intimidating the hell out of one person after another. I imagine those eyes, which tell a story I have yet to understand.

My phone buzzes again. "Another call," the receptionist says.

"This time it's a man named Chris Merit."

"What? Chris…Merit? The artist?"

"I don't know. Should I ask?"

"No. No, put him through." The line beeps, and I answer. "This is Faith."

"Faith. Chris Merit."

"Chris. Hi. I…thank you so much for including me in the show this past weekend."

"Thank you for being a part of it, Faith. I understand we have offers on your work."

"We do?"

"Yes, but your agent underpriced you. I'm going to adjust your prices, unless you have an issue with it."

I hesitate, but I say what I have to say. "I need that sale."

"You'll get your sale, and then some, and for what you're worth. Trust me, Faith."

When Chris Merit tells you to trust him and it relates to art, you trust him. "Why are you doing this?"

"My wife has decided to showcase a mix of new artists and established artists in her gallery in San Francisco. She and I both took a liking to your work. In fact, we'd like to showcase you in the gallery for our grand opening."

"You…I…" Oh God. I'm never speechless. "Thank you."

"I'd like you to present at least four pieces. You pick, but I'll need them in the gallery in four weeks."

"Of course. Not a problem at all."

"Excellent. We're holding a little VIP party at the gallery this weekend, Saturday night, which just happens to be Sara's birthday. We'd love it if you'd come. And bring a guest, of course."

"I'd love that. Thank you."

"You have talent, Faith Winter. Believe in you. We do." He ends the call.

I set the phone down, and I'm not a crier, not at all, but my eyes pinch. My chest is tight. This is my dream. This is everything.

I grab my cell phone to call Nick. That's my first instinct. To call Nick. But I don't dial his number. He's in a deposition. I can't believe he's the one person I wanted to call. But I still do. Instead, I dial Josh, and he answers on the first ring. "He called you," he says.

"You know already," I say, and my voice cracks.

"I know. So, are you in on this or not?"

"I'm in," I say. "How can I not be in?"

"Pick up the paintbrush and get to work."

"Josh—"

"I was out of line. I fucked up, Faith. I'm protective. That's personal, and there's no place for that in business. I'm your agent because you're good at what you do. The end."

"Thank you, Josh. I'm fortunate to have you in my corner."

"That said, on a professional note that has a personal influence: Macom is my best friend, but creative types are inherently insecure. He put down your work because of his insecurity. It affected you, and I think it's why you've used everything else as an excuse to stay away from painting. Make sure Nick Rogers does what you said. He inspires you to paint. If he does, I'll back off. If he doesn't, I'm not going to lose another two years of our work. Fair enough?"

"Fair enough," I say, appreciating the fact that he doesn't expect me to respond about Macom. He's right. Macom affected me in all kinds of ways. He still does.

"News on those sales soon, and the show. I'll be in touch." He hangs up.

I set my phone down and lower my lashes. I'm so confused right now. And angry. If my mother hadn't created this mess, I could just let Kasey run this place. Now, that man trusts me and lives for this place, and I might lose it. He might lose it. And Chris Merit called me. Chris Merit! And I am painting again, and that is because of Nick.

I look at the email again.

Faith:
What the fuck are you doing to me?

Nick
P.S. Don't stop.

I have so much I want to say to him, and I decide that in the sea of lies that is my life right now, honesty rules, and so I type:

Nick:
I hate what you made me feel last night, and yet when Chris Merit called me today to invite me to an event this weekend, I thought of only one person: you.
Faith
P.S. Stop being an asshole like you were last night.

I lean back in my chair and glance around my office, pictures of the winery on my walls. Not a one that is personal. Nothing in this office is mine, and yet, I guess if I inherit this place, everything is mine. My cellphone rings, and I glance down to find Nick's number. Adrenaline surges through me with crazy fierceness, and I look at the clock that reads noon.

"Nick," I answer. "Don't you have a deposition?"

"We're on our lunch break. How did I make you feel, Faith?"

"Like you're my enemy again."

"I'm not your enemy."

"Are you sure?"

"Why would I be your enemy?"

I inhale and let it out. "You're making me feel like the minute you discover any mistake I've made in my life, it's over. We're done. You're making me feel I can't ever let you see a flaw, of which I have many."

"That is not my intention, sweetheart. You're perfect to me. Too fucking perfect for my own good."

"See. I know you mean that as a compliment, but the underlying implication is that you want to find a flaw. Stop being an asshole, Nick Rogers."

"Right. Stop being an asshole. This is new territory for me, Faith."

"You said that. I get that. It is for me, too, and I don't even know what this is, but I apparently need to know."

"That makes two of us, sweetheart. Tell me about Chris calling."

"You have work."

"Tell me."

"He wants to showcase my work. I'll fill you in later, but I apparently need a date for Saturday night in San Francisco. Will you be my date, Nick?"

"You damn sure aren't taking anyone else. Yes, Faith. I'll be your date. I'll arrange to have a charter plane pick you up and bring you to me."

"That's not necessary."

"Can you come up Thursday night?"

"Friday night."

"I'll call you tonight with details. Faith?"

"Yes?"

"You're an artist. My artist." He hangs up.

I smile. I think it's my first real smile since my mother died. And for the first time in years, I am filled with possibilities, for my art and for this man who's taken my life by storm. And the possibilities are amazing.

CHAPTER TWENTY-FOUR

Faith

Friday afternoon comes quickly, but not quickly enough, and brings me to my house to pack, since I've been staying here all week. And I stayed here despite the fact that the winery has been crazy busy, but none of it has been collection calls. Nick assures me he has things under control and that I should trust him until he can give me a full update in person. And I do. I tell myself it's because he's an amazing attorney, and he is, but after spending hours on the phone with each other every night, it's the man I'm connecting with, not the attorney. And while our conversations have been more about our youths, his school and mine, it's groundwork. It's a path to more. It certainly brings more to my canvas. I start a new canvas. The gardens. My mother's gardens. It's somehow therapeutic.

But it's staying here, and I'm heading to San Francisco, where I hope maybe I'll get news of those sales that I still hear are pending, but I've had no confirmation. I'd really like to hear about the L.A. show, too, but Josh swears I've not been ruled out yet. More so, I am going to the Chris Merit event, with Nick by my side. Nervous and excited, I pack my weekend bag and fret over what to wear tonight. Nick wants to stay in at his place and have quality time together, so jeans should work. But jeans feel so plain. I've finally decided on black dress pants and a pink silk blouse when my doorbell rings. Dread that the bill collectors are back fills me, and I walk to the door to find a delivery driver standing there.

Frowning because I've ordered nothing, I open the door.

"Faith Winter?"

"Yes."

"For you."

He hands me a big box, and my stomach flutters because I know this is from Nick. "Thank you." I sign for it and carry it to the kitchen, where I set it on the counter. Feeling ridiculously nervous, considering it's a package, I cut away the tape and paper and find a beautiful silver box inside. I open it to find a card on top with neat, masculine script that reads: *Faith* .

I open the card.

I was going to send this earlier in the week, but I decided that if it pisses you off, I'll see you in a few hours to fight that battle in person. But know this. I'm happy to rip this version up, too, as long as it's on you at the time. And I owed you a pair of panties anyway.

I actually hope you want me to rip it off you again.

All of it.

Looking forward to it and you,

Nick

I set the card aside and pull back the paper to first find gorgeous royal blue lace panties that I do *not* want him to rip. They're too beautiful. Beneath them is a dress. I pull it from the box, and while it's not an exact replica of the one that was destroyed, it's close. I inhale and let it out. I wait for that feeling of being bought, but even with this and Nick flying me to San Francisco, I don't feel that. Maybe because he's done these things just because. Not to make up for something. And the dress. He turned it into something we shared and will share again. He made it special.

I gather everything up and walk into the bedroom. And right before I pack the panties, I take a picture of them and, laughing, text it to Nick with the words: *New challenge. And I love the dress. Thank you, Nick.*

He calls me. "You're not mad."

"No. Because you made it…about us."

"There's a lot of us going on this weekend, sweetheart. The plane is waiting on you. Hurry the hell up. The pilot is going to call me when you take off."

"I'm leaving here in fifteen minutes."

"See you soon, Faith Winter."

There is a deep, raspy quality to his voice that I feel from head to toe. "See you soon, Nick Rogers."

He ends the call.

With a grin on my face, I finish packing. I'm about to leave when I open the nightstand by my bed and find the card from my father. I still haven't read it. I stare at the script, and I shake myself before stuffing it in my purse. I need to read it, and I might just need that spanking I mentioned. I don't know that I want to be under Nick's hand to forget something this weekend, though. I think I'd rather be there just because. Still, I decide to leave the card in my purse.

My cellphone rings, and I remove it from the spot under that card, and the minute I see Josh's number, my heart starts to race. With a shaky hand, I punch the answer button. "Josh?"

"You're in, baby! You made the show."

"What? No. Yes. No?"

"Yes. Yes. Yes. You're in. I'm walking into a meeting, but I'll send you details. They love you. They say you are the next 'it' artist. So, drink some wine and start fucking selling it. I have to go. Congrats, baby."

He hangs up, and I dial Nick. "You can't be at the airport yet."

"I got in the show. I got in."

"The L.A. show?"

"The L.A. show. I got in."

"Then why the hell are you not here already so we can celebrate? Get your sweet, spankable ass to the airport."

"I'm leaving now."

"Faith."

"Yes?"

"Congrats, sweetheart."

"Thank you."

We disconnect, and in a rush of adrenaline I hurry to the door, exit to the porch, and lock up the house, then move on to load up my car. No. My mother's car. I hate driving this thing. I climb inside, and I swear I smell flowers. I can never escape the flowers, but I'm not trying anymore, I remind myself. I'm painting them. I'm facing them and every demon associated with my mother. I start the car and glance at the house. I love it. I always have. If I can live here and paint, and just be near the winery, maybe, just maybe, that's the path to compromise between my father's wishes and my own.

I'm about to place the car in gear when the rapidly setting sun catches on something in the yard. Frowning, I decide I must have dropped something. I place the car in park and get out. Walking to the spot I'd saw something, I bend down and pick up what appears to be a money clip engraved with an American flag. It must be Nick's, but I'm not sure I see that man with an empty money clip. Maybe it's the delivery driver's clip. I take it with me, slide back into the car, and stuff it in my purse. If it's not Nick's, I'll call the delivery company next week.

Fifteen minutes later, I pull into the private airport, and another fifteen minutes after that, I'm the only person on a small luxury jet with leather seats and even a bottle of champagne on ice. I pour a glass to enjoy while the pilot finishes his checklist and promises to call Nick. I've just taken my first sip when my cellphone rings. Certain it's Nick, I dig it out of my purse and freeze with the number. Macom. He heard about the show. And probably not even from Josh. He's an insider. He's a name in the business that I am not yet. But at least I can say *yet*. Not never. And while it's inevitable that I'll see him at the L.A. show and otherwise, if I'm to reignite my art career, I don't have to welcome conversation. I hit decline.

And I hate that as the plane starts to taxi, he's in the cabin with me. Old times. Old demons. A past that I don't want to exist. Of a me that I don't want to exist. Of a person I never want Nick Rogers to know. I'm reminded that, on some level, he knows that person exists. *What aren't you telling me, Faith?* he'd asked. *I will find out.*

And he will. I know he will. Maybe he's more forgiving than I am of myself. Then again, he's Tiger for a reason. He's vicious. He's cold. He's not forgiving at all. But my sins were not against Nick.

CHAPTER TWENTY-FIVE

Tiger

I've just heard from the pilot that Faith is on the plane in Sonoma when Rita walks into my office and sets a stack of papers on my desk. "You were served. It's all a bunch of nonsense meant to slow probate. Boy, the bank really wants to keep that place, don't they?"

I thumb through the stack she called "nonsense," and it's exactly that.

"What do you want me to do?"

"I'll let you know."

"Did she get the dress?"

"Yes. She got the dress."

"And?"

"And it's good."

"And you're happy with the other gift?"

"Yes. I'm happy."

"But not about that stack of papers. Got it. Removing myself from the line of fire." She turns and leaves, and I thrum my fingers on the desk. The bank wants Faith in default. I don't know why, and I don't care. They're gambling on the fact that I'll advise her not to pay the money until I'm sure she won't lose it. And without all the hidden facts they seem to know and we don't, that's exactly what I'd do.

I stand up and walk to the window, the fifth floor of the building allowing me the feeling of looking down on a city of millions, and it's here, doing just that, that I find answers. And now is no different. Faith can't pay that money, but I can. I dial my banker. "Charlie," I say. "I need a hundred and twenty thousand dollars delivered to SA National Bank by closing today in the name of Reid Winter Winery. I need you to personally talk to Montgomery Williams and confirm it's done."

"You got it," he says. "What else?"

"Note that this is back payments, fees, and six months in advance. And email proof to Rita and text me when the transaction is complete." I end the call and walk to my desk. "Rita."

She appears in my doorway. "Yes, boss?"

"You will be receiving proof that the Reid Winter note to the bank is paid to date and six months in advance. I'll be filing a slaughterhouse of documents Monday morning."

"In other words, be here at six."

"That will do it."

"Got it. What else?"

"Go home and do whatever people who have been married forever do."

She smiles. "We do the same things you do, Nick Rogers, but better, because we've been practicing. Have fun with Faith this weekend." She disappears, and I'm already back at the window and dialing Beck.

"I just paid Faith's past-due bank note and six months in advance," I tell him. "I like to know my enemies when I make them. And I pay you a lot of money to tell me who they are."

"I found a secretary at the bank who was at a party your father attended three months before he died. That same secretary visited Reid Winter Winery a year before Meredith Winter died. The interesting part about this is that that same weekend, Faith's agent *and* her ex were at the gallery where she just had that show."

"With Faith?"

"Faith was in L.A."

"That's odd."

"Yes. It is."

"It gets even stranger. Her uncle was in Sonoma that weekend, staying at his cottage without his wife."

"You think he was still fucking Meredith Winter?"

"I damn sure wouldn't rule it out."

Which will absolutely kill Faith. "How does the secretary connect to that bastard, Montgomery, I'm dealing with?"

"She's his boss's boss's secretary. I don't know what your father got himself into, but it's dirty. I'm gambling on that murder connection. And I'll figure it out, but you need every bit of evidence when I do to take this to the police. You still believe Faith Winter is innocent."

"I don't remember saying either way."

"Well, let her tell you if she's innocent or guilty. We need two bodies and two autopsies. If she's innocent, she'll request one on her mother. If she's not, she'll refuse."

"Just keep working this," I say and end the call, leaning a hand on the window.

Faith *is* innocent. The problem is, I'm not. I've lied. I've deceived her. And eventually, I have to tell her. And when I do, I'm at the risk of losing her, but I've never lost anything I wanted in my life. And I've never wanted anything as much as I want Faith Winter.

I'm standing in the private hangar when Faith's plane pulls to a halt, and the minute the doors open and she steps into my view, adrenaline surges through me. Her eyes meet mine, and I feel this woman like I've felt no other. I'm obsessed with her when I have never been obsessed with anything but success. With how she looks. With how she feels. With how she tastes. With the way she trusts me when I trust her. The way she doubts me when I doubt her. I have read people as well as I read Faith, but no one has ever read me the way she reads me. And out of nowhere, I think: *I'm falling in love with her.* Which is insane. I don't believe in love, and neither does she, and she's new to me. I'm new to her. But when does someone know they are in love? A day? A week? A year? It doesn't matter. It's not love. Whatever the hell this is, though,

Faith feels it, too. I see it in her eyes. She lowers her lashes as if battling what I'm battling.

I watch her inhale and let it out before her lashes lift and she starts walking down the stairs, her eyes on mine, and in them I see an echo of what I am thinking. We need to fuck this out of our systems. Fucking makes everything better. I meet her at the bottom of the steps, and in the quiet of the private hangar, I do exactly what I want to do. I mold her to me, and I kiss her like the starving man I am. And she tastes like everything I have ever wanted and didn't even know I wanted.

"Let's get out of here," I say, tearing my mouth from hers.

"Yes," she whispers, and I swear this woman's voice gets me hard and hot. I want her mouth everywhere, most definitely on my damn cock, and that's her fault for being so damn good at putting it there.

I grab her bag from the flight attendant and waste no time guiding Faith to the parking lot. Once her bag is in my back seat, I walk her to the passenger side of the vehicle, and when she's about to get inside, I pull her to me again and kiss her. "I'm really fucking glad you're here."

"Is this where you say 'too fucking glad'?"

"This is where I take you home and get you naked before I find a way to piss you off and it never happens."

She laughs, soft and sexy, and slides into the car. I'm inside with her in a few beats, and before I start the car, she says, "Can I get the bad stuff over with real quick?"

I angle toward her. "What bad stuff, Faith?"

"Anything with the bank?"

"I filed papers. They filed papers. I'm filing more papers. Bottom line, I made a big move, and I'll know more on Monday about how that plays out."

"What big move?"

"Legal stuff," I say, not about to tell her about the money. Not now. I'll swim in the shit I've created all at once and with a plan.

"And I'm asking you to trust me enough to set it aside until Monday. Okay?"

"Yes. Okay."

"Good." I lean over and kiss her because, fuck. I have to. And then I get us on the road.

"How was your flight?" I ask.

"Short and bumpy," she says. "But it was great. I love flying."

"But you've never flown internationally," I say. "We need to fix that. Paris is all about art and wine. We should go."

"That would be incredible, but right now I can't leave."

"We're going to fix that, and soon," I promise. "Tell me the details you know about the L.A. show."

"Josh just told me that I'm in," she says. "I'm sure I'll get more specifics by Monday."

"And you know which pieces were selected?"

"Nick. Don't be mad, but…"

I glance over at her and laugh. "You put me in it, didn't you?"

"I did. My first portrait, and on a whim when I was filling out the forms and submitting photos, I included it. You're not mad, right?"

"I don't care if you put me in the show, as long as it's about you."

"Maybe you are a little sweet, Nick Rogers."

"I'll put that idea to rest before the weekend's over, I promise you. And that means you have to let me see it."

"I will. When it's done. I have two weeks to finish. I think this weekend might just let me finish your eyes."

And on that note, I silently vow to make sure that every time she looks at me this weekend, she sees all the right things and none of the wrong.

Fifteen minutes later, we pull into the garage of my house, which is only a few minutes from my office. Faith is out of the car before I can round the BMW to help her, gaping at the dark gray sports car beside us. She bites her lip and glances over at me. "You are such a rich guy, Nick Rogers. What is it?"

"Audi R8 5.2 V10," I say. "And thank you. I work my ass off to be such a rich guy, and I owned that assessment long before I inherited my father's money."

"How did you make your first million?"

"A drug company whose best-of-the-best attorney wasn't as good as they thought." He was also my father, but I don't tell her that. Not now. One day when there are no more secrets. "Let's go inside, Faith."

"Yes. Let's go see what a man like you calls home."

"A man like me," I say. "You can explain that later. Naked."

She gives me one of her sexy, confident smiles. "I will."

I open the back door. "I'll get your bag. The door's unlocked. Make yourself at home."

She doesn't hesitate. She drags delicate fingers through her long blonde hair and walks to the door and up the short set of steps that leads to the foyer of my home. I take my time pursuing her, allowing her to decide what to do and where to go, curious as to where that takes us both. Intrigued by this woman all over again, I join her, leaving her bag by the door, to find her slowly walking the rectangular-shaped space, and I scan it, taking in what she sees. Pale wooden floors, a gray sectional. Parallel to the living area is a bar that is shiny white with four barstools, and opposite it are two modern steel-and-glass stairwells that climb the walls in two different directions.

She turns to face me with distance between us I don't intend to remain. "Clean, artistic lines. A house for a man who likes control."

"I do like control," I say, closing a foot of space between us. "I think that I like control."

She replies as if I haven't spoken those words. "It's a beautiful house, Nick. It smells like you."

"And how do I smell, Faith?"

"Like control. Like sex. Woodsy and sexy."

"And you, sweetheart, smell like—"

"Amber and vanilla."

"Yes, you do. And I'm obsessed with your scent. I'm obsessed with *you*."

"Obsessed," she says. "That sounds dangerous."

"It is dangerous."

And her reply is everything any man could want. "Where is your bedroom, Nick?"

"Up the stairs directly behind you."

She turns and starts up the stairs, her pace slow, seductive, calculated. She knows every swing of her hips makes me burn. And I fucking love it. I wait until she's upstairs, out of sight, and then, with my adrenaline pumping, I follow her. I find her sitting on the end of my king-size mattress, the centerpiece of my room, the gray headboard behind her. That card from her father in her lap.

"I need to read this. And you know that means I need *you*."

I inhale on a realization. Faith is once again using sex as a wall. And I almost let her. I had the word "love" pop into my head, and I just wanted to fuck. And she just wants to fuck. But I'm not letting her hide from me. Even if it means I can't escape whatever the fuck this unknown emotion is I feel for this woman. I walk to the bed and stand above her. She doesn't touch me. I don't want her to, and she knows this. I like that she knows. I shrug out of my jacket and remove my tie, both of which I toss to the center of the bed. I then set the card aside and do what I know she does not expect me to do.

I take her down on the mattress with me, rolling her to face me. "I'm not going to spank you, Faith," I say, sliding my leg between hers. "Not now. Maybe not even this weekend. I want you to see and feel me. I want you to remember me this weekend, not my hand."

"Nick," she whispers, and when I kiss her, she does that thing she does. She breathes out like she needed my kiss, like it's why she exists. And right now, this woman is why I exist. I kiss her. I touch her. I strip her naked, and me, too. I lick her nipples. I lick her clit. I lick every inch of her until she is begging for me inside her and I need to be there. And once I'm inside her and we're staring at each other, swaying together, I don't make love to her. I don't do love, but I damn sure don't fuck her, either. And when it's over, I hold her for long minutes before I settle my shirt around her and help her roll up the sleeves.

We order Chinese and eat in my bed, me in my pants, her in my shirt, and I like this woman in my clothes and my bed. It's only after we finish eating that I am ready to show her one of the gifts I have for her this weekend. I take her hand. "Come. I want to show you something."

"Now you have me curious."

"Good," I say, guiding her down the hallway. "That's the idea."

We stop at a room with the door shut, and I open it and motion her forward. She smiles and walks inside and gasps. "Nick. What did you do?"

I step inside the doorway to find her standing in the center of the massive triangle-shaped room, next to the canvas I have set up for her, a supply of brushes and paint nearby. "They tell me the floor cleans right up. I had it installed this week."

"Why would you do this?"

"I didn't want you to be away from your brush."

"This is incredible. It's such a cool, crazy-shaped space. What was this room before now?"

"Nothing. I had no idea what to do with it."

She inhales, her chest rising and falling. "What happens when I'm not around?"

I cross to stand in front of her, cupping her face. "That's where we're differing here, Faith. I'm thinking about every moment I have with you, and you're thinking about goodbye." I kiss her then, and damn it, I am obsessed with her. So fucking obsessed. And like she said, obsession is dangerous.

CHAPTER TWENTY-SIX

Tiger

I watch Faith paint for hours, a stack of work next to me that I barely touch. I just watch her work while my mind chases the puzzle that is her mother and my father together. Murder brought us together. Lies could tear us apart. I don't know what time I take her to bed, or how long I keep her awake once I get her there. But I wake with Faith pressed to my side, and I have one thought. In the right and wrong of things, there is nothing wrong about this woman in my bed.

The day is lazy, rain falling outside, and we have coffee on my balcony, talking, laughing, both of us in sweats and T-shirts with no plans to go anywhere until tonight. "Are you wearing the blue dress tonight?" I ask, sipping my coffee while thinking of the blue panties.

"I'm not sure," she says. "I wish I had asked about the dress code. I brought several choices."

I set my cup down and grab my phone from my pocket. "Let's find out. I'll call Chris." I punch in his number from my autodial.

"No," she says quickly, setting her cup down. "No, don't—"

"It's already ringing," I say, and Chris immediately picks up. I get right to the point. "What's the dress code tonight?"

"Translation. You're Faith's date tonight, and she doesn't know how to dress. Put her on with Sara."

"Good plan." I hand Faith the phone. "Sara."

She pales, glowers, and takes the phone. "Sara. Yes. No. Great. Nice to meet you, too. Yes. I'll see you then." She hands me back the phone. "Chris."

"I'm here," I say, placing the receiver to my ear again. "And I need nothing else."

"Works for me," Chris says. We disconnect, and I focus on Faith. "Blue dress?"

"You shouldn't have called them, and actually the blue dress is too fancy, and I want to save that dress for the L.A. event. It was lucky the first time."

"Luck is good," I say. "But you do have a dress to wear, right?"

"Yes. It's pink and doesn't require you to spend money on me."

"You're going to have to get over this money thing, sweetheart. I have it. I spend it. If I want to spend it on you, I'm going to, and that doesn't make me an asshole unless I use it against you in some way, which I won't." And those are words I'm going to have to repeat loudly when she finds out I paid the bank on her behalf. "Moving on," I say. "Your dress is pink. Do I get the royal blue panties underneath?"

"They're pink, and I don't want you to spend money on me."

"I like spending money on you, and I like pink."

"Don't rip them this time and you can like them twice."

"Twice is good. More is better."

"Do you know what you're wearing?"

"Why? Are you considering which knife you need to undress me?"

She grins. "I think that's a moment I need to capture on the canvas. That moment when you first saw the knife in my hand. It was priceless. I'm suddenly inspired to paint."

"Then go and paint a masterpiece. I've got work that I can dig into in my office. I'll come get you for lunch."

"Are you cooking?"

"If ordering takeout counts, then yes. At your service, Ms. Winter."

She laughs and starts to get up but sits back down. "I never asked what time the party is. Chris never said."

"I'll find out," I promise. "You go paint."

Her eyes light. "I actually can't wait to pick up a brush again."

"I prefer you with a brush than a knife in your hand."

She laughs and pops to her feet, rushing through the house, and I sit back and enjoy this moment. I could get used to having this woman around.

The day passes too quickly, when Faith will leave tomorrow unless I convince her otherwise.

It's nearly seven, and I'm standing on the balcony off my bedroom in a blue suit and blue tie, waiting on Faith to finish dressing, a glass of that whiskey Abel left behind in my hand. Outside, the storms of earlier in the day have passed, stars dotting the skyline before me, while the storm of lies I've told Faith is clear and present, haunting me tonight in ways it hasn't before now.

"Nick."

At the sound of Faith's voice, I down my drink, set the glass on a small table by the railing, and walk back inside. "Well?" she asks, holding out her hands to her sides. "How do I look? Is it too much? Too little?"

"Sweetheart, I don't let women in my house, let alone invite them to dress here. So no one has ever asked me if a dress was too much or too little." I close the space between us, my hands settling on her tiny waist. "But you look *beautiful*." And she does. The dress is pink lace and knee-length, which offers me the benefit of easy access to her gorgeous legs. Her shoulders are bare, her blonde hair caressing the skin the way my mouth will later. And the neckline is high, reserved, but still somehow sexy—but how can it not be? It's on her.

Her hands go to my chest, her eyes searching my face. "You don't bring women here?"

"Never," I say. "In the five years since I bought this place, not once. Just you."

"Why me, Nick?" she asks, her tone earnest.

"Because you're you, Faith. There is no other answer." And while it's the truth, it guts me to know that she'll see it as one of my lies, and do so sooner than later.

"Where did you go?" she asks. "To their place?"

"Anywhere but here," I say, when the truth is that I go to what is now my club—a place that doesn't matter to me, but she does. "You're nervous about tonight. Why?"

"Chris Merit is a big deal in the art world. His support could change my life."

"You admire him."

"Yes. He's talented and successful. And even though he's really not from Sonoma, he just always felt like a local, and if one local could make it, another could, too."

"Did you admire Macom? Was that part of the draw to him?"

"I met Macom before he made it. We both loved art and the creative process. And yes, he's talented, but it was different. I don't admire him." Her hands settle on mine at her hips. "He called me yesterday, and I just feel like I should tell you."

I go very still, that possessiveness I feel for Faith rising up inside me. "And?"

"I didn't take the call. I can guess what it was about. He heard, probably before me, that I was in the show."

"And he wanted to congratulate you?"

"More to gloat. He's been there, done that; but of course, he'd mask it as a compliment. I don't need that in my life right now and just wanted to tell you, Nick." She pauses and then adds, "*Thank you*. I've known you such a short time, and you've been more supportive of my art than anyone else in my life."

"It's self-serving," I say, leaning in to brush my lips over hers. "I want a beautiful artist in my bed, and if we don't go right now, I might rip this dress, too." I turn her toward the door.

• • •

We arrive at the gallery at seven thirty, and it's not long before we're ushered into a room full of at least fifty people, shiny white floors beneath our feet, wavelike rows of displays in random places. Faith and I work our way through the crowd, and when we're offered champagne for a birthday toast, we both accept. "My preferred drink," she tells me, sipping her bubbly. "It's sweet, and we don't make it. It's also low alcohol, and I don't tolerate much."

"You really don't like the winery, do you?"

"No," she says. "I really don't, but I've never said that to anyone but you. Just now."

My hand settles at her hip. "It's our secret."

She looks at me, shadows in her eyes. "That's trust, Nick. Just in case you didn't know."

Trust.

That I've already betrayed.

"Welcome, everyone!"

At the shouted greeting, I look up to find Chris Merit at the front of the room, the only person here in jeans, but it's rather fitting. He's a rock star in this world. "I just want to say happy birthday to my wife," he announces, "and to tell her how proud I am of her and this gallery. Enjoy the art and chocolate cake, because it's her favorite."

Everyone applauds, and there are shouts of "happy birthday." Chris catches my eye over the crowd right as soft music begins to play. He motions us forward, and I lift a hand to acknowledge him. "Empty that glass," I tell Faith.

Her eyes go wide. "I can't just down it."

"Chris is waving you over."

She downs the champagne, and I do the same with mine before handing our glasses to a waiter. I lace my fingers with Faith's and lead her through the crowd while cake begins to circulate on trays. Chris, however, is cornered by fans, and Sara appears in front of us. "Faith!" she greets her, hugging Faith, her brown hair a contrast to Faith's blonde, while waving at me over her shoulder.

I give her a nod, but she's fully focused on Faith, as it should be. "I love your work," Sara announces, leaning back to look at Faith. "Chris and I both love your work. Let's go talk." She motions us forward. "Come. Chris will catch up."

She starts walking, and we follow her through the gallery to where two glass doors lead us to a heated outdoor sitting area, which has at least a dozen seats and rose bushes surrounding the exterior. "This space is our newest addition," Sara says, claiming one of four seats forming a square while primly tugging down the skirt of her emerald green dress. "I want people to come here and talk art, then buy artists like yourself, Faith."

"I'm incredibly honored that you want to include me," Faith says, claiming the seat across from Sara while I sit next to Faith.

"We'd be honored to show your work," Sara says. "Just to be sure that you're aware—everything we do has a charity component, but we're going to make that worth your while."

"Exposure is everything," Faith says. "I'm not worried about the money."

"Thus why I'm her attorney," I interject. "Because I am worried about her money."

Faith glowers at me, and Sara laughs. "He's fine, Faith. He should be worried about you. Chris would be the same way." She refocuses on business. "I'm not sure what Chris told you, so I'll start from scratch. The gallery officially opens in six weeks, but we're basically letting people have VIP cards to enter a week sooner if they're here tonight. I'd like to get your work here by then."

"That would be incredible," Faith says. "And Chris said you need four pieces to make that happen?"

"Yes, please," she says. "But I need to know that you're a for-sure placement by next week. And I can talk to your agent if you wish." She laughs and glances at Nick. "Or your attorney."

Chris joins us at that moment, greeting everyone as he claims his seat, his hand instantly on Sara's. "Where are we on things?"

"I was just telling her the details on the gallery," Sara replies.

Chris flags down a waiter, who is immediately by his side. "I know you know what I want."

The waiter reaches into his apron pocket, removes a beer, and hands it to Chris. "At your service."

"Thanks, David," Chris says, eying Sara, who shakes her head but accepts his replying kiss more than a little willingly.

"Beer, anyone?" Chris asks as the waiter holds two more up.

"Don't mind if I do," I say, accepting it, while Faith and Sara wave off the offer.

"In explanation," Sara says as the waiter leaves. "Chris hates wine and champagne."

"You hate wine?" Faith asks. "But your godparents own a winery."

"And I still ask for a beer when I'm there," Chris replies.

In other words, he's his own man, the way Faith wants to be her own woman, and I squeeze her hand, silently telling her there is no reason she is that winery and not her art. She glances at our hands, the tiny gesture telling me that she hears me even before she squeezes back.

From there, the four of us start talking, and I take in this world of art that is Faith's now, listening to the ins and outs, interested in a way I wouldn't have been before meeting Faith. It's not long before we're eating cake, and Sara and Faith have hit it off so well that their heads are together, and Chris and I are left to our own devices.

"You care about her," he says, his voice low, the women too absorbed in talk of art to hear us anyway.

"She matters," I say without hesitation. "Yes." And admitting that to someone else, saying it and meaning it, tells me just how deep I am in with Faith.

He leans forward, elbows on his knees, and I do the same. "Does she know about the club?"

"No," I say, and while I have pushed this topic aside, with

bigger problems to face, I can't ignore the topic forever. "Now is not the time."

"It's never the time," he says. "And telling Sara was hard on us, but we had to go there to get here. And one small secret becomes bigger over time. The bigger the secret and the longer you keep it, the bigger the problem."

The bigger the secret.

He has no fucking clue how much bigger my secrets are than that fucking sex club. There's a hell of a lot that I have to come back from with Faith, and at some point I'll have to decide if I spill it all, fast and hard, or in pieces.

Chris has just leaned back in his seat when the music changes and an old seventies song, "Sara Smile," begins to play, a soft, easy, sexy tune. Chris sets his beer on the small table in between us and stands, walking to Sara and taking her hand. "I need to borrow my wife for a moment," he says, but he's not looking at us when he speaks. He's looking at her. And she's looking not at us but at him.

Chris pulls her to her feet and leads her inside the gallery, the words to the song filling the air:

When I feel cold, you warm me
And when I feel I can't go on, you come and hold me
It's you and me forever
Sara, smile

Faith stands up, and I catch her hand. "Where are you going?"

"Bathroom," she says, but she won't look at me.

"Faith."

"I need a minute, Nick."

She tugs against me, and I release her, but I don't want to. I watch her walk back into the gallery, and I know this woman in ways I should not yet be able to know her. Chris and Sara have this way of radiating love. You feel it. You almost believe in happily ever after. And then she suddenly feels like we're nothing but sex and goodbye. I'm on my feet in an instant, pursuing her, following a sign to the bathroom. I spy Faith just before she is about to round a hallway, and the minute she looks around that corner, she flattens on the wall as if burned.

I'm in front of her in a few long strides, my hands on her waist. Her eyes pop open in shock, and I lean around the corner to find Chris kissing Sara, and it's one hell of a kiss. Intense. Passionate. I refocus on Faith, and I cup her face. "We're whatever we decide to be, Faith." And I kiss her, just as passionately as Chris is kissing Sara. I kiss her my way. I kiss her and let her taste my words: *We're whatever we decide to be.* And when I tear my lips from hers, I say, "Instead of a hard limit, we have a new hard rule: *Possibilities*, Faith. We have them. Say it."

"New hard rule," she whispers. "Possibilities."

"Let's go back and wait on them until we can say goodbye and get out of here."

She nods. "Yes. Please."

And with her hand in mine, I lead her toward the patio, but footsteps sound behind us, and Faith and I turn to find Chris and Sara returning. "You're leaving," Sara says, seeming to read our body language, her focus on Faith. "You have my email and phone number, right?"

"Yes," Faith says. "And I'm excited about being a part of the gallery. Oh, and happy birthday."

"Thank you," she says. "I actually wanted you to come here tonight to give *you* a gift, Faith."

"Me?" Faith asks. "I don't understand."

Chris reaches into the pocket of his jeans and produces a check. "I negotiated your price for the showing last weekend, as promised, Faith. You now get twenty thousand a painting and accept no less, or I will personally come kick your ass." He looks at me. "Twenty thousand. Don't let her get screwed." He hands Faith the check. "Sixty thousand. You sold three paintings."

Faith starts to tremble, and my arm goes to her waist, my hip pressed to hers. Her hand shakes as she accepts the check and looks at it. "I think...I...I'm going to cry, and I don't cry."

"Don't cry," Chris says. "Celebrate."

Faith looks up at him. "I'm going to have to hug you," she says, taking a step toward him and then grabbing Sara instead.

Sara laughs and hugs her. "Best birthday gift ever," she says, and when Faith releases her, she adds, "You can hug Chris, too."

Faith laughs through tears. "No. No, I... Thank you, Chris. And thank you, Sara."

Chris grabs her and hugs her, giving me a look over his shoulder that is filled with admiration I see but Faith would dismiss. "She's talented," Chris says. "Take care of her and her gift."

I nod, and damn, I want to take care of this woman.

We say our goodbyes and cross the gallery to exit to the street. We're a few steps away from the door when Faith turns to me and holds up the check. "I can't believe this just happened."

"It didn't *just* happen," I say. "You started painting at age five."

"I know, but it feels... I don't know what I feel. But now the winery—"

I cup her face. "Do not make this about the winery. That is your money. That is your first big success."

"But Nick—"

I kiss her. "No buts. We'll deal with the winery. This is for you. Okay?"

"Yes. Okay."

"Good. Now. Let's go home."

"Your home."

"My home," I say. "That is far better with you in it." I turn her toward the car, and she's still trembling. And the depth of her emotional response affects me. Everything about Faith affects me.

Thirty minutes later, Faith and I are standing by my bed, her shoes kicked off, and she is finally coming down from her high, her body calming. "I'm completely wiped out," she says. "I think you are going to wish I was someone else tonight."

I cup her head and pull her to me. "What did you say?" I don't give her time to reply. "That came from someplace I'd most likely name as Macom. I'm not him. And we are more than the sum of how many times we manage to fuck each other. And for the record. To repeat what I've already said. I don't want anyone else."

Her lashes lower. "I think that was possibly the most perfect thing you could say to me right now."

In that moment, I remember her comment about Macom competing with her, and I decide Faith thinks her success comes with punishment. A problem I need to fix. For now, I kiss her, a soft brush of lips over lips, before I turn her around and unzip her dress, dragging it down her shoulders. Her bra is next. Then her hose, but I leave the panties, and as much as it kills me, I hold up the blanket and urge her to climb under. She turns around and faces me, pressing herself against me.

"You feel good, sweetheart, but you'll feel better when you're rested. Climb into bed. I'll be right there after I make sure I've locked up."

"You, Nick, are nothing I expected."

"*You*, Faith, are nothing I expected."

She kisses my cheek, a mere peck, which might be the best kiss this woman has given me, and I don't fucking have a clue why. It's a peck, but it's sweet. It's emotional in some unnamed way, and I like it. She climbs into bed. My bed. And damn, I like her there more now than I did this morning. She snuggles down in the blankets, and I walk to the door, where I find myself just staring at her, watching as her breathing slows and turns even. She's asleep. She trusts me. Damn it, I need to solve this mystery so I can tell her everything and deal with the aftermath.

I exit the bedroom and head down the stairs to my office, walking to a chair in the corner and removing a box I have shoved underneath it. Stacks of my father's papers. I shrug out of my jacket, pull away my tie, and start going through them again. Somewhere in here is my answer. I just have to find it. Time passes. Documents are read. My eyes are blurry. Finally, I decide I have to go to bed. I'm stuffing the papers back in the box when a small book on legal ethics falls to the ground and a piece of paper pokes from the side. I grab it and open it to read:

Faith Winter is the problem. She's dangerous. Far more than her mother. She must be stopped.

I stare at that piece of paper for long minutes, and I try to make sense of it. I return the box to its spot under the chair with that piece of paper inside it. I stand and walk upstairs, standing at that doorway again and at the naked woman in my bed, wondering which one of us is now exposed. Knowing it's time to find out.

SHAMELESS

BOOK TWO OF THE WHITE LIES DUET

CHAPTER ONE

Nick

Faith Winter is the problem. She's dangerous. Far more than her mother. She must be stopped.

Those are my dead father's words, scribbled on a piece of paper I found in his things only minutes ago. Words now burned in my mind, as I stand in the doorway of my bedroom, staring at Faith as she sleeps, moonlight from a nearby window casting her in a soft glow. Her blonde hair draped over my pillow. Her amber-and-vanilla scent a sweet whisper in the air on my skin. While the words *she's dangerous* repeat in my mind again and again, radiating through me like an electric charge, but not because I trusted my father's opinion about anything. But rather, there is no denying the fact that I did seek Faith out with the opinion that he was murdered, perhaps by her.

And he didn't say she's trouble or a problem or difficult. He said that she's dangerous.

And yet, as seconds tick by, I am riveted by the image of Faith *in my bed*, where I invited her to sleep, and holy fuck, I like her there. I *want* her there, when I never let any other woman in my house, let alone in my bed. I'm obsessed with this woman, and as Faith herself warned yesterday, obsession is dangerous. Some—most—would say fucking a woman you suspect killed her mother and your father is dangerous, but it doesn't seem to matter. I want her. I am crazy about this woman, and maybe that just makes me crazy.

Needing space to clear my head, I walk across the room toward the bathroom, my tie and jacket that I'd worn to tonight's event at the Merit gallery gone, and I don't even remember removing them. I remember Faith. Her smile as she'd been praised for her art. The way she trembled with the news of her success, when she is not a woman who trembles. Not unless it's with pleasure. And these thoughts are exactly why I stop myself from turning back to her, because what I really want is to be in that bed with her. But, when I'm with her, touching her, kissing her, just fucking holding her, even looking at her in my bed, I am not objective. And yet, knowing this, I reach the doorway, about to escape into the quiet sanctuary of the next room, seconds from the space I need to rein in my thoughts, and fuck me, I find myself pausing in the doorway, facing the bed again.

She stirs suddenly, as if she senses me watching her, a soft, sexy sound slipping from her lips as she shifts from her side to her back, her hand settling on the pillow next to her. She instantly rolls over to where I should be, reaching for me, only to sit up, the sheet falling away, and even in the shadows, I am aware of her naked breasts, her naked body, which I know feels so damn good against mine. "Nick?" she calls out, turning in my direction, sensing me here.

And the minute she says my name, her voice is like silk on the sandpaper of my nerves, and I know that if she's dangerous, I'm fucking high on the danger. And if that is what she is, I want that danger on my tongue, in my hands, in my bed.

I rotate and press my hand to the doorframe over my head, shutting my eyes. What the hell am I doing? Either I have a killer in my bed, which I reject as an option, or I have a woman I'm falling in love with who has to hate me for lying to her. *Love*. Damn it to hell, where did that come from? I don't do love. I don't do commitment, and once again, I have to remind myself that you don't prove guilt when you're looking for innocence. And yet, I know this woman is not a killer.

Dangerous, though. That word just won't let go of me. Why

the fuck did my father use that word?

"I just finished up some work," I say, lifting my face to the ceiling, lashes lowered. "I'm going to shower, and I'll be there in a few minutes." I haven't said the words before Faith is not only slipping between me and the wall, but resting against the doorframe under my hand. My gaze is riveted to her moon-kissed naked skin. My body arches in such a way that she can't easily touch me, and I don't touch her, but I want to, and I don't even remember in this moment why I resisted doing so before now.

"What's wrong?" she asks.

Aside from the fact that my dead father called you dangerous, I think, *or that your stunning, naked breasts should not be in my hands, I need time to think.* But since she doesn't know about my father, *can't* know about my father—not yet—I offer her the expected answer of, "Nothing is wrong."

"Liar," she whispers.

"Work is on my mind," I supply, and that's not wholly untrue. I was working on the mystery of two murders when I found that note.

"Liar," she repeats, her tone sharp, some unidentifiable jagged-edged emotions radiating off of her, or maybe I'm wrong. Maybe it's my jagged-edged emotions that are crashing into her and then slamming right back into me.

"I've been watching you sleep," I say, embracing every honest word I can speak to Faith when so much, *too* much, has been lies.

Her eyes open, and even in the shroud of shadows, I feel the punch of her gaze colliding with mine. "That's not an answer," she says. "That's a deflection, and deflection doesn't suit you any more than fear." It's a reference to the night that she'd pulled a knife on me and used it to remove my shirt buttons, and I understand the message: we feel like we did then—uncertain; incomplete in some way.

"I wonder," she continues, pushing off the wall, her hands pressed to my chest, the slight but firm heft of her body weight knocking me backward, against the wall, "if I held a knife in my

hand now, if you would trust me to cut the buttons off your shirt,
or if you would wonder if I'd cut you instead?"

I'm not sure if she's daring me to trust her or pushing me to do
the opposite. Pushing me away. Pulling me closer. It's all the same
with her. With one always comes the other. "We aren't where we
were then," I say, but I don't touch her. Once I touch her, I won't
stop, though I'm really fucking trying to figure out why the fuck
that feels important right now.

"And yet I feel the same now as then," she says, "and so do you.
And don't lie again. You know I'm right."

"It's not the same."

"It is. And we are. And that leaves only one of the possibilities
you had us proclaim earlier tonight. Me making us both forget
all the rest. Whatever the rest actually is, since you won't tell me
what's wrong."

Suddenly, she's peeling away her panties, the only garment
she'd worn when she'd gone to bed. The next moment, she's
kneeling, her hands on my knees, her head tilted down. I know
exactly where this is going, and if I intend to keep my head clear,
I should stop it now. Only the head on my shoulders isn't the
one doing the thinking. Not when Faith's hand strokes the one
between my legs that has been hard as a rock since she and all
her naked curves slid in front of me. Hell, since practically the
moment I met this woman. She tugs my shirt out of my pants and
starts unbuttoning it, her gaze reaching mine as she says, "If I
only had that knife."

I don't laugh. She doesn't laugh. The edge between us is as
jagged as those emotions beating through me and obviously into
her. I reach up and undo several buttons on my shirt, just enough
to then pull it over my head, tossing it into the bedroom. It's not
even hit the ground, and Faith has not only unbuckled my belt,
she's pulling it free of my pants.

It hits the floor, and she reaches for my zipper, wasting no
time freeing my cock. She grips it, her hold firm and confident.

Her eyes boldly find mine as she licks the end of my erection and then draws it into her mouth, her message clear: right now, she demands control, a response I strongly believe to be a reaction to the questions I've allowed to stir between us. She needs to own me right now. And while I don't let anyone own me, even if they do have their mouth on my cock, I'm oddly at peace with this woman's power. There's a message in that regard, which I'll analyze when I'm not hyper-focused on the silk of her tongue and the sweet suction of her mouth.

And damn, if she's not licking every last inch of me.

And damn, if I'm not at her mercy.

Heat and adrenaline pulse through me, and my hand finds her head, fingers slipping into her hair, but I don't even need to guide her. She's exactly where I need her, *how* I need her. There is something about this woman's mouth, her tongue, that is quite possibly heaven on earth. It's a bliss that I welcome, and yet, suddenly, I'm not in this heavenly moment. I'm flashing back to right before she fell asleep. To me helping her undress.

In my mind's eye, I see us standing next to the bed, her in the dress she wore to the Chris and Sara Merit gallery event, me in the same blue suit I have yet to fully remove. She'd just kicked off her shoes, finally coming down from the high of selling her art, her body calming. Me, I'd been reveling in her in my bed and in our vow that "possibilities" were the new hard rule we'd follow. *"I'm completely wiped out," she'd confessed. "I think you are going to wish I was someone else tonight."*

Those words had jolted me, and I cupped her head and pulled her to me. *"What did you say?" I'd demanded, but I didn't give her time to reply. "That came from someplace I'd most likely name as Macom," I'd said of her ex, whom I already knew used sex as a weapon against her. "I'm not him," I'd continued. "And we are more than the sum of how many times we manage to fuck each other. And for the record. To repeat what I've already said. I don't want anyone else."*

Her lashes lowered. "I think that was possibly the most perfect thing you could say to me right now."

And in that moment, I'd remembered her comment about Macom competing with her, and I'd decided that Faith thinks her success comes with punishment. A problem I needed to fix. I *need* to fix. I had intentionally put her to bed without touching her. I come back to the present, to her mouth on my cock, pleasure with every stroke, pump, and lick, and I am so damn hard and close to release. I want it. Holy hell, I want it so fucking badly, and I have no doubt that she would take me to absolute completion and rock my world. But this—what we are doing right now, and why we are doing it—is exactly what I *didn't* want tonight to be for her or us.

Suddenly, my orgasm doesn't matter, no matter how close I am to heaven or, sweet Jesus, how damn good it would be. "Faith," I say, and despite my determination and intention to end this, her name comes out a pained near-growl. "Stop." I slip my fingers from her hair and cup the sides of her head. "Stop, Faith. Sweetheart. Stop." She stills, as if the words and my touch finally penetrate her brain, and pulls her mouth slowly back until it's no longer on my cock. But her hand still grips my erection, and I swear just the idea of removing it is torture.

Confusion flits across her beautiful, desire-laden expression, and I pull her to her feet and to me, my hand at the back of her head. "I've decided that your mouth on my cock is the best thing in this world, outside of my mouth on you while you come for me and because of me."

"Then why did you stop me?"

"Because you were on your knees for all the wrong reasons, sweetheart. I don't need this to be with you, and that's what you thought, wasn't it?"

"You needed something. You were watching me."

"And wondering how the hell it felt so fucking good just to watch you," I say, relieved to speak the truth—and it is the truth. "Like I said. We are not the sum of how many times or ways we fuck, and that's new territory for me. I'm trying to figure it out."

"I'm trying to figure all this out, too," she confesses.

"Does that mean you like being in my bed?"

"I like many things about you, Nick Rogers, that I didn't expect to like, but yes. I do."

"We'll figure it out together," I promise, scooping her up in my arms, her gorgeous, naked body pressed to mine. She is so tiny, and yet she's seized my world in gigantic proportions, in ways I never thought any woman capable.

I stop at the side of the bed, setting her down on the mattress, and to ensure my control stays firmly intact, I adjust my cock back inside my pants. And I did so just in time, considering she's now scooted across the bed, then rolled to her side to prop up on one elbow. Her breasts are displayed; the curve of her waist, the rise of her hip are sexy as hell, and I'm hard as nails all over again. I toe off my shoes and slide into bed with her, pulling the covers over us, and before she can protest, I'm turning her back to my front and pulling her close. And just the feel of her next to me, the sweet amber scent of her, consumes my senses, in every right way. The truth is this woman is everything I've known right in this world.

"Nick," she says softly.

"Yes, Faith?"

"Why are you not naked with me?"

"If I do that, I'll end up inside you."

"And that's bad why?"

"Because," I say. "Tonight, I really want you to know that I see the beautiful, talented part of you, not just your body."

She gives an insistent tug and twist, rotating to face me, her fingers curling on my chest. "If there is anyone in my life who I believe sees beyond the surface, it's you."

"And yet you thought I was upset because we didn't fuck tonight," I say. "Which means you don't trust me, or us, yet."

"It's not about you," she says, "or us. It's about my own baggage that I wish didn't exist." She touches my cheek. "But whatever the case, I don't need a knight in shining armor."

"And I told you," I say, "I know that, but the more evident that becomes, the more I seem to want to be that for you. And I don't do the knight routine."

"Well, then, if you are going in that direction—and it appears that you are—you should know that my knight, should I want one, would be inside me right now." She leans in, her lips a breath from mine, her fingers tearing away the tie holding my hair in place before her fingers are diving into the loose strands. "Be inside me right now, Nick."

She presses her lips to mine, and the minute her tongue touches mine, I need her. I just plain need this woman, and I don't hold back. I kiss her and touch her, and it is not long before my pants are gone, and I give her what she wants, what I want. I press inside the wet heat of her body, my hand sliding up her back, fingers splayed between her shoulder blades, molding all her soft perfection to every hard part of me.

"Now I'm inside you," I murmur, my lips closing down on hers, my tongue licking against hers in what becomes a drugging kiss that has nothing to do with fucking and everything to do with how much this woman is inside me. And I still don't taste murder. I don't taste lies. There is just hunger. Hers. Mine. Ours. And we savor it, and each other, with slow kisses, our bodies moving in a gentle dance. My lips on her shoulder, her nipple, her neck. My hand everywhere I can find skin. But it's when she whispers my name—when she says, "Nick," in that same way she kisses me, like I'm the only way she can take her next breath—that I know *I can't breathe without her.*

I tangle fingers in the silk of her blonde hair and pull her closer, her mouth lingering one of those breaths from mine. "What are you doing to me, woman?" I demand, but I don't give her time to respond. I kiss her, and the instant our tongues collide, there is a shift between us, the hunger turning darker and more demanding, and I drive into her, pulling her against me, her face buried in my neck until she trembles into release. I quickly follow with shuddered finality, but there is nothing final about my desire for this woman.

I hold her close but force myself to release her and walk to the bathroom, returning with a towel I offer her. She's barely slipped it between her legs before I'm behind her, pulling her back into my arms, wrapping my body around hers. Neither of us speak, but I can almost hear her thinking as hard as I'm thinking. I want to clear my conscience and tell her everything, but tonight is about her art. Tonight is about us sharing her life, a life.

Fuck. That's what I want.

I could tell her the truth now, about why I sought her out with the hope that together we can solve the mystery of our parents' deaths. However, not only is this night her night to celebrate her art, and I would never strip that well-deserved joy from her, but she'd push me away before I solve this mystery and save her winery. Before I am certain that she is not in danger, more exposed without me than with me. And the moment I opened us up to possibilities, I knew, even if she did not, that I wanted her in my life, not just my bed. And the minute I decided she wasn't a killer, I became a liar who needs her to trust me, when her reaction to me tonight says she does not. Not fully; not yet. And somehow, while she exposes herself, while she gives me that trust, and before I reveal the truth, as I must, I have to convince her that just as we are not the sum of how many times or ways we fuck, neither are we the sum of my lies.

CHAPTER TWO

Faith

I wake to the soft glow of a new day, a barely realized sunbeam splaying through the bedroom windows, and the woodsy, wonderful scent of Nick surrounding me, his hard body wrapped around mine, and I don't want to wake up. I shut my eyes again, reliving this weekend in random little pieces, starting with our arrival at his house. His expensive cars in the garage. Me calling him a "rich guy," which he claimed with pride and a declaration of hard work, boldly himself, and it had stirred both envy and arousal in me.

"Let's go inside, Faith," he'd said.

"Yes," I'd replied. "Let's go see what a man like you calls home."

"A man like me," he'd repeated. "You can explain that later. Naked."

I'd hurried into the house, and once there, I'd taken in the stunningly gorgeous house, the pale wooden floors, the high ceilings, layers of beautiful decor and fixtures as complex as the man and all he made me feel. I'd turned to face him. "It's a beautiful house, Nick. It smells like you."

"And how do I smell, Faith?"

"Like control. Like sex. Woodsy and sexy."

"And you, sweetheart, smell like—"

"Amber and vanilla," I'd said before he could say roses. Or flowers. Because the last thing I wanted to be reminded of that night was the garden at the winery—my mother's garden.

"Yes," he'd confirmed, "you do. And I'm obsessed with your scent. I'm obsessed with you."

"Obsessed," I'd said. "That sounds dangerous."
"It is dangerous."
Dangerous.

I blink with that word, and in contrast to the reaction you'd think that word would evoke, I snuggle a little closer to Nick, my hand on his where it rests on my belly. And yet as I shut my eyes again, that word echoes in my mind, and I don't know why.

Dangerous.

Dangerous.

Dangerous.

Sex is safe. It's just sex. It's just fucking. Or it was with Macom. It was supposed to be with Nick. But now there is a new hard rule: possibilities, and possibilities are dangerous. They expose me in ways I don't know if I want to be exposed. And yet I crave every one I might have with Nick. In other words: *Nick is dangerous.*

Letting him get too close is *dangerous.* Maybe that's what I've been trying to capture in my paintings of him. Nick Rogers is dangerous. He has secrets. He'll discover *my secrets.* He once told me that he wanted to see the woman behind the wall. The real me, stripped bare and not just exposed. *Willingly* exposed. Will I ever be willingly exposed?

Do I dare?

My lashes open, and this time there is a beam of bright sunlight in my eyes, and I no longer feel Nick behind me. Rolling over, I find the space next to me empty. I glance at the clock that reads ten o'clock and suck in air. Oh no. I fell back to sleep and stayed asleep a long time. I sit up, frustrated with myself. I'm supposed to fly home today, and I've wasted the little time I have with Nick in bed without him. I assume he's up, dressed, and busy by now.

I start to get up, and my gaze lands on that card from my father, a knot forming in my chest. What does it say that I want to open it *with Nick* and have him spank me, to deal with the emotional explosion to follow? I wouldn't even tell Macom about that card. Never. Ever. In a million years. And I would not invite him to spank me to deal with it. Sex with Macom was the wall Nick talked about me putting up, a big, thick emotional wall I didn't even recognize until near the end of our relationship. Macom never knew it existed. And yet Nick knew from the moment he met me. And sex with Nick is raw and real. So damn raw and real that it is terrifyingly addictive.

I throw away the blankets and stand, feeling naked and exposed beyond the physical with Nick, and in some ways, I'm not sure I have ever felt naked and exposed with anyone. And I've been in some pretty intense, naked positions with Macom, that's for sure. I'm halfway across the room when footfalls sound on the steps, and I react to that emotion, darting forward and into the bathroom, where I grab my robe and pull it on, swiping at the wild mess on my head. And oh God. Why do I look like that *The Grudge* horror chick again, with mascara under my eyes? I need new makeup.

It's in that moment that Nick steps into the doorway, his broad shoulders consuming its width, his fierce masculinity consuming me. And while last night he was the picture of corporate power in a blue suit, refined with that hard, alpha edge of his, today, in black jeans, a black T-shirt, and biker boots, a light stubble on his jaw, his longish hair barely contained in a tie at his nape, he personifies that raw, real feeling of every touch and kiss that we share. Most definitely the ones we shared last night. I swear even the coffee cup in his hand somehow makes him sexier. I really, really think I need to lick him all over after watching him undress.

"Hi," I say, not even sure why that's what comes out of my mouth.

"Hi," he says, his eyes lighting. "You're looking bright-eyed this morning."

I laugh and shake my head, pointing at my cheeks and then turning to the mirror, hands pressed to the counter. "This is your fault," I say, looking at myself and then him. "I'm always naked and in bed before I get my makeup off."

He saunters toward me, setting the cup on the counter. "I'd apologize," he says, "but I just can't be sorry." His hands find my waist, and he turns me to face him, his touch somehow more electric than ever before, the collision of our eyes, which is always intense, now downright combustible. "I like you naked and in my bed too much," he adds, a rough quality to his voice that is somehow both silk and sandpaper at the same time. And as we look at each other, there is something I cannot name expanding between us. Something happening between us. Something rich with those possibilities we've vowed to explore.

And suddenly, I can't seem to catch my breath. "I...uh..." I swallow hard. "It turns out I sleep really well in your bed, when I haven't been sleeping well really ever." That confession is out before I can stop it, exposed all over again, and in turn, I change the subject: "Why didn't you wake me up? My flight—"

"Your flight leaves when I say it leaves, and I didn't wake you up because I like you in my bed." He reaches for the coffee cup. "I made this special for you, and on the nightstand there are chocolate croissants that I had delivered from the bakery on the corner."

"Thank you," I say. "For an arrogant bastard, you're very considerate."

"Let's keep that as our secret," he says. "I don't want anyone but you believing I've grown a heart." I'd ask if he has, but he quickly—almost too quickly—moves on, offering me the cup. "Try it."

I accept the cup, my gaze lowering as the brush of our fingers sends a zing of sizzling heat rushing up my arm, and I wonder if Nick feels what I feel. This crazy, fierce magnetic pull that wants me to just melt into him. I take a sip, the secret rich beverage surprising my taste buds, my gaze lifting to his. "Is that Baileys I taste?"

"You know your liqueur," he says.

"Only the sweet-tasting, wonderful stuff, like Irish cream," I say. "And are you trying to get me drunk? Because you know I'm a lightweight. Or if you don't know, you're about to if I finish this."

"Nothing wrong with a little buzz," he says, stroking my cheek, his tone sobering. "We need to talk, sweetheart, and I thought I'd help you relax a little in advance."

My defenses prickle, and the fear that I've read him wrong, *us* wrong, comes at me hard and fast. "Nick, if you regret last night and that talk of a new hard rule—"

"I don't," he says, taking the cup from me and setting it down. "We need to talk about the winery, and I need to be your attorney for a few hours. And I know that's not easy territory for you. It's not going to be easy territory for us."

"Oh."

"Oh," he says, cupping my face. "Sweetheart, I *am* an arrogant bastard. A ruthless, arrogant bastard."

"Your point?"

His lips curve. "Your point," he says at my obvious agreement. "My point," he says, softening his voice, "is that all the good that is in me is here with you—hell, maybe because of you. So, I don't just want those possibilities. I'm pretty damn sure that I need them, which means you. Stop looking for the bad. Unless you—"

"I don't want to back out," I say, realizing only then how much I mean that statement. "Hard rule: possibilities."

"Good," he says, his hands settling back on my waist. "Drink your coffee. Take a hot bath if you want, and relax. No one uses that tub, so you should. There's no rush. I'll be in the kitchen at the bar working when you're ready. Okay?"

"Okay," I say, and then he's releasing me and walking to the door, gone before I can stop him, though I'm not sure why I want to. I just do. I want to pull him back, but he disappears. I inhale as he departs and face the counter, staring at my mascara-stained face, which he actually seems to find acceptable. Macom would not have thought this was acceptable, and I think back to all the times I thought I was raw and *real* with Macom. I was never real with Macom, and as for raw, well, perhaps, but in a cutting, harsh way, not like what I have with Nick, which I can't even name or truly describe.

But if that is what Nick wants, raw and real, then raw and real means he's willing to let me see all those hidden pieces of himself I try to paint. And if he lets me see his, I'll need, even want, to show him mine. But I'm not sure I can take that risk, even with him. Even if I want to. And I do. I want to trust Nick. Maybe I can. Maybe he can handle all of me. Maybe I need to know before I get any further in this. Or maybe not. Maybe I just need to enjoy him while I can.

CHAPTER THREE

Faith

Maybe I will enjoy him while I can.

Or maybe I can't enjoy him past today.

Because I have secrets that I hold close to my chest, the ones I try not to think about, to deny even to myself, and at least one of them—the one that stirs guilt in me—leads to the winery. And Nick Rogers is not the kind of man or attorney to leave a stone unturned. That man will wade into the muddy, crocodile-infested waters of my family secrets and kill the crocodile. Which is good and bad. Good because I need that kind of attorney. Bad because I really care about this man and I haven't been honest with him about who and what I am. But how could I be? We were two strangers who crossed paths and chose to stay on one.

I down the whiskey-laden coffee like it's a shot, because Nick's right. I need it, and the fact that he knows that I need it suggests that he's already been diving into those muddy waters. But he hasn't found the crocodiles, or he wouldn't be offering me hot baths. Then again, he gave me whiskey. I glance at the tub and walk to the shower, eager to just get dressed and pack, so I'm ready to leave if things go south. Moving quickly, I step under a spray of warm water in no time, when the buzz of the Baileys hits me, numbing my brain. Numb feels pretty darn good right now, too, just like the water, and while I am in a rush to get downstairs, I am not in a rush to say goodbye, and I find myself lavishing in Nick's shampoo, conditioner, and body wash, rather than my own.

Soon after, I stand at *Nick's* sink, in *Nick's* house, feeling incredibly comfortable in the alpha domain of a man who might have his head in the mouth of my crocodiles. I apply my makeup and dry and flat-iron my hair while, of course, stuffing my face with croissants. Because why wouldn't you stuff your face with loads of calories when you're pretty certain the alpha man of the house won't be seeing you naked again after this talk? Once I've packed on five pounds, I spray on Nick's cologne, because he smells better than me, and I'm obviously feeling a bit more clearheaded, because I'm not vowing to eat carrot sticks, rice cakes, and nothing else tomorrow. Which is me lying to myself, the way I feel like I lie to the world. And I really hate carrot sticks and lies, I think, and part of me just wants to confess all to Nick and see if he can handle it.

I think I will. I'll confess all.

Or not.

I make my way to Nick's large walk-in closet, where I've hung my clothes, the neat, organized way his clothes are lined up exactly as I expect of a dominant control freak. Exactly as Macom's always were. There are similarities in the two men that I only just now am acknowledging, though on some level I've known they existed. But Nick is not Macom. Not even close to Macom, and it's an insult to him that I even think of them in the same box. And damn it, all I'm doing is justifying reasons to walk away when I get downstairs, and I know it. I shove my own nonsense away and get dressed, choosing black jeans and a lacy top, which I pair with knee highs and lace-up black boots. And when I'm done, I don't let myself pack my bag. Instead, I retrieve my coffee mug, and after a quick path through the bedroom, I'm traveling down Nick's glass-and-steel stairwell, toward the lower level of his home. The high ceilings and long, clean lines of the entire structure, as well as the pale hardwood floors, are as sleek and sexy as the man—everything in this house screams sex and power, like the man who owns it. I'm quite certain everything about my demeanor right now screams of guilt.

I step into the living area, a white rectangular island dividing the two rooms. And the man who is power and sex sits at one of the four gray leather barstools on either side of it, paperwork and a MacBook sitting in front of him. His eyes meet mine, his keen and intelligent—too intelligent for my own good, and I remind myself: I have attorney-client privilege. I'm protected, and Nick just told me himself that he's no saint. If he knows what I've done, he didn't exactly go cold and brutal on me. If anyone can handle the truth, he can. If anyone can protect me, he can. Of course, if anyone can destroy me, he can as well. And so, I have to decide, right here and now: can I trust Nick Rogers?

CHAPTER FOUR

Nick

Faith rounds the corner looking so damn good in a pair of snug jeans, with some sort of lace top that hugs her breasts, and that makes me wish my hands were hugging them instead. And for just a moment, I contemplate marching her back upstairs, stripping her naked, and fucking her one, two, or maybe ten times while having this conversation. Or perhaps before and after. But the problem with fucking is that it makes everything better while you're doing it, even lies, and I don't want to feel better about my lies or invite her to spin any of her own. Not that I think Faith lies. I came looking for a liar and a killer, and all I found was a liar: me. But today is not about lies. It's about the facts as I laid them out in my head while she slept last night.

"How was the coffee?" I ask as she steps to the opposite side of the island and sets her cup down, my gaze finding her delicate little hands—talented, gifted hands, her nude nails somehow simple yet elegant. I don't notice women's hands. But then, other women are not her, nor are they talented with a paintbrush, and Faith most definitely is talented.

She turns her cup upside down. "It's empty and dry. And as for how it was. It was strong enough to make me stuff my face with croissants and weak enough to have to devour three thousand calories worth of croissants to return me to sanity."

"Well then," I say. "Let's make you another cup."

I start to move away, and she catches my hand, and I don't remember ever feeling a woman's touch like I do Faith's. Like a punch in the chest, I feel it go straight to my balls, which, to a man, might just be the perfect contradiction. "I don't want to be impaired when we talk," she says, her pale-pink-painted lips tightening as she adds, "*Tiger*," my lawyer nickname. "You'll rip out your opponent's throat, right?"

I turn my hand over and close it around hers. "Your Tiger, sweetheart," I say, sensing the apprehension in her. "And the only throats I'm going to rip out are those of your enemies. You know that, right?"

"I do, actually," she says, her eyes meeting mine. "I know, and I needed someone on my side, and suddenly you were just there. Fate, I guess, if you believe in that kind of thing, and I'm not sure I've told you how lucky that feels."

"Then why are your nails digging into my hand?" I ask while guilt over the fate that I created jabs at me like a blunt, rusty blade, trying to bleed me dry.

"I'm sorry," she says, softening her grip on my palm. "Your 'we need to talk' clearly has me uptight. Maybe I do need that Baileys."

"And there's nothing wrong with that," I say. "I keep a bottle of scotch in my office. Sometimes you need to take the edge off."

"But you're Tiger," she says. "Confident. Arrogant and—"

"Sexy as fuck?" I supply, trying to get her to ease up a little.

And my feisty, amazing woman doesn't disappoint, smacking me down. "Are you?" she quips back, making a soft, sexy sound that has my cock twitching, before she adds, "I hadn't noticed, but surely someone as confident—scratch that—as cocky as you doesn't need a drink to take the edge off."

"Sweetheart, I prefer my moves—even the ones that require teeth—to be calculated, which is why taking the edge off serves me and my clients well. So, what do you say? One more cup?"

"I don't hold my tongue when I drink," she warns.

"Hold your tongue with the rest of the world," I say, "not with me." I grab the pot of coffee from the counter behind me, fill both of our mugs halfway, and then top them off with Baileys. "Let's go to the living room."

She nods, and we both pick up our mugs and head in that direction, and yes, I watch the sway of her heart-shaped ass, because she has a fucking amazing ass in those jeans. It, like her breasts, would be even more amazing in my hands. "What's that saying?" she asks as we sit down on the couch and angle toward each other. "Loose lips—something?"

"Sink ships," I supply, and fuck, I need to get my head back in this conversation where it belongs. "And so does letting your attorney, and the man you're spending every naked moment possible with, get sideswiped," I add.

"Because being naked with you comes with rules?"

"Yes," I say. "Like how I don't want you to fuck anyone else but me, but that's another conversation. For now, we stay on topic, which is your business and legal affairs. And I can't protect you or help you get what you really want if you don't speak frankly with me."

"The same goes for you," she says. "I don't want you to fuck anyone but me, and be frank with me. Treat me like your other clients. Don't talk around things, because that makes me uptight. And I'm not some delicate flower."

"First, no other woman could get my attention, and as for you not being a delicate flower, believe me, sweetheart. You've made me well aware of that fact."

"And yet I got softened up with Baileys and croissants. Is that a service you're providing your other clients?"

"Sweetheart, I have clients I'd pour a bottle of whiskey down to either shut them up or get them talking. The croissants, however, and the fuck after this conversation, I reserve for you."

"You're still not getting to the point," she says. "Thus all the bedroom talk. It's a distraction."

"Actually, it's not."

"So I'll just get to the point for you," she continues as if I haven't spoken, before sipping the coffee and setting the cup down on the granite coffee table in front of us.

"Okay then," I say, taking a drink before setting my cup down as well. "What's the point?"

"I need to write the bank a check for the sixty thousand dollars I got paid for my art last night. And yes, that sucks in some ways, but in another it doesn't. My art allows me to get out of this mess."

I move to sit on the coffee table in front of her, not quite ready to spark the anger sure to follow once she learns that I've paid off that note. "That money won't save the winery."

She pales instantly. "Oh God. Did I already lose the winery? Did the bank already take it?"

"Of course not," I say, my hands settling on her knees. "I'm your attorney, remember?"

"I know that, but you weren't until a few days ago."

"I'm your attorney," I repeat, "and I'm not going to let that happen."

"But why would you even have to fight the bank at all at this point? The money should be the end of the bank's involvement in my affairs. They can't hold up probate if the debt is up to date. Right?"

"Correct," I say. "Based on the documents that you've shown me."

"Implying there's something I haven't shown you?"

"Easy, sweetheart," I say softly. "Implying there's more that you don't have."

"Wouldn't they have to give that to my attorney?"

"Yes. But your attorney has to be smart enough to ask for everything, rather than assume he has it. And since I've talked to the bank and they're playing hardball, they could be bluffing, but they didn't back off when they heard my name. Thus, I'm of the strong opinion that your father—or your mother—signed documents that give the bank rights that I don't know they have. Any idea what that document might be?"

"None. No idea. That would have required trust and communication from my mother I simply never had." Bitterness etches her tone, cold in that way that tells me the chill didn't happen overnight, but then, I knew that already. "But regardless of what legal document was signed," she adds, "what's the end game here? If I sold the winery, the net after that note, plus all debt, would be seven to eight million. I know that's a lot of money, but enough for the bank to go to this much trouble?"

"It's not a lot of trouble to intimidate you into handing it over, especially when you have a limp-dicked attorney allowing it to happen."

"Nick!"

"I tell it like it is, sweetheart. If you haven't gotten that by now, it's time to wake up and see the Tiger roaring in your face."

"Frank is not a limp-dicked attorney. He's just old."

I arch a brow. "And your point? Or was that my point you were making?"

"I assume your point is you're not him."

"No one knows that better than you, sweetheart," I say, handing her the coffee and preparing her for what comes next. "Drink."

She holds up a hand. "No. I need to know what's happening here. If the bank takes us to court, then you just do your Tiger routine, rip their throat out, and it's over, right?"

"They want to have the property evaluated."

"What? Why? Can they do that, and again, *why*?"

"That crop destruction you had last year could lead them to believe the value is now below that of the note."

"That's simply not the case," she says. "I don't believe that. I hope not. But let's just say it is—then what? Does that allow them to call the note due in full?"

"Not according to the documents I've seen and read."

"But we think there are other documents," she supplies, following where I've been leading.

"Exactly," I say. "And again. They could very well be bluffing, but we just won't know until they choose to show their hand or until we get to court. But the good news here is that my involvement alone tells them that they can't push you into a rash decision."

"And the bad?"

"It may take me getting in front of a judge to find out what we're up against."

"Which will be when?"

"If the bank has a leg to stand on, they won't be afraid of a judge, which means—"

"Right away," she says. "And if they don't, they'll stall. How long can they do that?"

"A few weeks at most, and that's if everything works against me, and I won't let that happen. But they're in this deep. They will try to force you to crack under the pressure. In the meantime, we'll prepare to hit back, and hard."

"What about me paying down the debt? Why wouldn't I do that?"

I steel myself for her reaction and set down her mug, which I'm still holding. "Because I paid the past-due amount and six months in advance."

She blanches and holds her hands up. "I think I misheard you. I need to pay six months in advance? That's double what I have in the bank."

"I paid it, Faith."

"No," she says.

"Yes."

"No."

"Yes."

"Get it back," she says fiercely. "Tell them you want it back. I'm not taking your money."

"They will, and they did. It's done, and by cashier's check."

"I'm not taking your money, Nick," she says, her tone absolute.

"Thank you. I mean that, and those words feel too small for what you've done, but you don't know me well enough to do this. And even if you did, I don't want charity."

"It's not charity. It's a gift that I want nothing in exchange for.

And as I've asked before, when do I know *enough*, Faith? I can fuck you all I want, but I can't give a damn? Because I give a damn. I get it. It's early. It's new. But it is what it is, and I can't change that."

She presses her hands to her face, and I can see them tremble, as they did last night when she found out that she'd earned sixty thousand dollars on her art. And I don't know how it's possible, but I know this woman in a way that defies the time we've been together. I reach for her hands and pull them between us. "I'm alone in this world, too. You know that, right?"

"You don't seem alone."

"Why? Because I'm foul-mouthed, cocky as you say, and sexy as fuck?"

"Nick," she whispers, no laugh this time.

"I know that we are new to each other. I know it feels like you could count on me and then I'll be gone, but I'm not going to be. Even if you decide you don't want to be *us* anymore, I'm your friend. I will remain your friend. And I don't have a lot of friends, but the ones I have, I take care of. Okay?"

"The money—"

"Is not a big deal to me. I know that feels big to you, but it's not a lot to me. I've done well for myself, but my bastard of a father was rich as fuck, and now I have his money. And I'd like to do more than a few good things with it."

"How much was the check you wrote?"

"A hundred and twenty thousand."

"Nick," she breathes out. "You can't—"

"I already did."

"It's a lot of money."

"I just told you. I have a lot of money."

"It's a lot of money," she repeats.

I grab the notepad on the table, write down a number, and show it to her. "That's the current valuation of my holdings."

Her lips part in shock. "That isn't even comprehensible to real people. Did you— Are there too many zeroes on that number?"

"No, there are not."

"Okay. I… Okay. But even if you took two or three zeroes off that, I'm not taking advantage of you."

"No," I say. "You're not. Because it's a gift." I settle my hands back on her knees. "But let's talk about why I did it and what it does for us. I have documents for you that state this is a gift. You do not owe me anything in return. But I have a plan to make this go away, and we need it to go away. But it means you're going to have to trust me, and Faith, I mean *really* trust me."

"I trust you, Nick," she says. "Why do you think I slept so well in your bed?"

"You sure about that? Because you seem to have a calendar and a timeline for when we're allowed to do certain things."

"This is new to me, too," she says. "It wasn't like this with… I trust you."

"Macom," I supply. "It wasn't like this with Macom. You lived with him, Faith."

"I did."

"You trusted him."

"I'm actually not sure I did."

I study her for several beats, wanting to unwrap that package she just handed me but knowing now is not the time. I show her that valuation again. "That kind of money is power that we can use to end this, and I'm not talking about me spending more money, though that is not off the table."

"By disclosing your involvement," she assumes. "And therefore giving yourself a vested interest in the case."

"We have to go further than that. I drew up a separate set of dummy documents that give me an interest in the winery. But again, you'll have documents that cover all of this and protect you."

She doesn't even blink. "I trust you. What else?"

"I have a number of tools in the chest, but among them, I'll offer to move some of my money to your bank, which will have influence. But not until we have our day in court. I want to see their hand before I play ours."

"Ours," she repeats.

I reach up and brush a strand of the pale blonde silk of her hair from her beautiful green eyes, the many shades of torment in their depths accented by flecks of yellow. "Ours," I say. "I told you. I'm in this with you until the end."

Her hands come down on my forearms, then lift the right to stare down at the black-and-orange tiger etched into my skin, but her gaze shifts to my left, her fingers tracing the words there. "An eye for an eye," she says, reading them as she did once before. "I don't believe in an eye for an eye."

I believe her. She is a kinder, gentler soul than me, the moonlight on the water when I'm the sun bringing it to a boil. And I like that about her, about us. The contrast; the good and the bad. And I don't mind being the bad. "Only one of us has to go for the throat," I say. "I'll be the killer. You be the artist. And maybe you'll tame the beast along the way. But I wouldn't count on it."

"You'll be the killer," she whispers, letting out a choked laugh. "Right." She reaches for the coffee and gulps it down like water, then sets the cup aside. "I need air." She scoots around me, stands up, and walks away.

I'm on my feet almost immediately, watching her track across the room to exit the open patio doors onto the terrace. I'm aware that I've thrown a lot at her, but also that she's rattled when she doesn't rattle easily, and I don't like the word that had that impact: killer. Fuck. What is happening here? I pursue her, and I find her at the railing, her back to me, her attention on the city, the ocean, and the Golden Gate Bridge before her. I close the space between us, stepping to her side, close but not touching her, my hands also resting on the railing. And while there are times when I push people to talk, there are others when silence leads them to reveal what is there but not yet spoken. With Faith, I don't speak. I wait, giving her the opportunity to speak when she's ready. Confident that she needs to say whatever it is she hasn't spoken yet.

"When I went to L.A.," she says without looking at me, "it hurt my father. He didn't want me to chase a hopeless dream."

"Was *hopeless* his word or yours?"

"His," she says. "But I couldn't give up my dream for his."

"And his was for you to run the winery."

"Yes. Exactly. And yet, I almost stayed. I was going to stay, because I was worried about my father. But then the night of my college graduation happened. That disaster changed my mind."

"What kind of disaster?"

She looks at me. "You know the details on that already. It was when my mother got mad at my uncle. To get back at him, she told my father that she slept with my uncle."

"Holy fuck," I breathe out. "I still can't believe she slept with his brother and he forgave her."

"Yes. And the truth is that I hated my father a little afterward, too. I mean, he never spoke to his brother again, but he forgave my mother. I couldn't look him in the face and see the same man anymore." She cuts her gaze, staring out at the city. "I wasn't as angry at my mother at that point as I was at him. I mean, he was the one who'd become the fool."

"And then he died."

"Yes. On the same night I had an explosion with Macom that was the end of us—in my book, anyway. So, leaving felt right. It had for a long time. But I didn't think it meant leaving my art. But my mother was a train wreck, and I wasn't without a head for business. I wanted to protect my father's pride and joy, but also, one day that winery would be mine. And with a management team, I knew it would be an asset and an income that supported, not destroyed, my painting." She glances over at me. "I hated to think like that. It meant thinking beyond my mother."

"It's business. It's smart business."

"Yes. Well, I took it a step further. She refused to tell me what was going on, and the vines were lost and bill collectors were calling. I'd lost any hope of painting. I was consumed by her screwups, and I couldn't take it. I hired an attorney, Nick. I tried to take it from her. It was brutal." Her hands clutch the railing. "She threatened suicide. She cried. She yelled. She made scenes at the winery, and I was losing my mind. I wanted her to go away. I *needed* her to go away. And then...she was gone. Then she was dead. And Nick..." She looks down, her grip tightening on the railing. "I *killed* her."

CHAPTER FIVE

Nick

"*I killed her.*"

Faith's words, her tormented confession, roar through me like a tiger trying to rip *my* throat out. I didn't, I don't, believe she is guilty of killing her mother or my father, but my father's warning is burned into my mind: *Faith Winter is the problem. She is dangerous.* And mixed with her own statement, I need an explanation, peace of mind. I need to know what happened, and therefore what I'm protecting her—and myself—from, and I need to know now.

Still standing at the balcony, she has yet to look at me, like she doesn't want to see what might be in my face. Or maybe she doesn't want me to see what is in hers. Or both. Both, most likely. But I read people. It's what I do. It's who I am, and I glance down at her hands where they grip the railing, and her knuckles are white, telling the tale of dread and guilt. Urgency and need boil inside me, and not in the way they normally do for this woman. I step behind her, turn her to face me, and press her back to the railing, my big body pinning hers to it, my hands on the railing at her shoulders. "What the fuck does that mean, Faith?" I demand.

She looks up at me, her green eyes flashing with anger. "I shouldn't have told you. Get off me."

Her withdrawal stirs a spike of anger in me I can't seem to control, when I control everything around me—except this woman, it seems. It's a claw opening a wound I don't even understand, and I don't like anything I don't understand. My hands go to her waist, my tone hardening. "I'll let you when you explain yourself."

Her hands go to my hands. "Let go of me, Nick," she warns, her voice tight, icy. She tries to move.

My legs close around hers. *Not until you explain yourself.*

"I *shouldn't* have told you," she says again. "I shouldn't have trusted you."

"Attorney-client privilege, Faith."

This time, it's her anger that is hard and fast. "Are you serious right now, Nick?" The question rasps from her throat. "Is that what we are now? Or I guess we always were? Is that why you think I told you everything I just told you? Because I have attorney-client privilege?" Her fingers press into my chest, the prelude to the shove I steel myself for, as she adds, "I don't know why I thought we could be more than that," and then throws her body into pushing me away.

I don't budge under her impact, not physically, but I feel the emotional jab of those words. "I'm trying to give you the room to say whatever you need to say. I'm *trying* to protect you."

"Are you? Because that's not what I feel right now. Not when you're demanding what, a few minutes ago, I didn't need you to demand. I *wanted* to talk to you." Her voice lowers, but it's not less biting as she adds, "Get off me, or I swear to you, Nick-asshole-fucking-Rogers, I will make you. And don't think I can't, though maybe I should add: Don't worry. I won't kill you. I'm not quite as skilled in that area as you might think."

My grip on her legs and waist tightens. "I was not implying that you were a cold-blooded killer."

"Just a killer."

"Stop."

"Gladly. Let me go."

"Damn it," I bite out, feeling that urgency and need again. "Talk to me, Faith."

"Not anymore," she says. "Not ever again."

"Don't do this."

"*You* did this."

"I'm trying to protect you," I repeat.

"By acting like I *really am* a killer? Because that's not what I needed from you, but then, that's the problem. I know better than to need anything from anyone. Mistake noted. Lesson learned. Again."

That wall she slams down between us is far more brutal than any tone or word spoken, and I don't even think about what comes next. My mouth closes over hers, my tongue stroking against hers, and at first, she doesn't kiss me back. I mold her close, deepening the kiss, demanding she give me what I want, and finally, her fingers curl around my shirt and that tongue of hers licks against mine. And there it is—exactly what I want, need, know to be this woman. Desire, hunger, sweetness. And damn it, I know what she meant now, and I am such a fucking asshole. I tear my mouth from hers, my hands cupping her face. "I know who you are. I know how you taste. And you are not a killer. And yes, I know that I'm a fucking asshole."

"You don't know me. We are too new, and you—"

"Know you like I know my own smell. Know you like I don't know people I've known for years. I can't explain it, but you really are nothing I expected and everything I wanted. And needed."

"You came at me like—"

"I'm sorry," I say. "And I never say I'm sorry, but I'm fucking sorry. I go at things, Faith. I know you know this about me. I push. I want answers the minute something threatens what matters to me. And *you*, Faith Winter, matter to me." I lean back to look at her. "And no matter what you tell me right now, or when you're ready, I meant what I said. I'm in this with you until the end. I am not leaving. I'm not turning on you. I am not letting you go."

"And yet you thought the worst of me."

"Not you. But the worst, yes. Things happen that are sometimes out of our control." *Like everything I feel for this woman*, I add silently before I continue, "I always go to the worst place, because then I get ahead of what I'm facing. What *we're* facing, Faith. I pushed because—"

"Like I pushed *her*," she breathes out. "I pushed her, Nick. I pushed her until she was dead like my father." She buries her face in my shoulder and sobs, but in another instant, she's pushing away and swiping at her cheeks. "I think I'm going to keep crying. I need to go…"

"No," I say, cupping her face. "No. You do not." I thumb the tears from her cheeks. "You're right where you belong, Faith. *With me.*"

Her lashes lower. "You don't understand."

"Make me understand."

"Not now, or I'll cry, and that is weak and confusing." Her fingers curl around my shirt.

"Why is it confusing or wrong to cry?" I ask, my hands moving to her shoulders.

Her lashes open, her eyes meeting mine. "You haven't cried for your father."

"I didn't see my father for years before he died, sweetheart. It's different."

"I was with her. When she died. We were fighting, and then she just dropped dead. And the guilt—Oh God." Her hand goes to her forehead. "I told you. I can't keep talking now." Tears pool in her eyes again. "I can't keep talking…now." She leans into me and buries her face in my chest, her body quaking with silent tears that she clearly struggles to control. I don't want her to stop crying, to hide anything from me, and bastard that I am, I all but created that need in her.

I scoop her up, carry her to the sitting area to our left, and set her down on the couch, framed by a table and two chairs, her legs over my lap. But she doesn't let go of my shirt, her face still buried in my shoulder. And she hasn't stopped trembling, trying to pull herself into check, and still she says, "I'm okay." She pushes away from me, swiping her cheeks and sitting up. "I'm fine."

Guilt, plus my intense need to control every damn thing

around me, is now my enemy. I went at her. I pushed when she didn't need to be pushed. But saying that to her won't make her believe me now. I have to show her she can trust me again. I cup her head and pull her to me, giving her a quick kiss and saying it anyway. "It's okay to not be okay with me, Faith. I'm an asshole, but this asshole is crazy about you and on your side." I don't force her to reply. She doesn't need to do that. "I'll be right back." I kiss her again and release her, standing up and walking into the house.

I cross the living room, kicking myself for my reaction to Faith's confession. She baited me, and I let her, though I'm not certain she even realizes she did it. She's punishing herself. Maybe testing me at the same time. Trying to decide if she really can trust me. Fuck. I need her to know she can. And I failed whatever that was. Worse, I failed because I let that note of my father's mess with my head when I meant what I said to Faith. I know her in ways I'm not sure I've ever known another human being. I know she is not a killer, and yet I reacted as if I thought she was just that.

Entering the kitchen, I stop at the corner built-in bar, pressing my hand to the edge of the counter. "You're an asshole," I murmur. "Such a fucking asshole, just like she said." And why, I think? Because I felt, for just a moment, like control was lost, and I had to grab it and hold on to it.

I push off the counter and grab a glass, needing the drink I came in here to get for Faith. Scanning my many choices, I opt for my most expensive Macallan, pour three fingers, and down it. Smooth. Rich. Almost sweet in its perfection. I open the mini freezer under the counter, add ice to the glass, and refill it. Then, with the bottle in hand, I return to the balcony, where I find Faith standing at the railing again. Seeming to hear or sense my approach, she rotates and meets me back on the couch, her tears gone. Her hands steady. She sits down, and I go down on a knee in front of her. "Drink this," I order, offering her the glass.

"I'd argue," she says, accepting the whiskey, "but I never allow myself to be numb like I was a bit ago, and as it turns out, I'd like to feel that again." She sips, testing it, and then downs it before handing me back the glass. "Thank you. That was smooth and, I suspect, quite expensive."

"You're worth it, and I vote we sit here and down the entire bottle." I move to the cushion beside her and refill the glass, down the contents, and refill it again, offering it to Faith. "I know you didn't kill her."

She studies me a moment, takes the glass, downs the whiskey, and sets the glass on the table. "Do you? Because I don't. I think that's why your reaction got to me so much."

"I told you—"

"It's okay," she says, grabbing my leg. "In fact, I should apologize, because when you walked into the house, I realized something. I set you up. Not on purpose. But come on, Nick. I dropped the 'I killed her' bomb."

I'm stunned that she's self-analytical enough to come to the same conclusion I did, and in the same timeline I did. "Why, Faith?"

"Some part of me feels so much guilt that I wanted you to come at me. I wanted you to punish me." She gives an uncomfortable laugh. "I think I'm pretty fucked up and you should run, Nick." She tries to pull her hand from my leg.

I cover it with mine, holding it in place. "I'm not going anywhere, Faith, and I'm not letting you, either. Not without a fight. One hell of a fight. And as for being fucked up. We're all fucked up. Anyone who claims they aren't is lying."

"You don't seem fucked up at all. You're successful. You know yourself. You seem to know me."

"I do know you, but obviously you don't quite know me, yet, and I need to fix that. Starting with your current misconception of me. Of course I'm fucked up. My mother left my father for slutting around and then died and left me with that man. I blame her. I blame him. I blame me. I fear the fuck out of being just like that man."

"You aren't."

"I am, Faith. I'm calculated. I'm cold with everyone but you, and yet I say that after the way I just treated you. I'm a bastard made by a bastard, and he was a damn good attorney. I drive myself to be better than he was. And I am."

"Your version of being a bastard is a man who demanded to know everything from me. Not a man who assumed he did. Once I came to the realization that I'd pushed your buttons, I realized that, too, even if you did not."

"I pushed you."

"I pushed you, too. And for the record, it's pretty impressive that your version of 'fucked up' is to be amazing at your job."

"I've seen your art, Faith. Your version of fucked up makes you amazing at your job, too, and obviously, from your recent success, I'm not the only one who shares that opinion. But there's a difference between the two of us. I know I'm amazing at my job. You don't."

"I'm working on that," she says. "You've helped. Last night helped. But right now, in this moment, I'm consumed by the same demon I've been consumed by since my mother died. I go back and forth between anger and gut-wrenching guilt. But never grief, and that starts the guilt all over again."

I hand her another glass of whiskey.

"I shouldn't drink this," she says.

"Why not? Are you driving?"

"Right," she says. "Why? I'll just go slower."

"And as for your current demon," I say when she sips from the glass, "I predict that once we get the chaos your mother created under control, you'll find the grief. Or not. Maybe you'll find out things about her that make that grief impossible."

"Is that what happened with your father?"

"Yes," I say. "It is, but I feel like I should remind you of what I just said. I came to terms with what I felt for my father many years before he died. And he wasn't in my life; therefore, there wasn't anything to change those terms."

"And you really feel no grief?"

"I really feel no grief," I say without hesitation. "But you asked me if I feel alone now."

"You said that you don't."

"And I don't," I confirm, and when I would offer nothing more to anyone else, I do with Faith. "But, on some level, I have moments when I'm aware that I have no blood ties left in this world, and that stirs an empty sensation inside me. Maybe that is feeling alone. I just don't name it that."

"You have no family at all?"

"My mother's family has been gone for many years. My uncle on my father's side died a few years back, but I hadn't seen the man in a decade and, as far as I know, neither had my father."

"We live odd parallels," she says. "My father and my uncle hadn't spoken for about that long when my father died, either." She sinks back against the cushion. "And I'm feeling all the alcohol now." She shifts to her side to face me. "I'm not drunk," she adds. "Just kind of numb again, which is a good thing. It's better than guilt."

"How many employees do you have?"

"Is this a sobriety test?"

"If it is, will you pass?"

"Yes," she says. "I told you. I'm numb, not drunk. And I have fifty employees, at least part of the year."

"And your mother's mishandling put all of those jobs on the line. You had to protect the winery."

"I know. Especially Kasey's job, and another ten or so key people who have been with the winery for their entire careers."

"And yet you still feel guilt for fighting for them?"

"I feel guilt for not finding a way to fight for my mother *and* them."

"Your mother didn't want help."

"But she needed it," she argues. "She was clearly an addict, both with alcohol and sex."

"You said you hired an attorney?"

"Yes. An expensive one, too. That's what happened to part of my inheritance."

"Who?"

"Cameron Lemon. Do you know him?"

"In passing and by reputation. He's good. What happened with him?"

"One of my mother's many male friends was an attorney, too, and he knew just how to nickel-and-dime me to death with Cameron. I ran out of money, and with the winery in debt, I couldn't even promise him I'd pay him when we won ownership. I had to back off."

"Who was your mother's attorney?" I ask, steeling myself for the answer I am sure I will receive.

And as expected, she says, "Nathan Marks," her lashes, thankfully, lowering with my father's name on her lips. "Do you know *him*?" she asks, looking at me.

"Yes," I say, telling her every truth I can at this point. "I do. And your mother chose her friends wisely. He would have been a formidable opponent."

"She got naked with my uncle. She didn't choose wisely. She just chose often." She downs the drink. "I can't believe this, but the whiskey effect is wearing off. Maybe I wasn't really feeling it after all."

I fill her glass. "Try again."

"What if it hits me all of a sudden, and I wipe out on you?"

"I promise you that we won't fuck," I say, placing her hand on the glass. "Because I want you to remember every time we fuck."

Her teeth scrape her bottom lip. "You're really quite memorable, *Mr. Rogers*." She downs the drink. "I think my mother watched that program. I'm really glad that you don't wear button-up sweaters and sing like the real Mr. Rogers on the show."

"Last I heard, I was the real Mr. Rogers."

"Right," she whispers, giving a tiny laugh. "You are, but without a button-up sweater. Or is it button-down sweater?"

"I vow to never, ever wear a button-up or button-down sweater."

"It might be cute on you."

"I don't want to be cute," I assure her.

"What's wrong with cute? Women like cute."

"Only women who have been drinking really expensive, smooth whiskey or picking out a puppy."

"Or cat. I prefer cats. I really need to get a cat." Her hand goes to her face. "I was wrong. I'm feeling those drinks now, and I just drank more." She sets the empty glass on the cushion between us, as if she can't quite sit up and get it to the table. "What have I done?"

I set the glass on the table, lower myself to the cushion beside her, and roll her to face me. "I'll catch you if you fall, sweetheart."

Her hand falls from her face. "Will you? Or will you fall with me?"

I stroke her cheek. "What does that mean, Faith?"

"It means that if we're both fucked up, then sometimes, two fucked-up people fuck each other up more."

"We're all fucked up, remember? Which means that sometimes, two fucked-up people make each other whole again."

"That's like a fairytale ending. We don't believe that."

"Now we have each other, don't we?"

"*Do* I have you, Nick?"

"Yes, Faith, you do."

She reaches up and strokes my cheek this time. "Ah, Nick. I have to paint you again. You know that, right?" Her lashes lower, and her hand falls from my face. I catch it, but she doesn't open her eyes. I count seconds. One. Five. Ten. She sighs and seems to fall asleep. I sit there, staring at her, searching every line of her face, and I swear she grows more beautiful by the second. Her full cheeks. Her fuller lips. The confession that says she wants to trust me, even if she doesn't quite yet.

"I don't want to leave," she murmurs, her eyes fluttering and closing again.

"Then don't," I say, pleased that the first confession came when she was sober, and this one comes when she's just drunk enough to make emotional confessions.

She doesn't respond. She's dozing off again, and I stand and scoop her up. She curls into me again, her body soft in my arms. "Kasey—"

"Can handle the winery," I say, already in the house and crossing to the stairs. "If he can't, he needs to be replaced." I start the upward climb. She's silent until we're almost to the top, and then she seems to remember the conversation.

"But the collectors," she says. "I need—"

"You don't," I say, entering the bedroom. "Debate me after you take a nap—preferably after Wednesday, when I can return with you."

"You're very convincing when you're holding me like this. Even with your clothes on."

I laugh. "I'll have to remember that."

"That's not the alcohol talking," she murmurs. "I mean it."

"Even better," I assure her, setting her on the bed, which remains unmade. She plops onto the pillow.

"My head is spinning," she says as I take her boots off. "I really hate being out of control."

I lean over her and press my hands to either side of her. "No. You don't. You hate always having to be in control."

"How could you possibly know that?"

"Because I know how to read people, you especially. And now you don't have to be in control all of the time. You have me. And you don't know it yet, or you don't trust me yet, but I'll take care of you."

"No one takes care of me but me," she says. "That's just how it is."

"Was," I amend. "That's how it was. Like I said. Now you have me."

"Ah, Nick," she whispers. "I don't."

"You don't what?"

"Have you. At least, not all of you." She traces my brow with her finger. "It's in your eyes right now. It's always in your eyes. The secrets I try to understand when I paint you…things you don't want to tell me." Her lashes lower. "Maybe you will one day." She inhales again, and her breathing slows, evens, while my heart is racing. She knows I'm telling her a lie. She senses it. Fuck. Fuck. Fuck. I stand up and shove fingers through my hair before walking to the door, and just as I would exit, she whispers, "Nick."

I face her, and she's looking at me as she says, "When you're ready," before shutting her eyes again. "I can wait."

And therein lies the problem. I'm never going to be able to tell her. I'm never going to be ready to lose her. Because I need this woman. I need her like I need my next breath.

CHAPTER SIX

Nick

After leaving Faith in my bed, I end up on the balcony, where I sit down, pour the last glass of whiskey in the bottle, and down it. What the hell is this woman doing to me? No woman has ever consumed me the way Faith has and does. No woman has ever made me not just want her, but need her, like I need Faith. As I, in turn, need her trust that I do not deserve. Forced lies are killing me and most likely will kill us, a likelihood that only gets worse with each day I continue to let them become a divide between us. She senses it. She knows it. She knows me in ways people who have known me for years do not. I need to fix this. I'm damn good at fixing things. This can't be the exception. I will make things right with Faith. I will make everything right in her world, including me.

Which is exactly why I left Faith sleeping this morning and got to work doing just that, including a long conversation with Beck. Pulling my phone from my pocket, my finger hovers over the autodial with his number, but I remind myself that I didn't even send the man a copy of my father's note until early this morning. He's a damn good PI, but even he needs time to work. I punch Abel's number instead, who, as of a few hours ago, became more than my friend and personal attorney. He's now one of Faith's attorneys as well. She just doesn't know it yet. "Bring yourself and those documents I had you do up for me over here," I order when he answers.

"Have that bottle ready for me," he replies.

He means the Glenlivet Winchester Collection: Vintage 1964 bottle valued at $25k that was gifted to me first by a client, and now by me to Abel for taking care of Faith. "It's ready and waiting," I say without hesitation, more than happy to give up a bottle of booze to ensure Faith knows she can trust me. Which is the role Abel is going to play in this web I'm weaving for her enemies.

"I might let you taste it when I open it," he taunts.

"I'll gladly share a drink of anything the day you finally get smart and stop fucking the wrong women, like your ex."

"She's not my only fuck these days, and even if she was, *I'm* fucking *her*. She's not fucking me. We're going to talk about how that plays out with you and Faith. I'll be there in fifteen." He hangs up, and I stand, taking the empty glass and bottle with me to the kitchen. I don't refill that glass. I make an old-fashioned pot of coffee, because I like the insulated pot right next to me while I work, and on quick pour.

I then sit down at the island, my stacks of work in front of me, my briefcase locked and to my right. I punch in the combination and open it, pulling out my father's handwritten note to read it again, homing in on those poison words: *Faith is dangerous.* She was a threat. How? I grab a note pad and start writing down my thoughts:

—*My father had to have been after the winery, but why? Is it worth more than we think? It has to be. Actions needed:*

—*Get assessment done Monday.*

—*Beck needs to find out what might be beyond the obvious.*

Moving on...next item:

—*Why call Faith Dangerous? COVERED. He had to have felt she was dangerous to his plan.*

—*Seven to ten million wouldn't motivate a man who was damn near a billionaire at that stage in his life. Would it? No. COVERED.*

—*Why pay Meredith Winter one million dollars in staggered payments? Down payment on the winery? But she couldn't sell without Faith—is that why Faith was dangerous? She could stop the sale? Back to: Why is the winery more valuable than it appears?*

—*Autopsy results—WHEN?*

—*If someone killed my father and Faith's mother, doesn't that imply that my father and her mother were on the same side? Unless my father convinced Meredith Winter to be on his side. Or she convinced him to be on her side. Or they were both such players they were playing each other, but either way they both ended up dead, by the same means. The same person had to have killed them. And that person was NOT Faith.*

I move on to another key list, and one to discuss with Beck:

Suspects:

—*Someone associated with the bank.*

—*Ask Faith for a meeting with Cameron Lemon, with her present so he will talk.*

—*Faith's present-day attorney when she met me—he's her father's friend, but it appears her father's friends were usually her mother's friends as well, and in Meredith Winter's case, that's a problem.*

—*Faith's uncle—enough said.*

—*Kasey, or another staff member at the winery, but Kasey would be the one who knows intimate details of the winery and family— sleeping with Meredith Winter?*

—*Any one of Meredith Winter's lovers, with a focus on the long-term boyfriend right before my father that Beck has found.*

—*An unknown I have yet to identify or see a link to connect them to Meredith and my father.*

My coffee finishes brewing, and I fill a cup, bring the pot to the island, and ready it for future pours before reviewing my new list several times over. My focus is on why my father would pay Meredith Winter a million dollars and in installments. Somewhere in that act is an answer to every question I have and some I probably don't know to ask. Yet. I will.

The doorbell rings, which says the $25k bottle of booze has Abel showing some manners for once, and of course he chooses now, while Faith is sleeping. Fully intending to soften his edges where she's concerned, and before he meets her, I make fast tracks for the door. Abel doesn't wait on my arrival. Clearly impatient, he's used my back-up key and is opening the door as I arrive. He steps inside the foyer, his typical designer suit replaced with his weekend faded ripped jeans, plus a T-shirt that sports the Harley logo and supports the man's obsession with the brand and the bikes. "Take me to the wonderland of whiskey," he says, shutting the door and sliding his key back into his pocket. "Because I do have something to celebrate." He runs his hand over his buzzed blond hair as he adds, "Remember that Navy SEAL judge I buzzed my head to impress?" He doesn't wait for my confirmation. "He dismissed my case, and I landed a six-figure paycheck."

I back up to give him space to pass. "Not bad for a week's work."

"Not bad at *all*," he agrees, heading down the hallway.

I follow him, his destination the island or, rather, the long-ass bar that serves as the island, but he doesn't stop there. He drops his briefcase on a seat and heads to the bar. I walk back to my seat behind the island and face the living area, keeping the stairs that Faith would have to travel to join us in view. While Abel's view is on my many whiskey choices. "Was the client guilty or innocent?" I ask, thrumming my pen on the shiny, white granite counter.

"He says he was innocent," he replies, walking toward me with a bottle of scotch and two glasses in hand. "I have to believe a client is innocent to take a case." He stops at the end cap by the chair his bag has now claimed and sets the bottle and glasses down. "I have to believe, man." He opens the bottle and fills one of the glasses. "You know that."

I narrow my gaze on him, not so sure we're celebrating after all. "But was he innocent?" I ask, waving off the pour he's about to give me. "I've had my share today." I lift my coffee cup. "I'll stick to this."

"Suit yourself," he says, his tone impartial. He really doesn't care. That's one of the things that I like about Abel. He is what he is, and I am what I am. We are night and day in some ways, especially when it comes to women, who he tends to allow replays with that I do not. *Not until Faith*, I add silently and quickly refocus on Abel and our similarities. We like control. We like to win, and we hit hard. And considering we've known each other since law school, I know he has some baggage, as Faith calls one's history, and like me, Abel trusts almost no one. Which means he won't be quick to trust Faith.

"And as for my client's guilt or innocence," he continues, snapping me back to the moment as he downs the contents of his glass and refills it. "He was guilty as sin, but I didn't decide that until I got him off, when he smirked and said: 'Who says only the innocent go free?'"

"Ah shit, man."

"I know, right?" he says. "I thought I was good at reading people, but holy hell. I missed this one. But there wasn't even a semi-good case built against him, and I can't turn back time. Which is why I have to focus on the payday and celebrate that."

"What was the crime?"

"Murder," he says, his lips tightening. "And don't ask me who he killed. I don't want to talk about it." He scrubs the light stubble on his jaw. "I *really* don't want to talk about it." He refills his glass.

We're not celebrating. He's come to swim in the sea of guilt Faith is splashing around in, and I get it. Defending a killer sucks. Thankfully, Faith isn't a killer, but the guilt is killing her. I don't really understand guilt. I don't feel it. I do something. I did it for a reason. I own it. And so I only know one way to help with it. A good fuck—Abel is on his own on that one. And a good drink. I stand up and round the counter, open a cabinet above the bar, and pull out that $25k bottle of booze before returning to the counter and setting it down beside him. "This and a trip to the club and you'll forget the asshole you just banked on," I say. "But tell me again why you stick with criminal law?"

"Because the innocent ones need me, and paydays like this one let me help people who don't have a bank account as big as the likes of that asshole I got off." He taps the bottle. "You really going to give me that?"

"You need it."

"I need a trip to the club to get fucked ten ways to next Sunday, but I was never going to take that bottle, man. But hey. I'll work for the sentiment behind it." He opens his briefcase and pulls out a file. "The gift documents and the dummy documents," he says, setting the file on the counter. "But seriously, man. What the hell are you doing with this woman, Nick?"

"Protecting her."

"Protecting a woman who might be a killer."

"She's innocent."

"And you know this how?"

"Because I know, and you know when I say I know, I know."

"Like I knew my client?"

"I know Faith personally now."

"Yeah, well, you're fucking her, and that tends to cloud a man's judgment."

"Not mine. You know that."

"And I've never known you to mix business and your personal life." He taps the file. "And these documents tell me you've either lost your fucking mind or you're brilliantly working a woman who doesn't know she's being worked. And you can tell me either way. I'm *cool*. You know that." He removes the stopper from the scotch.

"She and I just downed a bottle of Macallan No. 6 together, and she's in my bed right now."

He's about to pour another drink, but he sets the bottle down, looking stunned. "You shared your No. 6, and she's in your bed?"

"Yes and yes."

"You don't share your No. 6 or your bed. What happened to keeping your women confined to the club?"

"Faith isn't going to the club," I say, once again wishing I'd never bought the damn place. "Ever."

"So she's vanilla and you're chocolate, and that shit will get old."

"Faith is not fucking vanilla," I snap.

He arches a brow. "Got it. Not vanilla. Not going to play with you at the club. Does she at least know it exists and that you own it?"

"No," I say. "Now *focus*." I slide the notepad I've been writing on in front of him.

He scans it, and his gaze rockets to me. "Faith is dangerous? When did your father say that Faith was dangerous?"

I open my briefcase and set the note in front of him. He studies it for several long beats before he glances at me. "You're sure Faith—"

"Faith is *not* a killer," I say tightly. "Assume I'm right on this because I am. Now. Where does that note lead you?"

"That your father wanted the winery, or something else, and she was in the way of him getting it."

"Exactly my thoughts," I concur. "But Meredith Winter. He was paying her. I can't make sense of that in my head."

"He clearly implies that Meredith was dangerous, as Faith was more dangerous, but the tone also implies that he had Meredith under control."

"It's almost impossible for me to conceive of my father paying someone off. But the evidence supports just that."

He refills his glass. "What if he was getting something in exchange?"

"But what?"

"Ownership of the winery?"

"Faith would have had to sign off on that," I remind him.

"Thus, she was a problem," he says. "Or more dangerous to his plan than her mother. He had Meredith pinned down but not Faith."

"But the bills were not being paid," I argue. "Meredith received a million dollars from my father and allowed a section of the vines to go untreated and therefore become damaged."

He thrums his fingers on the counter. "Could she have been trying to get Faith to sell? You know, making it seem that the winery wasn't worth owning?"

"Faith was working at the winery. She knew how well it was doing."

"And yet the bills weren't being paid?" he confirms.

"Correct," I say, "and finally, after trying to get her mother to come clean with her about what was happening, and failing, Faith took action. She hired an attorney and tried to take the winery from her mother."

"I can't say that I blame her. What was her mother's response?"

"She hired my father, who nickel-and-dimed Faith into giving up."

"I'm not sure that disproves my theory about Meredith wanting her to sell. Did she ever directly ask Faith to sell?"

"My understanding," I say, "is yes. But all of this gets more interesting. I paid the bank off. You know that. And they still plan to hold up the execution of Meredith's will while they get the property appraised."

"Ouch. That's not good. They have to have a document that says if it's under the value of the note, they can take it," he agrees. "Which would make anyone who signed that agreement royally stupid, but it happens."

"Obviously I get my own appraisal, but why would the bank want a property that is under the value of the note anyway?"

"And why would your father want it?" He doesn't wait for a reply. "There's something about that property. Something that got your father and her mother killed."

"I agree wholeheartedly," I say, sticking the note back in my briefcase. "And I'd get my bank to buy out her note, but obviously, the bank isn't going to let that happen if they feel they may own it outright, and with some back-end benefit we don't know about."

"You can try," he says. "But you'll have to disclose the bank's intent to have the property assessed."

"Agreed," I say, aware of the liability doing otherwise could incur.

"What does Faith think about all of this?"

"She doesn't have the luxury of knowing that my father and her mother are linked to truly evaluate the situation as we do."

"Tell her."

"If I tell her, she kicks me to the curb and I can't protect her."

"What *does* she know at this point?"

"She knows that my father represented her mother and that her mother was involved with him."

"Well then. Both of them are dead and connected. Use that to convince her to exhume her mother's body."

"I'm not lying to her any more than I have to. And that plan would lead me to more lies."

"Then just talk about her mother. Someone wants the winery. Her mother is dead. Have her do an autopsy."

I shake my head and refill my coffee cup. "Negative again. I'm not putting her through that hell unless my father's autopsy is suspicious. If there's nothing to find in his reports, we won't find anything in her mother's."

"While I agree," he says, "time is critical when a killer is on the loose, and when does that killer turn to Faith or even you?"

"That PI I hired has someone watching Faith."

"Does she know he's watching her?"

"No."

"Damn, man. I get it. All of it. I know why you can't tell her, but I don't envy you the moment she finds out. Especially the part where you sought her out and fucked her to prove she was a killer."

He left off the part where I wanted to ruin her. And I have to confess everything to her, in some brilliant way that convinces her I'm not her enemy. In fact, I am the man whose bed and life may never be the same again without her.

CHAPTER SEVEN

Faith

I killed her.

I blink awake with my confession to Nick in my mind, the scent of him surrounding me, his bed cushioning me. The taste of the rich whiskey I drank with him is still on my tongue, but it does nothing to erase the bitterness of those words or the way I feel them deep in my gut. I wait for the regret over telling Nick to follow, but it doesn't exist. I didn't plan to bare my soul to Nick, but I did, and the fact that I felt that I could, especially with my history with Macom and my mother, brings one word to mind: *Possibilities.* Considering Nick and I started with a vow for one night, the place we've landed is pretty incredible. And scary. Because I really am naked and exposed with this man. That means vulnerability. That means he could hurt me.

Oddly, my fear of him hurting me served as a mechanism to push me to trust him more. The minute he'd told me he'd paid my debt, I'd panicked. I was feeling emotionally exposed, and then he claimed control over the winery situation that I had failed to control myself. He'd been generous, protective—a hero, even—but unknowingly, he'd shifted the financial dynamic between us to resemble the one I'd shared with Macom. The next thing I knew, I was throwing out the "I killed her" statement and, in hindsight, wanting Nick to prove he wasn't worthy of my trust. Wanting Nick to judge me the way I was judging me.

And it had not only been a beautiful failure, it led me to share more of myself with Nick. He understood my choices and, I think, believed them to be more right than I do, even approving of my decision to try to take the winery from my mother. Unbidden, that thought has my mind trying to skip over Nick and go back to that night when my mother died. It is not a gentle memory, and I reject it, throwing off the blanket and sitting up, swinging my legs to the floor, feet settling on the ground. I really need my feet on the ground, but it's not enough to keep the past at bay.

I'm there, living it, my fingers curling on the edge of Nick's mattress, my eyes shutting as I return to the winery and that brutal night. I'd just finished being humiliated by a bill collector in front of several staff members. Furious, I'd sought out my mother and found her in her gardens on her knees, fussing over the ground around a cluster of some sort of white flowers. And the past is so vivid right now that I can almost smell the flowers, bitter and sweet in the same inhaled breath.

"Where is the money, Mother?" I demand.

Of course, she knows what I'm talking about but chooses to play dumb, glancing up at me and saying, "What are we talking about, dear?" which only serves to infuriate me more.

"Where is all the money we're making?"

She pushes to her feet, pulling off her gloves, her hands settling on her slender blue jean–clad hips. "You need to go back to L.A. and let Macom take care of you, because you clearly cannot handle the pressure here. And this is my winery anyway."

"It will be mine one day, and I'll inherit the debt and problems you're creating."

"Oh, so that's it?" she demands. "This is all about protecting your money. Wouldn't your father be proud? You finally give a damn about the winery, and it's about money."

"I have no choice but to care about the debts I will inherit."

"Like I said," she bites out. "Go back to your rich artist boyfriend and let him take care of you. This is my world, not yours. I bet your father turned over in his grave when you sued me."

"He's in his grave because you fucked my uncle and everyone else who would have you."

She laughs. "You didn't even know your father," she says. "He liked watching me with other men."

"He did not," I spit back. "He did not."

"He did," she insists, turning away from me, and she seems to take a step forward before she falls face-first into all of those dozens of white flowers.

My thoughts shift at that point to the place they always go after that memory: the funeral, and, as expected, the grave site, and the final goodbye. *There are rows of filled seats surrounding me, people lined up beside and behind me while rain splatters down atop a sea of umbrellas. Appropriate, actually, since my mother loved the rain. It also saves me when I didn't save her, because no one knows that I'm not crying. But I know. I know so many things I don't want anyone else to know. Like the fact that as the preacher speaks, I'm wondering how many of the random men here slept with my mother. And how many did my father know, too? Did he like to watch? God. Is that why he tolerated her?*

I shiver, wishing I had a jacket, my thin black dress doing little to offer me shelter. There just isn't shelter I can find anywhere. My grip tightens on the umbrella I'm holding, which someone gave me. I don't know who. I don't even remember how it got into my hand. I just keep remembering the moments before my mother had died. The speech and time tick on for what feels like an eternity, while time has now ended for my mother and my father. I'm alone in this world, and as the rain begins to fall with a fierceness rarely rivaled, the crowd scatters; a few people try to speak to me, but soon, I am alone here, too.

Everyone is gone, and I walk to the casket and just stare at it. I go back to then, to those moments in time, reliving the fight with my mother, the moment she'd tumbled forward. My knees are weak, and so is my arm, and I can't seem to hold on to it. I don't want to hold it anymore, so I don't. I just can't. I drop to the ground and let the force of the rain hit me, my black dress instantly wet, my hair...

"Faith."

At the sound of my name, I turn, and Josh stands there. "Josh? How are you here?"

"I wanted to be here for you."

"Where's Macom?"

"I'm sorry, Faith. He's not coming."

"Good," I say, "I told him not to come. I don't want him here." *And knowing how he operates all too well, I add,* "Being my agent doesn't require that you do funeral duty. I don't like that kind of plastic friendship, and I don't want it in my life or career."

"Faith—"

"Go home, Josh," *I say, and, needing to escape the obligatory sympathy from him and everyone else, I start to run toward my car.*

My cellphone rings, jerking me back to the present, and I grab it to ironically discover Macom's number on caller ID, feeling as if I've willed a ghost of my past into the present. I hit decline, noting this as his third call, and I really want to block the number. I'm about to do just that when my cell rings in my hand, and this time it's Josh's number. I answer immediately: "Why is my agent calling me on a Sunday?"

"To tell you not to answer Macom's call."

"You're a little late, since he's called three times."

"Holy hell. Please tell me he didn't get in your head about the L.A. Forum show."

"I didn't talk to him," I say, well aware of why he is concerned, since Macom pretty much declared my work an embarrassment the last time I wanted to submit. To protect me, of course. "And even if I had, I'm in the show."

"And I'd prefer you get there feeling confident."

"Why exactly is Macom calling me?"

"To give you advice you don't need."

My mind goes back two years, to me standing in my workspace, in the home I'd shared with Macom, while I'd proudly revealed new paintings. Certain that my work on the three pieces would finally capture the L.A. Forum's attention.

"*Stunning,*" *Josh had said, motioning to a Sonoma mountain shot I'd so loved. "This one," he'd said. "It's one of your best yet."*

"*Absolutely not,*" *Macom had said, shoving his hand through his spiky dark brown hair before motioning to the three paintings. "These are not what they're looking for. None of them. You'll look like a fool."*

The words had been like knives in my heart, and I'd instantly doubted myself, questioning why I was even picking up a paintbrush any longer.

"*I respectfully disagree,*" *Josh had argued, daring to go against his moneymaker Macom.*

Macom's gray eyes had flashed. "Who is the star of that show for the second year running? Not my fucking agent, I'll tell you that. I'll help Faith pick her submission."

"Faith?"

At the sound of Josh's voice, I snap back to the present. "He doesn't get to shove me back down a rabbit hole, Josh," I say vehemently. "I'm not that girl anymore. I was never that girl. I was simply lost in Macom's translation."

"Yet you let him choose your show submissions over and over, and you received a rejection in response over and over."

I think back to every rejection I'd gotten and Macom's replayed response: *It doesn't matter, baby. Paint for you, not them. I pay the bills. You don't need them. You have me.* Like I didn't need my own success because I had his.

"That man shuts you down," Josh adds. "You didn't paint after you left him. Not until a few days ago."

"Because I wasn't going to paint until it was for me again," I say.

"And if he gets in your head again, how long will it be before you get there again?"

"I'm past him. And this show is for me."

"And what about Nick Rogers?"

I frown. "What about him?"

"Is he still distracting you?"

"You mean inspiring me?"

"I take that as a yes. And I thought you were painting for you?"

"I am."

"And yet, one man convinced you to stop painting. Another convinced you to paint again."

That assessment hits me hard. "That's not—"

"I need to know that you're a painter no matter who is in your life or what is going on in your life." His line beeps, and he curses. "Macom's calling me. I'll handle him. You avoid him. And paint. Fuck the winery, Faith. Be a damn painter." He ends the call, and I grimace. Fuck the winery. He knows I can't do that, not with the money connected to it, but it doesn't matter to him. It's not his money. My art could be. It's a thought that reminds me that Nick understands why I can't walk away from the winery, and yet, he pushes me to embrace my art.

Glancing at the time on my phone, I suddenly realize I've been sleeping for two hours when I'm supposed to fly home today. I grab my boots, and my head spins while my stomach growls. I'm not drunk, but I'm not myself, and I don't like it. There is enough spinning out of control in my life without me drinking myself there, too. But then, doesn't the fact that I let this happen here with Nick say trust? On a core level, I didn't even recognize until today that I trust Nick. I'm not sure who I said that about last.

Finishing the task of pulling on my boots, I stand up, testing my footing, and decide that I'm light-headed but otherwise really okay. I walk to the bathroom to pee and fix my face, frustrated as my conversation with Josh replays in my mind, as does the memory of Macom that Josh had brought forth. And suddenly, I need to see Nick. I need to feel the connection I have with him, the trust. And the minute he touches me or kisses me or simply looks at me, I will.

CHAPTER EIGHT

Faith

On my quest to find Nick, I quickly make my way through the bedroom to the hallway. I head down the stairs, only to grab the railing with the queasy, dizzy sensation called foolishly drinking syndrome, which I'm fairly certain is a real medical term. Or perhaps it's the kind of college kid I never was and am not now, thus should not be using in my life—ever. A thought that has me taking slow, cautious steps down to the first level of stairs to ensure I don't tumble downward.

My feet are thankfully still on solid ground as I reach the platform below and turn the corner to take the second level of steps. Instead, I find myself halting at the sight of Nick and another thirty-something man, with buzz-cut blond hair, sitting at the island bar, both with files and computers in front of them. Aware that I'm about to interrupt their obvious work session, I fully intend to sneak back up the steps, but instead, I find myself staring at Nick. There's something inherently sexy about the way his brown hair tied at his nape, his high cheekbones, and his full mouth come together to accentuate his masculine beauty. The man literally oozes power and arrogance, reminding me that he is all about control. All qualities that remind me of Macom and my mother in different ways, and that I swore I never wanted in my life again. And yet, Nick might as well be a drug and me an addict, because I am officially incapable of walking away. Some might even call my attraction to him a form of self-destruction, and yet, Nick is more than the sum of those descriptive words. He's become the wings in the wind of change for me. The one person in my life who has ever truly lifted me up.

Shaking myself, I take a step backward, but the stranger with Nick sits at the end cap of the island facing me, and suddenly, his gaze lifts and lands on me. Nick follows his visitor's lead, his attention immediately rocketing to me as well, and when his gaze meets mine, I forget leaving. I forget the stranger. There is just this man taking my life by storm in all the right ways, and that connection we share that I was looking for. The bond I am now certain that we've shared in different incarnations since the moment we tangled words in my mother's gardens, our connection intense and fierce even then.

"Faith," he says, pushing to his feet, his voice warm, welcoming, the look in his eyes hot. "Join us."

"No," I say, holding up my hands. "Keep doing what you're doing. I just wanted you to know that I was going to do some painting." But he has already stuffed documents into his briefcase and shut the lid, and he is now crossing the room toward me, his stride long, confident. Everything about this man is powerful, intense. Riveting.

"I'm going to go paint," I say again, hurrying to meet him at the bottom of the steps. "I can tell you're working, and I didn't mean to—"

He pulls me to him and kisses me, his really wonderfully hard body absorbing the softer lines of mine. "Don't do that," he orders softly, a rough, intimate quality to his voice.

"Do what?"

"Act like you don't belong here, because you do. And since you obviously don't know that yet, I've got work to do. Abel's a close friend, of which I have few. I wanted you two to meet. And we ordered pizza with the intent of waking you up to join us."

"You did?"

"Yes," he confirms. "We did. How do you feel?"

"Unsteady," I admit, my hands on his upper arms. "I don't know what I was thinking, drinking like that."

"I'd like to think that you trusted that you were here with me, and safe." He caresses my hair behind my ear. "If you fall, I promise I'll catch you."

"You already did," I say, my hand flattening on his chest, my mind reflecting on the secret I sense in him and trying to understand when I paint him. "I'll catch you, too. You know that, right?"

His gaze sharpens and then darkens, a hint of that secret flickering in his eyes, here and gone in a few flashed seconds. "I'll hold you to that," he says softly, but I sense the wall he now throws up, even as he twines the fingers of one of his hands with mine. "Come sit down and meet Abel."

He attempts to put us in motion while I dig in my heels. "I'm not myself right now."

"I'm half a bottle in," Abel calls out, and Nick rotates to stand by my side, allowing us both to spy the bottle in Abel's hand. "We'll be speaking the same language, Faith," he assures me.

Nick glances at me. "He's an attorney," he explains. "And he just won a big case that he wishes he had lost."

My brow furrows. "He wanted to lose a case?"

"I did not want to lose my damn case," Abel grumbles. "I win. That's what I do."

"All right, then," Nick says drily. "Pizza for you both, and no more whiskey." And this time, he doesn't give me time to object. His arm slides around my shoulders as he sets us back in motion. I can't help but think that Abel and I oddly have similar reasons for drinking. He had an obligation to save a client who perhaps didn't deserve to be saved, much the same as what I felt with my mother.

"How are you this clearheaded?" I ask as we round the counter and Nick pulls out the barstool for me that sits between his spot and Abel's. "Didn't you drink with both of us?"

"I drank a pot of coffee," he explains, indicating the thermal pot on the counter as we both claim our seats.

"He drank his No. 6 with you," Abel comments, sounding less

than pleased. "My bottle is beneath him, and for the record, you better be damn special to score the No. 6 over me."

"Perhaps he needed No. 6 to deal with my version of crazy today," I rebut, with the full intention of dodging an awkward bullet.

He laughs and glances at Nick. "Quick-witted. I like that."

"Until she outwits you—and she will," Nick assures him.

"Game on," Abel says, glancing at me. "You know this now, but to make it official, I'm Abel. Especially when I'm not drinking."

I laugh, finding Abel—the official or not-so-official version—easy to like. "You're pretty humorous, Abel, especially when you're not drinking."

"A perfectly acceptable assessment," he says, "unless it's next week when I'm in court."

"Ah well," I say. "You might not be funny at all. I'm pretty sure I'm easily amused right now, considering my alcohol intolerance."

"That's a horrible condition, I hear," he says, refilling his glass. "Thank God I don't have it."

"As you can see," Nick interjects. "He's a phone book of bad jokes, sadly, even when he's not drinking."

"My jokes amuse people with a sense of humor," Abel comments drily, glancing at me. "In case you haven't noticed yet, Faith, Nick doesn't have one of those."

"You know what they say," Nick replies. "If you can't be the good-looking one, be the funny one."

Abel snorts. "If you are implying you're the good-looking one, then you drank more than I realized."

Nick offers me his cup in response. "Drink this. None of us need to numb our brains to the kind of stupid Abel's attempting."

Smiling at the banter between these two, and also eager to put the whiskey behind me, I sip Nick's coffee, regretting it as the bitterness hits my tongue. "Oh God," I murmur, unable to control the intense grimace on my face. "That is horrible." Both men laugh fairly ferociously, and I shoot glowers between them.

"It's not funny. That might be poison. I don't know how anyone drinks that."

"It's called lots of long work nights and building tolerance," Nick says. "You'd be surprised how good bad can taste when you need to stay awake and focused." His cellphone rings where it rests on the counter.

He grabs it and glances at the caller ID, his jaw setting hard as he stands back up. "I need to take this." Apparently, that translates to alone, because he's already exiting the kitchen.

"And then there were two," Abel says dramatically, pattering fingers on the table, as if creating music. "Don't worry," he adds. "I do awkward small talk better than the average guy. For instance, I hear you're not only an artist but that you made a big sale last night. Congrats."

"Thank you," I say, feeling a bit taken aback and awkward that he knows about my payday. "I guess Nick has been talking."

"Bragging," he says.

A warm spot forms in my chest with the realization that Nick doesn't just support me when he's with me, but even when he is not. "That's nice to hear."

"Nice," he repeats. "Nice and Nick don't really want to compute for me, but maybe it's the whiskey. What are you going to do to celebrate your payday?"

Pay back Nick a chunk of the money he paid the bank, I think, but that's none of his business, so I settle on a generic, "Pay bills."

"Huh. A new car or even shoes would be a sexy celebration. Bills. Not so sexy."

"Sexy has never been on the top of my priority list," I say. "And paying bills is much sexier than not paying bills."

"That's true," he says. "And I'm sure Nick will help you celebrate anyway."

"He did that by being with me at the gallery last night."

He arches a brow. "And gave you a gift, I assume? The man is rolling in money, which I'm sure you know."

A fizzle of unease slides through me. "I know he has money."

"A lot of money," Abel pushes. "You know that, right?"

"He told me," I say, my discomfort growing exponentially, as does my regret over the whiskey that still has me feeling less than sharp.

"Did he?" Abel asks in what feels like feigned surprise. "Huh. He usually doesn't share details because, you know, everyone wants something from him." He stares me down, all signs of humor gone now, his green eyes cold, hard, as he adds, "Do you?"

CHAPTER NINE

Faith

blanch at Abel's question and obvious accusation, but I recover quickly. "That's direct," I say, realizing what should have been obvious. He's sizing me up, looking for the vulture in a butterfly's clothing.

"Do you have a problem with direct?"

"Actually, I prefer it," I say. "Namely because I dislike secrets. So, to answer your question: yes. I want *many* things from Nick, but none of those things include his money." I think of my fake friends back in L.A. who turned out to be all about Macom and his fame, which spurs me to add, "And for the record, I find the idea of a friend who wants to protect him enviable."

Surprise flickers in his eyes, and when I believe he's about to reply, Nick reappears. "What's enviable?" he asks, claiming the stool next to me again.

"My hot body," Abel says, holding out his hands to his sides. "Which is why I stay single. I need to spread the wealth." The doorbell rings, and he is on his feet in an instant. "I'll get that," he announces, already walking toward the door.

"He's a piece of work," Nick says, and we face each other as he adds, "but I'm sure you figured that out."

"I did," I say. "But I think I might like him."

"Think?"

"I'll decide after I have more food than whiskey in me," I reply, appreciating Abel's loyalty to Nick but not necessarily his approach in showing it. "Do you two work together?" I ask.

"No," he says, "but we run cases by each other with surprisingly good results, considering our fields of expertise."

"You trust him," I observe.

"I call no one that I can't trust a friend."

A comment that brings my little chat with Abel full circle. "Because everyone must want something from you."

His hand settles on my leg. "Where did that just come from, Faith?"

"The number that represents your holdings," I say. "It's rather sobering, quite literally."

"Most people would find it intriguing."

"I'm not most people, Nick."

"With that," he says, "I would agree."

"Money changes people."

"I've had money all my life, sweetheart. Adding a few extra zeroes isn't a character-changing event for me."

"I get that," I say. "But just as money can make the holder less than genuine in many ways, it makes those around the money holder tend to be less than genuine. Nick, I don't want your money."

His eyes, which are always so damn hard, soften. "I know that, Faith," he says, seeming to understand that I'm speaking beyond the bank note.

"If anything, your money makes me nervous. It makes me—" I stop myself before I head down a path that leads to Macom and is better traveled when we're alone. "You have to know that I can't—"

Nick's hand goes to my face, and suddenly his cheek is pressed to mine, his lips at my ear. "*We* can, Faith," he says softly, leaning back to look at me; our eyes lock and hold; I feel the deep pull between us. "Together, remember?"

"Yes, but—"

"No buts," he says.

"Nick—"

"Faith."

"We aren't done with this, Nick Rogers," I warn.

"You most certainly are for now," Abel says, setting the pizzas on the counter. "Eyes on the guest and the food, people."

Nick lifts his brows at me, offering me the power of decision: do I push for a talk I can't really have in front of Abel or cave to the scent of spicy cheese goodness currently teasing my nostrils? The spicy cheese goodness wins. I rotate to face Abel, who rewards my attention by opening a box to display an impressive-looking pepperoni pizza. My stomach growls again, and I decide this delicious, calorie-laden lunch will either grow the brain cells I will need to negotiate a proper financial outcome with Nick "Tiger" Rogers or put me back to sleep, but the latter is a risk I will have to take.

Ten minutes later, we remain at the island, all with bottles of water and paper plates piled with slices of pizza in front of us. "How do you two know each other?" I ask, and one slice into my meal, I'm already feeling sharper and far more present in the conversation.

"We met in law school," Nick offers, his answer seemingly simple, when I've come to know that there is nothing simple about Nick Rogers.

Or silent about Abel, I'm learning, as he adds, "A long-ass time ago. Fourteen years ago?"

"I got my tattoos in July of 2003, and we met that week," Nick says. "So yes. That would be fourteen years ago." He glances at me. "Which I remember because he talked the entire damn time."

"Offering moral support when he almost backed out," Abel interjects. "You know the whole 'don't be a wuss' kind of support, though that wasn't the exact word I used."

"He's a big talker in every possible way," Nick says, holding out his bare forearms to display the black-and-orange tiger etched on one and the words "An eye for an eye" on the other. A phrase that I hate, and that still isn't about him to me. I'm not sure it can ever be about him. "Two tattoos," Nick continues. "Ask Abel how many he got while talking big? None. He was afraid it would hurt."

"It's a good thing you two aren't competitive or anything," I say drily. "Or else you might be enemies."

"Speaking of enemies," Nick says, shoving aside his plate. "Let's get serious and talk about the winery."

I stiffen instantly. "What are you doing, Nick?"

"Abel knows what's going on at the winery," he says, and before I can even register my shock at this announcement, he adds, "and he knows this because I've asked him to protect you from me."

I face Nick, my feet suddenly unsteady again, and I haven't even stood up yet. "What is this?"

"I promised you paperwork that protects you and the winery. And that needs to come from another attorney, who could be disbarred if he helped me deceive you."

His friend, who just not-so-subtly accused me of using him for his money. "I'm giving you my check from last night," I say. "That covers sixty thousand of the money I now owe you. After the L.A. Forum in a few weeks, I should be able to pay back the rest."

"You owe me nothing," Nick says, "which is exactly what Abel is going to guarantee."

"Abel doesn't decide this," I retort. "And neither do you. I'm paying you back."

"We can talk later," Nick states. "Let Abel do his part in this now."

"Abel's been drinking," I argue.

"Abel's had half a pizza," Abel says. "He's good. You can ask him yourself, though, if you prefer."

I inhale and face him, shoving my plate aside as I do. "I appreciate your efforts, but—"

"But I'm Nick's friend," Abel supplies, wrongly assuming, at least partially, he knows where my head is at right now. "Legally," he continues, "once you sign this document"—he sets a piece of paper in front of me—"I'm your attorney before I'm his friend." He taps the document. "It's an offer of representation. And for the record, I might be a criminal attorney, but I had a few years of corporate experience right out of college, and I spend a hell of a lot of time with Nick Rogers' cases. I know how to protect you."

"Nick's the one who needs to be protected," I argue. "He paid six figures on my behalf."

"That he doesn't want back," Abel replies, the simple statement contradicting his earlier tone, and I don't like it.

"How," I challenge, "can you possibly back up that thought process when you just implied that I want his money?"

"He did what?" Nick demands. "What the fuck, Abel?"

"I didn't imply you want his money," Abel bites out, ignoring Nick. "I was reading you, just like I do anyone who wants my representation."

"Except I didn't want your representation," I counter. "And I don't appreciate being read like a criminal using Nick for his money."

"And if I believed that now," Abel says, "I would have talked some sense into Nick and declined to offer you representation."

"Let me get this straight," I say, my temper flaring, my tone controlled but biting. "A few minutes ago I was a low-down dirty user, and now I'm worthy of your services?" I don't give either man time to say anything else. "That's it. I need out of here." I slide off my barstool, but Nick catches my arms.

"This is not the time to hold on to me, Nick," I warn, my gaze rocketing to his, the charge between us ever present, but this time the heat between us is my anger.

"This is exactly the time to hold on to you," he argues. "It's Sunday. We need these contracts signed by tomorrow morning."

My gaze rockets to his. "Then you give them to me."

"Abel's involvement not only protects you, it lawyers us up even further with the bank."

"You said my actions were enviable," Abel points out. "And I'm as good an attorney as I am a friend."

Angry all over again, I pull away from Nick and turn back to Abel. "It *was* enviable," I say. "But so is honesty, and your behavior with me was not honest."

"You're right," Abel surprises me by admitting. "And first and foremost you need to know that my actions were mine and mine alone." He eyes Nick, who is now standing beside me. "Nick did not know what I was doing." He looks between us now. "But that said, I won't apologize to either of you. Considering our timeline, I had to make a decision on where I stood in my involvement now, not later. And I'm all in." He refocuses on me. "And that's the case for you as well, Faith, which is why I've prepared some guarantees for you."

He reaches in his briefcase, pulls out a folder, and sets one sheet of paper on top of the representation letter, then creates two more stacks. "Start here," he says, indicating his offer letter. "I contacted your estate attorney, and without disclosing details, aside from my intent to aid Nick in your protection, I asked him to endorse the protection my agreement offers you. He not only read my representation offer, he scanned it back to me with a handwritten note to you that stamps it with his approval." He shuffles the papers and shows me the note, which reads: *Faith—this agreement ensures Abel's legal obligation to protect your interests and privacy. It's a sound document.*

"Sign the agreement," Abel says, "and I'm now loyal to you first and Nick second."

"Questions?" Nick asks, his hands settling back on my leg.

"Not about this," I say, my hand waving over the rest of the paperwork. "What is the rest of this?"

Abel indicates the second stack of documents, which is actually not a stack but one form. "Before I explain what this is," he says, "let me explain why it's important to you. When someone gives you a lump sum of money for a business interest, they could later claim it was with the promise of something in exchange."

"Even without a signed document?"

"Yes," Nick states. "Because a verbal agreement is binding, and it would be my word against yours, and I have the money to fight you on it."

"But that can't happen with this document in place," Abel interjects, "as it clearly states that the money he's given you is a gift, and it cannot be treated as leverage against you for any monetary gain. In other words, he can't claim it was a down payment on the winery, meant to kick in after you inherit. Additionally, the legal verbiage assures that this contract supersedes all others."

"Meaning," Nick says, "that nothing can be signed after the fact that voids its content."

"An important factor, since this final document," Abel says, indicating the last stack of papers, "requires one hell of a thought of trust. This is the dummy document that will be shown to the bank and in court, which gives Nick half ownership of the winery once you inherit."

This isn't news to me. Nick warned me this was coming, despite not warning me about Abel. I trust Nick. So why, right now, in this moment, are there warning bells going off in my head? Maybe it's Abel. I don't know him. Nick sideswiped me with his involvement. That has to be it, but as Nick's hand comes down on my shoulder and he softly says my name, I still find myself back at the art show where Nick and I had first connected, replaying a conversation about secrets that I'd had with him there.

"People have secrets, Faith," Nick says. "It's part of being human."

"My mother sure did," I reply.

His hands find my waist, turning me to face him, intensity radiating off him. "What kind of secrets, Faith?"

"Her kind of secrets," I reply, not sure why he is suddenly so very intense. "Like you have secrets," I add, using his nickname: "Tiger."

"My enemies call me Tiger. You call me Nick."

"Why do I keep feeling like you're the enemy?"

"Why are you looking for an enemy?"

I return to the present and ask myself that very question: Why am I looking for an enemy? *Am I looking for an enemy?* And if so, who is it that I don't trust? Nick? Abel? It has to be Abel. I've already established that I trust Nick. And he's earned that trust. He wouldn't lie to me. He wouldn't deceive me. And if he trusts Abel, I trust Abel.

So why am I still so uneasy?

CHAPTER TEN

Nick

Seconds tick by as Faith stares down at the documents Abel has given her, no words, no action, but I sense that wall of hers slamming into place. "Let us have a few minutes," I order Abel.

"No," Faith says quickly. "I have questions."

"As you should," Abel says. "We can go through every line of the documents one by one."

"I'll read them myself," she says. "These questions are not questions that these documents can answer." She looks between us. "For starters, I want to verify that we're all on the same page I believe us to be on. That page being that the bank would not be ordering a property assessment if they didn't believe it would somehow allow them to stake a claim on the deed. Correct?"

"Correct," Abel confirms.

"That's the assumption we're operating under," I add. "And while my preferred method of operation is not to assume anything, winning is about being a step ahead of our opposition. Which is also why I called my personal banker today and have him on standby to buy out your note."

Her eyes go wide. "At what cost to you?"

"Nothing outside of paying for a rushed property assessment of our own."

"We can't use the current one?"

"If my bank finds out your bank is questioning the property value and we don't disclose that, we're looking at a fraud situation."

"Right," she says. "That makes sense." She moves on. "And if that assessment comes back under the value of the current note?"

she asks. "Can we use the revenue the winery produces to justify the new note? I have that well documented."

"We not only can," I say, "we will. But set that aside, and let's talk about the worst-case scenario: my banker makes an offer, and they decline."

Her brow furrows. "Why would they do that?"

"That's our question," Abel says. "What do they know that we don't, beyond any piece of paper?"

Faith gives him a puzzled look. "I don't follow where you're going with this."

"Where's the money?" I supply. "What makes the winery or something connected to it worth money outside the obvious? Do you have any idea?"

She shakes her head. "None. And by *none* I mean that I'm a complete zero on this entire premise. That said, if that were true—if there is some hidden treasure, be it literal or not—the bank will fight hard, and that doesn't bode well for the outcome we're after. Which brings me to another question." She picks up the dummy document and focuses on me. "If you present this and the bank legally claims the winery, are you left with any liability?"

"No," I say. "I am not."

"Okay," she says. "Then can you use that dummy document to force them to pay you back the money you paid on not just my behalf but that of the winery?"

"I'd demand they compensate both myself and you," I reply, "and for all the monies paid on behalf of the rightful owner of the winery. And because under that treasure scenario, the bank would just want us to go away, I believe they'd settle with us. But we're a long way from that point."

"Nick's the expert here," Abel says. "I believe there would be a case to prove deceptive practices, among other charges, and force the bank's hand into backing off. But we have to find the proverbial treasure."

"Which is why, among other things," I reply, "that we have a private investigator working on this."

"The private investigator that you're paying," Faith says, gathering up the documents and turning her attention to Abel. "I'll read these and let you know if I have questions."

"This is time sensitive," Abel says before I have the chance. "Let's read through them together."

"Nick needs them by morning," she says. "It's afternoon. And I need two things from you. One is your fee agreement. I need to know how much you charge, so that I can budget to pay you."

"I've been paid," he states.

"By Nick."

"Not with cash," he clarifies.

"He's been paid, Faith," I reiterate.

She ignores me. "Please put together a bill," she says again. "And additionally, I need a contract that states that I will pay Nick back any and all money he spends on my behalf with fifteen percent interest."

My jaw clenches. "Faith—"

"And," she continues as if I have not spoken, "if I do not do so in a year, he receives thirty percent interest in the winery. There will need to be a financial ledger."

"He's not going to do that, Faith," I say.

She rotates to face me. "He is, or he isn't my attorney but yours, and I'm not protected at all."

"Don't be stubborn."

She looks at Abel. "I need those documents." She holds up the paperwork in her hand. "And I'm going upstairs to read these in detail."

"My cellphone number and email are on the offer letter," Abel says, drawing her attention again. "Email me and text me so that I have your contact information to get you those documents. And you can give Nick the signed documents, but if you have questions or concerns, text me, email me, call me. Whatever works for you, but do it this evening."

My cellphone rings, and I glance at the number to find Beck is calling for the second time in forty-five minutes, and just that fast, Faith has darted around me and is walking away. I hit the decline button and take a step in Faith's direction.

"Wait," Abel orders harshly, his tone insistent, his hands coming down on the counter. "Don't go after her yet."

"Now is not the time for whatever you plan to say," I say, taking another step, but he doesn't take "no" for an answer.

"Damn it, Nick," he growls. "*Wait.*"

With agitated reluctance, I halt, facing him, my gaze pinning his. "Now is not the time," I bite out again, "for whatever it is you want to say."

"Quite the contrary," he assures me. "It's the exact right time, considering you're about to go upstairs and bulldoze Faith. Let her do what she feels she needs to do."

"You're supposed to be working for *her*. Do that. Protect her, not me."

"I am working for her," he says. "Which is why I repeat: don't be a bull charging at her. If you—"

"I don't want her money."

"I know that," he says. "I get that. So does she." He grimaces. "Look, man. You don't deal with death with your job the way I do. I see how it impacts people. It steals your control. It makes you need to find it in other places, and finding it is part of healing."

"Death has nothing to do with this, Abel. Again. For the third time. Now is not—"

"Death *is* a part of this," he presses. "You both are dealing with its biting impact on your lives."

"There is no biting impact for me. I hated my father."

"And yet, despite hating your father, you had to solve the mystery of his death. Open your eyes and recognize how much you both need control right now. Because if you don't find a way to give Faith some of what you want to take, she will push back and perhaps even push you away."

I run a hand over my face, begrudgingly admitting that he's making sense. "Fuck," I grind out, stepping to the opposite end of the table from him and pressing my hands to the island. "Fuck. Fuck. Fuck."

"Go talk to her," he says. "But don't bulldoze her with your money or even with good intentions. It will make her feel unsettled. It will push her away, and frankly, if she was willing to just take your money, I'd be concerned. I *was* concerned until I met her and she stepped up to do the right thing."

"I want—"

"Her," he supplies. "I see that. But money doesn't buy love or anyone worth having. Providing that paperwork to her proved to her that you're honorable. The fact that she didn't just accept the money proves she is as well. That's not a bad thing, and neither is her having enough pride to want to pay her own way."

"I told you—"

"Even if," he continues, "you buy her a diamond the size of Texas and a wardrobe to match."

"Where *the fuck* did that come from?"

"You," he says. "It came from watching you with her and for years without her. And on a side note, you have an excuse for not telling her about most of this, which is for her safety. You don't have that excuse with the club. Obviously not now, but if you wait too long, that is going to bite you in your ass, which is already in deep shit."

He starts walking toward the door, and I don't move, his warnings radiating through me, as well as his comment about Faith and a ring. I have never considered myself a marrying man, and even if I did, the mountains I have to climb with Faith are many. The club matters. The truth about how I found her matters. Her safety comes first. And right now, I need to make sure that while I'm trying to destroy our enemies, I don't destroy us in the process.

Feeling the urgency of that need, I start walking, double-stepping the stairs, telling myself Faith trusts me. She told me about her mother's death, but did that come from a place of trust or guilt? Fuck. I need her to trust me. If she doesn't now, she damn sure won't when she hears about the club, let alone how I found her. Reaching the second level, I enter the bedroom, and Faith isn't in sight. Continuing on to the bathroom, I find her suitcase open on the floor. She's exiting the closet with her clothes in hand. "I need to go home." Her announcement proves that the control I seek is not mine.

"We talked about this," I say. "You're staying, and we're going back at the end of the week together."

"*You* talked about this," she says. "While I was drinking."

"The contracts—"

"I can read them on the plane and scan them back to you."

"I want you to stay, Faith."

She zips her suitcase and stands up. "I'm going to be honest with you, Nick, because you know: no one in my life has been honest with me, and I really need honest things in my life right now."

Holy hell. She's killing me. I take a step toward her. She backs up and holds up a hand. "Stop. When you touch me, I get more confused."

"Confused," I repeat. "That's what my touch makes you feel?"

"I can't think when you touch me, Nick."

"And that's a problem? Because I can promise you that if you can do a mathematical equation while a man is touching you, he's the wrong man. I'm not the wrong man."

"You can't just spend a hundred and twenty thousand dollars on me, Nick. Or more. You want to spend more." She presses her hand to her forehead. "I appreciate what you've done. You are acting like a hero, and I know in my heart that's your intent."

"And you don't want a hero."

"That's not it. I mean, no. I don't, but I'm not going to be foolish and not see that I'm pretty lucky to have one in you right now. But Nick. We decided on possibilities based on who we are together.

And I like who we are together so far."

"But?" I prod.

"Money changes people."

"I told you. I've had money all my life."

"I'm not talking about you alone."

"You think it changes us," I supply.

"Of course it changes us."

My mind tracks back to the references she's made to her ex's fame and stature. "I'm not Macom."

"I know that," she says, folding her arms in front of her. "I do. But I'm still being honest. Once he paid all the bills and made a ton of money, I was subservient to him in ways I should never have allowed myself to be."

"Again. I'm not Macom, but I have money. I won't apologize for that any more than I will spending it on you."

"It's a six-figure bank note, Nick. It's not a dress."

"Whatever it is. I don't spend money on women, Faith. They aren't around long enough for me to even think about it. But you. You are different, and if there was a dress that cost six figures and you wanted it, I'd damn sure buy it for you. The money is nothing to me."

"But it is to me, Nick. I need—"

"What you need," I say, closing the space between us, and before she can back away, my hands are on her waist and I'm pulling her to me. "What *we* need is to fuck, talk, and repeat." I cup her face. "Abel told me not to bulldoze you. That my money and the death of your mother had stolen your control, and I need to let you have some control. But what he—and you—don't seem to see is that you have stolen my control."

"No one steals your control, Nick Rogers."

"You have, Faith," I say, my voice low, a hint of rasp. "Because I can't think when I'm not touching you." I kiss her, a deep lick of my tongue against her tongue before I say, "I once told you that I wanted you naked and willingly exposed. I still do. And we aren't there yet, which means you don't trust me."

Her fingers curl around my shirt. "I do trust you. I just want to trust in us. I want to trust that I know what is real. And I don't want money to get in the way of that."

"You want real, sweetheart. I'll show you real." I scoop her up into my arms, and I start walking, heading into the bedroom. And as tempted as I am by the idea of stripping her naked and showing her my many different versions of real, I have another destination in mind. A place where I show her just how naked she's made me.

CHAPTER ELEVEN

Nick

I exit the bedroom with Faith in my arms, where I want her to stay in every sense of the word.

"Where are we going?" she asks.

"Somewhere that apparently speaks louder than I do," I say, my stride long as I carry her down the hallway toward the room I designed for her, entering her new art studio. Her place to paint, to escape, to forget that damn winery she doesn't even want to own but can't walk away from without foolishly leaving behind a small fortune.

Entering the room, the glossy white flooring that I'd had installed for her painting process beneath my feet, I don't stop until I'm setting Faith down in front of her current work in progress. "You want real," I say. "This room is as real as it gets." My hands settle on her waist. "I didn't just invite you to stay with me, Faith. I invited you into my life. I want to be a part of yours. That's real. We're real. What I *feel* for you is real."

"Which is what?"

Words fly through my head: Protective. Aroused. Hungry. Connected. Quite possibly love. "Everything, Faith," I say. "Everything I can possibly feel. Stay with me this week." My fingers flex at her waist. "Paint. Prepare for your show, and by the time we go back to Sonoma *together*, the bills will be paid, we'll know more about the bank, and we'll set up a plan to keep Kasey motivated."

"Kasey," she says. "Right." She inhales and exhales, then abruptly twists away from me.

I go to touch her, but she is just out of reach, and before I can correct that wrong, she is standing in front of the canvas that is her current work in progress, where it sits on an easel. And that space, really like this one, is her space. A place I do not want her to feel I can invade, take, and control. Inhaling, I hold my ground, seconds ticking by and turning into a full minute as she studies the black-and-white Sonoma mountain scape that has yet to find color, that one splash of red she always adds in completion.

"This room," I say, "is supposed to be the red you add to your works: the new life, the possibilities even before I asked you to consider the possibilities. *Talk to me*, Faith."

She turns to face me. "I've been asking myself that since I stood downstairs with you and Abel. I trust you, and yet I was uneasy, and I really think it comes back to control. You have it. I don't. You create the red splash, not me. Not us."

"Because I want to help you with Kasey?"

"Because you're taking over my life, Nick. You have the control. All of it. I have none."

"Sweetheart, I told you. You have control. More than you obviously realize."

"Really? Because I just walked downstairs and found out your friend, whom I had never met, knew things about me I had only told you. You should have talked to me about him before he was here."

Guilt slices through me with the realization that I never even considered talking to her and for one massive reason: he already knew. And he knew because he was involved with my quest to prove she was a killer. I don't make excuses. There are none. "You're right. I fucked up. I'm sorry."

"You're sorry?"

"Yes. I am. Why does that surprise you?"

"Because you always surprise me, Nick. I feel like I shouldn't be upset at all. Abel is helping me. And I know you are trying to protect me. But the truth here is that you blasted into my life out of nowhere, and refused to be ignored in every possible way. You singlehandedly inspired me to paint again when my agent and even my own desire couldn't do it. Not even the certainty that Macom was mocking me for failing could do it. But you did. You supported my art when no one else has. Cared about why I felt things and what I was doing. Made me feel I could share my secrets with you."

I narrow my eyes on her, reading where this is going. "But?" I prod. "Because there is obviously a but."

"But you also shared some of my secrets with Abel without talking to me first. Told me how to spend the money I got from my art. Hired yourself as my attorney without really asking. You just told me. Paid my bills. Told me how to handle Kasey. All with good intent; I know that. But you have completely consumed me. You are like a drug that I am high on, but what happens when that drug is gone? I don't know if I have it in me to get any higher and then crash without you, Nick. I don't know how I can get any more reliant on you and survive that."

"Obviously we are not on the same page, Faith. Because every decision I make is with the assumption that we're going higher, getting closer, and that I'm protecting my woman. And that's what you are to me."

"I know that you're protecting me."

"And every reaction you have to me, and to us, is with the assumption that we're crashing and burning. That we're ending. That's not good enough for me or for you. And that's not *me* controlling *you*. That's something—or someone else—controlling you because you let it. You want control? Take it, Faith. For now, and despite every fiber of my being wanting to undress you, strip you naked, and never let you leave again, I won't. Because like I said, I still want you naked and willingly exposed. *Willingly exposed*, Faith. Like I am to you. I'll call the pilot." I turn and start for the door, the sum of my lies and her push to distance us zipping through me like a razor.

"Nick, wait."

I don't wait.

Because besides the fact that "wait" isn't the response I'm looking for from her, there is a storm brewing inside me that I need to contain or she'll end up naked. And then I'll fuck her until this feeling goes away, which might be never, since I want to force her wall down, but my lies say that I don't deserve to see it fall.

"*Nick.*"

She's no sooner said my name again then she is in front of me, her hands on my chest, heat radiating through me, but I don't touch her. I don't want to drown truth in the fiction by way of fucking. "I need to say something to you," she says, a seemingly nervous breath trembling from her lips. And I tell myself to think about those lips on my cock, that mouth sucking me deep and hard. I tell myself to strip her naked, fuck her, and send her on her way. I tell myself she's every other damn woman in my life that meant nothing to me because that would be easier, but she's not.

And it pisses me off.

"I'm done talking," I say, my hands coming down on her shoulders, and I fully intended to set her aside.

But she fists my shirt and steps into me. "What part of 'you are a drug' do you not understand? A crazy, wicked drug that consumes me. I'm afraid of taking another hit, and another, and depending on that drug, and then it's gone. I've never felt that about anything or anyone but my art. You and my art. I don't know what to do with that. But I can't—I won't—let your money and power take control of me or us."

Still I don't touch her. "In or out, Faith?"

"What does that even mean?"

"You either decide that we are reaching for those possibilities, working through the ups and downs, not caving to them. Or you get out. But there is no in between for me. That's not how I'm wired. So. You have the control right now. Decide how this plays out."

Her lips tighten. "I *will* push back when you push too hard. And I won't back off."

"In *or* out, Faith."

"In," she says fiercely. "You know I'm in."

I'm not sold yet. I don't want a reply delivered by a cornered woman. "Maybe you need to think about it, because you aren't talking like you were a few minutes ago."

"Because like most addicts, we try to deny we're addicted."

"That's not a good answer." My hand is instantly under her hair and at the back of her neck, pulling her to me. "Is that what you want? To deny the addiction? Because I don't deny mine, Faith. I am very much addicted to you. I'm obsessed. And nothing but all of you will be enough."

"And if I want all of you, Nick?"

"You already have me, sweetheart. And you're clearly trying to figure out what to do with me, but that's okay. I'm here to offer suggestions." My lips slant over hers, my tongue licking into her mouth, a deep stroke followed by another, and when she moans, only when she moans, do I pull back and add, "Suggestion number one: you have on too many clothes." I catch the hem of her shirt and pull it upward, over her head.

Before it's even hit the ground, my hand is back under her hair, cupping the back of her neck and pulling her lips back to mine. "Suggestion number two: it's okay to do drugs when I'm your drug." I kiss her again, and she does that thing she does, which I swear I want to experience again and again for the rest of my fucking life. She sighs into the kiss as if she can finally breathe—as if I'm the reason she breathes. She's damn sure the reason I breathe and most definitely the reason my cock is so damn hard it could break glass.

At the feel of her hands under my shirt, on my skin, a heady rush of lust and adrenaline pulses through me, while my mind conjures all the places her hands could be next. Namely, the same place I want her mouth—my cock—though just about any place on my body would do just fine. But as much as I want her to touch me, as much as I want to be naked with her right now, I can't focus on fucking. And holy hell, I want to fuck. But right now we have to have a conversation about control. And control isn't about having no limits. It's about controlling the ones you have, about owning them. And that means I'm keeping my clothes on, at least for now, while she is not.

I reach for her hands and pull them from my shirt, holding them between us, walking her backward as I do. "Let's talk about the subject of the day. Control."

"You want it. *Sometimes* I'll let you have it."

My lips curve, and I press her hands behind her back, shackling them with one of my hands. "Is that right?" I ask, unclasping the front of her black, lacy bra, my hand settling between her breasts.

"Yes," she says. "*That* is right."

My gaze lowers, raking over her high, full breasts, her pebbled nipples, my finger lightly teasing one stiff peak, her back arching into my touch. "Can I have it now, Faith?" I ask, my eyes rocketing to her face. "Or am I being too controlling?"

"Not even close," she whispers, her voice low, raspy. Affected.

I respond to that bold sexual challenge in her that has been in the air between us from the moment we met and turned me on right out of the gate. I'm hot. I'm hard. My blood is pumping, but I am not blind to the fact that she ran from me minutes ago, vulnerability in that action, but now... There is none. Because being sexually daring is her emotional shield, something I suspect she learned at the club she and Macom frequented. Maybe that is even why the club worked for her. She didn't have to be present with him there. She didn't have to be present in life there. And that might have worked for her and him, but it no longer does for me or us.

I brush my lips over hers and release her hands, turning her to face the opposite direction while I skim her bra away, my hand flattening on her belly, my teeth on her shoulder. "I'm going to keep asking for more. You know that, right?"

"Yes."

"Can I have it?"

"Yes."

"Are you sure about that?"

"Yes."

I settle on one knee, my hands on her hips, my lips on her naked back, my tongue licking the delicate spot. And when she draws in a shaky breath, I stand up, my hands falling away from her. "Undress, but don't turn around."

I want her to turn and look for where my head is right now. To look into my eyes and see the test I'm giving her. To be present with me, right now, in this moment, in all possible ways. But she does it. She walks forward and starts undressing, so emotionally removed that she takes my commands that I'm giving her almost coldly.

And it both challenges me and pisses me off, and not at her. At me. I want her to be present, but I haven't given her a reason. I haven't let her know that I see her, *really* see her. Hell. Maybe I didn't until now. Until she almost walked out the door over a control issue we haven't even come close to solving.

Now I see that she is guarded in all the ways that matter, the ways that make her think we will end and I will leave. And now I refuse to let her hide. I walk around her and sit on the stool beside her workstation, directly in front of her. Our eyes meet, and still I see no trepidation. No vulnerability. She verbally said she was in, not out, but she has shut down on me.

She watches me watch her, stripping away her socks and jeans, gauging her control over me. Making sure her facade of submission still gives her control, and on that Faith understands sexual play, while I suspect Macom did not. The reality here is that submission, when done right, is all about the sub's control. But Faith is no submissive, and I want more than her body.

Her gaze finds mine as she twists her fingers into the thin black lace of her panties at her hips and drags them down the silky expanse of her legs. The way I plan to drag my tongue down them in the very near future. The tiny triangle of blonde hair in the *V* of her body is sexy as hell, but then, everything about this woman is sexy as hell to me.

I stand up and move behind the stool. "Come to me, Faith."

Her lips curve ever so slightly, oh so sexily, and she walks toward me, her hips and breasts swaying seductively, stopping in front of the stool. I could tell her to bend over the stool and stick that pretty ass in the air for me, and I suspect that is what she wants. For me to spank her. I give myself just a moment to think of her creamy, curvy, perfect ass waiting on my palm. The way her back would arch in anticipation when I warmed her cheeks. How wet her sex would be when I slide my fingers between her legs. How hot she would be when my cock followed my palm. But now is not the time for a spanking that would give her that ultimate rush and force her to forget everything. I don't want her to forget. I want her to be right here, with me, willingly, emotionally exposed.

"Turn around and sit."

Her teeth scrape her bottom lip, and she does as I say, sitting down. I move to stand in front of her, squatting down, my hands on my knees when they want to be on hers. "Open your legs for me," I say, the stool low enough to place her sex directly in front of me. My mouth exactly where we both want it.

Interestingly, though, it's in this moment that I see a flicker of vulnerability in her eyes, but it is there and gone in an instant, the way we will be if I don't build our bond and build it now. To my surprise, she doesn't open her legs. "Are you going to get undressed?"

"No," I say. "I am not, but I am going to lick that sweet spot right between your legs, and slide my fingers in, and make you come. Open for me, Faith."

Her lashes lower, but not before I see the flicker of vulnerability, the emotional kind I am after, in her eyes. My hands go to her ankles, and I slowly caress upward. "Look at me, Faith."

"No," she whispers, emotion radiating off of her.

I kiss her knees, tiny little clusters of kisses, and her fingers slide into my hair. I flick my tongue between her knees and then inch her thighs apart. She tilts her head back, looking skyward. Looking anywhere but at me. I don't force her to look at me. She's exposed when she didn't mean to be exposed. I stole the control she pretends to give to me. But this isn't about taking her control. This is about making her present, and that I did it as easily as I have pleases me. Makes me want to please her and give her that escape, that sanctuary that is sex for her.

My mouth travels up her thigh, and I lick her clit. Just once. A quick flicker before my mouth is at her other knee, my tongue teasing the inner curve. Faith trembles, and I look up at her at the same moment her gaze lowers, colliding with mine, the vulnerability I'd seen moments before still present, and she doesn't seem to be able to hide it.

And for a moment I feel a stab of guilt. I'd come for her. I'd wanted to make her vulnerable to hurt her, and for what? A bastard of a father I hated. But that bastard brought me to Faith. I caress a path up her legs, mouth on one and hand on the other, and I don't tease her any longer. I give her clit a gentle lick and then another before suckling, my fingers stroking the slick wet heat of her body. And apparently vulnerability is arousing to Faith, because I don't even manage to slide my fingers inside her before she's pulling at my hair and trembling into release.

I ease her into her release, licking and stroking until she calms, falling forward and catching herself on my shoulders. I stand up and cup her face, forcing her to look at me, that vulnerability back in her eyes, etched in her beautiful face. "This is what I want from you."

"What does that mean?"

"You were willing to be naked physically while I was fully dressed, but not emotionally, not at first. You are always willing to give me control of your body, Faith, even from the first night we met, but you aren't willing to give me the ultimate control I've given you."

"I'm naked. You're not. One of us gave the other control. And it wasn't you."

"I can be naked and fuck a million women and they wouldn't have anything but my cock, Faith. But you, Faith, are the one who is one hell of a drug." And I don't plan to say it, but suddenly the words are on my tongue, and I know I have to say them. I know she needs to hear them. "I'm falling in love with you, Faith."

She gasps. "What?"

"I'm falling in love with you," I say, my thumb stroking her cheek. "I've never said that to anyone. I've never felt it with anyone."

"I'm pretty sure lust and hate have evolved into something that I'm not sure I want to feel."

"Why, Faith?"

"You could hurt me, Nick."

"Sweetheart, you have pieces of me no one was supposed to ever have, and the many ways you could shatter them should have me running for the hills. But all I want to do is kiss you again. Hold you. Watch you paint." I brush my lips over hers. "Which you should do now. You have a show."

"Watch me naked," she says. "I need you inside me right now."

"As much as I like that invitation," I say, stepping back and pressing her knees together. "This was about you, Faith. Not me. I don't want it to be about me."

Faith is on her feet in an instant, her naked body pressed to mine, her fingers curling in my shirt all over again. "Let's be clear, Nick Rogers. That wasn't just for me. That was for you. That was about control."

"Not this time."

"Maybe you believe that, but I don't. And I could drop to my knees and take it from you the way you just took it from me. We both know I can. But I won't, because I now realize what I didn't before. You don't just want it. You need it. It's *your way, your wall.* It's how you keep people at a distance—me at a distance."

"I just told you I'm falling in love with you, woman."

"And you made sure I was vulnerable when you did because you were vulnerable. And I let you. I'll let you, but not forever, because I can't be as vulnerable as you just made me alone." She releases my shirt and tries to move away, but there is no way in hell I'm letting her get away. Not now. And not ever.

CHAPTER TWELVE

Nick

I cup the back of Faith's head, dragging her mouth to mine. "Sweetheart, you aren't alone, and if I have my way, you won't ever be alone again."

"That's a long time, Nick," she whispers, but I'm already kissing her by the time she finishes speaking my name, and as for that control she claims I am playing with, I let it go. I let her feel my unbridled need for her, and between the two of us, we are kissing, touching, all but crawling under each other's skin. That word I never meant to say—love—is now between us, and it's like freedom, a new kind of drug that stirs hunger in me for this woman, so fucking intense it damn near hurts.

My shirt comes off, my pants down, and it's only a matter of time before she's against the wall and I'm pressing inside her, lifting her, pulling her back off the wall. Holding both our weights the way I'm willing to hold us both up every moment of every day, if she'll give me that chance. If she'll forgive me for the way we first met. It kills me right now not to tell her. Guts me, and I have never wanted her trust so much. I urge her backward, and not just because I can now watch her breasts bounce as I pull her down on my cock and thrust it inside her—they are beautiful and fucking hot as hell—but she now has to trust me to hold her up. *She has to trust me.*

On some level, I know this is a fruitless endeavor. I can't force her to trust me, not if I want to have that trust be real. And real is what she wants. Real is what I want. My hand flattens at her back, between her shoulder blades, and I drag her back to me, her head buried in my shoulder, our bodies melded together. I drive harder into her, wanting out of my own head. Wanting more of her. So fucking much of her.

"Nick," she pants out. "Nick."

Her voice, the grip of her sex, the rush of blood in my ears and in my cock, and a deep pull in my balls say that I am here, in that place of no fucking return, only moments after she is. I quake, my thighs burning with the force of my release and our weight. I lose reality with the force of my eruption and come back to the present to discover I'm leaning against the wall, holding Faith against me in a bear hug. And I don't want to let her go.

My legs have another idea, and I shove off the wall, carrying her to the table next to her workstation and easing her sideways to allow her to grab a tissue. "Ready?" I ask before I set her down.

"Yes. I'm ready."

I ease her down my body and set her on her feet, righting my pants as she tries to put her tissue to use, only to stumble. She laughs even as she's about to go down, which makes me laugh, but I catch her arms, preventing her fall. "I've got you," I promise.

Our eyes lock, the mood darkening, the pull between us fiercely present. "I know, Nick. Just don't let go, okay?"

"Sweetheart. I'm not going to let go. That's a promise, but don't forget you said that and how I replied."

Her brow furrows, and I turn away, hunting down our clothes and kicking myself over the coded gloom-and-doom message I've just given her. I gather her clothes and set them on the stool, and my phone rings in my pocket. Assuming it's Beck, who's already called me with dead-end leads today, I almost ignore it but think better. I snake it out of my pocket and glance at caller ID. "It's Chris Merit," I say, glancing at Faith, who is tugging her pants over her hips.

"Answer it," she urges quickly.

"Too late," I say. "He hung up."

"Call him back," she says, pulling her shirt over her head, sans the bra she seems to have forgotten.

I snag the bra she's not wearing and hold it up. "I sure as hell hope you get this eager when I call," I tease.

"Sorry," she says. "I only get this excited for Chris Merit." She snatches her bra up. "But you're the only one I take my underwear off for."

"I can live with that answer," I say as my phone rings and I glance at the screen again. "It's him again," I say, hitting the answer button. "Chris."

"Sara, actually," I hear instead. "I was wondering," she says. "Is Faith with you? I seem to have written her number down wrong."

I glance at Faith. "She is. Hold on." I cover the phone. "Sara for you." I offer her the phone. She doesn't take it.

"Oh no. What's wrong? I wonder if my work got returned? What if—"

"Nothing's wrong," I promise, stroking her hair. "I'd sense it, and I don't."

"God," she breathes out. "I hope you're right."

"I am," I say, handing her the phone.

She places it to her ear. "Sara. Hi." She listens a moment. "Yes, actually I'm still here in the city." She looks at me. "I'm staying with Nick all week." She listens again, and those beautiful green eyes of hers light up. "I'd love to. Yes. Terrific. What time? Yes. I'll see you in the morning." She ends the call, and now her entire face is glowing. "She wants me to help her set up the show. Her right-hand person had a family emergency. This is such an opportunity to learn another side of the business. Oh, Nick." She closes the space between us, her hands settling on my still-bare chest. "Me being here opened that door. Once again, my love of art takes on a new life because of you."

My hand settles at her waist. "This had nothing to do with me. This is all you. All you. I'm just along for the ride and enjoying every fucking minute."

She pushes to her toes and kisses me. "I am, too. The ride and you being on it with me." She smiles, this sweet, happy smile, and then moves away to finish dressing. I grab my shirt and present Faith with my back, pulling it over my head as I endure my own conflicting reactions to what just happened. On one note, I'm happy as hell that Faith not only has another reason to embrace her art, but to be here, with me, where I not only want her but can ensure she is safe. On the other note, she's embracing that art with Sara Merit, who knows I own the club and whose husband used to be a member. The ticking clock gets faster, and the balls I'm juggling multiply.

Inhaling, I turn around to find Faith perched back on the stool, staring at me with expectancy on her face, her mood back to sober. "We never finished talking about money. I don't want it to divide us again. I really would like to finish that conversation."

And the bullets just keep coming.

CHAPTER THIRTEEN

Faith

Nick's response to my request to talk about money again is slow to follow, his expression unreadable, his energy dark. The wisps of his dark brown hair around his face are torn from the clasp at his nape, the aftermath of our turbulent encounter. Certain we're about to have a repeat, I stand from where I've perched on the edge of the stool. But as surely as I'm prepared for another battle over the topic, yet again, his mood seems to lighten, and he steps in front of me, his hands settling on my neck, under my hair. "We do need to finish talking. Let's go back down to the kitchen to talk, but bring your paperwork from Abel. I want to go over it with you."

"I'd actually really like your thoughts before I form my own."

He kisses me, and I hurry to the bedroom and then to the bathroom, where I've left my purse, which now holds the documents I planned to read on the plane. Finding it on the counter, I'm reaching for the paperwork when my hand hits the money clip I found in my yard Friday night. Still puzzled by finding it, I hear Nick's footsteps sound. I set the paperwork on the counter and rotate to find him leaning on the doorway between the bathroom and the bedroom. "Is this yours?" I ask, holding up the gold clip with the imprint of an American flag on its side. "I mean, it looks like it's souvenir-shop quality, and under your pay scale, but I thought it might be a sentimental thing." He pushes off the doorframe, and I close the space between us, stopping in front of him. "Then again," I add, offering him the clip, "you're actually not exactly sentimental. It's not yours, is it?"

"No," he confirms, taking it from me to give it a quick inspection. "Where did you find it?"

"My front yard as I was leaving for the airport. It must have been the delivery person who brought the package you sent me."

"Right," Nick says, the look on his face oddly serious, but he says little more. "A delivery person makes sense." He pockets the money clip. "I'll have my assistant call the delivery service. Do you have your paperwork?"

I grab the documents on the counter and hold them up. "All set."

"Well, then," he says, "let's go have that talk." He backs out of the doorway, giving me space to exit. The idea that we're going to sit down and have a formal chat is a positive signal to me that he plans to take my concerns seriously.

Once I exit to the hallway, Nick steps to my side, and side by side, we start down the stairs, my curiosity piqued. "I just realized that I don't know much about your work life. I haven't even thought about you having an assistant, which, of course, you do. And where is your office? How many staff members do you have?"

"Downtown. Twenty staff members. And my assistant is Rita, who is a mother and has been happily married for decades. She also tolerates my arrogance about as well as you do."

I cast him a sideways look and a smile. "So I'll like her."

"Without question," he says as we reach the living room, "and I'm fucked ten ways to hell if you two team up on me. That said, I'm brave. Once you know your schedule at the gallery, you should come to my office, meet her, and see the place."

"I'd like that," I say, stopping on this side of the island bar as Nick rounds it and steps directly across from me.

"How long do you plan to work with Sara?" he asks.

"She said this is just for this week, but I'd love to help her get to opening day."

"That's weeks away," he points out. "And you have a show to prepare for. How much work do you have left to complete?"

"Two paintings," I say, pleased that he's aware of my deadline. "But one is half done, and the gallery will inspire me. I should paint today, though. I'd actually really like to get a brush in my hand."

"I'm glad to see you embracing your work again. After we talk, just go hide upstairs and do what you need to do. We'll hang out here and order in dinner later this evening." He lifts the lid to a pizza box. "For now, we have this. Abel actually left us a few slices." He walks to the oven behind him and turns it on.

"You're hungry?" I ask incredulously. "How can you be hungry? We just ate not that long ago."

"Almost two hours ago," he says, glancing at his industrial-looking watch with a thick black leather band and silver face that fits well with his black jeans and biker-style boots. "That's a long time with all that fighting and fucking we just did."

I laugh, shaking my head, the laughter part something I'm not sure I did all that often before I met Nick. "The things that come out of your mouth, Nick Rogers."

"You get special treatment," he says, grabbing a pan from the drawer under the stove and setting it on top. "You should hear what I say to those I don't like. Because I'm not a nice guy, remember?"

"All too well," I assure him, joining him on that side of the bar and helping him load the tray with pizza. "I can just imagine what your courtroom must be like," I say, lowering my voice to imitate him. "Tell me, Mr. Murphy. Right before her death, were you fighting with her or fucking her?"

"First," he says, grabbing the other two pizza boxes. "My voice is much deeper than that. Second, I usually make those kinds of statements long before we ever get to court, and then we don't go to court."

"How often are you in court?" I ask, setting an empty pizza box on the counter beside me.

"A lot of my work is done for contracted, long-term clients, which means I negotiate and litigate on their behalf as needed. But overall, only about ten percent of my time is spent in court, while another thirty percent is spent in mediations." He sticks the pizza in the oven and sets the timer, his mood turning serious. "Let's sit and have that talk so you can get to painting. And to bed. You now have work tomorrow."

It's then that realization hits me. He starts to move, and I grab his arm. He turns back to me, arching a brow, so very tall, broad, and bigger than life in too many ways to count. Bigger in *my life* than anyone else has ever been. "What's up, sweetheart?"

"I just needed to say something."

"You have my full attention." His hand settles at my waist, and I swear I don't know how it's possible, but I feel this man everywhere when he touches me in one spot. "You *always* have my full attention, Faith," he adds, his voice low, intimate.

And what's really amazing to me is that I believe him. I feel his interest, his engagement, and not just now. Always. He is more present in my life than people I have known for years. "It just hit me that I didn't even consider saying no to Sara and rushing back to Sonoma."

"Is that a bad thing?" he asks.

"I don't know," I say. "That's what I'm trying to decide."

He tilts his head toward the table. "Let's sit and figure it out," he urges.

I nod, and we both claim our barstools from earlier and face each other. "Why don't you know?" he asks, returning to the point rather than moving past it, his hands bracketing my legs, our knees touching. "Just say whatever comes to mind, and you'll have your answer."

"I'm excited about working with Sara and painting and my show in L.A. and so many things, but the moment that I forgot to worry about the winery because of those things tells a story."

And instead of telling me what I mean, he asks, "And that story is what?"

"That I'm counting on the winery running without me, and that means that I'm counting on your help."

"Good. I want you to. Because you can. I'm not going anywhere, Faith, and clearly, I'm doing my best to make sure that you don't, either. I owe Sara for the assistance on that one."

"I'd already decided to stay," I remind him, wanting him to know that I'm here for him.

"I know you did," he says. "But let's face it. The winery comes with a long history of pulling you there. I have a short one of pulling you to me. I'd like to help you find a way to cut off the drain it has on you."

"You mean by paying off the debt and rewarding Kasey for taking charge."

"Among other things," he says, "but before we talk about money, I want to go over the documents with you, and, with full disclosure, I drafted them for Abel."

I laugh. "That doesn't surprise me at all. You have to be the driver."

He doesn't laugh with me as he usually does, not this time. "I do," he agrees, his tone serious. "It's who I am. You need to know that. My instinct will always be to take control."

"Type A personality on caffeine," I say, "and the truth is that I can pretend to be a type A, but I'm not. But that doesn't mean that you get to be in charge."

He gives me a shrewd look. "Unless you're naked."

A knot forms in my chest with what is clearly an observation and a question I'm not ready to answer yet. "That's a different topic for another time," I say, cutting my gaze from his, and because I need to do anything but look at him in the next thirty seconds, I reach for my bottle of water and unscrew the lid.

Nick's watching me, I feel his scrutiny—heavy, intense—and it makes my throat dry. I tilt the bottle back, drinking deeply, and when I lower the bottle, Nick takes it from me, holds my stare, and the bottle goes to his lips. I watch him chug the liquid, my fingers curling on my leg, acutely aware of the intimacy of sharing my water with him.

He sets the bottle down, and I don't even mean to, but I'm staring at him, and the look in his eyes tells me that his thoughts are with mine, and I suddenly realize his message even before he says, "You can be naked with your clothes on or off, Faith." He reaches up and caresses my cheek. "And I do like you naked, but as you said to me, tell me whatever you want to tell me, whenever you're ready to tell me. I'll still be here."

"I just—"

"No pressure." He eases back in his seat. "For now. You were telling me my control has to have limits."

"Are you capable of limits?"

"Control is all about limits. Is that what you want, Faith? Limits?"

I'm instantly aware of where he's leading me, and I go there. "Control is about limits. Possibilities are not. But me owing you money feels like a limit. It might not change you, but it *will* change me. I need to pay you back. And I need to give you that money I got from my art as a down payment."

He studies me for several beats, his expression unreadable. "You need this."

"Yes," I say. "I do."

"I won't agree to ever taking any portion of the winery. Period. No conversation. And no interest, Faith. I don't need the money. I won't take extra." I open my mouth to argue, and he says, "Compromise. I'm agreeing to a payback for you, not me. Agree to my terms for me."

"Compromise," I repeat. "Okay. Yes. And for the record, I actually like that word. I like it a lot, and perhaps I was unfair earlier. I know you just want to help and protect me. Just please communicate, Nick, and I think that makes all the difference."

"This seems like a good time to tell you that if I have to spend money to take care of the winery situation, I'm going to spend money."

"And if I say I don't want you to?"

"I'm going to take care of this for you and for us. You can't be who you really are while being forced to be what you aren't."

That statement punches me in the chest with my mistakes and pretty much defines a huge portion of my life. "I don't know how to take your help and not lose myself, too."

"You're putting too much emphasis on the money. Eventually you're going to have to accept that is part of who I am. I'm not going to pretend that I don't have a large bank account. I work too damn hard to get it. And I'm going to spend that money on you and with you." He leans closer, softening his voice. "Make me understand why this is an issue. Who used money against you? Your father? Macom? Both?"

"Am I that transparent?"

"Not transparent enough, or I'd already know the answers to those questions. I need to know. Communication, remember?"

"Yes. Communication. Okay. My father was more about emotional baggage. As for Macom, I don't know if it was money or fame or both, but it went to Macom's head."

"Meaning what?"

"He would throw the money and fame in my face."

"How?"

"Does it matter?"

"It affects you, Faith. So yes. It matters."

"He'd criticize me and then build me up and then do it all over again. I knew that he was inherently insecure, which made his actions about him, not me. I tried to build him up and support him. Eventually, though, with him and my father talking in my ear, it wore on me. Their negativity became poison, and I started to doubt myself."

"And the doubt led where?"

"I'm not sure it was the doubt that led me down a rabbit hole I couldn't quite escape." I think of the fight I just had with Nick. "Macom and I didn't fight like you and I fight."

"How do we fight, Faith?"

"We do what we just said. We communicate."

"And with Macom?"

"He never hurt me, but he threw volatile temper tantrums and destroyed things. The next day, he would buy me extravagant gifts to apologize."

"Well, to start. I'm not insecure, in case you didn't notice. I'm good at what I do, but you have a gift that I admire. You are brilliant, Faith."

My cheeks flush, not as much at the compliment but the vehement way he delivers the words. Like he means them so very deeply.

He doesn't give me time to reply. "And as for money. I'm going to spend money on you. Because *I want to*. If I want to do it just because, I will. Because *I want to*. And if I want to do it because I piss you off, I will. Because *I want to*. He doesn't get to change that. He doesn't get that kind of say in our relationship."

"I don't need you to spend money on me, but I don't want him to define me or us. I hate that we're even having this conversation."

"We needed to have this conversation. You lived with him. You must have thought you loved him."

"I did. The man I knew before the fame and the money."

"Money and fame don't change people, Faith. Those things simply expose their true colors."

"I don't dispute that, but I don't know how he hid those true colors so well. I've thought about that a lot. How did I miss so much?"

"Were you his submissive?"

"No. I told you. I'm not a submissive. You know that I'm not a submissive."

"But he tried to make you one."

"Yes. He did. I refused."

He narrows his eyes on me. "He found that world while he was with you, not before."

"Right after his first big sale, he was invited to an expensive, invitation-only dinner club."

"That wasn't a dinner club at all."

"Exactly. And I agreed to go because he was still the Macom I thought I knew."

"And what happened?"

"For us, it was voyeurism and sex that felt daring and sexy at the time. Looking back, I think something was always missing for us, and that night, in that club, it felt as if we filled some void."

"And so you went back."

"Yes. And for a while I liked it. In some ways I always did, but why and how changed."

"Meaning what?" he presses.

"Starting out, we kept to ourselves. Just going there made things exciting. But then he got darker at home. More demanding at the club." I rotate and face forward. "The first time he crossed a line, he tied me up and then invited people to watch us without telling me, without *asking*. It spiraled from there."

Nick rotates forward as well, both of us side by side, arms resting on the table. "But you kept going?"

I glance over at him, daring to look into his eyes. "It's like you said earlier. I use sex to protect myself. That goes back to what I said a moment ago. I don't know when or how it happened, but that club became the place that I trained myself to be something that I wasn't before. It was where I learned to be in control, even when I was seemingly not in control at all. Sex became a different kind of escape. I actually found those moments, when I could be in a room of naked bodies and still feel alone, sanctuary."

"From what?"

"Everything I didn't want to face. In reality, my control in that club was a replacement for claiming real control of my life."

"And then your father died," he says, and I cut my gaze. I look at his arm resting on the table, his tattoo partially exposed. The words etched there are taking me back to a place I don't want to be, but my father's death always leads me there. I reach over and cover those words with my hand. "An eye for an eye," I whisper.

"You keep going to it. You clearly want to tell me what it means."

Now I look up at him. "No. No, I really don't."

He studies me a beat and then says, "Then don't."

Just that easily, he has accepted my answer and offers me an escape. I take it. "I need air." I slip off the stool and start walking, but as I round the table, I realize that the past is in this room, when Nick is my present, maybe my future. I don't want to shut him out. I want to take him on the ride with me. I rotate to find him still at the table. "Come with me?"

His expression doesn't change—it's unreadable—but his actions are what matter. He stands, and it's only a minute later that we stand side by side on the balcony at the railing, and for several minutes we don't speak. We just stand there, the blue sky and ocean stretching far and wide before us, like paint perfectly inked on a canvas. The wind lifts over the balcony edge, and I can almost taste the salt water on my tongue and, with it, the words to be spoken—and not just for him. I need to face the past fully and be done with it. I inhale and let it out. "There was another artist who went to the club. Jim was his name." I rotate to face Nick again, and he does the same with me. "He was the one who got Macom the invite."

"They were friends then," he assumes.

"I believe that was Jim's intent, but he and Macom sat on a high-profile board for a charity together. They bumped heads, and Macom got kicked off. The day it happened, Macom called me at work and told me about it. I got home that night to comfort him and found him with Jim's wife, in our bed. He invited me to join them. 'An eye for an eye,' he'd said. I could help pay Jim back."

"Had you been with Jim and his wife before?"

"No. His wife was a submissive, and Jim was very possessive and protective of her. I'd actually found it enviable, until she hopped in bed with Macom. Anyway. They were still fucking when I got the call about my father. I left. Macom called the next day looking for me."

"And you never went back."

"No, and honestly I hated the L.A. scene. I went to college there and learned the world there, and it just made sense to stay. And it kept me from my parents' drama."

Nick moves then, turning me to lean against the railing, his big body trapping mine, his hands at my waist. "Faith, I need you to know some things about me. This isn't everything I need to share, but it's a start and an important one."

"I know you were in that world in some way, Nick. We've hinted at that in conversations."

"I was. Not now. But I've played in that world that you were playing in, and I did so for many years."

"What drew you to it, and why did you leave?"

"I was drawn there for the zero-commitment guarantee. There was just sex. No one believed I wanted more. No one asked for more. I left because I met you."

I inhale and let it out. "That was recent."

"Because I didn't want a woman in my life. Now. If I never see that place again, it will be too soon. I would never take you there."

"So it was one club?"

"Yes."

"And why wouldn't you take me there?"

"Because we are more than the sum of what I was there. Because we are better than that place. Because I damn sure have no intention of sharing you in any capacity, and just walking into that place would make many a man and woman want you."

"Did you have a submissive?"

"No. Never. I cannot stress this enough. Until you, I didn't do commitment, and that is a commitment. But I liked the games, and it was fucking without complication. Bondage. *Check*. Ménages. *Check*. Voyeurism. *Check*. No couple play, though. I was never a couple, and I don't need another man comparing dicks with me."

"And you're telling me this why?"

"I didn't want you to find out from someone else. And I didn't want you to think that I want to be there, not here. The past doesn't define me or you or who we are apart or together. It simply represents the paths that we each took to get here. To *each other*."

I digest every word he has spoken with the realization that I am not shaken by Nick's confession, which is not so unlike my own. How can I be? He has been boldly forthright, brutally honest about his interests. And he's just told me that while Macom needed the club despite having me, Nick only needs me. And I choose to believe him. I choose to believe that he is right. All paths have led us here, to a place where I have a paintbrush in my hand and this man in my life.

CHAPTER FOURTEEN

Nick

I once told Faith that I don't do guilt. I make decisions. I own them. I move on. But as I leave her in her studio to paint, just beyond our talk about sex clubs and that bastard Macom, guilt is gutting me. It's like I'm in a horror movie with some slasher sicko slicing and dicing me, then coming back for more. I fast-step down the stairs toward the living room, reminding myself that I told Faith all that I dared. I cannot risk sending her running for the hills and pushing me into the doghouse. Not when it appears that someone wants the winery, or something connected to the winery, and that they most likely killed her mother and my father to get it. And Faith is the only person standing in their way.

Clearing the last step, I cross the living room, grab my briefcase in the kitchen, and then make my way to my office. Once inside, I shut the door under the pretense of the client conference call I told Faith I'd scheduled. A lie to hide lies. Jaw clenching at that idea, I drop my briefcase on my heavy mahogany desk, then walk toward the bookshelf-enclosed sitting area at the far end of the room. Claiming a spot in the center of the brown leather couch facing the door, I mentally prioritize the gaggle of fucked-up shit in my head right now. My focus is on Faith's safety, which means keeping her close. Which means containing any threat that could push or pull her away from me. That means dealing with Sara Merit.

I pull my phone from the pocket of my jeans, and since I don't have Sara's number, I dial Chris. He answers on the first ring. "You're afraid Sara is going to tell Faith about the club. And I can tell you right now. She would not do that."

"You certainly know how to get right to the point."

"Then let me do it again. You have to tell her."

"I told her I was a member, with graphic detail," I say, and, aware Chris has a bit of a history himself, I add, "She knows the world. It's not been kind to her."

"And living the lifestyle versus owning a club that says you can't live without the lifestyle are two different things."

"Exactly. And I never really wanted the damn thing. Mark owned it. Mark was a client and a friend, and I picked it up."

"You're known. Someone could tell her you owned it, and even if that never happens, you really don't want that unspoken truth between you."

"I'll tell her at the same time that I tell her I dumped the damn thing."

"Smart move in my book," he says. "Do you have a buyer?"

"You interested?"

"Not a chance in hell, my man. But we both know money isn't an issue to you. Kurt Seaver runs that place from sunup to sundown. Give it to him."

"You read my mind. That's exactly what I plan to do."

"Good move. Good move." There's a voice in the background. "I'm actually walking into a meeting with a donor for my charity. Sara's with me. I'll fill in the holes she missed." He ends the call.

I pull up my texts and Kurt Seaver's contact information, shooting him a message: *Ten o'clock in my office tomorrow.*

I move on to the next situation. I remove the money clip from my pocket, set it on the dark wood of the rectangular coffee table, and shoot a photo I then text to Beck. My superhero PI, who had better start acting like a superhero. I punch his autodial, and he answers on the first ring. "How's the black widow?"

"Since you're supposed to be an ex-CIA agent/hacker, who I now pay one hell of a lot of money to do PI work, I'd think you'd know how to google 'black widow' and find the meaning. She's never been married. She hasn't killed her nonexistent husband or any lovers."

"Unless she was fucking your father right along with her mother."

My teeth clench. "Don't push me, Beck. You might be in high demand, but I'm paying you a hell of a lot of money to do your job. And that job now includes protecting Faith, not attacking her."

"Relax, man. I was just pushing your buttons. Faith isn't a killer, but considering that note you found, she was clearly fucking with your father's head. And I sent a gift to your inbox."

"Which is what?"

"That attorney she hired to go after her mother had a file on her that included correspondence with your father."

"How did you get that?"

"Don't ask what you don't want to deny later."

My jaw clenches. "Save me time. Summarize the findings."

"Validation of her story. She went after her mother. Your father nickel-and-dimed her into giving up. The interesting part of this to me is that your father was paying Meredith Winter while acting as her attorney. If he wasn't fucking her, I'd swear she was blackmailing him."

"I told you. My father wouldn't tolerate blackmail. He'd act on his own behalf and viciously. He was after the winery."

"Here's the thing. There are no dots connecting. I can't find Meredith's money. I can't find your father's money. This tells me that someone as good as me made it go away. I need to put feelers out in my underground circles and find out who, but that means two things: We need to offer cash in exchange for information. And we risk spooking someone into doing something we might regret."

"Do we have other options?"

"They're running out."

"Exhaust them," I say. "I don't want to spook the bank before I have time to steal the winery out from underneath them."

"If you do that," he says, "the net outcome could be the same as me going underground. You end up stealing someone's thunder, and they come after you. Or Faith."

"What the hell is it about the winery that would make someone want it badly enough to kill for it?"

"There is no record of anything that remotely sets off bells. I checked for oil. I checked for real estate developments. There is nothing. And I went back a hundred years."

"It could be a business deal," I say, thinking out loud. "Some kind of merger that has never been put on paper."

"Or the same person who made Meredith Winter's money trail disappear made a whole lot more disappear."

"We just need to make sure they don't make Faith disappear."

"If the winery is at the core of all of this, and it seems that it is, make her put the winery up for sale. If it's gone, she's no longer a target."

"You do have someone watching her, correct?"

"I have a man watching your place and two in Sonoma, watching her place and the winery."

"Which brings me back to the purpose of this call," I say. "I sent you a photo of a money clip. Faith found it in her yard Friday. Does that belong to one of your men?"

"I see it. And my guys working the Sonoma area don't make stupid mistakes. And since Faith has no cameras on her property, I can't see who is. We need to upgrade her, and I can do it without her knowing, but with her stamp of approval, we can get far better equipment installed."

"We're here until Thursday and there for the weekend. Schedule it for Friday."

"We're talking murder here. We need cameras at her house and at the winery, where we can watch her staff, now, not later."

I'm immediately hit by the fact that he's just stated: *We're dealing with murder*. He's no longer on the fence about how my father and Faith's mother died. He now believes what I do. They were murdered. "I'll get you in by tomorrow night," I say. "And

Faith is working here at the Allure Gallery all week. I need you to be sure that you have someone watching her at all times."

"Done. And FYI, I hacked your father's autopsy reports. Nothing yet." He hangs up.

Fucker.

I set the phone down on the table and stare at that money clip with a bad feeling in my gut, my fingers thrumming on my knee. "What the hell were you up to, Father?"

I pick my phone back up and dial my assistant. "And here I thought that new woman of yours would make you get a life," Rita says, bypassing a hello. In fact, I think she started bypassing hello with me seven years back. "Sundays are for church and reruns of *Friends*," she adds.

"And me," I say. "I need someone respected assessing the Reid Winter Winery in Sonoma tomorrow. They'll need to bring a full team. I need it done quickly."

"Tomorrow?" she asks incredulously. "No one is going to talk to me today, let alone be there tomorrow."

"Pay them whatever you have to pay them."

"That could be hefty."

"I trust you not to let me get raped."

"Oh, good grief. I could do without your visuals sometimes, Nick Rogers. Tuesday is more reasonable, even with a bribe."

"I prefer tomorrow. If anyone can get it done, you can. Text me when you know the details. And yes, I'll bring the donuts you like in the morning." I end the call and stand up, walking to my desk, where I stick the money clip in the top drawer. I consider digging through the boxes of materials I have on my father, but that's risky with Faith in the house. And I'd rather be upstairs with Faith anyway.

With that in mind, I open my briefcase and pull out the sensitive material related to Faith and my father, filing it away in my desk. Selecting several client files I need to study, I seal it up, head to the kitchen where my computer still sits, and, with it in hand, make my way upstairs. The minute I appear in the doorway, Faith turns to face me, a black cover-up over her clothes, her hair piled on top of her head, little ringlets around her face.

She motions to her white Keds, now splattered with black and gray paint. "Maybe I could sell them to some clothing designer?" she says. "They're stylish, right?"

"Very," I tell her, walking to the wall behind her, where I can watch her canvas take shape. "It could be an empire." I sit down and open my briefcase.

Faith removes her cover-up and sits down next to me, her black pants now splattered with paint as well. "Isn't it going to be hard to work like this?" she asks.

"I'll manage," I say, leaning over and kissing her, but it hits me that she stopped painting the minute I showed up. "Unless," I say, pulling back to study her, "I'm making you feel uncomfortable."

She covers my hand with hers, a sweet gesture, when sweet has never been my thing. "I like you being here with me," she says, and when she lets go of my hand, I want hers back. Apparently, I like sweet now. A whole fucking lot. "I just wish you had a better place to work," she adds. "You should put a desk in here."

Or I could just buy a new house. A thought that stuns me, but I don't fight it. I'd buy ten houses for Faith, who is now flushing at her own words. "Not that I'm suggesting I'll be here often, but—"

"Faith," I say. "I made this room for you. I want you here all the fucking time." I don't give her time to object. I move on. "And I'm fine right here. I have a ton of paperwork to review and emails to answer."

She rotates to face me, on her knees, her hand on my leg. "Hard limit: One night."

My lips curve. "That didn't go as you planned, now did it?"

"No." She laughs. "It didn't." She stands up and heads back to her painting station, and I decide I'll talk to her about extra security tomorrow morning. She's had enough hell today, and she needs to paint. She has a show coming up. I watch her cover up before she turns back to me. "We need music."

I pull my phone from my pocket. "What are you in the mood for?"

"Surprise me, and I'll see where it takes me on my canvas."

I tab through my music and choose Beethoven's "Moonlight Sonata," and the moment it starts to play, she sighs. "Perfection," she says, a smile not just on her lips but in her eyes.

I relax into the wall, intending to reach for my files, but when the music lifts with a dramatic chord, I find myself watching Faith. Every stroke of her brush mesmerizes me as I wait for that red streak that she has proclaimed the beginning of a story. To me this symbolizes a feeling of hope—a look forward, not behind.

My mind goes back to the night we met, sitting in front of her fireplace, talking over pints of ice cream:

"Why black, white, and red?" I'd asked of her trademark colors.

"Black and white is the purest form of any image to me. It lets the viewer create the story."

"And the red?"

"The beginning of the story as I see it. A guide for the viewer's imagination to flow. I know it sounds silly, but it's how I think when I'm creating."

I cringe with the words: the beginning of the story as I see it.

The beginning of our story is nothing like she sees it.

CHAPTER FIFTEEN

Faith

There are things in life that are inarguably perfect: Milk chocolate. Good ice cream. A perfect sunset. A cold night with a fireplace. And me with a paintbrush in my hand for the past few hours, while Nick sits a few feet away, working, with Beethoven lifting in the air. There is just something about that combination that inspires me. Nick manages to calm and center me, which is really incredible, considering he's intense, demanding, controlling, and arrogant, while I am someone who is far more zen. But as I reach for the red paint to put the finishing touches on the mountaintop of my painting, I debate the reasons that might be, and an amazing list of answers comes to mind that I decide I might just talk over with Nick.

Satisfaction fills me as I stroke a brush through the red paint to complete my work in progress. In another fifteen minutes, I set my brush down. I'm done, and Nick is behind me almost immediately.

"Stunning, Faith," he says, his hands on my hips, and I find myself leaning into him, his big, hard body like a shelter in a storm that he's now helped me quiet. He really is a shelter, and there lies the core of why he calms me, why he works for me. He makes me feel like the rest of the world can't touch me.

"I like it," I say, inspecting my work. "But I'm not sure I'm going to use it for the show."

He turns me to face him. "Why?"

"It doesn't feel special. It's safe. I have to be cautious everywhere else. I don't want to do it on the canvas."

"You don't have to be cautious with me, Faith."

I reach up and pull his hair from the tie. "I know." I run my hands through his hair. "Because you're…"

He arches a brow. "I'm what?"

"Tiger."

"Tiger is for my enemies, remember. Not the woman I'm falling in love with."

There is that word again: love. It's terrifying and thrilling. "It's okay to be Tiger, Nick," I say. "That name is a part of you. I've met him." My lips curve as I think of the many sexy times we've shared. "I'm okay with him coming out to play."

He doesn't smile. "Tiger's not a nice guy, Faith. You remember that, right?"

I flatten my hand on his chest. "He's tough. He's hard. He's cold. And I really like him best when he's naked."

He remains expressionless for two beats, then laughs. "Ah, Faith. Woman, what you do to me. Maybe you need to put a little Tiger on your canvas."

My brow furrows. "What do you mean?"

"*You* are nice, Faith, but you have a darker side. That part of you that can take on the Tiger side of me and hold your own. That's the part of you that wanted out when you were in the club; it just wasn't the right place or way for you to do so. *The canvas* is your place. Put whatever you found in that club on the canvas. We both know nothing about that will be safe."

It's as if a switch flips in my mind. I've been boxed by everyone's expectations of me on and off the canvas. I twist around in Nick's arms and walk to my canvas, and I start to pick it up and move it off the easel. Nick is quickly there to help. "Where do you want it?"

"Against the wall seems to be the best spot," I say, already grabbing a blank canvas and setting it on the easel.

"I'll order you extra stands for your completed works," he says as I turn to my blank canvas, inspiration starting to form. "We don't want your work to get damaged," he adds as I reach for my brush. Nick intercepts, catching my fingers and walking me to him. "The food will be here any minute, sweetheart." He glances at his watch. "And it's almost ten. We both have early mornings."

I blink. "We ordered food?" I ask, then shake away the cobwebs, giving a low laugh. "Oh right. We did."

Nick laughs, that deep, rough, sexy sound I could really turn on and play like music, if it were possible. "We did." He motions toward the doorway. "Let's head to the bedroom and settle in so we can go to sleep after we eat."

"Well, as much as I want to argue, my hands are cramped, and my stomach is growling."

He unbuttons the cover-up I have over my clothes. "You can spend some time with Sara at Allure tomorrow and then come back here and paint."

"Yes," I agree, "but you know what? Let me just put a few strokes on the canvas. Just to get the inspiration started."

"You've painted for *eight hours*, Faith." He is suddenly lifting me, and I yelp as he scoops me up and over his shoulder.

"Nick, damn it, the blood is rushing to my head." He smacks my ass, and I arch my back.

"Nick!"

"Now where is that blood flowing, sweetheart?" he asks.

"You're evil," I say, thinking about the spanking he teased me with earlier today. "Really evil."

He keeps walking and doesn't stop until he's set me on my feet beside the bed. "Evil is your beautiful ass teasing my hand, sweetheart. You do need a good spanking."

Oh God. Why is just the promise of this man's hand on my backside so incredibly sexy? My nipples ache. My sex clenches, and my hand settles at his hip, my thumb intentionally placed near his cock. "I asked," I remind him. "You didn't answer."

He cups my face. "Sweetheart, when I spank you again, you won't be hiding from anything, especially me. I'll do it because you trust me and you want to feel that trust, and no other reason."

The doorbell rings. "And that would be the food. I'll bring

it up here." He kisses me and heads for the door. I inhale on his words, which were sexy and intimate and about us, but I turn and stare at the card from my father lying on the nightstand, where I'd set it Friday night, my mind replaying my exchange with Nick. It was the first time I'd seen his house:

"Where is your bedroom, Nick?"

"Up the stairs directly behind you."

I turn then and start up the stairs, my pace slow, calculated. I feel overwhelmed by him. I need to seduce him, to get back to a place I have control. I know every swing of my hips makes him burn. He doesn't immediately pursue, though. He's Nick, after all. Always dominant and in control, except when I make him want me. It arouses me, and it's powerful when he responds, when he needs me the way I always need him.

I walk into his bedroom, taking in the king-size bed and the masculine decor that fits him so well, and it affects me for no real reason other than the fact that everything about the man affects me. I need something now that I can't even name. An escape. That's what it was. I think this is the first moment I really realize how much this man could hurt me. I reach into my purse and grab the card from my father before setting my purse aside.

And then I sit on the bed with every intention of reading it. I think my subconscious just needs me to focus on something other than the man I am falling so very hard for. That I have fallen too hard for. He enters the room, and I swear he steals my breath with his size and just how damn beautiful he is, masculine and intense in his dark suit and white shirt in a way that only some men—very few, in fact—harness. But Nick does. So very well.

He looks at the card on my lap, aware, I know, of what it is. "I need to read this," I say. "And you know that means I need you."

His chest rises and falls, expanding with delicious perfection. He closes the space between us, his stride long, graceful. He stands above me. I want to touch him, but I don't. I need some control. I need him to touch me first, but he always wants to be first anyway.

I know this. He shrugs out of his jacket and removes his tie, tossing both to the center of the bed. And then he surprises me by setting the card aside and taking me down on the mattress with him, rolling to face me. "I'm not going to spank you, Faith," he says, sliding his leg between mine. "Not now. Maybe not even this weekend. I want you to see and feel me. I want you to remember me this weekend, not my hand."

Inhaling, I return to the present with the certainty that he's achieved that goal. I see him and feel him in every possible way. And maybe he knew I didn't really want to read the card. Because I don't. I turn away from it now, rejecting its content and walking toward the bathroom. I don't need my father's input on my career right before my show. Once I'm inside, I move my suitcase back into the closet, where I strip down. I'm about to pull on a sleep shirt I've brought with me when I spy Nick's row of T-shirts, the idea of wearing one of them winning me over quickly. I search through the various graphic designs and smile as I find a Batman shirt of all things. Oh, how Nick it is.

I pull it on, letting it fall to my knees, then grab my pink fluffy slippers from my suitcase. Shoving my feet in them, I return to the bedroom at the same moment Nick returns as well, bags in his hand. "*The Dark Knight?*" I say, pointing at the shirt. "Really?"

"I told you, sweetheart," he says, walking around the opposite side of the bed. "I'm not a nice guy, and neither are my idols."

"Batman is your idol?" I ask, settling onto the bed and accepting one of the bags.

"That one should have your egg salad sandwich and a bottle of water," he says before answering me. "And I don't have an idol, but I like Batman a hell of a lot more than Superman. Better outfit, more money, less rules." He sits down and checks his bag, then takes off his boots.

We do some shuffling of bags and drinks, and soon we are sitting facing each other with our bags as plates. "What about you, Faith?" Nick asks, unwrapping his sandwich. "Apparently, my club sandwich is a Philly cheesesteak."

"Do you like Philly cheesesteak?"

"It's greasy and unhealthy," he says. "Who doesn't like a Philly cheesesteak?" he asks, not waiting for a reply. "Back to more important things. Who's your idol?"

"At one point it was my father, but that ended. You know that. Aside from him, I have many artists that I admire. I think I told you that I really look up to Chris Merit. Aside from his talent, his family owed a winery in Sonoma, and he became so famous that it felt within my reach."

"In reality, I happen to know that he lived in Paris when he started painting and was always filthy rich, so you two aren't much of a comparison."

"True," I say. "And now it feels weird that I kind of idolized him, since I know him personally. But I did, and I still admire him."

"He's a good guy," Nick says. "And talented. I have one of his paintings in my office."

"I need to see that," I say, about to take a bite of my sandwich when a thought hits me. "I haven't even told Kasey I'm not going to be there tomorrow. I should text him."

"I'd like us to take him to dinner Thursday night," Nick replies. "We need to make him believe that I'm a co-owner, just like we do the bank."

"Kasey, too?"

"Everyone. It's the only way we make the bank buy into this. Is that a problem?"

"No. Whatever we have to do."

"On a positive note and another topic to discuss with Kasey," he says. "While you were painting, I heard from my assistant. She's lined up a team to do the assessment at the winery, starting tomorrow."

"Oh. Great. That was fast, but I need to warn Kasey about that, too. I need to grab my phone." I scoot off the bed and walk into the bathroom, where I find it in my purse. Once I rejoin Nick, I text Kasey. "How soon will we get the assessment results?"

"It's a big place. I expect it will take a few days."

My phone buzzes, and I glance at Kasey's reply. "All set. Dinner Thursday night, and he knows about the assessment."

"While we're on the topic of business," Nick says. "One more thing. Beck, the private investigator I told you I hired, wants to install cameras at your house and the winery. And he'd rather the staff not know."

My brow furrows. "Is there a problem I need to know about with the staff?"

"He didn't express a specific concern, but he did stress that he absolutely doesn't want the staff to know. It's his job to trust no one."

"Right. That makes sense. When does he want to do it, and how should I coordinate getting him into the locations?"

"He can get into both locations on his own."

"Okay, well, the fact that he can get into both locations on his own says I need a new security system. But yes. Whatever he needs to do. Tell him to do it." I take a bite of my sandwich.

He pulls his phone from his pocket and sends a text message before snatching up a few chips. He is about to set his phone down when it buzzes with a reply already. He reads the message and glances at me. "He's going to get it done tonight." He takes a drink of water and sets it on the nightstand while I manage another bite of my sandwich.

"And he's had no other luck on anything?" I ask.

"No, which is significant, considering his skill set. He's concerned there is more going on than we know and someone has covered it up."

My brow furrows. "Like what?"

"Is there any reason the winery might be worth more money than you think? Something no property assessment can find."

"I don't even have to think about that answer. Absolutely nothing comes to mind, and I can't believe my father knew of any such thing. He'd have told me, or at least left the details in his will." My eyes go wide, and I rotate to the nightstand, picking up the card. "Could this be where the answers lie?"

"No," Nick says. "He left this for a specific birthday, knowing that you could inherit before that date. And your attorney gave you no indication it needed to be opened sooner, upon his death." He takes the card from me. "He didn't support your art. If you want to open this, do it after you prepare for your show, and preferably after the show itself."

"That was my preference, actually, but if there could be answers we need inside—"

"I'll make you a deal. If I can't shut down these issues with the bank this week, we'll open it. Together, and if you want that spanking for just that reason"—his lips curve—"this time, I'll be happy to oblige."

My cheeks flush. "Thank you."

He laughs. "Thank you, sweetheart, for having such a sweet little ass." He sets the card on the nightstand. When my cellphone rings, my brows furrow. "What time is it?" I ask as I'm digging in the blankets for the phone I've now lost again.

"Eleven," Nick says, glancing at his watch.

I locate my phone right as the call ends, drawing in a breath at the number on the caller ID and sucking in hair.

"What's wrong?" Nick asks.

"It was Macom," I say, tucking the phone under the pillow. "Josh called earlier and warned me that he's become obsessed with talking to me. Josh didn't want me to talk to him. He said he messes with my creative process." My phone starts to ring again.

"Let me talk to that bastard," Nick says, reaching for it.

"No," I say, grabbing it first and standing up. "That would just turn into him calling Josh and Josh calling me."

"Block him."

"I almost did that earlier today, but that gives him power and satisfaction, too."

He stands up, hands on his hips. "You know, Faith. I'm starting to get the feeling that he has a hell of a lot of power and presence in our relationship." He doesn't say anything more. He rounds the bed, but he doesn't come to me. He passes me by, and I rotate to watch him disappear inside the bathroom. And while he doesn't shut the door, he's just shut me out.

CHAPTER SIXTEEN

Faith

I am stunned by Nick's reaction, but I am quickly reminded of the many ways this man has put himself on the line for me. He's pursued me. He's set up an art studio for me. Fought for me with the bank, and, today, professed budding love. And now, I've given him a proverbial punch—maybe I've even hurt him. I don't want to hurt him.

Dashing forward, I enter the bathroom as he enters the closet. Crossing the room, I step into the doorframe dividing the bathroom and the closet to find Nick standing with his back to me at the same moment that he peels his shirt over his head, muscles rippling, the small space suddenly even smaller.

"Nick," I breathe out.

He hesitates, not just in action—I feel the emotional hesitation, and I know that my instinct was right. I've hurt him, and that means that *I* can't have that same hesitation. "I don't love him. I don't even like him, but he and my mother taught me not to trust. I can't just make that go away, and I wish that I could. It's going to take time, but what I can tell you is that you, and you alone, are the reason that I'm learning to trust again."

Still he doesn't turn, shutting me out, keeping me at the distance he rarely tolerates. He inhales, his face lifting to the ceiling for several beats that are just too long for me. I close the space between us, and I pretty much collide with him as he turns to face me, my hand flattening on his chest, his catching my shoulders. "I will make him go away," I vow.

"I don't expect him to be out of our lives any more than I do my fucked-up father or your mother. They fucked with our heads. They made us, and they still play us."

This is a revelation about Nick he's never shared. "Your dad fucked with your head?"

"Of course he did. You know that I was raised by a rotation of nannies he fucked. He's why I am who I am today. Everything I do is to be better than him and different than him. But I know it. I admit it. I deal with it. You have done a lot of avoiding things in your life, Faith."

"You're right. I have."

"I'm in your life or I'm not. It's me. Just me. I can deal with the aftermath that he's created because I understand it. But only the aftermath, when he's past tense."

"He is."

"He just called you, and you didn't shut him down. That makes me feel like you aren't ready to let him go. And if you aren't—"

"He is *nothing* to me. *You are.* I just didn't plan to talk to him ever again."

"You're an artist, and so is he. You're going to see him. *We're* going to see him. Are you prepared for that?"

"Honestly? Not yet, but I will be. I didn't think or even dare to dream about being in a high-profile show while I was trapped by the winery. I didn't mentally prepare. I'm not like you, Nick."

"If you want me to make him go away, I will."

"And then you'll wonder if I would have done it without you. I need to handle him, and I will. Actually, I just want this done and over with." I twist out of his arms and charge through the bathroom into the bedroom, only to discover my phone ringing again.

Anger burns inside me for about ten different reasons: I've let Macom get into my head and inside my relationship with Nick. The man actually expects me to answer his calls when I haven't spoken to him in over a year. And I could keep going with the list of reasons, but I'm at the bed holding the phone, and I hit answer. "What do you want, Macom?" I demand, turning to find Nick standing in the doorway between the bathroom and the bedroom.

"Faith," Macom replies, his voice low, intimate, familiar, and I feel it like a punch in my belly.

I sit down on the mattress, my eyes on Nick. "Why are you calling, Macom?"

"I heard the good news about the show. Congratulations."

"Why are you calling me, Macom?" I repeat.

"I want to see you. Come here. Our bed misses you."

I laugh bitterly and cut my gaze from Nick's. "Are you kidding me right now?"

"I messed up."

"Let me be clear. We are *not* friends. We will never be friends. I don't think we were ever friends. We will *never* be anything but a bad mistake. Don't call me. Don't even talk about me. Stay away from me at the show. And be professional. Leave Josh out of this."

"I'll come there and help you make your show selections," he says as if I've said nothing. "I want you to do well."

"I've moved on, Macom. I'm in a relationship."

"Of course you are, but I'm up for the challenge."

"There is no challenge. *Do not* come here."

Suddenly Nick is on a knee in front of me, taking the phone. "This is Nick Rogers, Macom. I'm the challenge. Faith was done with you long before she left you, and you were too self-absorbed to see it. But if we need to talk this out, I have a private jet fueled and ready. I can fly you here, and we can sit and chat. You can tell me all about your art."

Nick abruptly lowers the phone and tosses it on the bed. "He hung up."

"You were supposed to let me handle this."

"Yes, well, sweetheart, I'm a little more possessive than I realized." His hands slide under his shirt on my bare thighs. "And if you're angry—"

"I'm not angry," I say, leaning forward and tangling my fingers in his loose hair, his protectiveness—possessiveness, even—hitting a nerve, and not a bad one. "I'm not," I say, shoving away the memory now stirred and focusing on this man, the man that matters. "I need you too much, Nick. I need you to know that's scaring me because I'm afraid you'll see it as something it's not."

"Then we'll be scared together, because I need you, Faith. So fucking much it hurts. Don't make me feel that alone because you're afraid of getting hurt. Because I'm just as afraid."

I pull back to look at him. "You're afraid."

"Yes. And I don't do fear. I don't wear it well, remember?"

"God, Nick. You are—"

He kisses me, a deep, drugging kiss before he pulls back, those deep dark blue eyes meeting mine. "I am what?"

"Everything."

"I like that answer," he says softly. "And in the midst of everything, I am the man who very much wants to fall asleep with you in his arms and wake up the same way, ready to go kick the bank's ass. Let's make that happen."

I nod. "Yes. I'd like that."

"What's your bedtime ritual?"

"Before I stopped painting, I would lay in bed and listen to music and think about what I might put on the canvas. What about you?"

"I go to bed."

I laugh. "That's pretty basic."

"I keep what I can simple." He kisses my forehead and stands up. "I'll be right back." He walks into the bathroom, and it hits me that I haven't taken off my makeup, but right now, I just don't care. I slip under the blankets and flip out my bedside light, inhaling the spicy, wonderful scent of Nick clinging to the blankets.

Nick reappears in the bathroom doorway, still shirtless, his hair tied back again, his jeans replaced with pajama bottoms. He flips out the bathroom light, and it's not long before he's in bed with me, propped against the headboard, his phone in his hand. "Music," he says, and with a punch of his finger, the soft, soothing sound of Beethoven's "Moonlight Sonata" fills the air.

My lashes lower a moment, and I take in the delicate notes. "I love it."

"I remember," Nick says, flipping off the light. A moment later, he's lying on his back and pulling me to his chest.

"Name one movie this music was featured in," I challenge, snuggling close to him, my hand on his chest.

"*Interview with the Vampire*," he says correctly. "Your turn."

"Nineteen seventy. *Love Story*. And it was a tragic love story that my mother loved."

"What's your favorite movie, Faith?"

"I don't have one. You?"

"Me neither."

"What's wrong with us?"

He laughs, that low, sexy laugh that is both soothing and arousing. "Let's find one together," he suggests. "It can be the first of many firsts for us."

"The first of many firsts," I murmur. "I like that."

He strokes my hair. "Good. Now close your eyes and paint."

I shut my eyes. "Paint," I whisper, listening to the music, the delicate touches of piano keys, thinking of my canvas. I can see myself painting, feel myself slipping into slumber. I have red paint, not black, and my brush is moving with purpose, speed. Emotion. The scene fades away, and suddenly I am cold and hot and cold again. I fight to open my eyes, and for a moment I do, feeling myself slipping in and out of a dream or a nightmare, but I can't seem to escape it. And then I'm back in time, inside the memory Macom and Nick had stirred tonight with that phone conversation. I'm at the dinner club with Macom, and I don't want to be there again. Not tonight. Not ever again. I don't want to relive this. But as hard as I try, I can't stop it from happening now any more than I could then.

In my mind's eye, I see myself in a short, silk, red Versace dress with deep cleavage that Macom had bought for me that night. Too much cleavage to suit me, but Macom likes to show me off. Maybe this should please me. Maybe it's pride. It doesn't please me, though, nor does it feel like pride. Macom himself is dressed in a black sweater and dress pants, his dark, curly hair neatly trimmed on the sides, longish on the top.

We enter the fancy, five-star dining room, his hand at my waist, and men turn to look at me when they would not look at other women in this part of the club—only those whose men allow their woman to be shared. I would not allow such a thing. I expect us to sit down, but instead we pass through a curtain, entering a sitting room that I've never visited, complete with a couch and two chairs framing a fireplace. Tom, a young and good-looking investment banker who often flirts with me, is standing at the fireplace. He looks up at our entry, eyes lighting in a way that tells me he's waiting on us.

"What is this?" I ask, but Macom doesn't answer. His grip at my waist tightens, and he urges me forward. "Macom, damn it," I say, digging in my heels.

He rotates me to face him, tangling his fingers in my hair. "A new game."

"No, I—"

His mouth closes down on mine in a deep kiss I cannot seem to escape, but I press on his chest, and he finally pulls back. "Relax, Faith. Every game we play makes us hotter and better."

"You want to share me? Is that what this is?"

"You're mine. He's just going to borrow." I shove back from him, and I'm pissed. I start to walk out of the room, but anger gets the best of me. I turn and storm a path to Tom, stepping to him and kissing him. He molds me close, his hand quickly on my breast, but I am done.

I push away from him and find Macom standing almost directly behind me. "He tastes better than you." I step around him and keep walking, straight out of the club door. And I keep walking, tears streaming down my face. I wanted my man to be protective—

possessive, even. I'd wanted him to want me that much. But he doesn't, and I either have to leave or find a way to deal with the reality: there is no such thing as a fairy tale. And maybe that's the problem. I wanted that fairy tale romance that doesn't exist, and I have missed that point. Everyone in that club, including Macom, knows that but me.

The images go dark again, and I feel my heart racing, but the music returns to me. "Moonlight Sonata." Soft piano playing. My hand on Nick's chest, his breathing steady. Calm returns, and I slowly sink back into the music, reveling in the feel of Nick next to me. I fade into sleep, and my mind goes blank, a sense of relaxation overcoming me, but somehow I'm now standing in my mother's garden. Or above it, looking down. My mother and father are there, kissing and laughing like young lovers, the way I remember them from my youth, but then my uncle walks up, taps my father on the shoulder, and my father backs up. My uncle takes my father's place with my mother and starts to kiss her. My father just watches. I start screaming at him, not them, but it's like I'm not really there. Like he can't hear me—or won't hear me.

I gasp and sit up, blinking into sunlight, a new day already upon us, and Nick is no longer in bed with me. "Faith," Nick calls out, rushing from the bathroom, now dressed in sweatpants and a T-shirt. "Sweetheart. Are you okay?"

"Nightmare," I say, throwing away the covers and scooting to the side of the bed. "Why are you dressed like that? Don't you have work?"

"I have a gym in the basement of the house. I was going to ask you to join me, but you were dead to the world. You want to talk about the nightmare?"

I inhale and let it out. "Yes and no."

He settles on his knee in front of me, his hands under his shirt and on my knees this time. "You have a few hours before you leave for the gallery, in which you could paint. Maybe you need to paint to clear your mind?"

"How can you know me this well?"

"Because I care enough to pay attention, Faith."

"Would you ever take me to your club?" I blurt before I can stop myself.

Something flickers in his eyes, there and gone, in an instant. "Do you want me to?"

"Would you?"

"Never. Not even if you asked."

"Why?"

"Because you're mine, Faith, and I don't share. And for the record, in case you forgot already: I'm yours, too, in all my arrogant glory."

I'm his, and he's mine. "It was about Macom," I say. "The nightmare was about Macom. And, oddly, my mother."

"I'm listening," he says, his expression unreadable.

"I relived the first night Macom tried to share me at the club."

"Tried?"

"Yes. There was a man who'd always flirted with me, and Macom wanted to watch me with him. I was furious. I left him there to do what he would. I walked home, and at first I said that I'd never go back. But then I decided that everyone at that club was smarter than me. They knew that pleasure was pleasure and expecting fairytale endings was pain. That's how I went back. That's how I became truly involved. And that's how I survived Macom. That's how I convinced myself we were the best I would ever have."

"Where does your mother come into play?"

"The images shifted, and I was in my mother's garden. I watched my father kiss my mother, and then my uncle showed up, and he backed away. He gave her to him. I was screaming at my father, but he couldn't hear me. It's like I wasn't there. He settled for my mother. He convinced himself they were the best he would ever have. I decided before I ever met you that I was done settling. I just didn't know where that would lead me or how to get there. Just that I needed to go."

"And you needed to tell me this why?"

"It led me to you, and while I do not want you to be controlling, I needed you to be the man you were tonight with Macom."

"Explain, Faith. I need to understand."

"We have the clubs in our backgrounds. I think I needed… When you took that phone, you made it clear we are just us. I needed to know that we are just us. That you will protect us, not give us away."

He cups my face, his voice low, raspy. "I will always protect not just us but you, Faith. And everything I do, I do for you. I need you to remember that. Promise me you will remember that. Tell me you know that."

"I do now. I know."

He pulls away and looks at me. "Don't forget," he orders, and on the surface his warning is all alpha male, but beneath it, in his deep blue eyes, there is something more. He lets me see that he is not unbreakable—that perhaps I alone could break him. The way he could break me. Something shifts and expands between us in those moments that I have never felt before. A bond forming that creates a need between us. We need each other. It is wonderful. It is divine. But long minutes after he's departed for the gym and I stand at the easel with a brush in my hand, I cannot help but wonder—when two people become this vulnerable to each other, when we need each other to keep from shattering, does this mean together we are weaker or stronger?

CHAPTER SEVENTEEN

Nick

"**W**ould you ever take me to *your* club?"

That is the question beating me to death while *I* beat a treadmill to death with a fast, hard run, the torment of her question lessened only by my fantasy of beating the shit out of Macom. Though another part of me wants to shake the man's hand for being stupid enough to lose Faith. I'm the winner in this one, but he also hurt Faith, and that part of me that isn't a nice guy really wants him to pay.

I finish running, and the idea of Faith upstairs waiting on me has me flipping out the light and skipping the weights. And when I would normally stop by the kitchen for a bottle of water, I continue onward, up the next level of stairs and into the bedroom, where Faith is not. Certain she's forgot the time and is still painting, I walk down the hallway to her studio and step through the doorway. Sure enough, Faith is painting, but from the silky sheen of her loose blonde hair and the faded jeans peeking from her cover-up, she's already showered and is completely unaware of my presence.

Being absorbed with her work, she doesn't look up, and God, she's beautiful when she's this focused on her art. The graceful way she moves. The way her brow furrows randomly with the strokes of her brush. The way her teeth worry her bottom lip as she tilts her head to study another angle of her work. Curious myself about what is newly developing on her canvas, I ease several feet deeper into the room behind her, keeping a distance so as to not break her concentration, but still she doesn't seem to know I'm present. Bringing her canvas into view, I'm surprised to find red as her master color, rather than her favorite black or gray, the image created appearing to be some sort of skyward half-moon with a circle beneath it. I don't know what she's creating, but the red tells me that she's doing what we discussed and unleashing a different part of herself.

Several beats pass, and she remains immersed in her work, which is my signal to get lost and let her work. I'm about to exit the studio when Faith laughs. I glance back at her, and she grins. "You're pretty easy to fool, Tiger. Did you really think you were that stealthy?"

I laugh and take a step toward her. She points her brush at me. "Stop right there. You go shower and get focused on your game, counselor. That's the point in this little exercise. You motivate me to paint. I expect you to keep being a badass attorney who doesn't lose."

"I don't know *how* to lose, sweetheart," I say, giving her a wink and heading down the hallway, and I hit the shower, following Faith's order. I'm 100 percent focused, but that focus is on her. She's worried about my career. She's worried about paying me back. She's a good person who deserves the world. I'm an asshole who plans to give it to her, when I would give it to no one else. Maybe that's the definition of love. Heartless bastards like me grow hearts. Whatever the case, I'm her asshole, and she's stuck with me. I'm going to make sure of it.

Twenty minutes later, not only shaved to the fully outlined goatee I prefer when headed to court, as I will this week, I've dressed in a gray pinstriped suit with a vest and a pressed white shirt. I'm standing at the mirror, fitting the black tie I've chosen to match the pinstripe around my neck, when Faith not only appears but scoots between me and the counter.

"I'll do it," she says. "If that's okay with you?"

"Sweetheart, if it's on my body, you can touch it."

She laughs. "That is such a you thing to say." She works the tie with expert technique, and I dislike the idea of her doing it for Macom, and I don't even care how possessive that makes me. "How did you learn to do this?" I ask.

"My father," she says. "He always wore a tie at the winery, and I had this obsession with artsy ties even before I started painting. I'd pick his tie and then tie his tie." She pats *my tie*. "Done, and you look good in this suit. Powerful. But then, you always have that alpha-power thing going on."

"Do I now?"

"You do. It's very sexy, but I'm pretty sure you know that."

I stroke the hair behind her ear. "And I know you didn't know I was there until the end. I watched you with your paintbrush, and, sweetheart, that is what I call sexy."

"I knew," she says. "I always know when you're close, Nick, but I was finishing one little spot that I didn't want to screw up, and then you were leaving." She reaches for my arm and glances at my brown Cartier watch. "It's seven. You have to be at work at eight."

"I'm the boss. I won't get fired if I'm late."

She pushes to her toes and kisses me. "The boss of everyone but me. I'm going to change shoes and touch up my makeup, and I'm ready to go."

She tries to move away, and I bring her to me, my hand tangling in her hair as I drag her mouth to mine. Taking a long, good morning drink of this woman before I say, "Sometimes you like it when I'm the boss. At least when we're naked, and that's not a bad thing. You like it. I like it."

"I know that."

"Just in case you *don't know*. I'm never going to hurt you, and I damn sure will *never* share you. You know that, right?"

"I already told you. I like when Tiger comes out to play. And don't start thinking I'm some shrinking violet, Nick Rogers. I told you some stuff. You know. Move on. And if you underestimate me, I'll end up on top every time that way. And sometimes I prefer *you* on top."

"As long as I'm inside you, sweetheart," I say. "I'll be on top, bottom, sideways, or any which way."

She shoves against my chest. "Go make coffee or whatever you do before work."

I laugh and step away from her and leave her in the bathroom, taking a path toward the stairs, but once I'm there, I pause, my curiosity over how Faith's new work is developing winning me over. Walking in that direction, I enter the studio, cross to the painting, and stare at what has become a dramatically changed image that downright punches me in the gut. I'm looking at two eyes that I know represent "An eye for an eye." Words she connects to Macom's betrayal. Macom, who she dreamed about last night. Suddenly, I feel like the fool, on my knees for a woman who's on her knees for another man. I don't want to believe that's true, but I don't know how else to read this, either.

I cross the studio and don't even consider the bedroom. I have a job to do and, as Faith herself said, a focus I need to maintain. I gather my work from my office and end up in the kitchen, where I set my briefcase on the island bar. Faith hurries down the stairs, her blonde hair bouncing right along with her beautiful fucking breasts in a light blue V-neck t-shirt, her purse on her shoulder. In this moment, I do not want to want her, and yet, as she nears and I watch the sway of her hips, my damn cock decides to stand at attention.

Where the fuck is my discipline?

"I thought you'd be on cup number two by now," she says, stepping to the counter directly across from me.

"I took another look at your painting," I say, deciding my focus is important. And she's distracting the fuck out of me.

"And?" she asks, sounding almost hopeful.

"And what, Faith?"

"What do you think? If you hate it—"

"You dreamt about Macom, and now you're painting about Macom."

She blanches. "What? No. That is *not at all* the case."

"It seems pretty damn clear."

"Then it's you who doesn't trust me, Nick. You who don't trust us. Because I told you about the dream, and I told you that dream was about us. And I did what I told you I was going to do. I'm getting Macom the hell out of our relationship. I'm facing the past. I'm owning it. And I own things by painting them."

"Is that painting going in the show? Is it to get his attention?"

"Oh my God. Did you hear anything I just said to you?"

"Answer the questions," I bite out.

"You're being a complete asshole right now, Nick Rogers. That painting is for me. For us. It's not meant for any other eyes."

I stare at her several beats, and she stares right back at me, not a blink. And I believe her. "I'm an asshole," I say.

"Yes, Nick Rogers, you are. You *really* are."

"Because you make me crazy."

"So, it's my fault that you're an asshole? Considering you were an asshole the night I met you, I'm pretty sure you mastered that skill long before you came along."

"I'm apparently practicing that skill right now. How am I doing?"

"Exceptionally well."

"I might end up in jail when I meet this guy."

"At least you'll have Abel to represent you."

I laugh, never a step ahead of this woman. "Indeed. At least I do. Will you visit me in jail?"

"I'd prefer to just keep you out of jail." Her mood shifts, darkens. "He's not worth it."

"But you are."

"Is that your way of apologizing for being an asshole?"

"If I want to apologize, I'll apologize," I counter.

"So, you don't want to apologize?"

My cellphone starts ringing, and I grimace. "And so Monday begins." I grab my phone from my pocket and glance at the caller ID, then at Faith. "A client who never uses my cell," I say, answering the line. "Devon."

"Holy hell, Nick. The feds want to talk to me. I have a deal that went sour. I'm scared, man. I need help." When a hedge fund billionaire sounds like he might just start crying like a baby, you know he's in trouble.

"What the fuck did you do, Devon?" I demand and then quickly say, "Don't answer that on the phone. Meet me in my office in twenty minutes." I end the call and dial Abel. "Heads up. Devon Stein. He's getting a visit from the feds. I need you to consult."

"When?" Able asks.

"Now. My office. Can you do it?"

"I have court. I'll call you when I get out, but make sure he keeps his mouth shut." He hangs up.

"I need to run, sweetheart," I say.

"I can take an Uber. No problem. Go. Do your job."

"You're not taking an Uber," I say, reaching in my pocket and setting a key on the counter. "Take the BMW."

"No, I—"

"*Sweetheart*. Take the BMW. I'll drive the Audi. The code to get into the house is 1588 in case you need to come back here. I could have a late night. I hope that I won't." I round the counter and pull her to me. "I'm sorry, and I said that because I want to say it. And I meant it when I said that I'm crazy for you, woman."

"You said that I'm making you crazy."

"That too," I say, kissing her. "Enjoy today. You belong in the art world, and you belong with me." I release her and head for the door, and as I step into the garage, I eye my custom BMW, my pride and joy, which Faith will be driving today. And I no longer care if Faith drives it as well as she rides me. I'll let her keep the damn keys and the car, for all I care. If Abel heard me say that, he'd already be planning a wedding. And it might just take something that dramatic to make sure she doesn't leave me.

CHAPTER EIGHTEEN

Nick

I arrive at my office building in the financial district in fifteen minutes. I'm on my floor in another five to find Devon pacing in front of Rita's desk, looking like he's slept in the wrinkled mess that is what I know to be his standard ten-thousand-dollar suit—a symptom of his excess. While I enjoy luxury, there is a point where money starts to control you, not you it, and that can lead to trouble, which I saw coming a year ago with Devon.

Rita spots me moments before him, her relief palpable, her red hair worn long today, while her patience is eternally short. Devon follows her gaze and rotates to face me. "Nick," he breathes out, and he really looks like he might implode if he doesn't spill out his confession here and now.

Exactly why I need him out of this lobby. "Have a drink in my office, my man," I say. "I'll be right there."

The minute he's gone and my door has opened and shut, I step to Rita's desk, and she lets out a breath. "He's guilty of whatever he's here to talk about. He's a guilty, walking-dead mess."

"Which is why I need North on standby to file an action, if it becomes necessary," I say, speaking of my associate. "And get him on the response to the bank on the Reid Winter Winery that needs to be done today."

"He already has the documents and is working on them now."

"Any further information on the inspection?" I ask.

"A team of five will be there any minute, and they plan to finish by tomorrow night."

I grab a sheet of paper and write down Faith's number. "Faith isn't at the winery. She's here. Kasey is in charge, but text Faith and me when the team arrives. If you have any trouble at the winery, call Faith. She knows who you are, but I left quickly this morning and didn't tell her you might be contacting her."

"Left quickly? As in she's at your house?"

"Drill me about my personal life later, when you can really dig your nails in and do it with full, irritating force. I need to see Charles tomorrow after that inspection is complete," I say of my banker. "Get him on the schedule, and if anyone from SF Bank calls, put them through." I consider a moment and write down instructions for North before handing it to Rita. "Have North ready to file these documents with the court the minute we receive the new evaluation of the winery."

She glances at the information. "This will put you in court Wednesday. I'll move your morning appointments. What else?"

"If Faith calls, put her through. And I need Frank Segal, an attorney practicing out of Sonoma, on the line."

"Now?" she asks incredulously.

"The minute you can reach him," I say, pausing at my door, "so yes. Now."

"You are clear on the fact that one of your largest clients, who's about to wet his pants, is in your office, correct?"

She's right. He'll melt down if I take a call when I'm with him. "Get Segal on the line the minute Devon leaves." I turn and head for my office.

"I really deserve those donuts, Nick."

I pause at my closed door. "Which is why you will have them as soon as you send someone to get them who is not you or me," I say before entering my office.

And holy hell, the minute I shut the door, Devon spews a mess of shit out at me that all but guarantees he'll be needing Abel a hell of a lot more than me. I listen to him, and despite all I have seen in my years of practice, this man manages to blow my mind. He's brilliant, with a wife and kids and a hell of a lot to lose, and yet he made stupid choices. When he's finally done and we have a plan to connect him to Abel, I watch him exit, with my father in my mind. Greed catches up to people, and I tracked my father's business dealings. When he wasn't banging a new woman, he was banging a new payday, and usually at the price of others. And that shit catches up with you. For some, it lands them in jail. Others, a grave.

That's not a hard place to go with my father, but how the hell did Meredith Winter end up dead, too?

Kurt arrives right at ten as scheduled, and I meet him in the conference room, where Rita has him waiting at the rectangular glass table. I like glass tables. There's nowhere to hide; no hidden hand gestures or body language. As for Kurt, a former SEAL, he's a casual guy who prefers jeans and T-shirts but wears discipline like a second skin, and today is no exception. He stands when I enter, his expression stoic, all six foot four inches of him pure steel. An intimidating guy to most, and in physical combat, I'd keep my gun pointed at him and never let go of the trigger. In a boardroom, I'm the one everyone fears, but guys like Kurt usually take a bit longer than most to figure that out.

"I'll cut to the chase," I say, motioning for him to sit and claiming the spot directly in front of him. "The club is your life, not mine; therefore, I'm gifting it to you. I'll have the paperwork ready for you tonight, and your only expense will be the taxes on the value of the gift. I'll front you that money in the form of a loan, if you need it. Or you can sell. I paid three hundred and fifty thousand for it. You can easily turn it for that or more, and I'll broker the deal for you."

He narrows his eyes on me. "Why wouldn't you sell it for yourself?"

"I don't need the money, and after years of service to that club, you deserve the reward."

"Why wouldn't you sell it yourself?" he repeats.

"A woman," I say simply. "I need it gone."

"That's becoming a familiar theme, considering you bought it when Mark Compton met a woman."

"Technically I bought it because of his legal issues, but she wasn't just a woman. She's his wife."

"A woman is why he stayed away," he says. "And I will never let a woman dictate my life." Words that echo my own sentiments before I met Faith. "If the club is now mine," he continues, "I'm not selling, and I don't need a loan. You pay me well, and I've recently made a smart investment that paid off."

"Well, then, I'll have the paperwork to you tomorrow," I say, standing and offering him my hand as he pushes to his feet. "But I need it signed tomorrow as well."

"Get it to me tomorrow, and I'll have it back to you by Monday. I need time for my attorney to look it over."

"It's a gift," I bite out.

"That comes with potential liability. I'll look for the paperwork." He heads for the door and exits.

I smile, that hard-nosed SEAL in him predictable in his skeptical pushback. I knew he'd want to have an attorney review what seemed too good to be true, even if he didn't act like it was too good to be true. And I knew he'd push for Monday, which is after Faith and I get back from Sonoma and a full two weeks before Macom fucks with her head again in L.A.

The phone on the conference table buzzes. "Segal is on the line," Rita announces.

I sit down and grab the receiver. "What do you know that I don't know?" I say, skipping the formality of a greeting. "What is it about the winery that makes the bank want it?"

"I have no idea," he says.

"What makes that property valuable beyond the obvious?"

"Asking your question ten different ways doesn't change my answer."

"The note Faith's father left for her," I say, hitting him from another direction. "Do you know what's inside?"

"That note is between Faith and her father."

"She hasn't opened it. Do you know what's inside?"

"Yes."

"Is there anything in that letter that tells us why the bank is after the winery?"

"Absolutely nothing. It's personal. It's not business, and she'd know that if she just opened it."

"Right. I'll be in touch." I end the call, my fingers thrumming the table, when Rita buzzes again.

"Beck is here."

She sounds uncomfortable. Beck has that effect on people. "Send him back."

"He sent himself back," she says, and sure enough, Beck opens the conference room door.

He's thirty-five. Tall. Quiet. Lethal. The difference between him and Kurt: CIA vs. SEALs. No conscience versus conscience. I don't get up. I let him come to me. He saunters toward me, dressed in black jeans and a Metallica shirt, his longish, black hair spiky. He claims the seat previously occupied by Kurt, his stare meeting mine, his blue eyes so damn pale it's like looking into the eyes of a husky on the prowl, ready to attack. You want this man on your side, but you protect your throat.

"I hope this visit means you finally did your job," I say drily.

His lips quirk sardonically. "Meredith Winter had a gambling habit most of her adult life. Ten years ago, her husband reined her in and put her on a budget."

"And made no provisions to control her when he died."

"Exactly. And when he hit the ground, she did, too. The underground poker rooms—and those dudes are bad news. She lost her touch. She took out markers against the winery, which explains why there was no money trail for her spending and why your father was paying her cash."

"If you want me to believe they both ended up dead over a gambling debt, you're barking up a fool's tree. My father would not just pay off her gambling debt, no matter how good a fuck she was. Not without leveraging her for the winery, and he'd put that in writing. You need to find it."

"I told you. Someone wiped the phone and computer records. There are entire periods of time missing from your father's and Meredith Winter's records. But there is an obvious suspect here. The next person in line to inherit, even if he had to force it through the court system."

"Faith's uncle," I supply.

"That's right. Keep her away from him."

"He fucked her mother. She hates him."

"Interesting," he says, though he never sounds overly interested in anything. "When?"

"The year Faith graduated from college."

"He was married then," Kurt says, proving he's been studying up. "And his wife is the female Mark Zuckerberg; her company is Facebook's biggest competitor. He wouldn't want his wife finding out he bent over his brother's wife, as she, from what I understand, gives him an allowance and keeps him on a leash."

"He's filthy rich. No prize at that winery would be worth killing over."

"But protecting his secret would be."

"None of this connects dots that make sense." I circle back to where we were. "This gambling debt was a tool my father used as a weapon. You need to find out why he needed that weapon, because that's why they both ended up dead."

"If you're right—and I believe you are—Faith is now the target."

"Which is why I'm taking attention and pressure off of her. I'm going to get my bank to buy out the bank note, and we've done up dummy documents to make me a key stockholder. That brings the attention to me."

"Or you trigger a reaction you don't want by making whoever

wants that winery think they can't have it."

"Pissed-off people make mistakes, and we'll be watching."

"Or your actions ensure that history repeats itself. Your father and Meredith Winter got in someone's way. Now you and Faith are in the way. They died. You two die."

"And would you suggest I do something differently?"

"No," he says, standing up and, without another word, heading for the door.

CHAPTER NINETEEN

Faith

I arrive at the Allure Gallery right at nine, parking the BMW in the rear of the gallery, running my hands over the logo on the dash with a smile. And not because it's a BMW but because it's *this* BMW. Because this one is custom, sleek, and sexy, just like the man who owns it. I'm just about to exit the car when my phone buzzes with a text from an unfamiliar number. *Faith, this is Nick's assistant, Rita. He's in a meeting but wanted you to know the minute the inspectors arrived at the winery. They are there now and have already checked in with Kasey.*

I am pleased by this text. It tells me that Nick listened when we talked. He's trying to keep me involved and informed. I text Rita back: *Thank you. I am looking forward to meeting you.*

Rita replies with: *When will that happen?*

This week, I hope , I reply.

Looking forward to it as well. Let me know if you need anything, is her message.

I smile at her offer, but as my mind turns to Kasey, I suddenly feel selfish for being here, not there. He's dealing with everything I don't want to deal with, and I've never put that on him or taken that off of me. I hit his autodial, and he answers almost immediately. "Everything is fine," he says, greeting me. "I'm quite capable, in case you've forgotten."

"You are incredible," I say. "Which is why I never want to take advantage of you."

"Please, Faith. Use me. Your mother did."

"My mother abused you."

"Okay. Your father used me. Use me like he did, but with less involvement."

"How is the inspection going?"

"They're on the other side of the property," he says, "and we don't even feel like they're here. Does this inspection get you out of probate?"

"It's a step to getting us out of all this mess soon," I promise, reading the concern beneath his question. The winery has been his world for all his adult life. "And we're close. The bank note is caught up. The bills will be by next Monday. And Thursday, I'm going to talk to you about finally getting you the appreciation you deserve."

"I don't need anything from you but some trust. Your father trusted me. Now it's your turn. Let me run this place."

"My father would roll over in his grave if he knew I didn't plan to run the winery."

"I loved your father, kiddo, but on this he was wrong. His obsession with you running this place was illogical. You have a dream. Most of us never make ours come true. Be the exception."

"Thank you, Kasey. I'm looking forward to talking Thursday."

"Me too. Now. Am I safe to promise vendors money by next Monday? Because I have someone waiting for me right now."

"Yes," I say. "Monday at the latest."

He lets out a breath. "I have to tell you. I'm relieved."

"Me too," I say. "All is well."

"That is good news for us all."

We exchange a few more words, and when we disconnect, I am feeling really good about Nick's idea to offer incentives, maybe even some ownership, to Kasey. He deserves it, and with the financial troubles moving behind us, he'll be the reason that I can keep the winery and focus on painting.

Exiting the car, I lock up and slip my purse over my head, a flutter of anticipation in my belly as I race toward the door. Sara must see me on a camera somewhere, because she opens the door before I can knock, greeting me in a pink Allure T-shirt. I step inside the gallery, and she pulls me into a hug, greeting me with such warmth that I feel like we are old friends. Only I don't have any old friends, and certainly none I'd want to call friend again. It's not long before I have my own pink Allure T-shirt on and we begin touring the gallery while she shares her vision for the structure of the displays and actually asks for my thoughts. We get excited together talking about random ideas.

By ten, we enter the private business area, passing the reception area and several offices before Sara presents me with an office. "This is yours for as long as you can help." She shoves her long dark hair back from her face. "There is a break room on the other side of the office area with lots of coffee options. And"— she sits down in front of me—"these are all the new artists who have submitted for the gallery's consideration. I picked my top ten. What I'm hoping is to see what your top ten will be, and then we can debate, narrow it down, and take ten options to Chris. He's basically endorsing them, so he gets the final say, even though he says he trusts me. I want him to pick."

And they already picked me. Chris Merit endorsed *me*. "I'm excited to do this."

"I'm excited to have you here. Take your time. Chris is deeply absorbed in finishing a painting right now, and he won't look at our picks until he's done. I just need to pick this weekend. I'm in the back far corner office if you need me, or"—she grabs a sticky note and pen, scribbling down her number—"just text me." She laughs. "Because why wouldn't you text me a few doors down?"

We share a laugh, and she leaves me to work. I stare at the painting in front of me, which is, of course, an incredible Chris Merit black-and-white cityscape. I study the technique, and I really don't notice anything else about the office for a good ten minutes. Only then do I notice bookshelves lining the wall to my left, filled with art books I'd love to study at some point. Right now, though, I have work to do, and I remove my purse and I'm about to stick it in a drawer. It's then that my phone rings, and I pull it from my purse and note Nick's number.

"Hey," I say. "How is that client situation?"

"Bad. He needs Abel. We're meeting with him at two. How are things there?"

"Fabulous. I love this place and Sara. Thanks for having Rita text me, Nick."

"I'm not trying to run your life, Faith," he says.

"Not on purpose," I say. "It's your nature to take control, and in case I've sent you confusing messages, I do want to be informed, but I feel immense relief to have you handling this situation for me."

"I actually need to talk to you about your mother. Were you aware that she had a gambling problem?"

"No," I say, shaking my head. "But isn't that just perfectly priceless. That's where the money went, isn't it?"

"That's where this seems to be headed," he says.

"And here I thought her only destructive vice was sex."

"Sex is not a vice."

"It is when you're married and fucking half the state," I say. "Unless, of course, my father liked to watch her with other men, as she claimed. In which case, he was more screwed up than her. I don't know why I was hoping for her bank account to save me. I need to save myself."

"You have me now, Faith."

"I know."

"Do you?"

"I'm trying to get us to that."

"Try harder. And just so you know, we should have the new evaluation by tomorrow. I'm meeting with my banker tomorrow to be ready to move the note, but I'm going to decide when to act based on how all the players are responding to the situation at the time."

His intercom buzzes, and a female voice I assume to be Rita's says, "Devon is melting down again. He's on the line."

"I'm not babysitting that stupid crybaby prick," Nick bites out. "Feel free to tell him that."

"Now that you got that off your chest," the woman says. "What would you like for me to say to him?"

"Whatever the hell you want to tell him, Rita."

"You're in a deposition," she says. "Remember that."

I laugh. "I like Rita."

"She's a pain in my ass today."

"Isn't everyone?"

"Yes, which is why I really need you here to fuck me into amnesia. I'd come over there and do a little artistic fucking with you, but I have a lunch thing I need to prep for. Think of me, sweetheart. I'm damn sure thinking of you." He ends the call, and I laugh, but it fades quickly.

I really want to end this nightmare with the bank. I need to do something other than wait on Nick to be my hero. I inhale and tell myself to make the call I know I need to make. Only I don't even know the number to call. I turn to the MacBook sitting on the desk and key it to life, looking up Pier 111, the business my uncle's wife founded that he helps run. Finding the main number, I punch it into my cellphone.

"Pier 111, can I help you?"

"I need Bill Winter, please," I say.

"May I ask who is calling?"

"Faith Winter."

"Hold, please." A few beats later, she returns. "He'll call you back. What number can he call you back on?"

I give her my cellphone number and end the call. Why did I even bother to make that call? He's a bastard. My cellphone starts to ring with a call from an unknown number.

Expecting it to be him, I answer. "Hello."

"Faith. What a surprise that you called. We've needed to talk."

I open my mouth to ask him about the bank and the value of the winery when it hits me. He's a bastard. He could try to take it as well. My mind races for a reason for this call.

"Faith?" he presses. "Is something wrong?"

"I had a dream last night," I blurt.

"About?"

"You. My mother claimed that my father liked to watch her with other men. Last night I dreamed that you were one of those men. Were you?"

CHAPTER TWENTY

Faith

He didn't say no.

That's what haunts me for the rest of the afternoon while I sit at my desk evaluating the files Sara gave me. Even after Sara and I dine on Chinese food and enjoy great conversation, I replay it again. And now, at nearly five o'clock, I do it all over again.

"My mother claims that my father liked to watch her with other men. Last night I dreamed that you were one of those men. Were you?"

"Sex is what put us at opposite ends of the world," he says. *"We're the only Winters left. We need to put the past behind us."*

"That's a yes," I say.

"That's a refusal to discuss my sex life with my niece. How are things at the winery?"

"We are not friends or family," I say. *"I have zero desire to discuss my life with you. I simply wanted to know if you and my father were both sick enough to share my mother. That simple. I got my answer. What I don't understand is why my father was upset when he found out you fucked her on your own. I mean, what difference does it make? You know what. This was a mistake."*

My phone buzzes, pulling me back to the present, and I glance down to find a message from Nick: *Client losing his fucking mind. I'll be another two hours. I'll bring home dinner.*

My stomach does this funny loopy thing it's never done in my life with the words *bring home dinner*. Like home is something we share. It's just a phrase, of course. It means nothing, but then, Nick does nothing by accident. And I'm officially falling so damn hard for Nick that there is no turning back. I'm in this, no matter how broken I end up.

I text back: *I can make my famous pancakes.*

He replies with: *Only if you make them naked.*

I laugh and type: *Batter splatters.*

Good point, he replies. *I want every inch of that gorgeous body feeling good next to mine. Call you soon, sweetheart.*

Sara appears in my doorway. "It's getting late. Are you staying a while?"

"Are you?"

"Chris isn't answering his phone, which means he's lost in his work. I figure I'll work another hour or so and then take him dinner."

"Nick is working late. I figured I'd stay another hour and then head home." Home. Now I said home.

Sara catches it, too, her lips curving. "It's nice to have you here in the city. I want coffee. You want coffee? They make a killer white mocha next door."

"White mocha?" I ask, perking up. "I'm in." I grab my purse and slip it over my shoulder before sticking my phone inside.

"Great. We can dash over there and be back in a few minutes."

We make our way to the door and step outside, both of us hugging ourselves against a chilly wind, the smell of the ocean air touched by the scent of fresh, hot nuts from a nearby vendor. In that moment, I decide I love this city. The smells. The art. The energy. *Nick.*

"We have arrived," Sara announces, indicating a door only a block from the gallery.

"Rebecca's," I murmur, reading the writing on the door. "Didn't Chris paint something dedicated to Rebecca?"

"He did," she says, and rather than offering more detail, she opens the door, motioning me forward.

I enter the adorable little shop with paintings of people drinking coffee on the walls, clusters of wooden tables, and booths lining the left wall. Sara joins me, and we approach the register, where a glass display case allows me to drool over a tempting selection of cookies and sweets.

"Usual, Sara?" a tall man with dark brown hair and glasses asks.

"You know it, Mick," Sara replies, "and anything Faith wants is on the house now and forever." She glances at me. "We own this place, too. Mick is our manager and co-owner."

"Oh, well then, thank you to you both," I say, placing my order, and it's not long before Sara and I claim one of the cute wooden booths in the back of the shop, with Mick's promise to bring us our drinks.

"So, you own the gallery and the coffee shop," I say. "That's a great combination so close together."

"Well, there is a connection, which is Rebecca. It's a long story, but she worked for the gallery. She spent a lot of time here. We were going to rename the gallery Rebecca's, but we had some name recognition issues and decided to make the coffee shop Rebecca's. We remodeled it to add these cute booths and overhauled the menu. We wanted it to be her place."

Our order arrives, and by the time we're alone again, despite my curiosity about Rebecca, I never get the chance to ask questions. "Oh yikes," Sara says. "I just realized I left my purse and phone next door. I need to run back."

"Of course," I say, and we hurry to the door and back to the gallery.

"Before you go back to work," Sara says, "I want to show you something in my office."

I follow her to the corner office and step inside, my lips parting instantly. "Oh my God," I whisper at the sight of a mural on the wall behind the massive mahogany desk. A painting of the Eiffel Tower in Chris's signature black and white. "It's incredible," I murmur, crossing to stand behind the desk, studying the tiny details that few artists ever master.

"Look up," Sara says, and, obediently, my gaze lifts to find another European scene.

"The Spanish Steps," I say, and I can't help myself. I set my cup down and lay down on the floor, staring up at it. More details. More perfection. "Wow."

Sara laughs and appears above me. "How's the view from down there?"

"Spectacular. He's incredible, Sara. Each step is different. The shadows. The shading. The texture."

"Sara."

At the sound of Chris's voice, my eyes go wide, a cringe following. How did I let myself end up on the floor?!

"Chris," Sara says, whirling around to greet him.

"Fuck, Sara," he says, his voice growing closer. "Why aren't you answering your phone?"

Sara is around the desk in a heartbeat, and I don't know what to do. Stay down or get up?

"I forgot it when we went to the coffee shop."

"Baby," he breathes out. "It's only been a few months."

My brow furrows at the curious comment that seems to explain his over-the-top reaction.

"Seven months," she says. "I know that's still not a long time, but we both need to let it go. We need some semblance of normalcy."

"Normal?" he asks. "Have we ever been normal?"

"No," she says, her voice softening. "And I love that about us."

"Keep your phone with you, baby," he says. "Please."

"I will," she promises. "Stop worrying."

"I won't," he promises. "Did Faith already leave?"

"Actually," Sara says. "She's on the floor behind the desk."

I cringe all over again, and suddenly Chris is standing over me, big, blond, and wearing a T-shirt that displays the artistically perfect, multicolored dragon tattoo sleeve covering his right arm. "Why are you on the floor?" he asks.

"I was admiring your work. It's stunning. The detail is perfection, and yet you had to do it on a ladder." I sit up, hands behind me, holding me up. "Is it bad for me to admit I have a crush on you right now? Completely professional, of course, but it's powerful."

Sara laughs and hitches a hip on the desk. "A lot of people feel that way about Chris."

Chris squats down in front of me, his intense green eyes boring into mine. "But not you," he says.

I blink. "What?"

"Don't idolize another artist," he scolds. "Appreciate their skills. Study their technique, but when you idolize them, you can't see your own work clearly. Focus on your own work, and based on what you're doing thus far, I can promise you success will follow."

"In fact," Sara says. "Why don't you come to work here full time? Chris can mentor you, and I get two gifted artists helping me make this place a success."

I blanch. "I... I wish that I could, but I can't. I have the winery to think about."

"Don't you have a management team to run it?" Sara asks.

"Yes, but it's complicated. And I can't afford a misstep. I'm alone—"

"What about Nick?" she asks.

"Nick and I are new, and I don't expect or want him to take care of me."

"That's a conversation for you and Sara," Chris says, "but all I can say is that painters paint."

"I know," I say, "but my family has owned this winery for generations. It was everything to my father. He expected me to run it."

"Your father," Chris says flatly. "That's another topic for Sara. And on that note, I'm leaving." He stands up and turns to Sara, and I swear he doesn't even touch her, and they sizzle.

"I'll meet you at home."

"I'll be there soon."

"Your phone," he says.

"I know," she says.

They stare at each other for another few sizzling moments, and then he's gone. To my surprise, Sara then sits down on the floor next to me, cups in hand, and hands me my coffee. "Sorry about that."

"I'm sorry. I feel like I eavesdropped."

"You didn't. And Chris is protective, but he's not that over-the-top. There was...an incident in Paris." She cuts her gaze and visibly shakes herself, then rotates to lean on one shoulder and face me. "I can't talk about it. Maybe one day, I'll tell you. Not now. Even if we knew each other that well, I'm just not ready, but let me say this, Faith. The past year has reminded me that life is short. We only get one chance to live it. Painters paint."

"I know, but it's complicated."

"My father is very rich."

"Like Chris."

"My father is nothing like Chris," she says. "Chris is strong, tough, dark in ways I understand, but he is kind, generous, gifted, generous. Did I say generous?"

"And your father?"

"Brutal. Self-centered. He treated me and my mother horribly. And he wanted me to live the life he designed, and when I refused, he disinherited me. But even then, when I had the courage to walk away from him, I took a teaching job, even though art was what I'd studied and loved."

"Why?"

"Fear. Money. Stability. You know galleries don't pay much."

"What changed?"

"I found a journal. Rebecca's journal. Inside it were all her deepest thoughts, fears, and confessions. Impossibly, it seemed, she wanted to be in this world, too, but resisted for the same reasons I did. But then one day she walked into a gallery—this gallery—and her life changed. She dared to chase her dream. And she was younger than me. Braver. She inspired me. I came to look for her, and she was gone. I never met her. I took her job. She led me to my dreams. To Chris. And now..."

"I'm here," I say, rotating to lean against the desk. "And with Nick."

"Yes," she says.

"I don't want to get ahead of myself."

"Is that comment about your art or Nick?"

I glance over at her. "Both, I think. Nick and I are new."

"I moved in with Chris a few weeks after meeting him, and I was terrified. He was bigger than life."

I face her. "Yes. Nick is so—everything."

"Good. He should be."

"I'm not ready for him to be everything."

"Because you're scared?" she asks.

"Yes. He hasn't revealed all of himself. I know this. I sense it."

"Chris once told me that we are all the sum of all of our broken pieces. You can't grow if you don't risk more damage, Faith. You can't find the person who makes you whole again if you're afraid. Nick. Your art. Whatever it is, ask yourself: what if there is no tomorrow? Because there was no tomorrow for Rebecca. It can happen to any of us." She cuts her gaze and swallows hard, seemingly shaken, before she stands up. "I want you to work here," she says, pushing past the obviously upsetting topic. "I want you to paint one of the offices the way Chris did this one," she adds. "Pick one. Any one, but if you say you'll do it, you can't stop coming here until it's done."

"You want me to—"

"Yes. Say yes, Faith."

"Yes."

She opens a drawer and pulls out a key, offering it to me. "Your key. I'll pay you two hundred thousand dollars a year. I'm going home to my husband. The security system arms if you hit the button by the door." She starts walking toward the door.

"Sara," I say.

She turns to face me. "Yes?"

"Thank you."

"No thanks needed. I'm really glad to have you here." She disappears into the hallway, and I believe her. Sara and I are alike in ways few people could understand. And suddenly I have two people in my life who fit.

I've never had anyone in my life who fit.

But she fits. *Nick* fits.

I inhale on a ball of emotions. Fear? Is that what is controlling my decisions? And if it is, how did fear become that powerful in my life? How did I convince myself that fear was strength? Because I did. And it makes me angry. I hate that this is what I've become. My phone vibrates with a text, and I open my purse to find a message from Nick: *I'm outside.*

He's here. He is always here when I need him, and if I let it happen, that will be always. And needing him doesn't make me weak. It makes me brave. Suddenly, I want to see him; I want to feel what he makes me feel and see if it feels different after that conversation with Sara. I exit Sara's office and hurry to my new office, pausing with my hand on the light switch, envisioning Sonoma on the walls. Or maybe something new and daring. My lips curve, and I shut out the light, my pace hurried as I exit into the gallery, a little thrill in my belly as I think of my art on display. I reach the exit and open the door, punching the security button before I step outside. And there is Nick, looking like sin and sex in his tan suit, leaning against his Audi, the beam of a streetlight illuminating him.

My heart starts to race, and I start walking, his eyes—those intense, blue eyes—following my every step, a curve to his mouth. And the minute I step in front of him, he pulls me to him, that raw, sexy scent of his consuming me. "How the fuck did I miss you this much?" he asks, his mouth closing down on mine. And oh, what a kiss it is. Deep. Passionate. Hungry. Like he has been starving all day, and I didn't know until this minute that I have been, too. "I have something for you."

"That wasn't it?" I ask, sounding breathless. Feeling breathless.

"That was just hello, sweetheart." He strokes a lock of hair from over my eyes. "I was going to save it for your show, but I think it's a good way to celebrate you being here today instead of in Sonoma." He pulls a box from his pocket and opens it to display a jeweled necklace, shaped like a paintbrush and color palette.

"Nick," I whisper, completely blown away, and not because the stones glisten with reds, blues, and greens. It's the sentiment, the thought he's put into this. I push to my toes and kiss him. "Thank you. It's perfect."

"You're perfect, Faith."

"No, Nick. I'm broken. But I'm pretty ready to be broken with you, if you think you want to be broken with me."

"Not broken. Together. Whole. Us. We. You and me."

"Yes." My heart swells all over again. "I like how that sounds."

"Me too, sweetheart. And how's this for a plan for the night? We walk two blocks to the best Mexican food place in town. After we eat at Diego Maria's, we go home, where the process is: Fuck. Paint. Fuck. Paint. Sleep. No nightmares tonight."

I smile. "I like that plan."

"But do you love it, Faith?" he asks, his voice low, raspy, and I'm not sure if we're talking about the plan or us. Either way, I don't let fear win this time.

"Yes," I say. "I do."

CHAPTER TWENTY-ONE

Nick

Faith and I are up early the next morning, her in her studio painting again, and me back in the basement on the treadmill. I run with the same fierceness I did yesterday, but this time, my mind isn't on the club, but rather a replay of Beck's ominous warning about history fucking repeating itself, with a repeat of a double murder the outcome. I am stuck in one of those rock-and-a-hard-spot places that I've always called myth, and it pisses me off. I can't delay my actions and risk Faith losing the winery, but before I act, I need a better plan than "I hope like fuck not" when it comes to Faith and me living or dying.

I punch the stop button on the treadmill, and by the time I step off the belt, I'm already dialing Beck. "Once the inspectors give me an evaluation on the winery," I say the minute he answers, "I have to move. I have to file a petition and claim Faith's rightful inheritance. I can't give the bank time to undervalue it with their own inspectors, which could well lead to Faith losing the winery."

"What's the timeline?"

"We get the evaluation back today. I meet with my banker later this afternoon. If the evaluation comes back where I need it, we'll file an emergency request to be in court Wednesday or Thursday, at which time my bank will buy out the note. If the evaluation doesn't come back where I need it to be, I'll package it to get it there, and we'll be in court Thursday or Friday." I look up to discover Faith standing in the doorway, hugging herself, the look on her face telling me that she heard every word.

"I have dirt on three people in the bank, and I've used it. They aren't breaking. That means they are either scared or we're wrong. And I don't think we're wrong."

"And your solution is what? And don't tell me you need to think this time."

"Whatever action you take, at least getting rid of both of you is harder than getting rid of just Faith, especially with my team watching."

"Holy fuck. Is this really what I'm paying you for? Get me *answers*." I hang up and focus on Faith. "Hey, sweetheart," I say, crossing to stand in front of her, my hands on her shoulders. "How is painting going?"

"Why would you want to delay claiming the winery?"

"When you take someone out at the knees, you want to know what their reaction will be."

"If we're already with another bank, what can my present bank possibly even do?"

"The question is, what are they motivated to do and why," I say, sticking to the truth but leaving out murder as an option. "Let's grab some coffee while we finish this conversation."

"Nick—"

I kiss her. "Coffee. Conversation. Me. You. Upstairs." I turn her toward the stairs and place her in motion.

Once we're in the kitchen, coffee in hand, we lean on the same side of the island, facing each other. "I'm very confused by the conversation I just heard. And even your response. Is the bank going to lash out at you? Because I don't want you to end up with trouble over me."

"Sweetheart, you and I are in this together. And when someone goes to this much trouble to get something and you keep them from getting it, you have to be prepared for anything. Especially when you don't know all of the facts, and we don't."

"I need to just open that card from my father. Now. This morning."

She starts to move away, and I catch her arm. "I called Frank. He knows what it says, and it's not what we need."

"Did he tell you what it says?"

"Only that it's personal and it has nothing to do with business."

She inhales and sinks onto the edge of the stool. "Okay. Well, I always thought it was. You know. A good ole personal punch in the chest. The whole: Your destiny is the winery. It's in your blood. I'm counting on you. Art is a hobby. Set it aside. Focus."

I step to her and run my hand down her hair. "Don't do that. Don't let this get into your head. You're an artist. That is what you want. That is what *you are*."

"I called my uncle," she surprises me by saying.

Alarms go off in my head, and I pull back and rest my elbow on the table. "When and why?"

"Yesterday. I meant to tell you sooner, but last night was good, and I didn't want to ruin it with him."

"Why did you call him and what happened?"

"I got this idea in my head that he might know what the value of the winery is outside the obvious, but the minute I heard his voice, I had second thoughts. I don't trust him. I was afraid that if I alerted him to a potential payoff he might try to take it, despite being a wealthy man."

Smart girl, I think. "Then what did you say to him?"

"I blurted out that my mother said that my father liked to watch my mother with other men and asked if he was one of them."

"Holy shit, woman," I say, scrubbing the new-day stubble on my jaw. "What did he say?"

"He didn't say no. He talked around it."

"Holy *fuck*."

"I know. But what doesn't make sense is why my father would be furious about him sleeping with my mother if they'd already been together. As in all of them. Unless their fallout wasn't about sex at all." She shakes her head. "But then he swears he and my father made up before my father's death."

"Something with him doesn't add up, but Beck can't connect the dots between him and the bank. Whatever the case, I'm moving forward. I'm going to get in front of a judge and get you out of probate. But from a timeline standpoint, I may have been overly ambitious with that Thursday night dinner with Kasey. Let's make it Friday night."

"He'll be fine with that. I talked to him yesterday, and I'm feeling really good about him running things without me."

"Good. You've come a long way in a short while, sweetheart. And on that note. Show me what you painted this morning."

She stands up. "Not what I was supposed to be painting," she confesses as we start walking.

"What were you supposed to be painting?"

"Something appropriate for the show," she says. We start up the stairs, and she adds, "I'm obsessed with those eyes. And I don't even think it has anything to do with the whole 'face the past' motto I'd used when I picked up the brush. It's just different and challenging. I'm enjoying it."

"You know the saying. Do what you love and success will follow."

"I need to move on and work on my final show piece. Oh, and that reminds me. Sara wants me to do a mural in one of the offices."

"What kind of mural?"

"It will cover one of the walls, and it can be anything I want it to be, but it's kind of intimidating. Chris painted her office."

"You need to stop comparing yourself to Chris."

"Funny you say that. *He* said that."

"Maybe he'll be the mentor you need, then," I say as we enter the studio and cross to stand in front of her canvas, which is now well-developed. One of the eyes is now filled with a rainbow of colors. The other is red and black. Almost as if it's her past and her present. And I can't explain what it is about two eyes on a canvas, but it's brilliant. "You have to put this in the show."

"No," she says. "Macom will read into it, and I don't want that drama. The entire point of this painting was to face the past and get rid of it."

"You just said it had become about the challenge. And it shows. And if you want to stick to the original theme of facing your past, face Macom with this painting. Get rid of him in person. And if he doesn't get the idea, I'll handle him."

She narrows her eyes on me. "You want trouble."

"I love trouble."

"You want trouble with him."

"I want to beat the shit out of him."

"Nick. You can't—"

"I can," I say, pulling her to me, "but I won't."

"Promise."

"I promise, unless he makes it impossible to resist."

"*Nick.*"

"Sweetheart, I'm not violent, but I am brutal. Come get naked with me and I'll show you."

"How did you just make that sound sexy?"

"Must be love, sweetheart," I say, "and now, I'm going to do things to you that you won't forget for the rest of the day. And *that* is a promise." I scoop her up and start walking toward my bedroom and my bed, where she belongs. And I'm going to make sure she knows it.

I arrive at work with a box of donuts, which I set on Rita's desk, earning me a smile. "You remembered."

"I did," I say. "Because you, Rita, are like Glinda the Good Witch, who's a really good bitch to everyone but me, when *you are well-fed*. I like you well-fed." I head to my office. "Whatever I'm doing today, when that property assessment arrives, get it to me." My mind turns to my personal banker. "What time will Charles be here?"

"Four o'clock," she says. "And North is on standby for the emergency filing the minute you say go. It's prepped and on your desk. He, on the other hand, is sleeping in his office. He's sick. The kind of sick that makes being sick look good."

"Fuck. Send him home."

"I tried. He refused."

I walk back to her desk, pick up her phone, and dial his office. "North?"

"Yes?" He starts coughing.

"Get the fuck out of my office before you make me sick." I hang up, and Rita opens the donut box, pointing to a certain donut. "Your favorite."

I turn away and walk into my office. About the time I reach my desk, my cellphone buzzes with a text, and I have to sit down when I see it. "Holy Mother of Jesus," I murmur at the sight of Faith's uncle, naked, tied up, and with a woman—I think she's a woman—but whatever the case, he or she is spanking him. Rita's voice lifts from the lobby, and suddenly Beck is walking into my office without knocking. My intercom buzzes. "I told him to wait," Rita says. "He's impossible."

"Yes, he is," I say. "But it's fine. I'll deal with him."

Beck's lips twist sardonically with my comment, and he shuts the door, his dark hair extra spiky today. His T-shirt—an image of a middle finger with "fuck you" printed above it—is somehow appropriate, considering that photo he just sent me. He crosses my office and sits down on the arm of a visitor's chair—always a rebel, even in the smallest of ways. "You got my good morning calling card, I assume?"

"I did." I lean back in my chair. "Did he?"

"Not yet," he says, "and here are my thoughts. We both know that you already decided you're making your deal with your bank and hers. If her bank simply thought they could cash in on the winery, it's over. If there's more to it, it's not, and we have two sources of potential trouble: someone at the bank and the naked, perversely kinky uncle." He holds up his hands. "Married uncle. We both know you'll use your extremely large bank account to influence her bank. *I* will handle the naked married uncle."

"I didn't hire you to fly blind and tape on Band-Aids, Beck."

"We both like trouble," he says. "Maybe there isn't trouble to be found. Until we get the autopsy report, we don't know, and unless you want to wait on that report, this is where we're at."

"Are the cameras in place at her house and the winery?" I ask, concerned about Faith's safety.

"Yes, and we're watching her so closely that I can practically tell you what color Faith's panties are." He holds up his hands again. "Don't worry. I'll ask if I'm curious. I'm curious. What color—"

"Get the fuck out."

He laughs and heads for the door. The minute he's out of my office, Rita is inside. "Seems a good bribe works wonders. We have the winery's new evaluation."

"How much?" I ask.

"Forty million," she says. "Five million more than Faith's note with the bank."

"Fuck me in a good way. Get Charles—"

"He's on his way over now. Look over the filing, and I'll get it done myself. North and the trash can are now one."

I reach for the documents she needs, do a quick review of the key points, then hand them to her. "File it at four o'clock. I don't want the bank to have time to get someone to the winery before we end up in court."

"Can you get an emergency hearing tomorrow? Because the Nichols family is coming in at ten, and you know—"

"How they are. Yes. I do. Plan on Thursday."

"Got it," she says. "Is Faith prepared for court? She'll need something to wear."

"Fuck. Yes, she will, and no, she isn't."

"I can order her some clothes, but I have no idea on shoe size."

"Negative. If I just order her a wardrobe, she's going to be pissed."

She arches a brow, her hands settling at the waist of her navy dress. "Really? Most women would love for a man to buy them clothes. Interesting. I *like* her already. Did you say—or did I overhear—that she's working at a gallery here locally?"

"Allure Gallery."

"I'll put your black card on file at several boutiques nearby." She pulls her phone from her pocket and tabs to the gallery. "Chanel and Dolce & Gabbana are two blocks away. I'll get it done right away." She glances at me. "When do I meet her?"

"Go file the paperwork and eat a damn donut," I say.

She smiles and walks toward the door.

She's barely had time to get there before I've sent a text to Beck with the details. Next up, I dial Faith. "Forty million, Faith."

She breathes out. "Oh, thank God. It's lower than I expected but still good, and I can't believe the bank really thought that I'd come in under that."

"I suspect they would have come in with a much different number than our person came in with. Whatever the case, it's done. We beat them to the punch."

"So now what?"

"I work my magic, and you're not only out of probate, my bank owns your note by the time we return to Sonoma. But I need a complete ledger of all your vendors and outstanding accounts payable."

"You're going to pay off the bills, aren't you?"

"We talked about this, sweetheart."

"Yes. I know."

"And?"

"And I'll have Kasey and Rita connect. Does that work?"

"Yes. It does. This is good, Faith. If all goes as planned, we'll be going to court Thursday." I decide a conversation about money and shopping is better saved for in person, but she goes there on her own.

"I need to be in court?"

"Yes," I say. "You do."

"I have nothing to wear here. I have to go buy something."

"About that—"

"No. You're paying off my debt. I will not use your money to go shopping. End of subject."

"Faith—"

"No."

"Rita is putting my card on file for you at Chanel and—"

"No. *Move on*, Nick."

I move on. For now. "I'll have a plane on standby for either Thursday night or Friday morning, whichever we decide we prefer. Any thoughts?"

"Friday," she says. "I don't want to put that pressure on us Thursday."

"Friday it is," I say, pleased that she so easily chose to stay here instead of go there.

She's silent several beats, and then: "Nick."

"Yes, sweetheart?"

"Thank you. For *everything*. Even trying to spoil me with clothes."

"The only thank-you I need is you naked in my bed tonight. I'm going to be late, but I'll update you soon." I end the call, push away from my desk, and stand up, walking to the window. Maybe there were no murders. Maybe this is over the minute I get that autopsy report, but every day that passes, I feel the betrayal of my lies as much as I dread telling Faith the truth. How the hell do I tell a woman who has become everything to me, who I've asked over and over to trust me, that I thought she was a killer? I press my hands to my desk. I have to make her love me more than she can possibly hate me.

CHAPTER TWENTY-TWO

Nick

The "stupid" disease erupts not long after the evaluation comes in on Reid Winery. Every client I personally handle needs me personally, and why? Because they've done something stupid and the only pill that will fix them is me. It's nearly six p.m. by the time the eruption calms down, but I've still managed to secure my Thursday court date, coordinate action with Beck, and pound on Abel until he confirms that the autopsy on my father has become one big fuckup. We are weeks from answering the murder question, and therefore weeks before I can risk telling Faith the truth.

Rita appears in my doorway. "Your broker has called four times," she says, walking to my desk, an envelope in her hands. "I suspect that means he's called your cellphone at least that many times."

"I'll call him back."

"I know," she says. "You've told me that four times. And I know, Nick Rogers, that you're this mega-superstar attorney, but apparently, I'm older and wiser. So here is some sound advice. When someone controls as much of your money as that man does, and he calls that many times, call him back."

I scrub the back of my neck. "Right. I will."

"When?"

"Before I leave."

She gives me a keen inspection. "You haven't even started prepping for the Nichols meeting tomorrow, have you?"

"No. I have not."

"What do I need to do?"

"Go home. I've got this."

"You're sure?"

"Positive."

"A few updates first. Number one: Kasey sent me the accounts payable for Reid Winery. All the bills are now paid in full, and I have it set up for him to send me the bills once a week."

"Excellent."

"Number two." She sets an envelope on my desk. "This came for you. It's from Faith. And if it includes further accounts payable, I haven't paid them. I didn't know if that's what it was, and I didn't want to risk invading your privacy."

I arch a brow. "And you've cared about my privacy since when?"

"Since your privacy became Faith's as well. Do you want me to arrange dinner delivery?"

"No. I'll wait."

She gives me a knowing look. "To eat with Faith."

"*Yes*, my nosy-ass assistant. To eat with Faith."

"Good," she approves. "You've been alone too long. And on that note, I'm going home and leaving you alone."

She heads for the door, and I reach for the envelope, opening it up to find a check for sixty thousand dollars and a note:

Nick,

You promised to take this, and I believe that you're a man of your word. And I owe you this and so much more, and I'm not talking about money. I'll be waiting on you when you get home.

Naked.

Faith

My lips tighten, and I reread the note a total of three times before I set it on the desk. I don't want her damn money, but I do want her. And naked or not, I like the idea of going home to her. I exhale and tap the desk, and while it matters to me that she isn't in this for the money, I want her to take the damn money back.

My cellphone buzzes where it rests on my desk, and I grimace at my broker's number on caller ID yet again. *But* Rita *is* right.

The man has a shit ton of my money.

I take the call. "Ned," I greet.

"What the fuck is this fucking shit you're fucking doing to me?"

"Once a New York fuck-mouth, always a New York fuck-mouth," I say.

"I'll fuck-mouth you, Nick Rogers." He pauses. "No. No, I won't. Fuck you for even tricking me into saying that. I got you out of Blue Textiles. They were tanking."

"I had two hundred in them. How badly did they tank?"

"I got you out before you lost your original investment and fifty more."

"I was up a hundred and fifty."

"Fucking call me back when I call. In case you've forgotten, I shouldn't have pulled you without your approval. Bottom line. I got you out fifty up, man. And I have a deal now that will make up your loss and then some. This is a two-hundred-k buy-in, and it's hot. I need you in now, and the money will be big and fast." He gives me the pitch, and it sounds worth the risk.

"Do it," I say, and when I would hang up, I hesitate. "And," I say, an idea hitting me. "Do a separate buy-in of sixty thousand dollars, under the name of Faith Winter. Whatever you need on Faith, Rita can get you tomorrow."

"That's one hell of a gift."

"Do it without comment," I say, ending the call.

And now, I feel good about taking Faith's money.

It's two hours later by the time I've finished my prep for tomorrow's meeting, and I'm just about to call Faith and see if she wants me to pick up dinner when I hear footsteps in what I'd thought was the empty office. A few seconds later, Faith appears in my doorway, the sight of her setting my blood to pumping, and not because her black jeans and light blue T-shirt accent every one of her many curves. It's simply because she's here. She's Faith. And she rocks my world.

"Hey, sweetheart," I say.

"Hey," she replies, leaning against the doorframe and looking a bit tentative. "Rita helped me get past security."

"Remind me to give her a raise tomorrow."

She pushes off the door, shuts it, and then leans against it. "So, I'm not interrupting?"

"Come here," I order softly.

She gives me one of her seductive looks that tells me she's feeling out of control, which means sex is her weapon, her way of getting it back. That's going to be a problem, because in this, I'm not giving it away. She walks toward me, the sway of her hips a seductive, sweet dance, and I don't remember a woman ever making me this hard and hot this easily, but Faith does. She rounds my desk, and I roll my chair just enough to allow her between me and the desk, my hands settling at her hips.

Her hands go to my hands, her perfect backside resting on my desk. A fact that I'm certain I will think about many times in the future. "I like you in this office, behind this desk."

"Do you?"

"You're Tiger here. Powerful. Confident. Sexy."

I don't let her take me to the fuck zone. Not yet. "I'm always Nick to you, Faith. You know that."

She inhales, her mood shifting, softening, a tentative quality to her voice as she asks, "Did you get my note?"

"I got your note and the check. And I *still* don't want your money."

"You promised to take it."

"As you pointed out in the note. And I did promise; therefore, I will take the money. But we are at that place in our relationship where there is more ahead of us, not less. I won't try to define what that is right now, in this moment, but it's a hell of a lot more than how badly I want to be inside you right now."

"You want to be inside me right now?"

"I always want to be inside you, Faith. You know that, too. And you know that gives you control. You have a lot of control, but I need you to let me be who I am. And who I am is the man who wants to take care of you. I want to handle the bank. And I damn sure want to buy you the outfit you need for court."

"I bought something today."

"Faith—"

"You paid my bills at the winery today, Nick. I just couldn't let you do more today."

"I'm not Macom, Faith."

"Stop saying his name." Her hands come down on my shoulders. "I am not thinking about him. Nothing about you feels like him. Nothing about us feels like what I was with him."

"Then let me be me."

"Then you have to let me be me, too. It will take me time to lean on you, Nick. Because it's not natural to me."

"Because when you leaned on Macom, he abused that trust."

"Now who is making him a part of our relationship? But if you're going to go there, I *always* on some level felt alone with Macom. So. I've *always* been alone."

I stand up and cup her face. "So have I. But we aren't alone anymore."

"I'm going to protect you just like you do me, Nick. You need that, too."

"Sweetheart, you can't protect me by protecting my money. Money's been saving me my entire life. *You* are what I need." I kiss her, my mouth closing down on hers, tongue licking into her mouth, the taste of coffee and sweetness, *her* sweetness, exploding on my taste buds. It only makes me hungrier for her, for that certain little sexy thing she does and doesn't even know she does. And she gives me exactly what I crave. She breathes into the kiss in that way that says, "Now I can breathe." Now I have what I need, and it sets me on fire, burns me inside and out, and I don't play

the control game I'd been ready for when she entered the office.
I let myself go, deepening the kiss, letting her taste the hunger in
me, the unleashed passion, and she seems to feed off of what I
feel, molding herself to me.

I drag her shirt over her head, and I don't stop there. Her bra
follows. Her zipper is next, and then I set her on the desk, my
gaze raking over her breasts, before I reach for her leg and settle
the high heel of her boot on my knee. I unzip it and pull it away. I
repeat the process with the other leg before I set her back on the
ground, our bodies melding together, lips following, but I want
her naked. *Need* her naked. I drag her jeans down her hips, and,
since impatience is my virtue right now, her panties with them. I
lift her and maneuver her jeans away from her feet. And now, once
again, she is naked and I am not.

Trust.

The word comes to me, clawing at me, my lies cutting me the
way I fear they will cut her, and I am not a man who feels fear.

She pushes off the desk and reaches for my pants, my zipper. I
shrug out of my jacket, and by the time it's off, her hand is slipping
inside my pants, pulling my cock free. I wrap my arm around her
and lift her, her legs wrapping my waist just long enough for me
to walk us to the sitting area to my right. Ignoring the couch, I
stop at an oversize chair, which I sit in, and I pull her on top of
me, straddling me.

"You have on too many clothes," she whispers, reaching for my
tie that I really don't give a damn about right now.

I cup her neck under her hair, bringing her closer, breathing
with her as I say, "I don't know if I've ever needed inside you as
much as I do right now," before I pull her lips to mine, letting her
taste how real those words are, and she sinks into the kiss, into
the heat of the moment.

In the midst of that kiss and the next, I manage to get just
what I hunger for. Her sliding down my cock. Her taking all of
me, naked, exposed, *mine*. "The next time I sit in this chair with

a client across from me, I'm going to be thinking of this." I press her backward, wanting to see her, all of her.

She catches herself on my knees, arching into me as I thrust—her hips, her back, her breasts high in the air, nipples puckered. We grind together, a slow, hard, melding of bodies, and I wrap my arm around her waist, my free hand cupping her breast. My mouth lowers, tongue lapping at her puckered pink nipple. She pants out my name, and I drag her to me again, her lips to my lips, and a frenzy of kissing and swaying follows—slow, fast, hard, fast again. Hard again. Harder now. Faster now. Her arms wrap around my neck, breasts molded to my chest, her body stiffening a moment before she trembles in my arms and quakes around my cock. I shudder into release with her, and I lose time. There is just how she feels. The way she smells of amber and vanilla. The way her taste lingers on my lips.

When I finally come back to the present, I am instantly living that clawing guilt from my lies, remembering my own thoughts from earlier. I need her to know how much she means to me. I need to know when the truth is revealed, she can't just walk away. Because I can't lose her.

"Faith." She leans back, and I rest my hand on her face. "I can't lose you."

"Then you won't," she says. "Because if there is one thing I know about you, Nick Rogers, it's that you don't lose anything you really want."

She's right. I don't, and I want her. "Move in with me."

She blanches. "What?"

"Move in with me, Faith. We'll split our time between Sonoma and San Francisco, but wherever we are, we're together. We're home."

"We've only known each other a few weeks, Nick."

"And I want to know more. I want you to know more. Find out who I am, Faith. Find out that my money won't change us or me. The dynamic we've shared this week here won't change. You don't have to answer now. Think about it. Decide when you're ready, but expect me to ask again. Expect me to—"

"I should say no."

"Why?"

"Because it seems smart."

"But what feels right, Faith?"

"You. Us."

"Then move in with me."

"Yes."

"Yes?"

"Yes."

CHAPTER TWENTY-THREE

Faith

I said yes.
This is my thought as I fall asleep in Nick's arms only hours after actually doing so. And I said yes without hesitation, with Sara's words in my head: *What if there is no tomorrow?*

I wake Wednesday morning with a smile and those same words in my head: *I said yes.* I feel lighter in some way with this choice, I realize as Nick kisses me before he heads down the stairs to run while I head to my studio. It's as if a weight has been lifted from my shoulders. I'm no longer fighting my connection to Nick. No longer letting that fear, which I'd inadvertently let rule me, rule me. And as I step to a fresh canvas, preparing to work on my final show piece, I step back to what I call *An Eye for an Eye.* I want to finish it. And I do. I finish what I know to be the most daring piece I've ever painted. It's not my trademark black and white and red. It's not my trademark landscape.

I love it.

I love Nick.

And when I walk back into the bedroom to shower, I spy the card from my father lying on the nightstand, and I realize now that the reasons I don't want to open it run deeper than I've allowed myself to admit. On some level, even after I left Sonoma to chase my dreams, I still needed his approval. I feared never having it. I really don't need to open a card that tells me I never had it. But one day, when the winery is running magically again and my art is just as magical, maybe I'll read it to prove to myself that I never needed his approval.

It's in that moment that Nick walks into the bedroom, loose hair dangling around his face, obviously having escaped during his run, his snug T-shirt damp, his body hard. He glances at the card in my hand. "It's calling to you?"

"No," I say. "Actually, it's not calling to me at all. Nothing that drags me back to the past is calling to me." I shove it under the mattress, and like the past, I leave it behind me.

Nick steps to me, his hands settling on my shoulders. "One day, it will feel right."

In that moment, I think of the shadows I sometimes see in his eyes, the secrets he hasn't shared, hoping that this new chapter in our relationship will free him to share them with me. I push to my toes and kiss him. "One day," I say, but I'm not talking about the card.

He knows. He always seems to know. He inches back, his navy blue eyes meeting mine, and for just a moment, I see what he never allows me to see: Vulnerability. And that is progress. That is one step closer to him being as exposed as he's made me.

By the time I reach the gallery, I'm leaning toward including *An Eye for an Eye* in the L.A. show. Excited about my choice, I chitchat with Sara, then settle into my new office with a cup of coffee beside me. And then I do it. I pull up the forms for my submissions and type in my selections, but I can't seem to get myself to push send. Sara appears in my office and claims the seat in front of me, setting a photo on the desk. "What do you think of this painting?"

I study the waterfront beach scene and smirk. "Average."

She sighs. "My thoughts, too. The artist is quite lovely, but she just isn't ready for the big league. I dread telling her we won't be selecting her work. Anyway. On to brighter topics. Have you thought about painting the office?"

"Yes. I'm excited to start, but it's going to have to be next week. I need to take care of the management side of the winery. I'll be gone Friday to Sunday and back Monday. But can I ask your opinion on something?"

"Of course."

"I made it into the L.A. Art Forum."

"Oh, wow. That's a big deal. Congratulations, Faith."

"Thank you. I need to pick all my pieces and submit them this week."

"And you're having trouble picking?"

"Yes and no. See, they picked me after they saw my work at the show you guys set me up with. That show had my classic work. The definition of who I've been publicly as an artist. But I want to include something different and daring for me. But should I? Or should I stick to safe over daring?"

"Safe is average," Chris says, stepping into the doorway. "Decide if you want to be average, and you have your answer." He disappears into the hallway.

Sara lifts a hand. "There you go. Your answer."

"Well, the thrust is that I'm not feeling like playing it safe or being average. As proof, I'm not only here instead of at the winery, but I agreed to move in with Nick."

"You did? Wow. Yay! That's huge."

"It is, and it was also an easy decision thanks to you."

"Me?"

"Yes. You. You said: *What if there is no tomorrow?* Those are my new words to live or die by."

She smiles and stands up, exiting the office. I pull up the Forum paperwork in my email and fill it all out. I enter *An Eye for an Eye* as my final piece. I then text Nick: *I did it. My entry for the Forum is complete.*

He surprises me by texting back a picture of *An Eye for an Eye* that I didn't know he'd taken: *Did this masterpiece make the cut?*

I smile and type: *Yes. It did, and why do you have that picture?*

His reply is instant: *Reminding myself to be the same kind of badass you are today.*

I smile, warmed inside and out by this man in ways I didn't know I could feel warm. As for being a badass, Nick is the ultimate badass, while Macom is the ultimate asshole. I try not to think about how that might look when the two meet. Because they will meet, no matter what painting I place in that show. And they will clash, no matter how I try to stop them. And I'm not sure Nick is capable of war and peace. I'm pretty sure it's all war to him.

And Macom aside, God, it's sexy.

Our Thursday morning court date has arrived, and I'm a nervous wreck. I can't paint, and I'm done with my show pieces, so I work out with Nick, and even a hard run doesn't calm me down. Nick's attempts at distracting me in the shower are completely effective, but the minute we're dressed, my nerves are back. He dresses in a navy blue suit, and I pick a blue-and-silver tie to match and then help him knot it. My dress is black, with a tapered waist and flared skirt. My shoes, classic pumps. I have no idea why I picked black when funeral black is the last thing I need to be wearing today, but it's too late. It's what I have.

"Let's go on to Sonoma when we're done today," Nick says, leaning on the doorframe.

"I thought we were going to wait until tomorrow. What if something goes wrong today?"

"It won't. It's going to go well. And rather than flying, we'll drive. It's not far, and we'll have the BMW when we're there."

"You don't want to drive my broken-down Mercedes?"

"Nothing against your broken-down Mercedes, but I prefer the BMW."

I laugh. "Okay then. Let's pack."

"You don't have to pack. You live here now. But I do, because I live there now, too."

"Yes. You do. You need things there. Your things."

His lips curve, and he says, "You're my thing. But I'll take some stuff anyway."

"I'll help you," I say, and for the next few minutes, I busy myself gathering items for his suitcase and packing up the few items I want to carry back and forth with me. Once we're done, we load up the car.

And then for the first time all week, Nick and I leave in one car, him behind the wheel of the BMW. By the time we get to the courthouse, my palms are sweaty. "Relax, Faith," Nick says after opening my car door and helping me to my feet. "I'm an arrogant bastard for a reason. I'm good. Really damn good, and we're going to win today."

"But we've talked about this. What if someone is angry you got me out of this nightmare and they lash out at you? What if I'm the reason—"

"Stop," he says, his hands on my shoulders. "Don't start fretting over me. I pack a big punch. Anyone who comes at me is going to feel a hell of a lot of pain, and they know it. I got this, sweetheart, and I got you. Okay?"

"Yes. Yes, okay." I flatten my hand on his lapel. "You *are* a badass."

He rewards me with a curve of his delicious mouth. "You inspire me."

I manage a laugh. "I'm not sure that is the way a woman wants to inspire a man."

"If a woman doesn't inspire her man, he's not her man. Now. Come see me in action."

Literally thirty minutes later, Nick and I step out of the courtroom, and the bank has approved the buyout, I've inherited the winery, and Nick has shut down every attempt my bank made to stop it from happening. "I don't believe it," I say as soon as we're in the car. "It's done."

"You doubted me?"

"No. I did not doubt you."

"Sounds like you doubted me." He leans over and kisses me. "And that, I do believe, earns that sweet little ass of yours a spanking."

"Hmmm. Promise?"

"Oh yeah, sweetheart. I promise." He settles back in his seat. "Let's go to Sonoma."

A few minutes later, we're on the road, and life is good. Almost too good to be true.

CHAPTER TWENTY-FOUR

Faith

"We're here, sweetheart."

I blink and open my eyes. "Nick?"

"Yes, sweetheart. *Nick*. You fell asleep. We're home."

I blink again. "Home?"

"Sonoma."

"We are?"

He strokes my hair. "Yes." He smiles. "*We* are."

I sit up and look around to find we're parked in the driveway of my house. And instead of the warmth and happiness "home" should create, there is an instant ball of nerves in my belly made better by only one thing: Nick. "We," I say, glancing over at him, "because we're really doing this thing, right?"

"We've been really doing this since the moment we met."

He leans over and cups my head in that way he does and kisses my forehead. "Come on. Let's go inside and get settled. And I vote for taking you out to lunch and a trip to the grocery store, or I'll starve this weekend." He grabs his jacket from the back seat and then exits the car. I grab my purse from the floorboard, where I'd left it when we'd gone into the courthouse. Slipping it over my shoulder, I exit the car and join Nick at the trunk, and the minute I'm beside him, the intimacy between us seems to take on a living, breathing life of its own. It wraps around us like a warm, soft blanket that I want to snuggle inside of and never leave.

He opens the trunk and pulls the two suitcases out before shutting it again. And then, together we roll the suitcases toward the house. "I'll get them the rest of the way," Nick says when we reach the stairs leading to the porch.

I hurry up the steps, key in the code to the door, and push it open. Nick joins me, and that charge between us intensifies the instant we are both over the threshold. He sets the suitcases inside the foyer and drops his jacket on top of one of them. I shut the door. And suddenly we are facing each other, our eyes colliding, that word "home" radiating between us.

The air thickens, crackles, and I move. Or maybe he moves. Maybe it's both of us, but suddenly my purse is on the ground, and we are kissing, a deep, drugging, intimate kiss. His hand is on the back of my head, and God, how I've come to love the way he does that. I breathe into the kiss, sink into it and him, and it only seems to ignite us further. And of course, my phone rings. I ignore it. Nick ignores it. I reach for his tie. This time I'm getting it off, along with every inch of clothing he's wearing. My phone stops ringing. I pull the silk from his neck, letting it fall to the ground. My phone starts ringing again.

Nick and I both groan. "You better get that, sweetheart," he says.

"It's not important." It stops ringing again and starts again. "Okay. It might be." I squat down to open my purse and remove my cellphone, frowning when I see the number. "Kasey," I say, standing up and answering. "Is everything okay?"

"Of course. Why wouldn't it be? The bills are paid. All is well."

"You called three times."

"No. I just called once."

"Oh. The other calls must have been someone else. Hold on one second." I glance at the caller ID. "Josh," I mouth to Nick, and I don't miss the tiny smirk on his face at the reference to my agent, who he clearly does not like.

"Rita was fantastic," Kasey adds, pulling me back into our conversation. Nick's own phone buzzes, and he pulls it from his pocket, looking at the caller ID. "I gave her the accounts payable list," Kasey continues, "and within two hours everything was paid to date."

Nick points to his phone and motions down the hallway off the foyer. "No more bill collectors," I reply to Kasey, following Nick, but as he continues to the living room, I cut right into the kitchen, rounding the island to sit on a barstool.

"Are we sure?" he asks. "This isn't a one-and-done kind of thing?"

"Not at all," I assure him, settling onto a barstool. "We're past the challenges that started when we lost my father."

"Then you finally got into the bank accounts."

"Everything is now in my name," I say, avoiding the topic of my mother and the bank accounts I won't have access to until Monday but already know are empty. "That means I'm free to discuss the future with you, because I know we have a future and one worth your time."

"Hiring Nick Rogers really made a difference, it seems."

"Nick has made an incredible difference," I say as he appears in the doorway, his eyes meeting mine, and I add, "in every possible way."

Nick's lips curve slightly, and he walks to the island, sitting down on the barstool across from me. Meanwhile, Kasey delivers a stilted, "That's great news," followed by an awkward pause.

Dread fills me. "Oh God. You're quitting."

"No. Of course not. This place is my life."

Relief washes over me. "Then what is it that I'm sensing?"

"Full disclosure. I just had coffee with your uncle. And since I know how you feel about him—"

My gaze rockets to Nick's. "Why did you have coffee with my uncle, Kasey?"

Nick doesn't react, and I have a sense that he knew before I did, perhaps from his phone call. "He bought a thousand bottles of wine for a weekend event," Kasey says. "And not the cheap stuff. Once the transaction was complete, he cornered me about you. He wanted me to try to convince you to talk to him. Apparently, he's left you several messages you haven't answered."

"He hasn't left me any messages," I say. "Okay. Not recently. And I talked to him two days ago and have no desire to talk to him again."

"I know that your father had issues with him as well, but they did make peace in the end. And now Bill wants to make peace with you."

I stand up with the impact of that statement. "My father and Bill reconciled?"

"They did. And just in time. It was only about a month before your father's death."

"Do you know what the falling-out was about, Kasey?"

"No. Do you?"

"I thought I did, but I have a hard time believing they reconciled under the circumstances as I thought I knew them."

"I can't help you there. Your father never shared that with me, and Bill didn't, either. All I know is that the man seems sincere in wanting to call you family." He hesitates. "Look. I'm just the messenger, and I wanted to talk to you about this now, not tomorrow night, simply because I didn't want you to hear I'd met with him through another source. We do have some wagging tongues in this town."

"I appreciate that, and I'm sorry to put you in the middle of this. I'll call him. I'll make sure he leaves you out of this."

"I'm not concerned about me, but I am concerned about you. You're alone, Faith. He's family."

"He's not my family," I say, and suddenly I want to get the meeting with him over and done with. "Hold on a second." I cover the phone and speak to Nick: "Dinner tonight?" He nods, and I uncover the phone. "Nick and I actually just got into town. Can we move dinner back to tonight?"

"Of course. Where and when?"

"How about the Harvest Moon Café at eight? That gives you time to close up shop there."

"That works. I'll see you then."

I end the call, setting my phone on the island. "Your uncle's timing is suspect," Nick says. "What did he want?"

"He bought a thousand bottles of wine and then convinced Kasey to soften me up and look at him as family."

"On the day you now own the winery," Nick says. "I've thought for a while now that he was behind the bank withholding your inheritance."

"He's filthy rich," I say. "He doesn't need the winery, nor has he ever approached me to buy it."

"But he might have approached your mother."

"Yes. He might have."

"And she would have told him that you wouldn't sell."

"That's true, too."

"His wife is filthy rich," he says. "And the word is that she treats him like a kept animal on an allowance."

"So, he wants his own assets?"

"It could be that simple," Nick says, "but I'm still of the belief that there is a hidden financial resource within the winery. And that call I got. That was Beck, letting me know about Kasey and your uncle. He didn't like how familiar they seemed."

"They've known each other longer than I've been alive," I say. "And they were friends at one point. But I can tell you this. When my father shut Bill out, so did Kasey. He was my father's best friend. And this is over now, anyway, right?"

"It is, but if I'm right and your uncle was behind this, expect him to try to buy you out."

"You think he's still a problem."

"I think he upsets you and that's a problem I'm going to make go away. Send him to me. I will bust the fucker's balls. The end."

My phone rings again. I glance at the number. "It's just Josh." I decline the call.

"We're here for thirty minutes, and you're ignoring your agent who is suddenly 'just' Josh. Call him back."

"You don't even like him."

"Irrelevant point, pulled out of a hat and meant to deflect. He's a horny piece-of-shit asshole, but he's your agent, and your career is connected to him."

"He can wait. Right now, I need to finish this conversation about my uncle and talk about Kasey's incentives."

"Call your agent back." He rounds the counter, snags my hips, and pulls me to him. "The man wants in your pants. I don't like it, but professionally, he's your agent, and your career is taking off. Everything else can wait and will be far more tolerable if he's delivering good news. *Call him back.*"

"You're being obnoxiously pushy."

"And this is unusual how?"

"Nick—"

"Faith."

"Nick—"

"Faith. How many times are we doing this? Because I have all weekend, but just in case you've missed the obvious. If you won't fight for your art, I will. That's what I do. I fight. And you could have already called him back in the time we've had this exchange."

"Fine." I grab my phone, and Nick releases me while I hit select on the most recent call.

Josh picks up on the first ring. "You have another sale from the Chris Merit show, darling."

I perk up, that ball of tension that had formed when we arrived easing just a bit. "I do?"

"Yes. You do."

I turn to Nick and mouth "another sale." He gives me a wink that does funny things to my belly while Josh adds, "And thanks to Chris Merit and your amazing skills, your price is now twenty thousand a painting. After this show, we're going to make it thirty. You need those paintings shipped out in a week. How are they coming?"

"I'm done. I copied you on the submission form."

"Done? As of when?"

"Yesterday."

"And you didn't run the pieces by me?"

"I knew what I wanted in the show."

"I need photos. Send me photos. We can still change them out if—"

"No. I'm not sending you photos or changing things out. I told you. I'm painting for me now, not for you or anyone else."

"As you should be, but come on, Faith. I've been in this with you a long time. Send me photos."

"On the condition that you offer no opinions."

"Agreed. And get them shipped in advance. Don't take risks. The details on how and where to ship are on your forms."

"I'll pull it, and it will be handled."

"You need to have all pieces there in a week."

"I know, Josh. Deep breath. I'm not going to let either one of us down on this. And you know what. I'm not sending you photos. I don't want you to freak yourself—or me—out over my choices. They are made. I stand by them. You need to just see them when I get there."

"Faith—"

"No, Josh. No. And FYI. I'm working at the Allure Gallery with Chris and Sara Merit now."

"What about the winery?"

"I have a staff."

"You've always had a staff. That didn't keep you painting."

"My situation here has changed."

"Here. So you're finally back in Sonoma?"

"Actually, I'm moving to San Francisco. Sonoma will be my weekend home."

"You're moving in with Nick Rogers."

"Yes."

"I told you—"

"That he'll fuck me and leave me? I think it's pretty clear that's not the case. I'll get you the new address."

"Okay. I get it. You want me to back off. And I will, after I say *be careful*, Faith."

"I've done a lot of that all my life. It's not worked out so well. I'll see you in two weeks." I end the call and face Nick, both of us settling elbows on the island.

"You sold another painting," he says, warmth in his eyes. "You're going to be famous before you know it."

"I don't want to be famous. It's about being good enough, and, as is the case in many careers, money is one of a number of validations. I've made eighty thousand in a week, Nick. From my painting. That's crazy good."

"Yes," he agrees. "It is. You told Josh you were moving to San Francisco."

"Because I am."

"What about here?"

"What about it?"

He snags my hip and walks me to him. "The minute we arrived here, you tensed up. I don't like what this place does to you, but we're both going to like what I'm about to do to you." He scoops me up and starts walking and doesn't stop until he's laying me down on the mattress, his big body over mine.

"Now we celebrate. You sold another painting. And we won the war."

"Are you sure we won?"

"Yes. I'm sure we won."

"Why do I feel like there is more?"

He rolls us to our sides, facing each other, his leg twined with mine. "There is more. More fucking. More loving. More us."

"Because you think you—"

He strokes hair from my face. "I know I love you, Faith."

"You do?"

"I do."

"I love you, too."

"Then there's more. There's always more. But whatever it is, good or bad, we do it together. Say it."

"We do it together."

CHAPTER TWENTY-FIVE

Nick

*M*ore.

That word stays with me as I make love to Faith, and even afterward as we dress in casual wear—Faith in jeans and a V-neck blue T-shirt that shows off her necklace, which she keeps touching. I like that she keeps touching it, as if she's remembering me giving it to her. As if she connects me to her art, and since she loves her art so damn much, I'll say "paint me, baby" any damn day.

I dress in black jeans, boots, and a black T-shirt that reads: *Lawyer—Let's just save time and assume that I'm right*, which gains me the laugh from Faith I'd been looking for. Because her laugh is sexy as fuck and damn addictive. Like the woman herself.

"You are not always right, Nick Rogers," she proclaims when she sees it, stroking my cheek. "But don't worry. I'll catch you when you fall."

"Don't I owe you a spanking?"

"It really is starting to seem like you're all talk and no action," she replies, twisting away from me and giving me a sexy glance over her shoulder. "Come, my hungry man. I have the world's most perfect burger for you."

My man.

She's learning.

I am her man.

I follow, but not for the burger. For the shake of her curvy and perfect ass in those jeans, and somehow my mind still works enough to ask, "Do you have the instructions for shipping your paintings? We need to arrange to have someone pick them up."

She pauses at the door and faces me. "I looked it up when I submitted my final paperwork. They have special arrangements with FedEx, and there's a location right up the road."

"Then we'll go after lunch," I say, stepping beside her, and because I just can't help myself, which is pretty damn unfamiliar to me, I give her a quick kiss and open the door.

"Food is literally three minutes away," she says once we're in the car and pulling onto the main road. "Just turn right, drive a mile, and we're there."

"Got it," I say. "Food. One mile." I glance over at her. "Dessert when we return home, and it's not ice cream."

"Oh. We need more ice cream. I have to have ice cream when I'm here. It's kind of like Sonoma survival. A survival kit that is cream, sugar, and calories."

"Why do you need a survival kit?"

"You're about to find out," she assures me but doesn't give me time to press for details. "So," she continues, "we eat. Then we need to go by FedEx and the grocery store."

"And to get boxes so you can pack some of your things to ship to San Francisco. We can arrange to have FedEx pick them up tomorrow with your paintings. Then it can all be waiting on you when we return Sunday night." I pull us into the restaurant parking lot and park.

"That's expensive, Nick." I open my mouth to object, and she holds up a hand. "Don't tell me not to worry about money. You didn't get rich by throwing away money. Don't expect me to start throwing it away for you."

"And I appreciate that, sweetheart, but the sooner you're with me in San Francisco, the happier a man I'll be."

"I said yes for a reason. I'm already with you, Nick."

I lean over and kiss her. "Keep saying yes. I like that answer." She smiles, and I like that, too. I'm so fucking in love with this woman, it's insanity, and I am happily insane. I have no fears. No regrets. No second thoughts. I want her. I need her. She's mine.

"I'll come around and help you out," I tell her.

"Because you have such good manners," she teases, a reminder of our little bathroom encounter on the first night we fucked, when I promised to make her come about a half-dozen ways, but only when I thought she was ready.

"You know it, sweetheart," I say, exiting the car, and the moment I'm outside, a sense of being watched hits me, right along with a blast of cool wind. And yes, logically, it's Beck's people. It had better be Beck's people, but I don't like how it feels. I round the car and help Faith out, wrapping my arm around her shoulder and holding her close. Making it clear she's mine. She's under my protection.

We enter the restaurant, and that feeling doesn't fade, even as the rush of attention falls on us as people who know Faith greet her. By the time we are at a table, it becomes apparent that pretty much everyone in this city knows her and *her mother*. Her dead mother, who is connected to my dead father. And that sensation of being watched is magnified with that realization.

Faith hands me a menu. "Now you know why I need a Sonoma survival kit. Everyone knows your business here."

As if proving her point, another guest steps to Faith's side, and after I am introduced, I text Beck: *Are your men following us?*

His reply: *Of course. Why?*

Mine: *Because I don't see them, but I feel them.*

His: *Huh.*

Mine: *WTF does huh mean?*

His: *I guess lawyers are never wrong. And if you believe that, I have a million dollars I want to sell you for fifty bucks.*

He's obviously referencing my shirt, telling me he has eyes on me and us. But something still doesn't feel right, and I discreetly scan, not just for his men but for the source of my discomfort. An old lady to our right. A cluster of businessmen in deep conversation in one corner. A mid-fifties man by himself in another corner in jeans and a T-shirt. Another cluster of businesspeople. A college-age woman by herself, with headphones on. My gaze shifts to the hostess stand, where a fit man in his mid-thirties is flirting with the woman showing people to their tables.

"The entire town is going to be talking about us now," Faith announces, drawing my attention back to her.

"Hopefully they mention my shirt."

She laughs. "I'm sure they will. You can't hiccup and not have it be part of the story."

"But you want to live here?"

"If I gave you that impression, it's wrong. I love my house, because it was an escape and my home outside of the winery. But I went to school in L.A. and stayed in L.A. for a reason, beyond my aspirations in art. I never wanted to live here."

"And you do want to live in San Francisco?"

"I do," she says. "You're there."

"But do you like it? Because if you don't—"

"I do," she repeats. "I *really* love it there, and I always have. The art. The food. The way it's a small city but you can still get lost in a crowd. The views. The art."

"Always the art. San Fran is a great hub for your craft. Why L.A.?"

"L.A. had wider opportunities for school, work, and a connection to agents and industry professionals."

Our plates arrive, and once we've tasted our food—and I've given the burger the thumbs-up Faith is looking for and that it deserves—I focus on what she's just told me. "You don't want to be here. That means we need to make sure the winery is self-reliant."

"I feel like I should offer Kasey stock."

"I suggest you start with a large bonus plan. Make sure he really does handle things when you or your father aren't looking over his shoulder."

"I'm sure he will. Of course he will. But what kind of bonus?"

"I have several plans I've helped clients set up over the years in my briefcase. You can look them over, but I'd suggest feeling him out tonight. We can send him whatever you decide on Monday. But, that said, I would like him to work with Rita on the accounts payable and have our CFO audit the books once a month."

"Is that really necessary?"

"I've seen people get screwed, Faith. And it's always by people they trust. Additionally, you need someone to play your role."

"That'll be expensive."

"The right person will grow revenues and more than pay for themselves. And since you don't want to sell and you don't want to work at the winery, the idea is to make it an investment. It pays you profit monthly. And when your art starts generating million-dollar payouts, you spend more money on the winery and end up with tax write-offs."

"I'd love to have that problem," she says, despite the fact that her inability to see her own success and skill is a product of a past she hasn't quite escaped.

But she will.

"Eighty thousand in a week," I remind her. "Success isn't an option. And I get to call you my crazy talented woman."

"And I get to call you my arrogant bastard?"

I laugh. "I told you. Anything but Mr. Rogers. And you forgot that when you were drinking."

"I didn't forget. I saw opportunity."

I laugh, and our waitress chooses that moment to reappear and present us with the check, and damn, I want her to go away. Or maybe I just want to take Faith away from this place and this intrusive little town. I reach for the ticket, and as I hand the waitress my card, I have that same sense of being watched all over again.

We stand up to leave, and my gaze travels toward the sensation and the man sitting at a table in the corner, flirting with our waitress, when he'd started out flirting with the hostess. Faith and I start walking, and my eyes catch on the tat on his hand: a flag, like the money clip. It's a long shot, but it could be a connection, and I don't let long shots go just because they're hard. I pause and turn back to the table, looking for something I haven't lost. Faith turns to help me, and my hand settles on Faith's shoulder, lips near her ear. "Be discreet," I murmur. Trying not to scare her, I say, "The guy talking to our waitress is familiar, but I can't place him. Glance over as we exit."

She nods, and we start walking, passing through the restaurant and stepping outside. "I've never seen him," she says. "He must be a tourist. Maybe from San Francisco?"

"Maybe," I say, opening her door for her and pulling out my phone.

I round the trunk and text Beck: *If the guy at the corner table isn't your guy, find out who he is. He has a flag tattoo.*

Once we're on the road, stopping at FedEx and then the grocery store, the trend of a waxing and waning feeling of being watched continues, as do the references to Faith's dead mother. By the time we arrive back at the house, there is no denying the relief I feel when we step inside and shut the door. And the word in my mind is no longer *more*—it's murder. It's not a good thought, but not one I can risk setting aside. Murder brought me here. Faith kept me here.

We're unpacking the groceries when Faith's phone rings on the counter where it rests. "Josh again," she says, answering and having a short conversation that finishes with, "No. No. No. I'm not. I'm hanging up now." And she does. "He wants to see my submissions so he can make me second-guess my choices, and I'm not going to do it."

"Good for you," I say. "So now I say we pack you up. Where do you want to start?"

"My closet. My clothes are the most important thing for me to take. And my shoes, of course. A girl has to have her shoes."

I'd tell her I'd just buy her all new things, but I'm smarter than that, and her phone rings again anyway. She grimaces and answers it without looking at the caller ID. I walk to the fridge and grab a bottle of water as she says, "No, Josh. Stop calling." I've just opened my bottle and tilted it back when she snags my shirt, and I turn to face her as she says, "Bill. Why are you calling me?" She puts the phone on speaker, and I join her at the island and set my water bottle down.

"I'm concerned that I gave you the wrong impression when we talked," he says. "I wasn't implying anything about your mother or father. I simply don't feel the topic is appropriate between myself and their daughter."

"They're dead," Faith states flatly.

"I'm aware of this fact every day of my life. We're family, Faith. Your father and I found our way to a truce. I'd like to do that with you as well."

"No," Faith says. "I have no interest in reconciling with you, and you've already proven that you won't answer my questions."

"Not if they're related to their sexual preferences."

"You did have a threesome with them, didn't you?" She doesn't give him time to answer. "Why, if you already had sex with both of them, did he get pissed when you had sex with just her?"

"Our falling-out wasn't about sex."

"Then what was it about?"

"Brother stuff. We're family, Faith."

"Stop saying that," Faith bites out. "Don't call me. And don't call or visit Kasey."

He's silent for several beats. "I have some old photos of your father I just stumbled onto. I'll drop them by the winery. I think you'll enjoy them. Maybe we can have coffee." He softens his voice. "I really hope that you have a change of heart, Faith." He hangs up.

I reach for the phone and ensure the line is disconnected.

"He had a threesome with my parents, Nick."

"Yes," I say. "I believe he did. He also wants to buy the winery."

"Even if I was willing to sell, which I'm not, I'd never sell to him. You'd think he'd be smart enough to just lie and say he didn't do the whole ménage à trois thing with my mother and father."

"He doesn't know what you know. That's obvious. And he knows that right now, you won't sell to him."

"So, he tried to drive me into the ground so I'd be desperate."

"Most likely," I agree. "And it's a smart guess that he made a deal at the bank to pay someone off for helping him pick it up for a steal."

"I will never sell it to him. I'm not going to sell."

"But he knows—everyone knows—that you want to paint."

"Oh God. You don't think he bought my work to give me some facade of success so I'd dump the winery, do you?"

"Don't do that. Don't let him downgrade your success. It's yours. You own it."

"Can you do what you do and make sure he didn't buy those paintings?"

"Yes. I will. But those sales are your sales. You own them, but if I confirm that he owns the hell you just went through, I'm going to ruin that bastard."

"No," Faith says. "Don't ruin him. I don't need justice. I just need him to go away."

"Faith—"

"No, Nick. Promise me."

"I'm not going to make that promise, because it would be a lie."

"I just want to make this go away." She grabs my arm and covers my tattoo with her hand. "Revenge: an eye for an eye. That's you. Not me." She lets go of my arm. "I'm going to start packing." She heads out of the kitchen, and I don't immediately follow.

I text Beck: *Bill Winter is trying to get into Faith's good graces. He's behind all of this.*

Beck: *Agreed. I'm working on it.*

I inhale and press my hands to the counter, the word murder in my head again. Bill might be trying to get into Faith's good graces now, but as Abel has always said, once a killer, always a killer. Only I'm not my father. I won't just cause pain. I'll draw blood, and I'll make sure it's first blood.

And I'll do it for Faith.

I push off the counter and seek her out, her frustrated groan drawing me toward the front of the house. I find her in the foyer trying to put together one of the boxes we picked up earlier, frustration in her face before she tosses it. "I can't get the stupid thing together. I've been living alone and doing just fine, but now, I cannot get that box together."

I walk to her and ignore the box, pulling her to me. "Implying that I've made you weaker?"

"No. No, that's not it. I'm sorry." Her hand goes to my chest. "If anything, your badass-ness has brought out my own."

"The eye-for-an-eye-revenge thing is a trigger for you. I know that. But he broke laws if he did what we think he did. And if he will go after his own niece, think what he'll do to others. He deserves to pay."

"You're right. But that means justice, not revenge. To me, they're defined by different intent."

"You're right. They are. And I might be brutal, sweetheart, but the law is my bitch, and so are your enemies."

"I know that. I'm not really upset at you, Nick. I wasn't even reacting to you. I'm upset to realize my father was someone I didn't know him to be."

"His sex life doesn't change who he was as a man, Faith."

"A little kinky sex doesn't. I, of all people, know that."

"Then what's bothering you?"

"He played the victim, and that feels like a lie. It's like I didn't really know who he was, and that is such a deep betrayal. I don't want to talk about this anymore. Not before we meet with Kasey. Can you just please help me with the stupid box?"

"Of course." I kiss her temple, my lips lingering there, because damn it, it's like she was talking about me. And it feels like she has that kitchen knife in her hand again and she just plunged it in my chest.

CHAPTER TWENTY-SIX

Faith

I don't like who you are here...
Nick's words play in my head the entire afternoon as we box up my belongings for the move to San Francisco. Namely because there isn't much to do or that I want to take with me—most certainly not how I act and feel here. All I want are my clothes, shoes, and basic items I use every day. Nick notices, too.

"You know," he says about an hour into packing my bedroom, "you can take anything you want. You can take *everything* if you want."

"I'm taking what matters," I assure him, holding up a pair of pink panties. "See?"

I successfully distract him, and we move on to the living area and make the rounds from there. The entire time, he builds the boxes and tries to overstuff them, and I pull things back out. Time gets away from us, and it's nearly sunset and time to get ready for dinner when it hits me that I haven't packed a box of random items like gloves and scarves that I keep in the closet. Afraid I'll forget again, I rush to the bedroom and the closet. Grabbing a decorative wooden container where I have various accessories stored, I stick it in an empty box in the center of the small room.

I rotate to leave and find Nick leaning in the archway, his hair half around his face and half tied at his nape. His blue eyes are stark. "Are you having second thoughts?"

"What? What are you talking about?"

"You aren't taking anything with you, Faith. It's as if you aren't committed to leaving or, rather, staying with me." There is a hint of vulnerability in his voice, his eyes, that Nick Rogers doesn't allow anyone to see. But he does let me now. He lets me see that I could hurt him the way he could hurt me.

And I am instantly in front of him, my hand settling on his chest. "I am committed," I assure him. "I want to be with you."

"Then why do you read like someone packing for a vacation and planning to come back home?"

"Because you're looking for one thing and not seeing what's really going on."

"Which is what?"

"I just don't feel connected to anything here. Only my studio."

"You bought this house. You designed it."

"Because I needed something of my own."

"And now you're accepting something that's mine."

"No. It's not like that. I don't want your place to look like mine."

"It's not my place anymore. It's ours, and I've never wanted to share my home with anyone, and I have zero hesitation in this. I need to know you feel the same."

His cell phone rings, and he draws in a breath, then breathes out. "Why do our phones ring at the worst possible times?" And when I would expect him to ignore the call, he doesn't, which tells me he's the one shutting down now, withdrawing.

"Nick," I say, but he's already looking at his caller ID with a frown.

"Rita. This is an odd time for her to call." He answers the line. "Rita?" He listens a moment. "Kasey?" he asks, and after a pause: "Right. She's standing right here. She'll call him." He ends the connection and offers me his phone. "Call him. There's a problem."

"I guess I don't know where my phone is," I say, punching in Kasey's number, and the moment it rings, he answers.

"Faith?" Kasey asks.

"Yes. Sorry. I was—"

"We have several busted water lines in the west vineyard. It's bad. I'm trying to get someone out here, but I'm struggling at this hour."

"How bad is bad?"

"It's flowing from numerous locations, and flowing isn't even an appropriate description. Gushing is more like it. If we don't get someone out here soon, it's a total loss."

My stomach knots. "We'll be right there."

"Faith, I don't know if we can save it even if we get someone out here," he adds, pretty much repeating what he's just said but obviously trying to prepare me for what he feels is the inevitable: we've already lost the west side.

"Do what you can," I say, ending the call. "We need to go there. There are several broken—"

"I heard," Nick says. "Grab your purse and phone. We'll go now."

I head into the bathroom, grab my purse, and hunt for my phone, which I can't find. Frustrated, I shout, "I can't find my phone!" and Nick appears in the bathroom, holding it. "Oh, thank God," I breathe out, racing toward him and grabbing it. "This is bad, Nick. He can't get anyone out there."

"You drive," he says, handing me the car keys. "Let me make some calls."

"Thank you," I say, nodding, and it's less than a minute later when we're in the car and he's already on the phone. "Rita. Be a superwoman right now. We have several broken water lines in the west vineyard. Pay whatever you have to to get help out there now." There is a pause. "I should have known. Yes. Call me." He ends the call and glances over at me. "She already knew and is already looking. And the woman is magic. She'll get us help." He's already dialing again. "Beck," he says. "Do you know what's happening?" He listens for a few beats. "Right. I'll find out if it's intentional once we're there, but get fucking cameras on the vines. I want every inch of the property covered." He doesn't wait for a reply. He hangs up.

That knot in my stomach doubles in size. "You think this is payback for us winning in court."

"I'd bet my bank account on it, sweetheart. Beck has the cameras in place that we discussed, and men here locally watching the place, but he didn't have eyes on the vines."

"I'm sure that didn't feel important," I say, turning us down the main road leading to the vineyard. "Why would it be? Until it is, obviously."

"Aside from us winning in court," he says. "You shut your uncle down today."

"Why would he do this? This isn't squeezing me financially. This is destroying the vines that produce profit for the winery we're assuming he wants to own. It doesn't make sense."

"It does if the real treasure isn't the vines but the property."

"You've said this before, but what treasure, Nick? What could it be?"

"The options are many: A highway or development coming through here that he's gotten an ear on. Some natural resource. Leverage on another deal. Even some sort of big-dick play for his wife. *See me. I have this family vineyard worth forty million dollars. I'm the man.* The reasons are many, and they don't matter at this very moment. Bottom line, I don't believe this is an accident even if it ends up staged as an accident. And about those cameras that I just ordered Beck to put in place—those are between you, me, and him. No one else."

"Not even Kasey?"

"No one. And it's not about me not trusting him. I don't know him to trust him or not trust him at this point. But even if I trusted him, we have to worry about who he might decide to trust himself. There's a saying I never forget: betrayal doesn't come from your enemies."

"That's the bitter hardcore truth," I say, turning us down the drive to the mansion, the now familiar flutter of dread in my belly. It's present every single time I've come here since my father's death, no matter how many times I come here, and even when I was living here. I pull us up to the valet area, and Kasey waits for Nick and me at the top of the steps, his gray suit uncharacteristically rumpled, his thick, dark, graying hair also in rare disarray, as if he'd been running his fingers through it.

Nick and I walk up the steps, and the two men greet each other, shaking hands. "We aren't saving those vines, are we?" Nick says, giving him a keen look.

Kasey's hands settle under his jacket on his hips, his expression stark. "No," he says, proving Nick has read him right. "Now we just need to stop the bleeding of gallons of water and start thinking about recovery. A witness saw two teenage boys in the fields, but that makes no sense to me. The pipes were hammered and broken in numerous locations."

"Do we need to go out to the vineyard?" Nick asks.

"Every staffer I could get my hands on is out there, knee high in water with buckets," Kasey replies. "You don't want to be out there."

"Knee high," I murmur, acceptance sliding through me. "Yeah. The vines are lost."

Nick's phone buzzes with a text, and he pulls it from his pocket, reads it, and says, "Rita has a team on the way."

Several customers exit the door behind Kasey at the same moment the crew Rita sent turns down the driveway. From there, chaos erupts. I leave the vineyard to Nick and Kasey, while the customers are mine to manage. It's nearly two hours later that the guests are cleared out of the mansion, the staff that can be sent home are home, and I find my way to the closed restaurant and sit down at a corner table, a number of things rushing through my mind. One of them is giving whoever did this exactly what they want. *I need to sell this place.* But I won't be bullied into doing it now or to sell to any one person.

Nick appears in the entrance and crosses to sit next to me, his hand on my leg. "The crew is good. They shut down the water flow in ten minutes, and they're extracting the water. We'll get the right kind of teams out here tomorrow to start the repair process."

"Thank you, Nick, for helping."

"No thanks needed. Ever. You okay, sweetheart?"

"Whoever did this won."

"No. They did not. We'll rebuild the west vineyard."

"That's not what I mean." I rotate to face him, the realization coming to me. "Keeping this place wasn't just about satisfying my family legacy for my father. It was safe, although that's almost a laughable statement right now."

"An excuse to fail at your art."

My throat tightens. "How did you know that? I didn't even know that until just a few moments ago."

"I pay attention," he says, and not for the first time. "I care. Everyone was telling you that you'd fail, and this place was both a sanctuary and a prison. But you need to think about this when we're out of the heat of this fire."

"I want to sell it, Nick, but I have to rebuild those vines first or it won't give me a nest egg."

"Agreed, and anyone who thought I'd let you be crazy enough to sell it under those conditions didn't think ahead. A year from now, we can not only have it rebuilt, we'll have time to figure out the hidden value. We'll get you that nest egg, sweetheart, and I have a pretty good nest egg for us both."

Trying really hard to get out of my past and my own head, I don't reject that idea. Instead, I press my hand to his face. "Is it okay if I contribute to it?"

He presses my hand to his lips. "I'm really turned on by the idea of having a famously wealthy artist in my bed."

My lips curve. "That was a pretty perfect thing to say, for such an arrogant bastard."

"Even arrogant bastards have our moments."

Footsteps sound, and a frazzled-looking Kasey appears, and he doesn't hesitate to cross the room to sit with us. "I need to know a number of things," he says, his focus landing on Nick. "You're a stockholder now? Because Rita said that you are."

"I am," Nick says, "which means you have the resources to fix today's problems."

"You'll want a return," he says. "Do you plan to sell?"

Nick squeezes my leg. "Have you heard a rumor?"

"This place has always drawn offers," he says, "and you're filthy rich, man. Money loves money."

"Did my father consider selling?" I ask. "Is that why you assume I will?"

"You know your father would never let go of this place, though yes. People tried to buy it."

"What is it about this winery that makes people want it?" Nick asks.

"We are part of the core history of Sonoma," he says. "It appeals to buyers. I know one wanted to restore the house and get it designated as some sort of landmark." He refocuses on Nick. "Are you going to force a sale?"

"I don't need a return," Nick says. "I'm here for Faith. And what she wants, I will make happen."

Kasey's attention turns to me. "Are you going to sell?"

"I'd be a fool to sell now," I say. "I'd lose money."

"That's a maybe," Kasey says. "Just not now."

"Not for a long time," I correct.

"And now you're devoted to being here and fixing things," he assumes.

"No," I say. "I'd like to offer you a new compensation package with bonuses. And if I sell, I'll include an incentive for you. I want to take care of you."

"Are you saying you're going to let go of the day-to-day operations?" he presses.

"I'm moving to San Francisco with Nick, unless you tell me I need to be here to run this place."

"You don't," Kasey says. "You're free."

Free. Am I ever really free of this place as long as I own it? I have to try to be. "Would you like to take over the living quarters in the mansion?" I offer.

His eyes narrow. "You're offering me the mansion?" His tone is incredulous.

"Yes," I say. "Rent free."

"I'll draft a contract with your compensation," Nick interjects. "We'll include the mansion, but I will need you to work with my team to manage the finances. If this sounds acceptable to you?"

"It does," he says, looking at me. "This place was never your place."

"No," I say. "But it has always been your place."

"Yes," he says. "It has been. And yes. I want the mansion quarters."

"Great," I say. "I ah… I haven't cleared out my mother's things."

"I wondered about that," he says. "I can do it."

"Thank you," I say. "Donate what you don't want. And my mother's car. It's yours. Sell it. Keep it. Whatever you want. I'll sign the title over to you."

"We'll authorize additional staff as well," Nick says. "Someone to report to you but do what Faith would have done to support you." Nick grabs a paper napkin. "Can I borrow your pen?"

Kasey removes it from his pocket, and Nick sets it on his knee, then writes down a number and a percentage, showing it to me for confirmation. I nod at the numbers that equal a substantial—and deserved—pay increase for Kasey. Nick slides it in front of him. Kasey looks at it and then between us. "Very generous. Thank you. And on that note, I'm going to go check on the work crew."

Nick quickly adds, "Coordinate with Rita to get a new team out here to start the repair process."

He gives an incline of his chin, stands up, and leaves. "Could a historical marker be a reason to want this place?" I ask when he disappears around the corner, while Nick sends a text message.

"I don't know enough about that topic to say, but we'll find out. I just told Rita and Beck to investigate in different ways, but I'm doubtful. Otherwise your father would have done it on his own and pushed up the value of the winery."

"Unless it costs a lot of money to do it, and my mother was gambling then, too," I say.

He glances over at me. "Good point."

A thought hits me. "And I'm officially brilliant," I murmur. "I just gave him the only working car I have."

Nick turns to face me. "Don't get angry, but—"

"You had it fixed."

"Weeks ago, and that old car is beneath my woman. We'll buy you something you want that I know is safe."

"You can't just—"

He leans in and kisses me. "Give him both cars, Faith. And if you don't want something new, there are two cars to choose from."

"You'd let me drive your Audi instead of your BMW?"

"Fuck. I must be in love, because yes. I'll not only let you drive it; I'll let you call the damn thing your own if you—"

I lean in and kiss him. He cups my head and slants his mouth over mine, his tongue licking into my mouth before he glances at his watch and says, "It's half past. You should be naked and riding my cock right now."

"That's crass and horrible."

"And it turns you on, right?"

I sigh. "Yes."

He laughs. "Let's get out of here."

Leaving the winery behind in the many ways that currently apply comes with relief, but arriving to the house I'd bought as an escape from it doesn't feel like an escape anymore. It feels like a part of that excuse this entire town had, unknowingly, become to me. Once we're on the porch, we find packaging left by FedEx to package up my art. Nick and I pull them inside and start carrying the supplies upstairs. Once we set the first lot down, he heads for the stairs. "I'll get the rest, sweetheart."

Scanning the work I'll soon ship off to L.A., my attention lingers on the painting of Nick—his eyes, and the secrets in their depths, my focus. I don't have any secrets left. He knows who I am. He knows what I am, and yet he still holds back. I grapple with an array of varied thoughts and where they lead me, but Nick's footsteps sound before I reach a conclusion.

I walk to the floor-to-ceiling window and stare out at the night sky, the canvas of a full moon and the twinkle of at least a dozen stars. Nick steps to my side, his hand at my waist, a possessive quality to his touch. "You need a studio like this in San Francisco. We'll hire someone to build it, or we'll just buy another house."

I face him. "You want to buy a new house because of me?"

"I want a place that you feel is yours, not mine."

"Because I didn't pack this one up to take with me?"

"I want you to feel like you're home. Like you did here."

Like I did here, I think, those thoughts I'd started to have when he was downstairs charging at me again. "The day I moved into this house with all my renovations done, I stood right here and watched the sun set, and I told myself: now I could be happy in this town. But once the sun set, do you know what I did? Nothing. I didn't paint. I built this beautiful studio and told myself it would inspire me, but I didn't paint. And when I was packing today, your words kept coming to me."

"My words?"

"You said you don't like who I am here. And I don't like who I am here. So, no. I don't want to take a lot of my stuff with me. This place was a placeholder. It's time to move on. I don't want to be here. I want to go home, to San Francisco, with you, Nick. Tonight. Or tomorrow when FedEx picks up my art."

"Then we'll leave tomorrow."

"Good. But I do think that, if I'm honest with you, I'm not without hesitation. I keep thinking that you will break me or me you."

"We've already determined that we're both broken. But we're better together than we are apart."

"Anything too good to be true is too good to be true."

"Sometimes it's just good, sweetheart."

"But you're not a good guy, Nick, remember?"

"I'm not good," he says, "but I'm a hell of a lot better with you than without you."

"Then you need to confess your sins, Nick."

He goes completely, utterly still. "What sins, Faith?"

"The ones you haven't told me. The ones you don't want to tell me. Trust me that much. Because it's not what you haven't told me that feeds distrust. It's about your unwillingness to tell me."

He snags my hips and pulls me to him. "When I'm ready, remember?"

"Yes. Agreed. But I'm already exposed and on the line with you, more so than ever by moving to the city with you. So, when do you think you'll be ready?"

"When I've made it impossible for you to live without me."

"Because you think I'll want to leave when you expose yourself?"

"Yes," he says solemnly. "I do. But you need to know that I'll fight for you."

CHAPTER TWENTY-SEVEN

Nick

Tonight, I tell Faith about the club.

After a hell of a good weekend with Faith, I arrive to work early Monday with that vow in my mind—and a sense of relief. Not only will she know that I owned the club, she'll know that I sold it and that she was far more important to me than it ever was.

By eight, I've already drafted Kasey's documents, contacted Faith, and sent them to her to review. Rita shows up about the time I've hit send, dressed in a red dress, with the redheaded attitude. "Oh, look," she says, waving her hands over her voluptuous figure. "We match. Your tie and my dress. Aren't we adorable?"

I give her a deadpan look. "Sometimes I think you forget it's me you work for."

"Sometimes, I think you forget it's me who works for you. And moving on. Landmark properties. It comes with regulations on property improvement but the potential to create a tax-exempt organization."

"Yeah. No. That would be tricky and potentially illegal."

"Everyone doesn't care, as you know." She sets a document on my desk. "That is the detailed breakdown, but from what I can tell, it might push up revenues, but not much. And I still cannot find any documentation that indicates a development, highway or otherwise, that would affect Reid Winter Winery. As for oil or minerals, there's certainly been gold and various other findings in the state, but nothing specifically in Sonoma or on that property. At least any not that is properly documented."

The same answers Beck gave me yesterday, but I'm still not satisfied. North walks into my office, still just as Clark Kent, super geeky, but extra damn skinny. "Did you almost die or what?"

"Yes," he says, shoving his thick glasses up his nose. "I did."

"You're fine now?"

"Yes."

I eye Rita. "Have him do everything you already did on Reid Winter Winery. See if he finds anything else."

"Typical Nick Rogers," she says, not even the slightest bit offended. She sets a stack of documents on my desk and spreads them out. "Sign. Sign. Review. Review. Sign. I'll be back in thirty minutes." She heads for the door and motions to North. "Follow."

They exit my office, and my cellphone rings, and a glance tells me it's Beck. "Tell me something I fucking want to hear for once," I say.

"Well, hello sunshine," he replies drily. "Fuck you in the morning, too. You never asked about flag dude again."

"I wasn't aware I needed to micromanage you to do your job. What about him?"

"Jess Wild. Ex-CIA. Does contract-to-hire work and makes my kind of bank."

"Which tells us what?"

"He has a thing for wine. He spent time in wine country investigating a French operative who also liked wine."

"You're telling me he was vacationing?"

"I'm telling you he showed up there last week at the same time a married female executive of Davenport Data showed up. And since he's banging her, we suspect she's either his client or his target."

"Does she connect to Faith or anyone connected to Faith?"

"Not that we know of, but we aren't stupid, despite your general opinion that we are. Banging a powerful hot chick as a cover is what I'd call brilliant. We're watching him."

"And the problems at the winery?"

"I have nothing new. Obviously, someone is still squeezing Faith to sell. And all I can say is history—"

"Do not repeat that history-repeats shit again."

He changes the subject. "I hacked the autopsy report again."

"And?"

"The written form filled out to order the proper testing was scanned and marked correctly, but when it was input into the database for actual completion, the data was incorrect. The important tests were left off. It could have been an input error, but per the internal memos, the person who input it insists she didn't make an error."

"It was hacked."

"That's my conclusion," he says. "Someone knew you ordered the autopsy and made sure certain toxins were not checked for. And we both know that there are substances that won't show up if you aren't looking for them."

"Jess Wild," I say. "That flag-wearing ex-CIA agent. It has to be him."

"Except that he let you know he was there. That's a stupid move with someone like you. Then again, he could be such an arrogant prick that he wants to challenge you."

"I need to buy us some time," I say. "Play the game. Give them what they want."

"If you mean put the winery on the market, you risk someone like Bill fearing the bids will get too high. Once a killer—"

"Always a killer," I supply as he repeats my thoughts from the other night. "We need to reel in the uncle. Make him think he can get in with Faith, and that's a big order."

"You can be her voice of reason," he says. "Of course, you'll have to convince Faith that this makes sense without sharing your suspicions." He laughs. "Good luck with that one."

My phone beeps, and I glance at the caller ID to find Kurt's number. "I'll be in touch," I say to Beck and disconnect, answering the other line. "Kurt," I greet, eyeing my watch. "I'm expecting you in the next hour, correct?"

"My attorney can't look at this until this afternoon."

"Then get another attorney," I say. "You've had time, and this is a gift. I can insert another name in this paperwork in sixty seconds. Have the signed documents here by three or I will." I hang up and start counting. One. Two. My phone rings again.

I answer. "I'll just sign the damn thing. I'll be there at two." He hangs up.

And I have the outcome I'm after. That club is not mine. Faith is.

I spend the fifteen minutes that I manage to spare for lunch on the phone with Faith, sharing her excitement that her paintings have officially been received. By two, I have my document from Kurt. By four, I have about ten crisis situations that ensure I'm going to have to work late. I text Faith: *I'm going to have a late night. I'll text you on the way home about dinner.*

Faith replies with: *Why don't I bring you dinner?*

I reach for the sandwich I've had sitting on my desk since noon, toss it in the trash, and type: *Chinese?* Because she was craving it before bed last night.

Perfect, she replies. *I'll text you when I'm on my way.*

I think of her spending her money to pick up that meal, and I dial Charlie, arranging to add Faith to my fast cash account and ordering her a credit card. Once I'm done, I buzz Rita. "Come."

She appears in my doorway almost instantly. "Come? That doesn't work when my husband says it, and it won't work when you say it."

"I said come, and you're here," I say. "It worked."

"Only because I have work for you." She marches to my desk and again sets a stack of documents in front of me. "Sign. Read. Sign. Call about this and be the bastard that you are. Sign."

"I need the top three realtors you suggest and the top three remodeling services."

She gives me a keen look. "Are you buying a new house?"

"Faith and I are going to buy a new house."

"And she hasn't agreed; thus, you want to make her feel in control by her choosing the contacts you work with."

"You know me a little too well sometimes."

"I'll get you the names." She starts to turn and seems to change her mind. "A jeweler takes quite some time to customize a ring—perhaps six to eight weeks. Shall I line up a few for you to interview?"

A ring. A wedding. I wait for the hesitation, the wall, the pushback, but there is none. "Yes. Line them up."

"Price range?"

"Whatever it takes to get perfection."

Her lips curve. "I'll let them know."

A ring, I think. A wife. Holy fuck. This is happening. I'm going to make it happen.

I send Rita home at six. Faith sends me a text at six thirty on her way to pick up the food. At seven, I toss down my pen, pressing fingers to my eyes, finally done with a brief I need by morning. The elevator dings, and Faith appears in the doorway, giving me a shy smile, her pink lipstick the same pale shade as her Allure Gallery T-shirt, which she's paired with faded torn jeans.

"Hungry?" she asks.

"Starving," I say, standing up and closing the space between us to take the bags. "For you, but I'll settle for what's in the bags until we get home."

"Home," she says, biting her lip. "I can't get used to that."

"You will," I promise, motioning with my head and leading

her to the small round conference table to the left of my desk. Once we've settled into our seats, takeout containers in front of us, I reach into my jacket and set a small sheet of paper on the table. "These are the names and numbers of the top realtors and remodelers in town. I want you to pick the ones you want to work with."

"You really want to do this, don't you?"

"I do. Don't you?"

She hesitates, but a smile hints at her lips. "I guess it couldn't hurt to look."

Baby steps, I think, but I don't heed that warning. I reach into my pocket again and set a bank card on the table.

She stiffens instantly. "What is that?"

"You're with me now, sweetheart. All the way. No half way. I had your social from the legal filings I did. I had you added to my account and ordered you your own card. That's good for two hundred, so you can get pretty much whatever you want when you want it."

She blanches. "Two hundred *thousand* dollars?"

"Yes."

"Nick—"

"I know you're going to fight me on this."

"I still owe you money."

"You don't owe me money, but we won't beat that up. Humor me. Put it in your purse. Have it with you in case you need it." I pause. "Please."

"Please? Nick fucking Rogers just said please?"

"I have very good manners, remember?"

She scowls. "No. You have horrible manners." Her voice and expression soften. "I'll keep it, but I'm—"

I lean in and kiss her. "Going to fight me on this. I know. Put it in your purse." She nods and unzips her purse where it rests at her hip, then sticks it inside a zipper pocket.

"Now," I say. "Tell me about the L.A. show. Did you hear

anything more about your work?"

"What the fuck, Nick?"

At the sound of Abel's voice, alarm bells go off in my head. I'm on my feet in an instant. "Abel—"

He appears in the center of the office. "You sold the fucking club and didn't give me a chance to buy it? Nick? Where the hell—"

"Abel," I bite out, and holy fuck I'm going to murder him.

Faith stands up at the same moment that Abel rotates to look at us, his eyes going wide. "*Oh* shit. Nick, man—"

"Get out," I all but growl at him, stalking toward him as he turns to leave, shutting the door behind him.

I face forward, and Faith is in front of me, hugging herself. "What club, Nick? What was that, and why do you, who is always cool and calm, look like you want to throw up right now? Is it the club you used to—"

"Yes."

"You own it?"

"Owned. I sold it. And I only owned it for a year. I bought it from a client to save him—"

"You didn't tell me. You know what that world did to me, and you didn't tell me you *owned* a club."

"I planned to tell you tonight."

"Of course you did. Tonight. The night Abel spills the secret."

"Abel burst in here because he heard I sold it today. Today, Faith. Actually, I gave it away. I took a three-hundred-and-fifty-thousand-dollar hit because I just wanted it gone."

"You didn't tell me," she repeats, rotating to face the opposite direction and starting to walk toward the window.

I move toward her, intending to pull her into my arms, and she seems to know. She stops dead in her tracks. "Do not even think about touching me right now."

CHAPTER TWENTY-EIGHT

Nick

I ignore Faith's order not to touch her, snagging her wrist. When she tries to pull away from me, I step into her, catching her hips and guiding her to me. "You are what matters to me. You, Faith. Not some damn sex club."

Her chin lifts in challenge, her eyes meeting mine. "Take me there."

My rejection is instant. "Not a chance in hell."

"Take me there, or I will go there on my own."

"You're not a member. You won't even find it."

"I've been in that world, Nick. *Your* world. Because I'm not naturally a bull like you does not mean I can't be one if I need to be. And if you think I can't make a few phone calls and find out where that club is, you underestimate me."

"I have never underestimated you a day that I've known you, but you won't get in the door."

"Then I'll stand there until they call you and you can let me in."

She will. I see it in her eyes. "Why do you need to do this?"

"I need to know who you really are."

"*You know* me, Faith."

"I don't want any more surprises."

Those words grind through me and make my decision. Because there are more surprises to come. I have to let her resolve this one from start to finish before we get there. I take her hand and lace our fingers together. "Come with me," I say, and I start walking, opening the office door and leading her into the lobby. I don't stop until we're at the elevator, and I don't give her a chance to withdraw any more than she has already.

I punch the call button and pull her in front of me, and when the doors open, I say, "There are cameras inside."

"Which won't matter if I'm alone. I need space."

"Too bad," I say as I walk us inside, holding on to her every step of the way. In a matter of seconds, I'm holding her in front of me again, nice and close, my hand on her belly, and we're riding toward the garage. "You don't have to do this," I say near her ear, as if me saying this will miraculously make her believe it.

"I do," she says, her hand coming down on mine, fingers closing tightly around it, barely contained anger in the death grip. "And on some level, I know you know I do."

I didn't know this would be her reaction, but in hindsight, I should have. I know Faith. When she spins out of control, she rebels against the free-spirited artist that she is at her core and tries to force control. The car halts, and the doors open, and I take her hand again, leading her into the garage. She digs in her heels. "I'll follow you. I'm parked—"

"Negative," I say. "You ride with me. You stay with me. Or you don't go. And before you even think about arguing, this is nonnegotiable, Faith."

Her expression tightens, but she clearly reads just how insistent I am on this. "Fine," she says. "I'll ride with you."

I'm already walking, leading her to the Audi and clicking the locks. I open the passenger door and hold it open for her, reluctantly letting go of her hand. She inhales, as if steeling herself to be trapped in a cage with me, before ducking into the vehicle and settling into her seat. I stand there for several beats, fighting the urge to pull her out of the car again, kiss her, and force her to listen to reason. But I can't force Faith to do anything, and if I could, I doubt I'd want her so fucking much. She's made up her mind, and I have to ride the ride with her.

Still, as I shut her inside the Audi and round the rear of the vehicle, I mentally argue a case to go home instead of the club, knowing she'll rebel but wanting to do it anyway. I'll take her there. I'll tie her to the bed, and I'll make her come so many times she forgets the club ever existed.

But she won't forget.

Fuck.

I open the driver's side door and join Faith inside, that sweet amber-and-vanilla scent of hers colliding with the punch of anger filling the car and proving to be a brutal cocktail. Wanting this over with, I crank the car in reverse and pull us out of the space. I don't turn on the radio. I want Faith to talk to me, to ask questions, but she doesn't. Once we're on the road, silence consumes us. Thick, heavy, a weight that promises to bury me—and us—alive. I want to say something to fix this, but I go back to knowing Faith. If I push her right now, she will thicken the wall she's now thrown between us.

So, for fifteen minutes, we endure a wordless ride, until finally we pull up to the private gates of the club, a mansion that sits on the edge of an elite neighborhood. I roll down my window and key in the entrance code, making it painfully clear that I still have access to the facility. The gates open, and I pull us through them, and we travel the long path hugged by trees and manicured foliage. Once I turn us onto the horseshoe drive, I stop in front of the mansion, holding up my hands to both windows and valets.

I turn to her, and before she knows my intent, I have cupped her neck and pulled her to me. "While we are here, I am your fucking king. You do what I say. You stay by my side. You hold my arm or hand. This, too, is nonnegotiable, and I swear to fucking God, Faith, if you disobey me on this, I will throw you over my shoulder and carry you out of here. Do you understand?"

She breathes out. "Yes."

I want to kiss her, but I don't. I hate her being here too damn much, and I will not risk her reading me in any other direction. "Stay," I order instead. "I'll come around and get you."

I don't wait for her agreement. She doesn't get a fucking

opinion while we're in this place. I exit the car and speak to the valet, a thirty-something guy named Rick who's been with the club for a decade. "Hold the car up front," I tell him. "We won't be long. Is Kurt here?"

"He is."

"Have him meet me in the foyer if he's not indisposed at the moment." I palm him a large bill and round the car, where Faith thankfully has listened and stayed inside. I grind my teeth and force myself to open her door. She slides her legs to the ground, and I offer her my hand. She hesitates, damn it, she hesitates, and it kills me. It also pisses me off. I squat down, lowering my voice for her ears only. "You aren't getting out or going anywhere without touching me," I assure her, "so slide back in and we'll leave or"—I offer her my hand again—"take my fucking hand."

She presses her palm to mine, and I stand, taking her with me and moving her to the curb. The car door shuts behind us, and I lace my fingers with Faith's, bending our arms at the elbows and fitting her snug to my hip. We start the walk up the stairs leading to the entrance, each of the dozen steps a walk of doom I reject. If this goes badly, I will lose her.

I'm not losing her.

We reach the top, and a doorman in a suit—everyone in the place wears suits—well-trained at the kind of discretion the club requires, does not make eye contact. He simply opens the door for us. Inside the foyer, the mansion instantly drips of money, from the expensive paintings on the walls, to the tiles and thick oriental rugs on every floor, to the enormous glass chandelier above our heads. "Where do they lead?" Faith asks of the set of wooden winding stairs directly in front of us, a primarily red multicolored oriental carpet up their center, while a second stairwell leads downward.

"No place you want to go," I assure her, redirecting her attention. "To the left is a cigar and whiskey room that is just that. Nothing more. No sex. No play allowed."

"The stairs, Nick," she says tightly, still keenly focused on them.

"Upstairs is group play. Downstairs, a dungeon and bondage area, among other things. I didn't go to those places without you, and we won't be going to them now."

She faces me. "I want to go to both areas. All areas."

"I told you, Faith. I didn't go to those places without you. I won't take you to them now or ever." I glance to the left to find Kurt, looking stoic in a black suit and gray tie.

Faith follows my gaze, and Kurt closes the distance between us, standing in front of us in a few moments. "Faith is my guest," I announce. "She is not, nor will she ever be, applying for membership." He doesn't react, but he's smart enough to know that she's why he now owns the club. "Faith," I add, moving on. "This is Kurt. The new owner of the club. Kurt. How long did I own this place?"

"Roughly a year," he says.

"Who owned it before me?"

"I'm not at liberty to name names, but one of your clients."

It's a good answer—the right answer—which sets up the story I'm trying to tell right now. "And this person owned it how long?"

"He created it," Kurt explains. "It was his from day one ten years ago."

"And did I ever claim the ownership duties?"

"You did not."

"Did I ever spend time in any of the places those stairs lead?"

"No, you did not," he says.

"And why should Faith trust that you aren't simply protecting me?"

He looks Faith in the eyes for the first time since joining us. "I protect my members, but I don't lie. I'd decline to answer rather than lie, as I did when asked about the prior ownership. This was never Nick's place. It was mine. It's simply official now." He looks at me. "Room eleven is yours."

I nod, and he gives Faith another look but says nothing more. He simply turns and walks away. I don't speak to Faith. I lead her down the hallway, and I don't stop until we're at room eleven. I open the door and allow Faith to enter what amounts to a giant bedroom with a wall of sex toys on the left. A massive canopy bed is on the right. A bondage stand is in a half-moon space at the back wall that is covered by a curtain. Beyond that curtain are seats, should you decide to invite viewers, which I never did.

I've barely shut and locked the door before Faith is already moving deeper into the room, walking up to the wall of toys. She pauses and grabs a black silk face mask, then walks toward the bondage stand. She steps inside it, her back to me as she starts undressing. I move to a spot a foot back, watching her, waiting, telling myself I'm about to show her that we are still us here and anywhere. That I am still me. Once she's naked, standing there, her perfect, heart-shaped ass on display, she puts on the mask and then turns to face me. Her arms are at her sides, hands gripping the bars on either side of her. Her breasts are high, full, nipples tight pink nubs. And yeah. My cock is hard. Hard as Sin City is to beat on a good day for a casino, which is every fucking day. This is Faith. She can smile and my cock sees it as an invitation.

"Tie me up," she demands, her voice quavering, and I don't miss the way her knees tremble, and that jolts me with realization. She's trying to be that person she was in the club with Macom. But she's not that person. And I'm damn sure not Macom.

I walk to her, and I grab the bars above her hands, but I don't touch her. I lean in, my lips near her ear. "You will never learn how to fuck me and still be alone, because you will never be alone again, Faith. And I won't touch you in this place." I remove her mask. "Get dressed. We're leaving."

"No. Nick." She grabs my lapels, her naked body pressing to mine. "I need—"

"To put your fucking clothes on," I say. "And let me be clear, Faith. If you don't get dressed, I will dress you, and that's going to be awkward for us both. I'll be in the hallway." I turn and walk to the door, opening it and stepping outside, running a hand over my face, adrenaline I didn't know I'd triggered pumping through me.

I lean against the wall, inhaling and willing my body to calm the fuck down. I am always calm. Until now, apparently. The door opens, and Faith exits the room, thankfully fully dressed, and I don't look at her, nor do either of us speak. I take her hand and lead her down the hallway, getting us the hell out of here. We exit the mansion and start down the stairs. By the time we're at the bottom, the car is pulled directly in our path, and I open the door to allow Faith to enter. A minute later, we're in the car and are back where we started. Her scent and her anger is a powerful cocktail, and I turn to look at her.

"That anger of yours can burn me alive, sweetheart, but I'm still going to be here, and I'm still not going to let you go."

CHAPTER TWENTY-NINE

Nick

Thankfully, the drive home is short. Ten minutes and I pull us into the garage and kill the engine. I'm out before it even dies, walking around the car to get Faith. She's out of the Audi by the time I'm there, facing off with me. "I should go back to Sonoma."

She just burned me, all right—scorched me inside and out. I'm pissed. One hundred percent certifiably pissed. I don't say a word. I walk toward her, pick her up, and throw her over my shoulder, just like I did the last time she tried to leave.

"Damn it, Nick," she hisses. "You can't throw me over your shoulder every time I want to leave."

I don't respond. I'm already walking, opening the garage door, and stepping inside the house, my hand on her pretty little ass, my path straight through the living room and up the stairs.

"Nick, damn it."

"You already said that," I say, entering our bedroom and walking through the bathroom to the closet that used to feel too big and is now just right with Faith in the house. I flip on the light and then set her down in the center of the room. "What do you see, Faith?" I don't give her time to respond. "Look around. Your clothes and my clothes. This is two people sharing a life, and when you share a life, you don't just leave because you're upset." Realization slices through me. "And if you really want to leave, then maybe you aren't in this the way I am in this."

"That's not true."

"Words versus actions, Faith. I can't keep picking you up every time you want to leave? Stop trying to fucking leave. Or don't. I told you. In or out. You said you were in."

"You *should* have told me, Nick."

"I took an enormous hit to give that damn place away, Faith. For you. I did it for you. Because after I heard what a club and Macom equaled for you, I wanted you to know the minute I told you that buying it was a *favor*, not some defining piece of my character. Not an indication of who I am or who we are. I waited to tell you. That was a judgment call, but I did it for the right reasons."

"You *gave* it away?" she confirms in disbelief.

I close the space between us and cup her face. "Yes. I did. Because you mean that much to me."

"Please tell me you have a way to get the money back."

"I don't care about the money, Faith. I care about you." My mouth closes down on hers, and I kiss her, deeply, passionately, drinking her in, so damn in need of her right now, and that need claws at me. "Get undressed," I order. "We need to be naked together."

"Yes," she whispers. "We do. I do."

I brush my lips over hers and shrug out of my jacket, and we watch each other undress, the anger between us shifting to something just as dark, just as intense and demanding. Lust. Love. Need. And when we are naked, both of us, we stand there in the fucking closet, but neither of us are looking at the other's body. Our eyes connect. That mask she'd had on and that I'd stuck in my pocket is in my hand, to her, it was a weapon against me and us. A way she made the sex nameless, faceless. To me, it's a way to show her that that will never be possible. Not for us.

"Do you trust me?"

"I trust you."

I walk to her, stopping a lean away from touching her. "*Do you trust me?*"

"*Yes.* I trust you."

"You didn't react like you trust me."

"I obviously have triggers. I realize that now. It's about me, not you."

"It's about us, Faith. Everything is us now."

"I know."

She doesn't, but I decide right then that I just have to accept the challenge. I'm not a patient man, but I am in love with this woman, and I will help her, not force her, to see how devoted I am to her. I snag the fingers of her hand and walk her into the dressing room connecting to the closet—a small room with one oversize blue-and-brown plaid chair, a dresser, a standing mirror, and a full wall that is all windows, the view the ocean, the city.

I lead Faith to the chair in front of the ottoman, which is large enough that it might as well be another chair. I then hold up the mask. "Trust," I say softly.

She reaches for it and, in the process, presses to her toes, leaning into me, her hand on my shoulder, her nipples brushing my chest. Her lips are a breath from mine. "Because it's different here."

"Is that a question or a statement?"

"A statement. It feels different. I'm glad you made me leave."

I cup her head and kiss her, savoring the sweetness of those words on my tongue before I say, "Me too. But I'm glad we went, Faith. You needed to know. I just don't want us in a place like that."

"I felt that. I needed to feel that." She pushes away from me just enough to slip that mask on her face.

My hands settle at her waist, my lips near her ear. "You know I like control."

My fingers tease her nipple, and she arches into the touch and gives a choked laugh. "You love control."

"Can I have it now, Faith?"

"I love that you ask," she whispers.

"I don't have control that you don't give me. You know that. I know that. And I wouldn't want the lie that is any other form of control. Do you know what I want right now?" I don't give her time to reply. "I want you to feel me so completely that you know, absolutely know, that if there is one person on this earth you can be free with, it's me."

"I do."

"No. But we're a work in progress, sweetheart. You will. I promise, I will make you not just feel those things. You'll know them."

My hands fall away from her, and I take a step backward. She reaches for me, and I am just a finger out of reach. Her hands fall to her sides, and for nearly a full minute, I just stand there, letting her feel the absence of my touch, letting her wonder what will come next. What I will do to her. I step closer to her again, letting her feel my nearness, and she does. She inhales my scent on her instincts that tell her I'm in front of her. I lower myself to my knees, but still I don't touch her. I hold my hands at her ankles, but still I don't touch her. I move my hands upward. But still I don't touch her.

"Nick," she breathes out, and when she reaches for me, my lips curve, and I allow her fingers to tunnel into my hair.

It's what I wanted. I wanted her to reach for me, to need me. And now that she has, then, and only then, do my hands come down on her hips, my lips to her belly. I cup her backside and lower my mouth until I'm a breath above her sex. Her fingers tighten in my hair, and I give her a tiny lick. She rewards me with a sexy, sweet moan. I suckle her nub, then swirl my tongue around it, and already she is trembling, and I can feel how on edge she is, how easily she will shatter for me, but it's not enough. I want more. So much more. An explosion. A connection. More than an orgasm.

And suddenly I know I need to test the waters. I need to know that we are not only moving forward but that we haven't gone backward.

I stand up, and she breathes out, "Nick," and my name is a plea.

I answer by cupping her face and kissing her, letting her taste *her* on my lips. "I'm going to spank you, Faith," I say, needing to know she won't hesitate. "I am not going to give you any other warning unless you tell me otherwise. Answer now. Trust me or not. Yes or no?"

"Yes."

I sit down and take her with me, pulling her across my lap so that the cushion cradles her body, my hand on her backside. I start rubbing her cheeks, warming her backside, when I feel the punch of ignorance overwhelm me. Of course she said yes. I spanked her the first night. She knows how to shut down. She knows how to escape, and *hell*. I'm letting her escape me. I'm hurting the level of trust between us, not creating trust.

I inhale and lean over her, kissing her back, her shoulder, one of my hands sliding under her to her sex, fingers stroking the silky wet heat. I slip fingers inside her, my thumb still working her clit, and she was already so damn close that she stiffens and trembles into that orgasm I denied her. I don't let her ride it all the way out, though. I want her to finish with me inside her. I shift our entire bodies, pulling her backside to my front, and I press inside her, my hand covering her breasts.

Her hand is immediately on my hand, and I thrust into her, pleasure radiating through. "God. You feel good," I murmur next to her ear. "So damn good."

She arches into me. "Nick, you...I..."

I pull out of her and turn her to face me, pulling away her blindfold. Pressing inside her again, I cup her backside to pull her down onto my cock before I repeat her words—"You and I is exactly right"—and then kiss her, a deep, drugging kiss, even as I do a slow thrust followed by another, and when I pull back to look at her, to breathe with her, there is a shift between us, an expanding need.

Our mouths come back together, our bodies grinding, pumping, thrusting. It's dirty, it's sexy, it's fiercely addictive, and yet it is sultry, intimate. She tugs my hair free, her fingers tangling in it, tugging at it. Her teeth scraping my shoulder, mine scraping her nipple. The rise of our orgasms is slow, it seems, until it's not. Until they're upon us and I am cupping her breast, pinching her nipple, thrusting my cock, and she is panting out my name in such a fierce, demanding way that I am helpless to stop the explosion. I shudder, and she trembles, and we cling to each other until we collapse against each other.

Seconds, maybe minutes pass, and we lay there like that until she says, "Why didn't you spank me?"

I pull back to look at her, stroking hair from her face. "I wanted to, but for the wrong reasons."

"I don't understand."

"A spanking is a power play. We both enjoy the give and take that it represents. But it is about power, my power and control, and that has no place between us with a fight in the air and that damn club playing with our heads."

Her hand settles on my face. "The club isn't between us. It's gone. It's done. And Nick Rogers. If I wasn't in love with you before this moment, I would be now."

She presses her lips to mine, and I slant my mouth over hers. In the depths of that kiss is what I have craved, what I have needed: a new level of trust, a willingness to risk it all with me. But hours later as I lay in bed, holding Faith close, I am not reveling in the mountain we've climbed today. I'm too busy looking for a way to battle the sea of sharks that are my lies.

CHAPTER THIRTY

Faith

A new day dawns for me with the emotional high of conquering "the club incident," as I call it in my mind, and with Nick and me a little stronger and a lot closer.

And with my car still at Nick's office, I hitch a ride with him, with a Starbucks drive-thru detour a few blocks from our destination. "That Chinese food we left on your conference table is going to reek this morning," I say as we wait at the window for our drinks.

"Rita is going to give me absolute hell about it, too."

"What are you going to say to explain it?"

"Absolutely nothing."

I laugh. "That sounds like you." I inhale and let it out, dreading the nagging concern that sparks my next question. "Did you ask Beck to confirm my art was bought by legitimate buyers?"

And as if waiting for his answer isn't torture enough, a woman appears at the drive-thru window to take our money. Seeming to sense my nerves, though, Nick ignores her, looks at me, and says, "Your sales are one hundred percent legitimate," before he turns to her and offers her his credit card. A minute later, he hands me my white mocha and sets his double shot espresso in the drink holder, rolling the window back up, which is my cue to press for more information.

"Did Beck check out my sales, then? Or, rather, the buyers?"

He places the car into gear and glances over at me. "This is going to make you doubt yourself, isn't it? You do remember you got into the L.A. show for a reason, right?"

"I do," I say as he pulls us onto the road. "But I'd like a firm grip on how well I'm doing. And the bottom line here is that if those sales weren't real sales, they might track back to my uncle. That could be the link we need between him and this hell we've been through with the winery. If he was behind those broken water lines, Nick, I want him to pay."

"And he will. I'll make sure of it."

"We need to buy some time for you and Beck to make those connections. I'd say we could place the winery up for sale—just for show, of course—but it would freak out Kasey and the staff. But it might bring our enemy out of hiding."

"And perhaps not in a good way," he says. "Whoever is behind this could see that as my negative reaction as a new investor to the vineyard water damage. They'll also see me as someone who will try to push the price upward despite that loss. In which case, they might try to further drive the price down by creating another problem."

"But they had to suspect that could be your reaction to the financial blow," I say as he pulls us into the parking garage and parks next to the BMW. "Maybe that's what they wanted."

"I'm leaning more toward them thinking I'd bow out and leave it to you, while you would end up just wanting out."

"Which brings me back to my recent sales. To someone trying to give me motivation to get out."

"Your sales are legitimate, Faith, and as for the rest, we can speculate all day, but I'm not ready to take calculated risks just yet. Let's give Beck a little more room to do his job. And the reality here is that now that we've bought out your note, this might fizzle out."

"The water damage says it won't."

"Or it was unrelated, or one last blow delivered by a bad loser." He reaches for his door. "I'll come around to get you."

I don't give him time to help me out of the car. I slip my tan purse, which I've paired with my favorite faded jeans and a matching pair of brown ankle boots, over my shoulder, and open my door. By the time I'm standing, Nick has arrived and is now towering over me, his navy blue eyes a perfect match for his suit and the dots in his black tie. And really, truly, I could stand here and take a deep blue swim in those eyes for a few minutes, or even hours, and be perfectly happy.

"Let's talk cars," he says.

My deep blue spell is broken. "What about cars?"

"Let's buy you something you want and love, and not because I care if you drive the BMW or the Audi. Because you need to pick what you love."

"I like the BMW."

"Then we'll custom order you one with the specs you like."

"I can just drive this one."

"What color do you want?"

"Blue like your eyes."

"Interior?"

"Black like my uncle's soul."

"Black like your uncle's soul," he repeats drily. "There's no question what's still on your mind. You, my beautiful woman, need to let go of the stress. Get your butt to Allure and paint that wall you're supposed to start painting today. And pick a remodeler, if you aren't going to pick a realtor. Let's get your studio up to standard."

"The studio you made me is fine."

"It's not fine. In fact, it's well-known that the male population— at least the smart ones—realize that when a woman says 'fine,' it's never fine."

I'd answer that claim, but a shout from the distance interrupts. "You have a meeting in ten minutes!"

At the sound of the female voice delivering that message, I turn to find a redhead rushing in our direction, her black high heels, which she's paired with a black dress, clicking on the pavement. "That would be Rita," Nick says, leaning in to kiss me. "I'll call you in a few hours." He takes off but calls over his shoulder, "Call the realtor. Any realtor."

Rita steps in front of me. "Faith. I've been dying to meet you, and I can't even chat. I have to go deal with a million things. Let's have lunch soon."

"I'd love that." She starts to turn away, and I stop her. "Wait. He has a meeting?"

"Yes. Why?"

"Chinese food on his conference table."

"Oh my God. It's the CEO of a bank. It's going to smell to high heaven up there."

She takes off for the elevator, and I laugh, walking to the BMW and climbing inside. Happy. I feel happy. Nick and I moved mountains last night, and I feel that success between us. But I also feel the heavy weight of knowing that I have an enemy who has now become Nick's. And I really need a paintbrush in my hand before I start thinking about all the ways that enemy might strike next.

By midmorning, Sara and I have made our final artist picks for opening week, and I've been sketching ideas for the wall, which isn't my normal method of working, but this isn't my normal canvas. It's also a really big canvas to mess up. I'm on what must be sketch number one hundred when Chris appears in my doorway, looking his normal, jean-clad, tattooed, cool artist self. "Nick called me."

I set my pencil down. "About?"

"Every customer that bought your work has bought from the gallery on numerous occasions. And every painting was purchased by an individual. He didn't give me details on why you wanted to know this information, but I'll use my imagination. No one bought your success. You made it." He motions behind me. "You going to paint that thing or think about it?"

"Paint it," I say, and that seems to satisfy him, because he disappears into the hallway.

I smile on a sigh with the realization that despite his meeting, Nick made me a priority again. He gave away that club because he made me a priority. He reaches for me constantly in so many ways. It's time for me to reach for him. I need to show how committed I am to him, and I open the drawer where I stashed the piece of paper with the realtor choices listed. I'm reaching for it when I pause with a thought. Nick *is* reaching for me. Helping me. Protecting me. I need to protect him. I need to make sure that my enemy doesn't turn on him and hurt him in some way. I need to buy him and Beck some time to investigate further.

I pick up my cellphone and, assuming that my enemy is my uncle, dial his number. Unsurprisingly, he answers on the first ring. "Faith," he greets. "I'm shocked you called. Happy but shocked."

"Yes, well, I keep thinking about those photos. I really miss my father, and I'd like to see them."

"I'll bring them to you. I'm in New York on business, but I can head that way this weekend."

"I actually moved to San Francisco, and I have craziness going on getting ready for the L.A. Art Forum in two weeks. And... I'd rather start with the pictures."

He's silent a beat. "Understood. What's your email? I'll shoot you over a few of them and bring you the box when we meet after your show."

He's teasing me with the photos and setting me up for the meeting. It irritates me, but it also buys me that time. I rattle off my email and continue with, "Thank you. I'm looking forward to seeing the photos."

"Of course. Shoot me back an email and let me know what you think of them."

"I will. Goodbye." I end the call knowing the twig I've given him is enough to buy some time for Nick and Beck to figure out what's really going on. Assuming, of course, that my enemy is my uncle.

It might not be him. In which case, I've bought no time at all.

CHAPTER THIRTY-ONE

Faith

Two weeks later...
"Good luck tonight and tomorrow."

I look up from my desk to find Sara in the doorway. "Thank you. I was nervous two weeks ago when I shipped my work, and then I just put it aside. I didn't think about it. But right now, my stomach is at my feet, and I think it's pretty clear that I saved all the nerves for now."

"Nerves are good," she says, walking to my visitor's chair and perching on the arm. "They mean you're experiencing life, not just going through the motions. And I went through the motions for too many years myself. I wish I could be there for you. Chris and I both wish we could be there, but it's just too close to the grand opening here. When are you leaving?"

"Now, actually," I say, standing up, still in jeans, boots, and a royal blue silk blouse, which I will trade in for something fancier tonight in L.A for the Forum launch party. "Nick had a meeting this morning or I wouldn't have come in at all. He's picking me up in a few, and we're actually looking at a house on the way to the airport that the realtor swears we have to see and could lose if we wait."

"Oh really? Where is it?"

"It's a penthouse in some new high-rise. I wasn't keen on being in a building, but the views are supposed to be stunning. Nick really wants to look."

"We're in a high-rise, and it's pretty lovely to have the service and security as well as the views. We love it." She motions to the wall behind me. "It's beautiful, Faith."

"Thank you. I'm so happy you like it."

"Our opening day guests are going to love it, too. We're going to allow only those who attend opening night to visit your room and Chris's. And we'll display a collection of your art on the walls here as well as in your display area. If you think you can spare a few more pieces? I know it's short notice, but—"

"Yes. Yes, of course I can. Thank you. So much, Sara."

"Thank you, Faith, for all you've done. And I know it's a pipe dream, but I'd love for you to take the job I offered you and stay here full time. And since I really just threw it at you without explanation, let me share a little backstory. When Mark owned this place, it was a normal, public gallery. We had full-time hours and full-time staff. He was going to close it. He shuttered it for a while but was going to reopen it with us."

"Shuttered because it wasn't making a profit?"

"No. Aside from Rebecca's situation, which affected Mark deeply, his family owns the Riptide Auction House in New York. He took over the management of that operation sooner than he'd expected. Chris and I didn't want to take this place on as a full-time job, so we paid the staff big bonuses and considered closing it down."

"What changed?"

"We started talking and got excited in a new way. We're going to develop new talent and do so mostly with special events, with a healthy portion of the profits going to charity. And because I still travel with Chris, we need someone who understands art and can become passionate with us while also running the place in my absence. My point here is that if the money is an issue—"

"Yes. Yes, I want to stay. This sounds wonderful, and the charity focus is inspiring. I'm really not worried about the money."

"Holy fuck," Nick says, stepping into the doorway, looking delicious in a navy suit that matches his eyes almost perfectly. "What am I going to do with you, woman? Of course you care about the money."

Sara laughs and stands up, placing us both in profile. "Should I negotiate the salary with you?"

"No," I say. "Nick does not get to negotiate my salary." I look at him. "You do not get to negotiate my salary."

"Technically, you're my client, and—"

"Stop while you're ahead, Tiger," I warn, "because you won't like the hotel sofa."

His lips curve ever so slightly, but he manages a stern look at Sara. "Do right by her."

"Yes sir, Tiger," she laughs, then glances at me. "We shouldn't let our two men spend too much time together without some rules. Their shared tendencies to control everything around them will have them feeding off each other, and we'll be forced to check them."

"Check me, sweetheart," Nick says. "Just make sure it hurts."

"On that note," Sara says. "I'll leave. Text me pictures from the show. And I'm talking to both of you."

She darts past Nick, and she's barely left the office before he's crossed the room to stand next to me, facing my wall. "The gardens," he says, studying my work before looking at me. "You painted your mother's gardens, and you did it in color."

"It felt like a way to make peace with the past."

"Did it work?"

"It helped," I say. "And I think it opened me up to variations of color in my art."

"With good reason," he says. "The details alone are exceptional, but the way you used color to create that detail is astounding."

"Thank you, Nick. You are always so supportive."

"Sweetheart, this isn't me being supportive. That sounds like you have a hobby, not a career I admire." He snags my fingers and pulls me to him. "We're going to have an amazing weekend, starting with tonight's welcome party." He kisses me. "Correction. Starting with this penthouse we're about to look at." He glances at his watch. "We better get moving. It's noon now. I want to be in the air by three thirty, so you have plenty of time to relax and dress for tonight. I'm parked out front."

"High places make me nervous," I say as we walk through the gallery toward the front door.

"Since when do high places make you nervous?"

"Since I considered living in the penthouse of a high-rise."

"If you don't like it," he says, opening the door and holding it for me, "we'll keep looking, but I saw pictures. I think you're going to love it." He motions to the Audi sitting a few spaces down at the curb. We hurry in that direction, and right as I've settled into my seat and Nick's shut me inside, my phone buzzes with a text. It's one of the many random photos of my parents my uncle has been sending me the past two weeks.

"Why are you scowling?" Nick asks when he joins me.

"Bill sent me another photo."

"And?"

"They're about thirty years old and standing in front of a 'Welcome to Las Vegas' sign, both laughing." I show him the photo. "His caption: *They were happy. I know there are a lot of things you feel and think about them, but I really think once we chat, you may change your mind.*"

Nick studies it for several beats and looks at me. "How do you feel about what he said?"

"Part of me really craves whatever information he has to give me."

"I assumed you would, but you started down this path to hold him at bay while Beck did his thing. And since nothing else has gone wrong, we can speculate that if he's our enemy, your plan is working. The timing of that particular photo and message, considering you told him you'd meet him after this show, is suspect."

"It does seem rather curious."

"In other words," he says, "you're playing him, sweetheart." He starts the car. "Make sure he doesn't start playing you."

"What do you think about the Vegas photo?" I ask as he pulls us onto the road.

"I think he's going to tell you she had a gambling problem. And I'll be interested in where that goes, considering he supposedly didn't talk to her or your father for almost a decade."

"And Beck has nothing for us?"

"Beck makes me want to return to my childhood and play pin the tail on the donkey again with him as the damn ass. He's dry. And I pay him way too fucking well for him to be dry."

"Could it just be over, Nick? I mean, maybe it really was just the bank trying to take advantage of me?"

"It could be."

"But you don't think so," I say, reading into his tone. "If Bill was up to something, you'd think Beck would find something on him."

He turns the corner. "I hate that he sent you that picture tonight of all nights, and got your brain wrapping around this again. Set it aside." He pulls us into the parking lot of a shiny glass high-rise. "We're here, and only a few blocks from your job, because we both know you're going to take that job at Allure."

I smile. "Yes. I am."

He stops at the front of the building, and two valets are instantly at our sides. A few seconds later, he palms both of the men money and joins me at the sliding glass doors. "The key," he says, holding it up. "I told the realtor we didn't have time for conversation."

We enter the lobby, a beautiful pale gray wood covering the floors, with gray furnishings and thick cream-and-gray curtains on the walls. The elevator is all glass, and as it starts to move, I face Nick. "What do people do if they forget stuff in the car in one of these buildings?"

"The staff will get it for you, or you get it yourself."

"The staff will do that?"

"It's a full-service building, and if you tip enough, the staff will know you and be happy to help."

"That sounds expensive."

"Most people living in the penthouse aren't worried about money."

The elevator dings, and we exit, turning left to be greeted by two massive arched wooden doors. Nick opens the doors, and I enter, finding myself skipping quickly past the dark wooden floors and balcony to the curved room, and floor-to-ceiling windows with a view of the ocean everywhere I look. "The ceilings are eighteen feet high," Nick says, shutting us inside. "And there's electronic shading for the windows."

"It's incredible." I look over at him as he steps to my side. "What do you think?"

"The same. Incredible."

"Do I even want to know how much?"

"I don't want to tell you."

"Tell me anyway."

"Fifteen million." I gasp, and he snags my hand, walking me to him. "It's just a number."

"A huge number."

"Forget the number," he says. "We've been instructed to go upstairs for your possible studio, but let's walk the rest of the place first."

"Nick, that price—"

He cups my face and kisses me. "I've wanted to do that since the moment I saw you in your office. You do know the place we have now is almost as expensive, right? And that I'll sell it?"

"Yes, but—"

"Money doesn't matter, Faith. A place we love does." He strokes my hair. "Okay?"

"I can't say okay."

"I will, then. I've worked my ass off to be in a position to pick a home with the woman I love and not worry about how much it costs." He kisses my forehead and then joins our hands again.

"Let's explore."

A few minutes later, we've seen five bedrooms, a den, an indoor pool, and an incredible kitchen with a white marble island with black finished cabinets. And finally, an outdoor space that stretches far and wide, with ivy-covered walls and brick steps. We finally head upstairs, and I step into a room with arched stained glass windows at each end and the same floor-to-ceiling windows lining the entire front wall. And above me is a skylight, a view certain to be moon and stars at night.

Nick steps behind me, his hand on my belly, lips at my ear. "What do you think?" he asks. "Could this be your studio?"

"Oh yes. I love this place. I love it so much. There's inspiration everywhere. The sky and the ocean."

"And an office already built in. I can work while you paint."

I rotate to look at him. "Have I told you that I can't paint when I'm being watched?"

"I watch you all the time."

"You're the only one I can let watch me, Nick."

"Why?"

"Because you're you. It's the only answer I have."

"Do you want to live here with me, Faith?"

"Yes," I say. "I do, but the impact of this is hitting me. This is big. Buying a new place to be with me is big. Are you—"

"In love with you? Yes. Obsessed with you? Yes. I am. Shamelessly."

"Obsession is—"

"Dangerous. Yeah. I know. Sign me up for more." He kisses me. "Let's go drink champagne on the plane and celebrate our new home and your show."

"We don't have a new home yet, and I'm feeling really nervous about my show. Let's celebrate after it's done."

"You're going to shine, sweetheart. And we'll have a home by the time we get to the airport. I'm pulling this place off the market."

He drapes his arm around my shoulder, and we start walking,

but I twist around to look at the space one more time. "I really love it."

His hand settles at my back. "We could get that cat you've wanted."

I turn to face him. "Do you like cats?"

"I had a cat growing up."

I blanch, surprised at this news. "Really? What was his name?"

"Asshole most of the time. Jerry the rest of the time. He hated my father. I loved him."

I laugh but sober quickly with a thought that seems important, considering the steps we're taking. "Do you want kids, Nick?"

His eyes meet mine, sharp, dark edges in his. "Kids break," he says. "Parents break them. I decided a long time ago I wasn't going to break any of my own."

Relief washes over me. "You know my family history. I feel the same."

He strokes a lock of hair behind my ear, those blue eyes of his softening, warming. "Possibilities, sweetheart. We'll start with a cat. We'll see where it—and life—lead us."

Thirty minutes later, we're in the lounge area of the plane, champagne-filled flutes in our hands, when the realtor finally calls Nick back. I listen as Nick negotiates, his hand on my leg, touching me—he's always touching me, as if he is truly obsessed. And I like it.

Five minutes later, he ends the connection and leans over to kiss me. "I made sure it's ours. We just need to line up a remodeling expert and decide what we want to do with it before we move in."

"How long will that take, do you think?"

"If I push them, I'd say we can be in the place in eight weeks."

My cellphone rings, and I grab it from the table built into the floor in front of us, glancing at the caller ID. "Josh," I greet.

"I got your email about your arrival," he says. "I'll pick you up at the airport. Five o'clock, right?"

"I don't need a ride, but thank you."

"I'm your agent. I'll give you a ride."

"I'm not your only client at the show."

"If you mean Macom, he can drive himself. He lives here."

I firm my tone. "Thank you, but I don't need a ride."

There is a heavy pause. "Nick's with you."

"Yes," I say, my eyes meeting Nick's. "Nick is with me."

Nick's lips curve in amusement, and he refills his glass.

Josh is silent for several beats before he replies with, "You need to make some time with me, without him, to meet the people I want you to meet tonight. And we're having breakfast in the morning to talk about those meetings, without him. Don't push back on this, Faith. I can't get you the thirty thousand a painting I want to get you if you don't let me agent."

"I know that," I say, wishing he'd been this eager to sell my work before Chris aided my career. "And I understand."

"You better." He hangs up.

Nick arches a brow.

I sigh and set my phone on the table. "How much did you hear?"

"Enough to know that he has his panties in a wad," he says drily, "because my very existence guarantees he can't get your panties in a wad."

"Stop saying things like that. It's all I will be able to think about when I am with him."

"Good. You need to be aware of his intentions."

My brow furrows. "You're in a mood. Should we talk about Macom before we get there?"

"Haven't we talked the shit out of Macom as it is?" he asks.

"Yes. And you made reference to—"

"Wanting to beat the shit out of him?" He doesn't give me time to answer. "I do, but I'm really good at fantasizing. Like right now, I'm thinking about you naked, straddling me at about thirty thousand feet, but despite how fucking hard I am just thinking about that, I'll most likely refrain from making it happen until the ride home. And likewise, I'll most likely refrain with Macom."

"Nick—"

"Faith. Are we doing this again?"

My cellphone buzzes with a text this time. I glance at it in my hand to find Bill has messaged me. I read it to Nick. "From Bill: *Just making sure you got the picture and my message?* He's giving me an uneasy feeling tonight. Maybe I'm just nervous that my paintings will be mocked or the man I love will punch the man I never loved, but he is. What should I say?"

"Fuck you, you lying, cheating, lowdown bastard." He downs his champagne. "Another fantasy. Stick to reality. Keep playing him, sweetheart. Soft and sweet. It's your magic, and I love the fuck out it."

I inhale and think a moment before I type: *Yes, sorry. That topic is emotional, and I have my big show this weekend, which I'm nervous about.* I show it to Nick.

"Magic," he says. "He'll eat that up."

My phone buzzes with a new message I read to Nick again. "His reply: *Yes, honey. Sorry. I didn't even think about this upsetting you. Go. Make your mark. Make the Winter family proud, and I promise you, your father would have been proud.*"

He's hit a nerve, and my stomach knots with the very thought of my father's thoughts on my art. But there is more. Something nagging in the back of my mind that I just can't put a finger on.

"You played the player," Nick says. "Now come play me." He cups my neck and pulls my mouth near his mouth. "Forget Bill, Josh, and Macom. They're making you nervous. Think of me. Think of us." He kisses me, and he makes me forget, but the minute his lips part mine, that nagging feeling returns.

CHAPTER THIRTY-TWO

Faith

We arrive at the L.A. hotel where the art show is being hosted with just enough time to shower and change. The doorman leads us into the fancy suite, which is, of course, glamorous; my first view is of a large outdoor area framing a living area, with a connected dining room and a grand piano. Hallways lead to additional rooms, and to my left and right are fancy, winding stairwells.

The bellman delivers our bags to the master suite, which is apparently down the right hallway. The minute he disappears into the room, I turn to Nick and softly say, "This is not a hotel room. It's the size of a house."

"You never know when you might want to invite a few gallery owners over or whoever else might help your career," he says, snagging my hips and walking me to him. "And I think you should consider doing just that before we leave."

"That's an incredible idea, but I will be too nervous to do that this time."

"Well, keep your possibilities open," he urges. "Bring it up with Josh. See what he thinks."

I soften with those words. "You hate Josh, but you really are willing to support him as my agent, aren't you?"

"As long as he keeps his hands to himself," he says, the light catching on a hard glint in his blue eyes.

The doorman reappears, and Nick tips him. I follow the path I now believe to lead to the bedroom, finding it is indeed at the end of the hallway. It has thick gray curtains, a cream-colored fluffy rug, a bed so high I need a step stool, and a sitting area. Our bags are nowhere in sight, and I walk to the bathroom to seek them out. It is, of course, as luxurious as the rest of the suite, with an egg-shaped tub, shiny white and gray tiles, and a massive tile-encased shower.

My hunt for the bags leads me to the walk-in closet, where they sit on suitcase stands, but there is more. There is a collection of dresses with the tags still on them. Six dresses. My heart starts to race, confusing emotions rushing through me. Nick's footsteps sound, and I turn to face him. He appears in the doorway, bigger than life, I swear, and so good-looking, so damn dominant in every situation. "You're very overwhelming," I blurt. "Everything you do is big, bold, and extravagant."

"Agreed."

I smile. "That's it? You agree?"

"Yes. Do you like the dresses?"

"I haven't looked at them yet."

"Why not?"

I walk to him and push to my toes to kiss him. "I know you want me to enjoy your money. I know that I can't be with you and not experience your money. I see that."

"But?"

"No buts other than me suddenly really needing to say something to you."

"Okay. You have my full attention. As I often say, you always have my full attention."

"You will never be the sum of a fancy hotel room or fancy dresses to me. I'm going to tell you that a lot because I don't want you to forget. And on that note. The dresses are exciting. The room is wonderful. Thank you for working so hard to make this weekend special." I give him a quick kiss, and when I would turn away, he pulls me to him. His fingers tangle in my hair, and his mouth closes down on mine, and in the depths of that kiss I taste torment that I do not understand. But there is love and hunger and need, too.

He pulls back, stroking my cheek. "I'd better stop, or we'll be late. Look at the dresses. And if you don't like any of them, we'll trade them in."

"What is it that I'm sensing?" I ask. "What's wrong?"

"Nothing you in one of those dresses can't solve." He brushes his lips over mine and releases me, and before I can press him for more, he turns and disappears into the bathroom.

I stare after him, and I have no idea what it was about that exchange, but every instinct I own now says that the club wasn't the big reveal I'd thought it to be. That secret that he fears I won't accept, that I've tried to reveal with my paintbrush, has yet to be exposed.

CHAPTER THIRTY-THREE

Faith

I'm still struggling to decide on a dress when the shower comes on. I step into the bathroom and find Nick's already inside. Still bothered by the exchange we've just had and by the idea that we might go into this night—and an encounter with Macom—with something I don't even understand brewing between us, I strip my clothes away and step around the tiled wall.

Nick is under the water, eyes shut, head tilted upward, suds pouring over every naked, ripped, perfect inch of him. He must sense my presence, suddenly lowering his chin, his eyes finding me. His gaze skims my naked body. His cock now thick, hard. I walk toward him, and he doesn't move, a dark edginess about him that confirms what I'd sensed in the closet. There is still a wall between us—a secret. I stop a lean away from touching him, but he doesn't reach for me. I lift my hand and press it over his heart, and that touch is all it takes. He is suddenly kissing me, his hand closing around a chunk of my hair, the taste of him wild hunger with a big dose of that torment I'd sensed. His hands are all over me, his mouth on my nipple one moment, fingers tugging it the next.

Before I know it, I'm pressed into the corner, and he is lifting me, his cock pressing inside me, stretching me, filling me. That wild hunger dominates, and it consumes me right along with him. I want him deeper. I want him harder. I want his mouth on my mouth. We don't last long, though. Both of us are too aroused, too urgent. I shatter, my sex clenching the thick width of his shaft. He shudders in response, and soon we are holding on to each other, breathing together—fast and then slow.

He eases me to the ground. "That wasn't supposed to happen."
I tangle my fingers into his wet hair. "We needed that."
He inches back to look at me. "Why do you say that?"
"I don't know. I just felt it. I needed it."
He studies me for several beats, his expression unreadable.
He kisses me again, a deep stroke of tongue followed by another
before he says, "I love you. Finish your shower."

And then he is gone, and for reasons I can't even explain that
have nothing to do with how hot and naked he is or how much I
love him, too, I want to pull him back. So much that it hurts to
deny that need.

I finish my shower, slip on a robe, and step to the sink next to Nick,
who is in a towel only, with shaving cream on his face and a razor
in his hand. I slip in front of him. "I'll do it."

"You need to get ready. It's late."

"I have time."

He gives me a heavy-lidded look and hands me the razor.

"Goatee or no goatee?" I ask.

"You tell me."

"I like the goatee," I say, stroking the foam from his face. "It
gives you a dangerous edge."

"And you like dangerous?"

"Only when it's you."

He takes the razor from me. "This is going to get us naked
again. Go get ready." He kisses me and foams up my face. I laugh
and move away, the mood decidedly lighter.

I dry and flat iron my hair to a blonde shine, choosing neutral
colors for my makeup, except my lips. I choose a deep rose that is
almost pink, and it will match the colors in my necklace, which I
now never take off. I walk to the closet and stand in front of the
dresses again. The blue one he got me weeks ago is for tomorrow

for sure. Tonight, though—hmmmm.

My gaze radiates to a simple, elegant dress with a beige underlay and ivory lace overlay. If I want to appear as an artistic type, it's muted and beautiful, but I don't reach for it. My attention rockets to another dress, an evergreen shade with a silk sheen that so perfectly matches one of the stones in my necklace that it can't be an accident. It fits my newfound love of colors, and I smile. This is the dress.

I quickly pull on a pair of thigh-high black hose I've packed in my suitcase, then inspect the shoes Nick also had delivered, choosing a pair of black heels with a sexy double ankle strap. And then I pull on the dress, the deep *V* managing to show skin, not cleavage. The skirt flares to the knee while a full sash ties at the left hip. It's stunning. And of course, Nick remembered purses—or the shopper he hired remembered. Four expensive purses that are all Chanel. I choose a small black bag with a sparkly logo and a bit of shine to the rather traditional and perfect style.

And then I inspect myself in the mirror, nerves attacking my belly. Tonight is big. Tonight, I am in a world I'd dreamed of not just visiting but embracing. And I'm there with Nick, who I'm suddenly eager to see. I fill my purse and slip it over my shoulder before hurrying through the bedroom to the living area. I find Nick in a sharp black suit with a black tie.

His eyes light on me, and he ends his call, the two of us walking toward each other, meeting at the back of the couch, a brown contemporary style that matches the two chairs framing it. Nick whistles as we grow near. My cheeks heat, and a smile touches my lips as I realize the dots in his tie are *evergreen*. I run my hand down it. "How did you know that I was going to pick this dress?"

"It matches your necklace perfectly."

"You chose it."

"I did."

"When and how?"

"I sent the shopper photos of your necklace, and she sent me back options."

He just made the romantic surprise that was those dresses even more romantic and personal. "I love this dress."

"It's beautiful on you."

There's a knock at the door, and he kisses me. "I'll get it."

"Who is it?"

"No idea," he says, leaving me to find out.

Curious, wondering what Nick is up to—because this has to be Nick being Nick, doing something unexpected and wonderful—I inch up a few feet to try and see who is at the door. It opens, and I hear, "I have a delivery for Ms. Winter."

"From who?" Nick asks, wiping out the idea that it's from him.

"I'm sorry, sir. I don't know."

Nick opens the door to allow the bellman to enter, and he's holding a giant bouquet of flowers and a box of some sort, but I think it's Godiva chocolates. My stomach clenches with the certainty this is a problem. The bellman sets the delivery on the coffee table, then gives me a nod and a "Good day, ma'am" before departing.

Nick joins me, his expression indiscernible. "You should read the card."

I wait until the door shuts behind the exiting bellman before responding. "It's going to be from Bill. He's laying it on thick now."

Nick rounds the couch and pulls the card from the bouquet, holding it up, an invitation in the action. Dreading what is to come, I join him and take it, tearing it open. And then cringe with what I read:

Faith,
Congratulations, baby. You did it.
See you tonight, FINALLY.
Macom

I hand Nick the card. He takes it and reads it.

"I'm sorry," I say.

He glances up at me. "For what? Godiva is good chocolate. Let's try some." He sits down and opens the box.

I blanch, confused by his reaction. He takes my hand and tugs, urging me to sit. "Chocolate, sweetheart. We missed lunch."

I ease onto the cushion, and he sinks his teeth into a piece of chocolate. "Did you know that I have a weakness for chocolate?" He holds a chocolate to my mouth. "Try this one."

I take a bite.

"Well?" he prods.

"It's delicious," I say, and it is, but the chocolate is not my focus right now. "You're not upset at all?"

He leans in and kisses me. "Sweetheart, if a box of chocolate and some flowers win you over, then you weren't ever mine to start with. But you *are* mine. He just doesn't know it yet."

There is a promise that he will capture me in those words that makes me nervous, but he pops another piece of chocolate in his mouth, stands up, and takes me with him. "Let's go show off that dress and your art." And then he kisses me again, and when his tongue touches mine, the heady taste of sin, satisfaction, and chocolate overwhelms my senses. He overwhelms my senses, and I forget to worry about anything and everyone else, Macom included.

But when we reach the elevator and step on the car, me in front of Nick, him holding me from behind, I remember the phone call they'd shared, and the obvious realization I've ignored hits me. I turn to face him. "He just issued you a challenge, didn't he?"

Nick arches a brow. "Did he? Because you of all people know that I can't turn away from a challenge. And that could be very bad for him."

The elevator opens to the busy lobby, and when I turn, I find myself facing the devil himself: Macom is standing with Josh a few feet away.

CHAPTER THIRTY-FOUR

Faith

Seeing Macom again punches me in the chest, and a world of dark, jagged emotions slashes a path through me. A moment later, Nick's hand settles at my lower back, and all is right in my world, and not because I feel protected. Because he's here. Because he's Nick. That's all my mind has time to process before we're crossing to meet them, both men watching us approach, both in expensive suits. Josh in navy blue, his dark hair as perfectly trimmed as usual. Macom stands out in a tan suit among dark colors, his curly hair a bit wild. The color choice is expected, as is the disarray of his hair; I know that he believes it to be sexy. He likes to be different, and I used to see that as artsy and unique. Today it reads as tasteless, as was him sending me those gifts, when I know Josh has to have told him I was with Nick. When both Nick and I told him that I was with Nick.

Josh leans in to speak to Macom, clearly telling him to leave. Macom quite obviously snaps back at him, most likely throwing around his power. Macom won't back down. Not here. This is his castle, and he's king. He thinks that makes Nick a peasant, but he's wrong.

Nick and I arrive to stand in front of them, me directly in front of Macom. My gaze meets his, and the heat in Macom's stare is awkward and so blatant, so "I want to fuck you again" that there is no way Nick doesn't see it. I look to Josh, who smiles and winks. "Looking gorgeous, darling. We want people to know your work, but it doesn't hurt for them to remember you're as stunning as art."

"Thank you, Josh."

"You've always been stunning, Faith," Macom dares.

Nick looks at him. "Macom, right?"

"Yes," he says. "Macom Maloy."

Nick arches a brow. "I believe I've heard the name, outside of what Faith has shared in graphic detail, of course. Up and coming, aren't you?"

"Up and coming?" Macom replies tightly. "Not many people call me up and coming."

"Ah well, they will, I'm sure. Hang in there. You'll be a Chris Merit in no time—who is a big fan of Faith's, by the way."

Macom's lips tighten. "So I hear."

"On another topic," Nick continues, "I should say thank you. Aside from the fact that you lost Faith, which led her to me, I love chocolate. Faith and I ate that shit up." He glances at me. "Didn't we, sweetheart?"

Considering Macom looked at me like he wanted to lift my skirt, clearly baiting Nick, I don't so much as miss a beat. I look from Nick to Macom. "Yes, thank you. The chocolate and the flowers were lovely. And it was unexpected, considering our last communication."

Macom's lips twist wryly. "That was interesting, but something tells me this night will be as well." He glances at Josh. "I need you at the stage in forty-five minutes." And on that note, he leaves.

Josh exhales. "Holy hell. Let that be it. Awkward, fucked up, but done." He pins me in a look. "Head to the second level. That entire floor is the party. At eight o'clock, there will be a ceremony, at which time they will announce the top new artists of the year. And I'd tell you that might be you, but I won't see your work until I walk up those stairs."

"It's displayed tonight?" I ask, suddenly anxious.

"Some of it. Each year, the show's top two executives pick the top three pieces for each artist. No one is allowed to see those picks in advance."

"Isn't Macom a part of the board in some way?" Nick asks.

"He is," Josh says, "but his role is more public show than anything. He didn't get a vote on entries, and he didn't get a vote on the winner that will be announced tonight. He does most likely know the winner, as he's presenting the award. Which, unfortunately, means it's not Faith. If it were, he'd have told me."

I didn't even know about the award. I didn't hope to win, but that announcement still cuts.

"Well, as far as I'm concerned, her accepting that award from him would be poetic justice for the way he put himself above her."

Josh declines to comment, which isn't a surprise, since Macom is his biggest client. "You're already a winner tonight," he says to me. "I need to handle a few things. Go upstairs. Drink. Eat. Revel in this night. In half an hour, I'm going to find you, and you will come with me. We will meet some powerful people you need to know." He leaves.

Nick turns me toward the lobby, his arm around my shoulder. "You okay?"

"You loved the chocolate?"

"I'd love it better melted and on you, so I could lick it off. Let's decide that's going to happen sometime this weekend."

I laugh. "You're so damn bad, Nick Rogers."

"In case you didn't get the memo, I'm not a nice guy. You think Macom noticed?"

I laugh, and we're about to head up a winding set of stairs when a couple in their late fifties to early sixties, and in casual wear, steps in front of us. "Nick Rogers," the man says. "Holy hell. It is you."

"David," Nick says, shaking his hand before looking at the woman. "Elizabeth." His hand returns to my back. "This is Faith."

"Nice to meet you, Faith," they both murmur.

"What brings you to L.A.?" the man asks. "Playing shark, or what is it, Tiger?"

"Actually, Faith is a gifted artist who's in the L.A. Art Forum." Pride fills his voice and warms my heart. This man supports me. He loves me. Life is good, and Macom is a blip on the screen.

"Oh my," Elizabeth says. "You're an artist, Faith? That's why we're here. We're going to the public event tomorrow. I can't wait to see your work. We love to discover new artists."

"Thank you," I say. "I'd love to have you view my work."

"And with that," Nick says, "we have a party to celebrate her art tonight."

"Understood," David says. "But as a quick side note, we're actually considering taking our company public. We'd like to have you on board."

"That's a conversation for Monday. This weekend is about Faith."

"Of course it is," Elizabeth says. "We will see you tomorrow, Faith." She touches my arm. "Good luck."

And then they are gone and we are walking up the stairs. "Were they important?"

"He's worth about a billion dollars."

"Nick. You just blew him off."

"Tonight isn't about him. If he has a problem with that, fuck him."

"Nick Rogers," I say, giving his sleeve a tiny tug that earns me the focus of those navy blue eyes.

"Yes, sweetheart?"

"I'm a little too crazy about you."

"Not yet," he says, giving me a wink that does funny things to my belly. "But we're getting there."

We reach the second level, and the entire floor is literally the party, clusters of women in fancy dresses and men in sharp suits everywhere. Elegant multicolored chandeliers dangle at random locations from above. Waiters work the crowd with drinks, and there are tables filled with finger foods. "We still haven't eaten," Nick says. "Shall we grab a few snacks?"

"I'll drop it, spill it, and generally make a mess." I glance at him. "I need to know which three pieces they picked."

"I'd like to know, too," he says, motioning me toward a sign that leads to the display room while another next to it points to the ceremony's location.

We walk that way. "Why am I suddenly so nervous?"

"Because in your mind you know your top three picks," he says as we reach the doorway, "and you're about to find out if the judges agree." He halts us and turns me to face him. "Name your top three."

"You. *An Eye for An Eye*. An older piece I called *Sonoma Sky*. What do you think?"

"My picks as well."

"Do you know *Sonoma Sky*?"

"I studied and admired it when we packaged it up. Let's go look." He starts to turn, and I catch his arm.

"I want you to be there."

"Why, Faith?"

"Because that painting was the first one I painted for me in a very long time. And you're the first thing I've done for me in a very long time."

He reaches up and drags his knuckles down my cheek. "I'll show you how much that means to me later, *alone*." He motions to the door. "Let's go look."

I nod, and we enter the room, people milling about displays, and, of course, Macom's is the centerpiece. And maybe it's my nerves, but heads turn as we walk the crowd, seeming to land on Nick and then me. Which is quite possible, since my heart is racing so fast that I can barely breathe. Finally, we reach my display, and I step inside to find exactly what I'd hoped for: Nick, *An Eye for an Eye*, and *Sonoma Sky*.

Nick's hand settles at my back. "How do you feel?"

I glance up at him. "Validated."

"Good. You need that. You lack confidence you need to find. I should buy the one of me."

"If you buy it, then it looks like I can't sell it. I'm still inspired. I'll be painting you again."

"Is that right?" he asks, heat in his eyes.

"Oh yes. And I'll know every piece of your story before you tell me your story."

Something flickers in his expression that I can't name, there and then gone, but before I can ask him about it, Josh suddenly appears, standing beside us and cursing under his breath. "Holy hell. Who painted these?"

I face him. "You hate them."

"I fucking love them. They aren't you."

"They are me. The real me."

"Interesting." He glances over my head at Nick and then back to me. "Come. Let's go meet important people. Alone."

I turn to Nick, and his hand settles at my hip. "I'm fine, sweetheart. This is about you, not me."

"I know, but—"

"Go. Meet people."

"What are you doing to do?"

"Drink insanely expensive whiskey, watch people, and find us a spot in the ceremony room."

Josh steps to my side. "Time is ticking."

I push to my toes and kiss Nick. He cups my head and kisses me again, this time with a sexy slide of tongue. We share a smile, and I join Josh, who looks more than a little irritated, but any thought that he might voice that irritation is quickly sidetracked. Almost instantly, within a few steps, we're intercepted by one of the show's sponsors, who wants me to meet another sponsor out on the party floor. It snowballs from there, though not many of the meetings feel important. I search for Nick and occasionally find him in the crowd, sharing a small smile with him.

This continues for a full hour before Josh points at a small standing table that is now free. "Let's talk," he says as we claim our spots across from each other, his fingers thrumming on the wooden table. "I hate to do this here, but it's important, since the rest of the weekend will be open to the public. And it's clearly a challenge to get you away from Nick 'fucking' Rogers."

"Nick 'fucking' Rogers is supportive of me and you. He rented the bungalow in the hotel with the thought that you could invite clients for a private party this weekend."

He ignores the offer. "You painted *him*."

"Yes. And obviously it was a good decision. Every person we met mentioned that painting."

"The painting is good, but as your agent, I see a habit."

"Habit?"

"Things become bigger than your art. Macom. The winery. Nick."

"You and Macom made him bigger than me."

"That's not true," Josh says. "He was my client before you. I was trapped in your own submission to him. And now it's happening with Nick. You didn't want to leave him to meet people."

"He's my guest and inspired me to paint again. He helped me get a grip on the winery."

"And there it is. I told you. He fucks you and uses you. He wants the winery."

"He does not want the winery."

"Make sure before it becomes a devastating realization that shoves you into a corner again. Because we're going to get offers. I don't want either of us to look like fools. Better yet, sell the damn winery, Faith. It's a distraction. You've made eighty thousand dollars in two weeks. More will follow."

"The winery isn't a distraction," I say, though those words might be a bit half-hearted. "Additionally," I add, "I moved to San Francisco, and I'm working at the Allure Gallery with Chris and Sara Merit. The pay and the opportunity are both great."

"Why am I just now finding this out?"

"You knew I was part of the gallery opening."

"Why am I just now finding this out?" he repeats.

"I don't want Chris used to move my career ahead," I say, only now admitting that very real concern. "Chris and Sara are my friends. Promise me."

"I'll talk to Chris—"

"No. No, you will not. Promise me."

His lips tighten. "I promise." He is silent for several beats before he says, "We're friends. I care about your success. Come to L.A. in a couple of weeks. *Alone*. Let's do some career planning."

Nick's warnings ring in my head, driven home by the way he's kept me far away from him tonight. "Are we too personal, Josh?"

"I care. Most people want an agent that cares."

"But are you too personally involved with me?"

"We're friends."

"Macom is your friend."

"You are, too, Faith. And I'm the best damn agent out there. You need me. I deserve you. I've ridden the highs and lows with you. You don't get to leave when you have some success or when I push too hard. We're a team. Agreed?"

He's right. He has stuck it out with me. "Yes. But you need to know that I have moved in with Nick. He's not going away, so please treat him accordingly."

"You moved in with him," he states flatly.

"Yes. Please treat him—"

"Understood," he says, glancing at his watch. "We need to get into the ceremony."

"I am going to go freshen up," I say, not about to let him come up with a reason to separate me from Nick for the ceremony. "I'll see you inside."

He studies me several beats. "Are we okay?"

"Yes. Of course."

He gives a short incline of his head. "You need to be seated in ten minutes." He leaves then, and I turn to find a bathroom and run smack into a hard body, big hands catching my waist. The musky scent of familiar cologne washes over me even before my gaze lifts, and I find myself looking into Macom's gray eyes.

CHAPTER THIRTY-FIVE

Faith

I push away from Macom, but he tightens his grip on my waist. "We need to talk. Let's set a time and place."

"Let go of me, Macom, or I will *make* you let go of me."

"When the ceremony is over. I'm in room—"

"You need to be on stage," Josh says, suddenly by my side. "They're looking for you."

Macom's eyes meet Josh's, anger crackling in their depths. "Now?"

"Now," Josh states firmly.

Macom's jaw tenses, and he looks down at me. "Ten ten. After the show." He releases me and fades into the crowd.

I turn to Josh. "Thank you."

"I told him not to pull this shit, but look, Faith. For what it's worth, he talked to me last night. He was torn up. He has regrets. He feels like shit. He seems to just need to apologize in person, and if you don't want him, he'll accept it."

"He doesn't want to apologize. He wants to make me another conquest."

"All I can tell you is my take, and I don't see it that way. But moving on. I'll see you inside." He steps away from me, and there is a ceremony announcement. The crowd immediately starts moving, and I end up in the crunch of bodies, a sardine in a can, as we slowly ease toward the door. Impatient, I slip my purse across my chest, then try to find a hole to break free.

More aggressive actions work, and I push through the bustle of people with a good amount of speed. The bodies bottleneck

near the door, though, and I'm stuck, unable to proceed. That's
when a hand comes down on my arm, and suddenly I'm folded
into Nick's arms. "Hey there, sweetheart."

I smile with the realization we're just inside the ceremony
room, against the wall and out of the rush. "You saved me again."

"I'll always save you, but I think you know that by now."

"I had a Macom encounter."

"And?"

"I ran into him, literally. He took that opportunity to corner
me. Josh intervened, and Macom backed off. But I don't think
me avoiding him is going to work. I need to just handle him, once
and for all."

"How?"

"I need to get through this ceremony and then figure it out.
Let's sit at the back so we can escape when it's over."

"You sure you want to do that?"

"Oh yes. I've met everyone and anyone, and that's an entirely
different story."

There's another announcement. "Please take your seats now,"
someone says over the intercom.

Nick drapes his arm around my shoulder, and we quickly scan
the rows of seats facing the stage before locating and claiming
back-row seats. Not more than a minute later, one of the event
founders that I'd met earlier steps to center stage and begins to
speak without wasting time on fluff. She gets right to the point
of the event: the artists. A big screen is lowered, and it starts
rotating with images of this year's artistic participants, as well
as the top three picks for each that were on display tonight. The
name "Winter" places me at the end of that lineup, and when they
read out *An Eye for an Eye*, I cringe with the certainty that it will
garner Macom's attention. Nick knows, too. His fingers flex on my
leg where his hand rests. But soon, the moment is muted as the
speaker launches into an anecdote about the first event held by
the organization fifteen years ago.

Finally, it's time for the award to be announced, which means Nick and I can escape, and the real experience, the show, will be only hours away. Macom steps to the podium to announce the winner, thankfully a really long way from myself and Nick. "Each year one blossoming talent is picked from the show's participants," he says. "Tonight is no exception. Tonight I will announce one shining star who will be featured at tomorrow's show at the entryway as all visitors enter the showroom. In the past, we've named such artists as Mallery Michaels, Kat Martin, and Newman Wright. Famous names I know you all recognize. If you're lucky, you own one of their creations. And so tonight, in the tradition of greats, I will announce a new great. I have to tell you, this one is special. I'm close to this person. She has always been a shining star in my eyes."

I suck in air at the "she." Nick leans in even before my name is even called and says, "Poetic justice, sweetheart."

"This year's winner," Macom says dramatically, "is Faith Winter. Faith, come to the front, please."

Shock rolls through me. "This can't be happening," I whisper, applause clamoring around me.

"It is happening, sweetheart," Nick says. "Go accept your award."

"I'm trembling," I say. "Nick, I'm trembling hard."

"I got you, sweetheart," he says, standing up and taking me with him, guiding me to the center row, which, from the back, now looks incredibly long for someone as unsteady as I am right now. Nick seems to know this, hitching my hand to his elbow before taking a step, walking that one and every one that follows with me. "Deep breath," he murmurs softly.

I nod and draw in air, holding it before I let it out, while my mind focuses on one coherent thought: *My dream of a career as an artist is becoming real.* I repeat this thought about ten times before we reach the stage. "Congrats, sweetheart," Nick says as a man in a suit offers me his arm and helps me up the stairs.

In five steps, I am on the stage and completely unprepared for a speech. I'm most certainly unprepared for Macom's greeting, which includes pulling me into a hug. "It was fate that I presented this award," he murmurs in my ear. "We're going to celebrate tonight." He releases me, and I'm too overwhelmed right now to do anything but dismiss him immediately and step to the microphone.

Suddenly, lights are shining on me and unknown faces are looking up at me. Seconds tick by before I realize this is where I need to speak. "Hi, everyone." Audience voices reply, and smiles abound, which eases my nerves. "To say that I am stunned and appreciative would be a gross understatement," I continue. "It seems I almost forgot how to walk while trying to get to the stage. Which brings me to the person who helped me make that walk and who not only encourages me daily but inspired one of the paintings on display tonight." I search for Nick and find him at the edge of the stage. "Thank you, Nick. I know that I would not be here without you. And I know you would tell me that I would have found my way no matter what. But it's a better journey with you." He presses two fingers to his lips and then does a little motion toward me before I refocus on the audience. "Thank you specifically as well to those who saw my entries, and then my work, and offered me this amazing recognition and opportunity. I hope everyone enjoys the show tomorrow."

I step away from the microphone to the clamor of more applause, and I fully intend to join Nick at the bottom of the stage, but the man who'd helped me up the stairs stops me. "We need you for a photo op backstage."

I'm then ushered away, and I try to turn to find Nick, but the lights are in my eyes. The next thing I know, Macom is at my elbow and cameras are flashing around us. "Congrats, baby," Macom says as we shove through a curtain.

I'd tell him not to call me baby, but I have no idea who the other man at my opposite elbow is, and I'm swarmed by people before I can reply anyway. Cameras flash at close range, and I'm hurried to stand in front of a photo backdrop. I'm also holding a statue that is a paintbrush and palette that I'm pretty sure I was given on stage, and the fact that I don't remember getting it is a testament to just how consumed by nerves I am.

Suddenly, Macom is sent back to my side for additional photos, along with a show sponsor, both instructed to stand beside me. Both place their hands at my back, but Macom's is low—too low for comfort. I don't want to seem as if I can't support the organization when my ex is involved, and I try to be savvy in my avoidance. The minute the shot is done, I step to the opposite side of the sponsor, placing him in the center. And this kind of push and pull with Macom continues until I can take no more.

"Excuse me, please," I say to a man who seems to be in charge. "I need to attend a meeting. Thank you for everything." I hold up my statue. "Really. Thank you." I dash toward an exit sign, and I don't stop. I close the space between me and it and push the bar on the door beneath it. On the other side, I find myself in some sort of narrow hallway that renders me trapped if Macom tried to follow. Wanting out of this maze, I head down the path, and I'm close to an archway leading to another room when a door opens in front of me and Macom steps in my path.

I start to back up, but he's fast, and already he's in front of me, his fists on the wall on either side of me, caging me. And with the statue in my hand, I'm at a disadvantage that reaches beyond his size versus mine. "Please move," I say, not because I want to be civil but because I know him. If I set him off, this gets worse.

"Baby, please talk to me. Don't put me through seeing you with that man for another minute. I saw the painting. I know what it means. I hurt you. I get it. But you've punished me."

"That painting wasn't about you but me. *Step aside*, Macom."

"It killed me to hear you thank him tonight. It's you and me. It's always been y*ou and me*."

"There is no you and me."

"I'll be more supportive in all things, your art especially.

Whatever he's doing to help you at the winery, I'll do ten times as much."

I laugh without humor. "Priceless. Josh took all of thirty minutes to run his mouth to you. And you can't do ten times what Nick does, because Nick is a hundred times richer than you. *Move.*"

"Faith—"

"Move or I will put a knee in your groin so hard that your balls will retract and disappear."

He reaches for my face and leans in, intending to kiss me, and I don't hesitate. I raise my knee, and I don't hold back. He grunts and doubles over. "Fuck, Faith. You fucking bitch." He sucks in air and straightens, leaning close again, his breath warm on my cheek. "You will pay for that. You will not get into another gallery in L.A., ever." He turns away from me and starts walking, or, rather, hobbling in obvious pain.

I sink against the wall, aware that I've provoked the vicious monster I was trying not to provoke right up until the moment I stuck my knee in his balls. But I also know him well enough to know that he's gone. He's not coming back.

"What the fuck," he growls, and I look right to discover Nick is standing under the archway, his shoulder pressed against the wooden frame. "Move out of my way," Macom orders, trapped the way I was just trapped.

"Here's the thing, *Macom*," Nick says. "No. Not until I'm ready."

"You don't want to fuck with me."

"I have compromising *naked* photos of you," Nick says. "I have IRS documents, bank records, and the list continues, all of which have your name on them. And if you don't believe that I will use those things fifty ways to Sunday, you haven't researched me the way I have researched you. Touch Faith or her career again, and I *will* come for you."

They stare at each other for all of two beats before Nick steps aside and Macom quickly leaves. I walk to Nick, and he immediately folds me into his arms. "How long were you there?"

"The entire time," he says. "And I let you handle him as you wanted to handle him, certain that he'd give me a reason to punch him. But then you went off and retracted his balls before I got the chance."

I laugh. "I can't believe I said that." I cringe. "I can't believe I told him that you're a hundred times richer than him."

"Why? I am." He softens his voice. "You okay, sweetheart?"

"Yes. I am. Really okay, actually. And ready to go upstairs."

He slides his arm around my shoulder, and we start walking through what looks like an empty banquet room. Thankfully, we make it to the elevator without being stopped, and we wait on a car. The doors open quickly, and Josh steps out. "Faith. Holy hell. I've been looking for you. You rocked it tonight."

"You're fired," I say.

He blanches. "What?"

"You told Macom about our conversation. We're done. I won't change my mind."

Nick catches the door as it begins to shut, and I step around Josh. Nick and I enter the car, and when we face forward, Josh has turned and is staring into the car. Nick punches in the code to our floor, and the doors shut us inside. "That was unexpected," Nick says.

"But necessary. I'll deal with a new agent hunt next week."

I rotate to face the window, the stars and city lights flickering in the night sky. Nick steps behind me, holding me close. "I thought you didn't like heights."

"I changed my mind," I say. "I'm not going to be afraid of anything."

And as Nick murmurs, "Congratulations, Faith," I feel as if the past is now behind me, and a new beginning before me. Everything that was once wrong is now right.

CHAPTER THIRTY-SIX

Faith

The morning of the show, I'm nervous. By afternoon, I'm so high I'm flying. Macom and Josh stay away from us, and the interest in my work and invitations to events overflow. And Nick and I have so much fun together. Sometime around lunch, we hear that the apartment is ours, and Nick takes me to an incredible restaurant to celebrate it all. On Sunday morning, we have breakfast in our room, and I gift my flowers to the maid. Nick refuses to give up the chocolates, and we proceed to eat most of them on the plane home.

Come Monday morning, Nick is scheduled to begin the negotiations on a merger that he warns me will make for an intense few weeks. He leaves the house wearing one of his sharpest suits and a dark, cutting edge that says he's already in battle mode. I am feeling rather fancy today, and since a dress doesn't make much sense for a pre-opening at the gallery, I trade in my jeans for dress pants, boots, and a soft, pink V-neck sweater that pairs with the classic flagship Chanel purse that had been in the items Nick bought me over the weekend.

I arrive at Allure with a smile on my face and a stack of cards in my pocket. I settle behind my desk to find a random list of things Sara needs to accomplish before the gallery opening, along with a formal offer of employment.

Oh yes, I think. *Life is good.*

Sara appears in the doorway, looking adorable in jeans and Keds. "Well?" she asks, claiming the visitor's chair in front of my desk. "How was the show?"

"Amazing. The Forum picks one up-and-comer to watch every

year, and they chose me."

"Oh my God. Woohoo! I'm so excited for you. You said nothing of this when you sent me photos this weekend."

"It just didn't feel real," I say. "It's a bit surreal."

"Of course it is. Are you still riding the high?"

"In a big way, and even after I fired my agent."

"You fired your agent?"

"Yes. And it was past due. He's my ex's agent, and it just got sticky." I set the stack of cards on my desk. "And I have all these people wanting to buy work or book me for events. I'm going to start a hunt today."

"Let Chris help."

"No. No, I don't want to intrude or seem like I'm using you or him for my own benefit."

"I'll call my agent," Chris says, appearing in the doorway in a brown Harley shirt after clearly hearing our conversation. "If he can't take you on, he'll help you find the right match."

"You don't have to do that," I say quickly.

"Why the hell not?" he asks. "You wouldn't be here if we didn't believe in you."

Sara twists around in her chair to look at him. "She won the Forum's up-and-comer award."

"Not a surprise to me at all," Chris says, pulling his phone from the pocket of his jeans and punching in a number. "Gabe," he says. "Yeah, man. I have a new artist for you. I'm behind her. We're trying to convince her to work here at Allure with us. She's helping us launch, and she's on display here. Yes. Call her here."

Sara holds up a hand, and when Chris offers her his attention, she points to the stack of cards. "All offers she needs managed."

Chris gives an incline of his chin. "She comes with offers from an event she just did. A stack of them she needs managed." He listens a moment. "I'll tell her." Chris ends the call. "He's headed into a meeting. He's going to call you this afternoon, but he's on board."

"That's incredible of you," I say. "Thank you. I…hate to seem unappreciative, but I've been through Macom being Josh's star. I don't want Gabe to sign me because of you."

"A valid concern," Chris says, "but that's not Gabe's style. He's got a mind of his own and balls the size of Texas. You'll like his balls, I promise."

We all laugh, and Chris glances at his watch. "I need to head to a meeting." Sara pushes to her feet and hurries to Chris, kissing him before he departs. I smile because I have a lot to smile about, and I sign the offer letter. And when Sara turns to face me again, I hold it up. "I'll get to work on your things-to-do list, boss."

Now Sara is smiling. "You're staying."

"Yes. And I'm thrilled to be here."

We chat a few minutes, and she leaves me to my work. About an hour later, I receive a call from Gabe. Fifteen minutes later, I send him samples of my work. Another fifteen minutes later, and I have a new agent. I'm dying to call Nick, but he's in those intense negotiations. I could text, but that is a distraction he doesn't need as well. Sara and I celebrate by walking to the coffee shop, and we return with white mochas and chocolate chip bagels. Nick sends me a text at noon: *Hell here. I'm going to be silent and late tonight. You okay?*

My reply is simple: *I'm great. You focus on your negotiations.*

He doesn't respond, which tells me hell is real for him right now. I consider all the ways I can ease the stress when he gets home tonight.

Home.

Our home.

I revel in those words.

It's nearly six, and Sara has just left the gallery. I'm finishing some paperwork before I leave as well. I file away the documents I've

LISA RENEE JONES 501

just finished, and I'm reaching for my purse when my phone buzzes with a text. I glance at the message to find Bill is the sender.

I need to speak to you urgently. I'm at the coffee shop next door.

My heart starts to thunder in my chest. He's here? I text him back: *What coffee shop?*

Rebecca's, he replies.

How does he know I work here? Did I tell him? Did Kasey?

My fingers hover over the call button for Nick, but I think better. I dial Rita. "How busy is he?"

"At the moment, he has ten people sitting at a conference table, and they all want to kill one another."

"All right, then," I say, and because I don't want to freak her out and have her freak him out, I add, "now is not the time to talk dinner."

She laughs. "No. Not right now. He could be a while. Or not. Sometimes these things end abruptly."

"Okay. Thanks, Rita."

"Congrats on your show, Faith. Nick came in this morning bragging up a storm."

"He did?"

"Yes. He did. He's incredibly proud of you."

"Thanks, Rita. He says it to me, but it's pretty special to hear it from other people."

My phone buzzes again. "Talk to you soon," I say and end the call to read the new message: *It's an emergency, Faith.*

He's going to press me about the winery. I know it. And I'd decline the meeting if I wasn't afraid he'd go after the winery in some way again and hurt the employees. Or Nick. He could go after Nick, and while Nick can take care of himself, he doesn't need to fight a war I create when he has his own he's fighting right now, in this moment.

I stand up and slip my purse over my shoulder, dread in my belly, but I can do this. I'll navigate whatever he throws at me, milk him for information and missteps, and then hand it to Nick. Ready to get this over with, I hurry through the gallery, lock the doors, and make the quick walk to the coffee shop. I step inside and wave to the regular girl, June, behind the counter before my gaze lands on Bill sitting in a booth.

I cross the space between us and sit down. "What's the emergency?"

"Look, honey. You're the closest thing to a daughter I have. I know you don't believe I care, but I do. And it killed me to be shut off from you."

"And yet you slept with my mother."

"That's a complicated story that I still believe is not my story to tell. But I need you to set that aside, just for now. Because I need to tell you a story that ends right back here, in the present, with you."

"I'm listening."

"I heard rumors that you were struggling to pay the bills, and I called the bank. They told me you bought out the note."

"I did buy it out."

"You mean Nick Rogers bought it out. He's an owner now, right?"

"Emergency," I say. "You said there was an emergency."

"We need to go back in time. Way back. Your mother had a gambling problem, and they were in a lot of debt. Your father contained it the best that he could. Back before he and I had our falling-out, some men came to him. They offered him a hundred million to sell out."

I blanch. "A hundred million? Why so much?"

"They were bad men, *and* there's mercury on the property, a fact that I had buried way back then. No one else knew."

"Mercury? I assume it's valuable, then."

"It's used for weapons, and these men were the kind of men who knew all about weapons."

"How do you know this?"

"Your father came to me in dire straits because they're also the kind of men that don't take no for an answer. They'll pay you, but you take what they offer."

"But they did take no for an answer."

"Only because I hired an ex-CIA agent to help us. He tipped off the right people, and they handled it."

My brow furrows. "Why would they pay my father at all if they were that bad?"

"They couldn't just take it without question, not with the way your father loved that place. And they knew that. They ran everything through a legit investment operation, and the truth is, that mercury might not be worth much to you and me, but to them it would net billions."

"Obviously there's more," I say, not liking where this emergency is leading.

"Your mother started gambling again when your father died, and this time she went off the deep end. She came to me for money. I helped her and tried to get her into rehab, but she pushed back. She wanted to sell. She wanted to find the men who wanted the mercury."

"Oh no."

"I'm afraid so. She told me you wouldn't sell and that I had to find a way to get around you having to sign off on the deal, and that if I did, she'd split the profits. I won't lie to you. Your father and I had disagreements, but I agreed with him on the mercury. Selling to those people would be blood on his hands he didn't want, and neither do I. I told your mother I'd look into pushing you out of the deal, but eventually I told her there was no way around it. I urged her to go to you and confess the gambling issues. I told her I'd even buy the winery and give you both a profit."

"She said no."

"She said no, and I told her I was going to you. That's when she showed me a video of the two of us together and threatened to take it to my wife. I was out then, but I kept tabs on things, waiting to see if you needed me. And that brings me to where this is headed.

I knew when you sued her for the property, and I wanted you to win. I would have offered to fund your legal fees, but you hated me and wouldn't even speak to me, and if your mother found out, I was at risk with my wife."

"Why would my father want me to inherit the winery if it put me in danger?"

"This was ten years ago, Faith. I buried the mercury. The CIA buried the mercury. And you were not going to sell, which means no one who wants the mercury could get it."

"I still don't see where this is going. What is the emergency? Are those men back? Did my mother contact them?"

"If those men are back on the radar, they're working smarter this time."

My heart starts to race. "What do you know? Just tell me."

"I followed the legal case between you and your mother. I know who your attorney was, and I know who her attorney was."

"And?"

He sets a folder in front of me. "Look inside."

I flip it open, and I'm staring at a birth certificate for a Nick Marks. Mother: Melanie Marks. Father: Nathan Marks. The attorney who represented my mother. My heart is now skipping beats. I flip the page to find a court document changing the name of Nick Marks to Nick Rogers.

I swallow, and I almost choke. I can't catch my breath. I can't breathe. "I need to go," I say, but he catches my arm.

"Easy, honey. Let me help you."

"No. No. I—"

"Listen to me," he says firmly. "If he's involved with the mercury hunters, this is bad news. We need to come up with a plan together."

"I need *to go*," I say, pulling away from him. "I'll call you. I just… Not now." I all but run for the door and barely remember the moment I get in the car. Nick's car. Oh God. My entire life is wrapped around a man conning me. So many things don't add up, but the bottom line is that Nick is Nathan Marks's son. He never told me that. I start the engine, and I don't even know where I'm headed. I end up parked in the parking lot of the high-rise that is supposed to be our new home.

I sit there thirty seconds, or maybe thirty minutes. I have no concept of time. My phone rings, and I reach for it, my hand shaking as I find Nick calling. I answer it.

"Hey, sweetheart," he says.

His voice, rich and masculine and beautiful and deceitful, tears holes in my heart. "I know," I say.

"What?"

"Nick Marks. I know who you are."

CHAPTER THIRTY-SEVEN

Nick

*N*ick Marks.

That name is a blade in my heart. The connection to my father that brought me to Faith. It's also the connection I've always known could rip her out of my reach. "Faith, sweetheart—"

"Don't speak," she orders, her voice breathless. "It won't help you. And it just hurts me."

"I don't want to hurt you. I would never hurt you."

"And yet you did."

"Where are you? I'll come to you and explain."

"You made me trust again, and now you made sure that I will never trust anyone ever."

Rita and North walk into my office. "Get the fuck out," I snap.

Rita's eyes go wide, and North is already tucking tail and running. Rita backs out and shuts the door.

"Where are you?"

"Was it the mercury? Were you after a big payoff? Of course you were. Money loves money."

"What mercury? Faith, talk to me."

"So you can lie again. And again. And again."

"We have to talk. *Where* are you?"

"I don't want to see you, Nick. Not now or ever."

"I love you, Faith. I love you so much it hurts."

"Liar," she says, her voice quaking.

"Faith—"

"Don't find me. Don't call me. And let me be clear. If you show up at my work, at the winery, at my home, I will call the police.

Don't test me. You think you're a badass, but liars aren't badasses. They're just bad people. I left your BMW in the parking lot of your new apartment."

She ends the call. I try to call her back, and it goes directly to voicemail. "Fuck." I call again. And again. "Fuck. Fuck. Fuck." I face the window and press my hand on the glass, my head tilted downward. "Fuck. I cannot lose her."

I straighten and dial Beck. "Mercury. This is about mercury. I don't know how or any details except that. Connect the fucking dots. I need answers. And hack the autopsy report. I need that now, too."

"Faith knows."

"Yes, she fucking knows."

"Then Bill is behind this. He showed up near her office, and I couldn't get through to you to tell you."

"So he told her who I am and that there is mercury on the property."

"He made her believe you want the property for the mercury."

"Obviously. He turned his intentions into mine, and my damn lie allowed it to happen. Where is she now?"

"She went to Sara and Chris Merit's apartment."

"Of course. The one place I can't get to her, and she knows it." I scrub my jaw. "At least she's safe. Get me answers. I can't go to her and make my case without answers."

"I hack that report daily. It hasn't been input yet."

"You have mercury now. Connect the dots."

"If he believed that connected the dots, he wouldn't have given it to her."

"Connect the fucking dots." I hang up and dial Abel.

"Hey hoe, what the fuck is up?"

"I don't care whose house you have to go to or what you have to do, but you get me those autopsy reports."

"She knows."

"Yes. She knows. Get me the reports." I hang up.

My phone rings, and it's Chris Merit. "What the hell did you do, man?"

"It's not what it seems, and I'm not going to explain that to you. All I will say is that I love her. I love her the way you love Sara. I ordered her a ring. I bought an apartment to customize a studio for her."

"Well, I'm not an advice kind of guy, and she's not saying anything other than you betrayed her in an unforgivable way."

"I didn't cheat. I knew who she was before I met her and didn't tell her. At the time, I didn't plan on fucking her, let alone falling in love with her. And that's all I'm saying."

"Fair enough. What's your move?"

"What I want to do is pick her up, tie her to my bed, and make her stay until she listens."

"You do that and you had better have a way to justify lying to her, because this cuts deep. She's not good, Nick. You hurt her. You hurt her bad."

"I know. And that guts me."

"Get your ducks in a row and give her some time to process."

"Right. Time. A barbaric form of torture."

We end the call, and I say "fuck you" to time and waiting. I text Faith: *Your uncle set me up. It's not what it seems. I love you. I want to marry you, Faith. Please talk to me.*

I get an error message. She's blocked me.

CHAPTER THIRTY-EIGHT

Faith

*T*he *first night without Nick…*
I lay in Chris and Sara's spare bedroom, staring at the ceiling, an invisible knife carving holes in my heart. I replay the conversation I had with Bill, and the implications. And then I replay the conversation with Nick, how sincere he sounded. God. I'm a fool. And he's such a good liar. Everything he did felt real. We felt real.

I have no place to live. I need an apartment and clothes. I have no clothes. I don't have a car. At Nick's recommendation, I gave both of the cars to Kasey. Nick made me dependent on our life together. I roll to my side and tell myself not to cry. He's not worth it. I don't cry. I won't cry for him. But somehow my cheeks are wet.

The first Monday and my first morning without Nick…
I wake up to coffee and Chris and Sara. Watching them together is both beautiful and salt in an open wound. An hour later, I arrive at Allure with Sara, wearing Sara's jeans, my own boots, and her Allure T-shirt. We have interviews today for several staff members, and that means no time for self-pity. I dive in and get to work. By midmorning, my new agent has sold every piece I had in the L.A. Forum for thirty thousand apiece. Even the painting of Nick, which kind of guts me, but it's probably for the best. I have this instinctive urge to call and tell Nick, and that guts me, too. And so I don't tell anyone, not even Sara. I refocus on what's important. I have a great agent, a great job, and money,

which is suddenly important, since I need new everything. It's a relief. I call a realtor.

Come lunchtime, we've hired a receptionist to start on Monday, and I already have two apartments to look at after work. At nearly four, Sara pokes her head into my office. "Delivery," Sara says, setting a large envelope on my desk.

I stare at the handwriting on the front that is clearly Nick's and let out a breath. "Thank you." I look up at her. "I'm looking at apartments tonight and going to buy some clothes."

"Don't feel rushed. I have clothes, and we have the space."

"I know you mean that, but I think I'm going to rent a hotel room until I find a place."

"That's not necessary. You know that."

"I do. I really do, but honestly, you and Chris are so damn wonderful together, I can't take it. That sounds horrible. I'm sorry."

"It sounds honest. Do you want me to go shopping with you?"

"No. Last night I needed you badly, and you were there for me, and I can't thank you enough. Tonight, I need to be alone."

"I can fully understand that, but if you change your mind, our door is open."

"Thank you."

She disappears in the hallway, and I stare at that envelope, my throat constricting. I throw it in the trash. I pull it back out. I throw it in the trash. Damn it, I pull it out and open it. Inside, I find my favorite paintbrush with a note.

Faith:

I came to you looking for answers to questions I didn't even know I needed to ask. I found those answers in you. Paint me. You'll get your answers, too, because there is only one answer: Us.

I'm coming for you, and I'm doing it with proof that I don't want anything but you.

I love you,

Nick

I read that note over and over: *I'm coming for you.* And he will, and I'm going to send him away, no matter how much I hurt all over again.

My first Tuesday without Nick…

I wake in a hotel room and order room service. When my coffee and omelet arrive, I eat it alone. Alone is safe. I forgot that. I won't forget again.

Bill tries to call me about a dozen times. I ignore him. It's probably not fair, but I feel angry at him for telling me what I needed to hear.

My first Wednesday without Nick…

I don't order room service, but I walk to work and stop in at Rebecca's and get coffee. I carry it with me to my desk at Allure. I drink it.

Alone.

I end the day with a text from Josh. He's wiring me my twenty thousand dollars minus his fee. I don't reply. Bill calls me. I don't reply. When he sends me a text, I *do* reply: *I need time.*

I say nothing more.

My first Thursday without Nick…

I have settled into my hotel, bought a frugal wardrobe, and found an apartment a few blocks from the gallery that has an upstairs perfect for a studio. It's an expensive rental, but I need a space that I can make mine.

I'm about to leave for the day when I get a strange phone call. "Faith Winter?"

"Yes."

"Name's Ned. I'm your broker."

"I don't have a broker."

"You do. You invested sixty thousand in a hot stock. I want to cash you out."

"Nick did this, didn't he?"

"Yes. He did. Good fucking news for you, too. You're up a hundred and fifty thousand, but you need to get out while you're on top. Do it?"

I'm stunned. Blown away. Confused.

"Do it? Snap. Snap. This is time sensitive."

"Yes. And send the money to Nick."

"Can't do that. He put it in your name. You have to send it to him yourself. Gotta go. Toodle-oo and all that shit." He hangs up.

My first Friday without Nick...

I start the day feeling Nick's silence. I don't want to feel it, but I do. I comfort myself by putting the down payment on my apartment, but by evening the idea of a weekend alone is pretty much gutting me. I need things to fill my apartment. And when Bill calls, I answer. I agree that we need to meet. And I decide to rent a car and head to Sonoma for the weekend, talk to him, check on my house, the winery, and Kasey, and gather some of the leftover personal stuff I still have there.

Because being alone is not better, even if it is safer.

CHAPTER THIRTY-NINE

Nick

My first night without Faith...
Hell.
My second night without Faith...
Hell.
Every night without Faith...
Hell.
If she's going to Sonoma, so am I.

The minute I hear Faith has rented a car, I know she's driving to Sonoma. And I don't want her there with Bill. I don't want her there—or anywhere—without me. And I'm done waiting on the autopsy report and answers. All fucking week I've waited without Faith. And so, I hit the road in the BMW, heading for Sonoma with a ring in my pocket and my heart shamelessly on my sleeve.

Because being alone is fine, as long as being alone is with Faith. Otherwise, *alone is hell.*

CHAPTER FORTY

Faith

My new landlord calls about the time I am on the road to Sonoma, confirming I can move in next weekend. I tell her how excited I am, and I try to sound convincing, but reality is setting in. I'm leaving Nick behind. I use my Siri feature to call Kasey.

"Hey, Faith," he answers. "Good to hear from you, stranger. I guess you meant it when you said you were going to let me run the show."

"I did. I do. I am coming into town just to get some of my things this weekend. You want to have dinner?"

"Of course. When?"

"Saturday night?"

"Perfect. I'll come to you after we close up."

I have Siri dial Bill next. "Faith. Are you on your way here?"

"I am. I think I'm ready to talk. How about coffee tomorrow morning?"

"That works. When and where?"

"Do you just want to come by the house? I'm afraid I might get emotional about my parents, and I really don't want to be around people if that happens."

"Eight?"

"Eight."

"And I understand you getting emotional, but we'll get through this."

"Thanks," I breathe out, and when I hang up, I'm pretty sure I've misjudged him for a really long time.

I reach for the radio, but it starts to rain, and I listen to the thrum of droplets on the windows. I love the rain, but tonight it feels like I'm in an empty hole. *Alone.*

And it doesn't ease up. In fact, the rain is heavier and the night pitch dark when I pull up to my house, and I am hollow inside except for a stabbing pain. I don't belong here anymore. I don't know why I wanted to come here. I almost turn around and leave, but I set up meetings. And I have random things in there. And I really need things that feel familiar.

I walk up the steps, key in my security code—miraculously getting it right the first time—and enter the house.

Nick

The rain is making me crazy. It taunts me. It repeats Faith's words: *Liar. You hurt me. You made sure I will never trust again.*

I dial Beck, desperate for anything I can share with Faith. "I'm going to see her. Your time is up."

"I'm onto something," he says. "One of my CIA contacts has a ping on that mercury, and flag boy got a hit. There's a connection there."

"Where is he now?"

"Hanging out in a cabin on the outskirts of Sonoma. He tells locals he is having a zen retreat."

"The autopsy report."

"Nothing yet, but I'm working on it. I'll be in touch." He hangs up.

Fifteen minutes later, in an absolute downpour, with adrenaline surging through me, I pull into the driveway of Faith's house. Our house. I'm going to fix us. I park behind her car and shrug out of my jacket and tie. The rain doesn't ease up, and I toss them in the back seat and just say screw it. I exit the car and take off running, stomping a path up the stairs, and I am literally so drenched I might as well have stood in the shower. But I'm here. She's here.

I ring the doorbell, and nothing happens. I ring it over and over, then start pounding on the door. "Faith! I know you're here. Talk to me. Faith!" Still nothing, I stomp back down the stairs and into the rain, the real storm raging inside me. I face the house and look for a light in her studio that I don't find. "Faith! I'm not leaving until you talk to me. Open a window. Anything. Faith!"

The front door opens, and I run up the stairs to find her standing in the doorway, behind the screen. I reach for it, but it's locked. "Open the door, sweetheart."

"I need you to leave."

"I'm not going to leave. I need to touch you again, Faith. I need to kiss you."

"You will never touch me again. Leave or I'll call the police."

"Nothing your uncle told you about me is the truth."

"Nathan Marks isn't your father?"

"He is, but it's complicated. I'll explain everything. Let me come in."

"No. You're still you. You still affect me, and that just makes me angry. I am not as stupid as you made me. And I'm not ever going to be stupid again. *Leave*, Nick." She shuts the door.

I press my hands to the doorframe and lower my chin. "Damn it." I sit down next to the door. Eventually she will figure out that I'm not leaving.

Fifteen minutes later, it's clear that she gets that point when a police car pulls into the driveway.

I stand up and walk to meet the officer, and after some smooth talking, I get in my car and drive to my rental house down the road. I don't dry off. I walk in the door, skip the lights, and head to the huge brown leather chair in the living room, where I sit down to think through what comes next.

Because I'm still not leaving. Because *I have* to touch her again. *I have* to hold her close to me in *our bed*. *I have* to put that ring on her finger and call her my wife. And I want to watch her paint every day for the rest of my life. I need to think. I can figure this out. I know I can figure this out.

Time ticks by: seconds, minutes, an hour. I've been in this damn chair *an hour* with no good plan when my cellphone rings. Hoping like hell it's Faith, I yank it from my soaking wet pocket to find Abel's number. "The autopsy report," he says immediately.

I sit up straight. "Tell me."

"It's not logged yet, but my insider says it's being sent to the DA. It wouldn't be sent to the DA if they didn't come to the same conclusion we did."

"My father was murdered. I need to call Beck."

I end the connection, and, knowing I can't get close to Faith right now, I autodial Beck with one thing in mind. Making sure Faith is not next.

CHAPTER FORTY-ONE

Faith

I wake Saturday morning with the same thought I fell asleep thinking, the same thing I'm thinking now standing at the kitchen island: *I can't believe I called the police on Nick.* Just seeing him made me weak in the knees, and he stood in the rain for me. I wanted to believe that meant we had something real, but he lied to me. Over and over, he lied to me. That is not the kind of "real" I want in my life. But Lord help me, I wanted to open the door and feel him, taste him one last time.

The sound of rain pattering on the windows sends a chill down my spine as I walk to the bedroom to pull a V-neck black sweater over the black tank that I'm wearing with black jeans. Apparently, I'm back in funeral mode. The doorbell rings, and I race down the hallway and inhale on a rush of nerves before reaching for the door. I open it to find Bill standing there in khakis and a button-down, a jacket over the top that has rain droplets all over it.

"Come in," I say, backing up, but he shrugs out of his jacket and leaves it on the porch rail.

He joins me inside, and I motion toward the kitchen, hurrying that way. He shuts the door and follows, his footsteps heavy behind me. I round the island, and he claims the spot across from me. His tall frame and broad shoulders are paired with his blue eyes, which are so like my father's that it hurts my already broken heart.

"Coffee?"

"I'd love some, but you stay where you are. I can see your supplies here. I'll mix me up a cup." He rounds the island, and I have this odd sense of claustrophobia, but maybe it's not odd. I have spent a lot of years distrusting him, hating him. That won't go away overnight.

It's not long before we are sitting on stools across from each other. "What have you done about Nick?"

"I left him."

"What about the winery?"

"It's mine," I say. "It's handled." But as I assure him of this, I realize I've not thought about this at all myself. Nick doesn't own the winery, but maybe he just did that to seem honorable and planned to convince me to sell?

"Really?" Bill says, pulling me back into the moment. "It was that easy?"

"Yes. It's handled."

"Well, I don't know how you managed that, but I'm damn glad. I'm concerned about his connections on this mercury, though. I have some people looking into it." He gives me a level stare. "It's okay to want to focus on your art and just sell. You know that, right?"

"I don't want to sell," I say, making that decision as I speak the words. This place is stability for me. I need it, but what I say to him is also true. "I will protect this place, just like my father wanted to protect it. And I have a good team. I'm okay."

"Are you sure? Because I could buy it and protect it for you. And heck, I'll do some improvements and get a tax write-off."

He says it so lightheartedly that it feels innocent, but I don't know. He does like money, and he, too, might find a hundred million dollars appealing. "I'm not selling. More now than ever, I know that's the right decision." A thought hits me. "You know, you sent me that Vegas photo with a note."

"I just wanted you to know that yes, your father did some things with—and for—your mother that went against his grain, but he loved her deeply. And she loved him, too. She just had issues. And as much as I hated to see him hurt, I often thought that few people love like he loved." He knocks on the counter. "I forgot a meeting I have this morning, but I wanted to see you. I am going to leave you to enjoy your Saturday on your own. If you need me, I'm here. I'll show myself out." I stare at his spot for several moments, remembering a conversation with my father. It had been just him and me at the kitchen table:

"I want to go to Vegas for my twenty-first birthday, and I want you to come," I'd said.

"Honey, I hate that place. I went once when I was twenty-five, and bad stuff we won't talk about happened. It's bad luck. I won't go back. Ever."

"But Mom loves Vegas."

"Yeah," he'd said tightly. "I know."

He'd gotten up and given me his back as he walked to the sink.

I grab my cellphone and tab through the photos Bill sent me, and there is only one of my mother and my father, and that's the Vegas shot. I study it now, and I can't be sure that's my father and not Bill. Did Bill send me a photo of him and my mother cheating on my father as a way to lure me into meeting him?

Nick's words come back to me: *Nothing your uncle told you about me is the truth.* Was Nick telling the truth? I shut my eyes in frustration. He's Nathan Marks's son. That is the absolute truth, and Bill told me that truth. I shove a hand through my hair. "Stop, Faith. Stop looking for a reason to forgive Nick." *No matter what,* I add silently. I remind myself that Nick lied to me. I know he knew that his father was my enemy. So the bottom line is that Nick feels right and good while Bill still feels bad and even a little scary. But Nick is the one who carved out my heart.

CHAPTER FORTY-TWO

Faith

Nick haunts me the rest of the day.

I can't get him out of my head, but I try. I spend most of the day packing up the house, even though there really isn't much of what I pack that I want to take with me. I don't go to my studio, but once I've thrown on dressy jeans and a sweater for dinner with Kasey, I am ready early. I walk upstairs and stand in my studio. And I see Nick everywhere. I painted him here. I got naked with him here. I fought with him here. God, I love him. This is gutting me. I need to understand. Maybe then I can move on.

I sit down against the wall and unblock Nick's number on my phone. I sit there, trying to decide if I really want to do this, and the answer is yes. I'm ready now to do this. I dial Nick.

"Faith. Sweetheart."

I love his deep, rich voice, and I love when he calls me sweetheart. "I need to understand."

"Let me come to you."

"No. Because when you touch me I forget everything else, and don't tell me that's a good thing. It's not. Not right now."

"I need you to look into my eyes and see the truth."

"Please just tell me."

"My father was giving your mother large sums of money. It made no sense. And then he was dead, and he'd never had a heart problem in his life. It didn't add up. I thought your mother killed my father, but then she was dead of the same cause."

"Oh God. You thought I did it, and yet you fucked me?"

"I knew you didn't do it as soon as I met you."

"Did you?"

"Yes. I felt it. I didn't want to admit it at first, but I know now that I felt it from the beginning."

"You *thought* I was a killer," I press, still stunned by this news.

"For a hiccup of a moment, Faith. But no more lies. I didn't come to you with good intentions, and I damn sure didn't come to you planning to fall in love. But I did. I love you, Faith Winter. So fucking much. Which is why I couldn't tell you."

"Lies are not love," I say, unable to even try and mask the anger and pain in those words.

"If there was a murderer on the loose, I was afraid they'd turn to you. I needed you close. I needed to keep you safe. I knew you'd react like you did this week. I know you. And I don't blame you, but, Faith…I had an autopsy done on my father."

"And?"

"It's being referred to the DA."

"He *was* murdered."

"Yes. Which means so was your mother."

"I don't know how to digest that fact. My mother was *murdered*."

"I know. I feel the same way about my father. I wasn't close to him, but nobody was supposed to take down that bastard but me. And full disclosure. Beck has men watching you. To protect you."

"I'm suddenly comforted by that news. You should have told me. I would have been angry, but I would have understood. Finding out how I found out was pretty horrible. It cut me."

"I know. I don't know if I'd do it differently, though, Faith. Protecting you was everything in my decisions."

"The mercury?"

"I knew nothing about that until you said something about it. And Beck thinks there's a connection to a man I saw with a flag tattoo that afternoon we went to lunch."

"Flag? There was a flag on the money clip I found."

"Yes. We believe that was his."

"Which means he was at my house." I don't give him time to

reply. "Who is he? What is he?"

"Jess Wild is his name, and he's ex-CIA."

Alarms go off in my head. "Bill said he hired someone who was ex-CIA to help him with the men who wanted to buy the winery for the mercury. He came here today. He tried to buy the winery."

"As I predicted he would."

"Do you think he wants to sell it for the mercury?"

"Yes. I do. And sweetheart, he would have a strong claim to inherit if you were dead."

I shiver. "He gave me the creeps today. Are you sure Beck has someone watching me?"

"Yes. He does. And Faith, before we move on. I can prove everything I'm telling you."

"I don't need proof. I should have listened sooner, but you hurt me. You hurt me so badly. There was the club thing, and people around me are never what they seem to be. You know this. I thought my heart was going to explode with the idea that you were one of those people."

"I know I hurt you, but if you give me the chance, I will spend the rest of my life making it up to you. Let me come over."

The doorbell rings. "Oh God. I'm having dinner with Kasey. He was supposed to call first. I can't cancel. Or maybe I can. No. We were just supposed to bond. I wanted to see how the winery is doing. But I feel nervous now."

"Talk him into ordering in. I'll come over the minute he leaves."

"Yes. Come over."

The doorbell rings again.

"I'll text you when I head back here or when he's gone if we stay in."

"Don't have dessert."

His voice is raspy and affected. It affects me. "No dessert," I promise and hang up.

For a moment I stand there, and I can breathe again. The doorbell rings, a third time and I hurry across the room and down the stairs. I reach the door and peek out of the window. Sure enough, it's Kasey. I open the door and motion him inside. "I thought you were going to call?"

"My phone died, and I didn't have a charger on me. Are you hungry?"

"I am. Where do you want to go?"

"Freda's?"

"Oh yes. I love that place. What do you think about ordering in so we have more time to talk?"

"That sounds good."

We head to the kitchen, and I find the number for Freda's. Once our order is placed, Kasey comments on the decor. "I love the place. And don't you have an amazing studio here? I'd love to see it. I watched you grow up. This stuff makes me proud."

"Of course. Come on." I motion him forward, and we head up the stairs.

Nick

I am the luckiest fucking man on the planet. After Faith hangs up, I'm relieved. I'm so damn relieved, and considering I'd been jogging when she called, trying to calm my fucking mind, I head to the shower. I make it fast and dress in the closest pair of jeans I can find and a T-shirt from the Art Forum. I open the nightstand drawer and pull out the velvet box there, opening it to display the ring: classic, round, elegant, and one of a kind, just like Faith. The important item, the ring, goes in my pocket. I'm proposing now, tonight.

I've just pulled on my boots when Beck calls. "Listen and listen carefully. I just pulled my man off Faith's house. I had no option. Jess Wild is in play. He's a bad dude, and while my men are good, they don't have his skill or nastiness. I can't risk one of them without the other with this guy. But he's the dangerous one.

We have him in our sights. Faith will be fine."

"Jess Wild meaning the ex-CIA flag guy?"

"Yes."

I'm already walking toward my car. "Tell me what the hell you've been working on."

"My CIA pal connected us to the right people. Turns out the agency has had eyes on Jess and Bill for a while now, but Jess went off radar several months ago. Jess disappeared after you saw him that day, but we have eyes on him tonight, and they want us to detain him."

"Fuck me," I say, climbing into my car and starting the engine. "I don't like how this sounds. I'm going to Faith's house just to be safe."

"And just so you know, there's another player."

"Who?"

"The guy who runs the winery. Kasey. But there is reason to believe he's being blackmailed."

"Holy fuck. He's at Faith's house." I back out the drive and disconnect Beck, dialing Faith. She doesn't answer. "Fuck. Fuck. Fuck." I dial again. And again.

I round the corner, and there are flames coming from the direction of Faith's house. Everything goes into slow motion from there. I call 911, and the minute I turn onto Faith's long drive, it's clear the house is engulfed. I end the call and gun my engine, screeching to a halt in front of her house, and I'm out of the door the minute I'm in park. I launch myself forward and up the stairs, but I can't get the door to open. I try the code. Still nothing. It's jammed. Wasting no more time, I kick the window over and over until it cracks. I yank the pieces away, my hands bleeding, but I don't care. I enter the house, and holy hell, the entire downstairs is on fire. "Faith!" I shout. "Faith!"

"Nick! Nick, help! I'm upstairs."

I jump flames left, right, left, covering my mouth as I reach the stairwell, which is all but consumed by flames. "Go to the window!" I shout.

"It doesn't open!"

This is not good news, and I study the top half of the steps that are not yet engulfed. I don't think. I act. I jump over the flames and grab the railing, launching myself over the top, flames scorching my jeans and my fucking hair and neck. I pat it out, or I hope I do, but keep moving. The minute I see Faith, I breathe out, relieved, but I stay focused. "We have to break the window," I say, the sound of sirens lifting in the air.

"I tried," she says, coughing, using one of her smocks to cover her face. "It won't break."

"Call 911 and tell them we're trying to break the glass." I use my shirt to cover my mouth and run into the office and dig around, finding a tool kit and grabbing a hammer. The flames are now at the door. I find the spot near the tree I know climbs her house and start pounding the glass over and over, harder and harder, and finally it cracks, but not enough. And smoke is everywhere, the thick air challenging my lungs, but I keep moving. I kick the glass again and repeat, then go at it with the hammer again. Another crack follows. Then another.

Finally, there's a hole.

That's when there is movement and noise outside, shouts lifting in the air. A firefighter sticks his head through the hole I've created. "Stand back!" he shouts, and I don't miss how he looks ominously at the flames quickly encroaching on us.

I pull Faith with me to the wall, flames a few feet from us. An axe hits the hole I've created, and in a matter of seconds I have Faith at that window, handing her off to a firefighter. I follow, and the minute my feet hit the ground, I grab Faith and we're ushered away from the building. We collapse under another tree, and almost immediately she's grabbing my face. "You're burned. Nick, you're burned. Your hair is scorched."

"I don't care about my hair," I say, pulling her forehead to mine, cupping her head. "God, woman. I almost lost you. I can't believe I almost lost you."

"I can't believe you came after me. You could have died."

A paramedic squats beside us, quickly checking our vitals and then focusing on me. He bandages my hand and neck. "Your neck needs to be treated at the hospital," the EMT says. "And that hair of yours is going to smell to high heaven. Cut it off."

"It's fine. I'm fine."

The man gives my neck a concerned look. "Really, you should—"

Beck appears and squats beside us. "He's fine, man. Move on." The EMT gives him a scowl but obeys, standing up and leaving. Beck eyes me. "Did I mention I was on my way here?" He looks at Faith. "I'm Beck. Glad you lived. Sorry your house didn't." He looks at me again. "Kasey, Bill, and Jess are in custody. Kasey and Bill are singing like birds. Jess is not. But the bottom line here per Kasey is that Bill threatened Kasey's sister, or so he says. He agreed to set this fire and take a payout a little too quickly for me to buy into that."

"Kasey set the fire?" Faith gasps.

"You didn't know?" I ask.

"He said he had a surprise for me and ran downstairs. He told me to wait in the art studio. The next thing I knew, the place was on fire. I don't know how it didn't get to me sooner. The stairs were on fire from the beginning." She covers her face. "I can't believe this." She drops her hands. "Did he kill my mother?"

"Bill says Nick's father was controlling your mother. He wanted the winery, too, and I assume he knew about the mercury. Per Bill, they both became a problem. Like you did, Faith. And that's all for now. I need to go hand off Jess to those who shall not be named." In typical Beck form, he just stands and leaves without another word.

I turn to Faith. "Your house—"

"Doesn't matter."

I cup her face. "I can't lose you."

Her lips curve. "Then you won't."

I reach in my pocket and retrieve the ring. "Marry me. Be my wife."

She breathes a heavy breath. "Your hair and skin are scorched, and you're proposing?"

"I'd propose if my entire body was scorched. Marry me. The ring is—"

"Gorgeous. Stunning. Huge. I'll need a bodyguard."

"Does that mean you'll marry me?"

"Yes. Yes, I will marry you."

I pull her lips to mine and kiss her like I might never kiss her again. And I plan to kiss her that way every day for the rest of her life.

EPILOGUE

Faith

It's our first morning at our new apartment. Nick and I sit down at a table on the patio with plates of pancakes in front of us—made, of course, from a mix, because that's my specialty. I'm still in his T-shirt that I slept in last night, while he's in his pajama bottoms and another T-shirt that fits nice and snug across his chest. That snug fit is exactly why I haven't stolen that particular shirt just yet. His hair is loose, longer now again, though he tested out the shorter style for all of about a month. Nick just doesn't do conventional.

He fills our glasses with fresh mimosas. "How does the new place feel?" he asks.

"Exciting," I say. "I'm dying for the studio to be done next week. I have orders and shows and painting to do."

His phone buzzes with a text, and he glances down at it. "Rita made it down to the winery to help Carrie this morning. Rita says that she is impressed. And we both know that Rita is not easy to impress."

Carrie being Kasey's longtime second-in-charge who is now running the winery. "I like Carrie, too," I say. "I always liked her, but she was just overshadowed by Kasey. And now that the government came in and claimed the mercury, we don't have to fear another problem. I can't believe Bill and Kasey went to jail so quickly."

"A plea deal works that way, but he's still going to be inside a long time, while Kasey will be out in a year."

"I still can't believe he was involved. And Jess Wild. We'll never know what happened to him, right?"

"The CIA deal with their own." He changes the subject. "Back to the winery. No regrets over keeping it?"

"No regrets at all. You know how the fire affected me. I gave myself the freedom to live and to let it go."

"But you didn't let it go."

"No. We've made it possible to maintain my father's legacy while I'm creating my own—at least I hope that I am."

He holds up the card from my father. "Then you're ready for this."

I swallow hard. "Oh."

"No?"

"Yes." I firm my voice. "Yes I am." I stand up and take it from him, walking to a small sofa seat a few feet away. Nick joins me, and I slowly peel open the seal and remove the handwritten note. Just seeing my father's script steals my breath. I start reading out loud:

Faith,

If you aren't painting right now, it never really mattered to you. It wasn't your passion. Because when something is your passion, you can't let it go. You can't walk away. The winery was that for me, and so was your mother. Both had flaws, but it's the imperfections in things that are often perfection. I always assumed that one day I'd tell you how proud I am of you for fighting for what matters to you, for embracing your passion. I just needed it to be the right time. If you're reading this, I never got the chance to pick that time, and the moral of the story is that life is short. It could end tomorrow. All or nothing, Faith.

I love you forever.

Dad

Tears are streaming down my cheeks, and Nick is on his knee beside me. I lean forward and press my hand to his cheek. "All or nothing."

He kisses my hand and says, "Let's set the wedding date. We were waiting until things calmed down. That's now."

"Let's elope. Now. Right away. All or nothing."

Nick smiles. "All or nothing. Name the place."

THE END

ACKNOWLEDGMENTS

To Emily, for everything you do. I can't even list everything. It's just too much. Thanks to Zita and Alyssa for proofreading this duet and so many books over the years. And thank you, to my husband Diego, for all the support in my writing endeavors in so many ways. I'm also excited to thank Passionflix for intending to turn this series into a film project. And to my agent, Louise Fury, and my publisher Entangled and Macmillan for giving this story a chance to be in print and reach a broader audience.

Much love— Lisa

AMARA
an imprint of Entangled Publishing LLC